BLOOD

BLOOD

JACK REMICK

CAVEL
PRESS

Seattle, WA

Published by Camel Press
PO Box 70515
Seattle, WA 98127

Cover design by Sabrina Sun
Cover illustration by M. Anne Sweet
Contact: info@camelpress.com
Copyright © 2010 by Jack Remick

ISBN: 978-1-60381-804-9 (Paper)
ISBN: 978-1-60381-805-6 (Cloth)
ISBN: 978-1-60381-806-3 (ePub)

1.

It's hot in the laundromat. Hot and moist as the inside of a woman's mouth. Sitting on the hard-backed metal chair beside the door, I wait for the red-headed woman to return. The magazine, an old issue of Car and Driver, splays open on my lap to an article on the Audi R8, a street version of the racing machine that re-wrote the history of auto racing at Le Mans, making it the perfect vehicle of the upward-bound young man with two hundred thousand dollars to burn on new wheels. But I'm not interested in the R8 or the Audi record book or anything to do with wheels. I am interested in the contents of the red-headed woman's dryer. The huge dryer spins to a stop.

I check the wall clock: 11:30 PM. Maybe she fell asleep at the TV. Maybe her lover called. Maybe they are having phone sex, their words burning up the cell towers. Maybe he paid her a surprise visit and their moans are scorching the walls of her apartment.

Standing, I close the article on the R8 and look out the window at Third Avenue at 11:30 PM. It is gray with mist and the vague, complicated shadows of moonlight and sodium-based street lamps with their yellow glow and orange tinge. I look again at the dryer, see the whiteness in the glass door, see the strip of white panties forced against the door, the hooked strand of a bra strap buried in the waist band of the panties. I check the clock again—11:33. I feel the itch in the palms of my hands, that dry rancid anxiousness in my mouth. The door opens. I turn. Cool night air pushes in. I expect to see the red-headed woman, but instead two men wearing Chargers jackets and carrying duffel bags enter chatting about sports and scores. One of them tackles the duffel of his friend and they both laugh, ignoring me standing at the window. Their reflections in the glass move like ghosts. They dump their duffels into side-by-side washers, pour in Tide—too much detergent for the size of the loads—and then they search for quarters. Click, clang, click, clang and then one of them says, Shit, I'm short and he looks at me.

Hey pal, he says, you got change for a few bucks?

I point at the change machine on the wall. He follows my finger. Grinning.

Right, he says. The change machine.

Slipping dollar bills into the machine, he scoops out quarters and then, glancing at me, pumps the quarters into the washer. Then he and his friend walk outside.

As the door whishes closed, I run to the red-headed woman's dryer, open the glass door, unhook the tangled bra strap from the white lacy panties and, reaching into the still warm body, feel the heat of the mass of white. My heart beats faster and I stuff the still warm underwear into the sleeves of my jacket, feel the heat radiate through me, my heart hammering. I empty the dryer, close the door, feel the heat of the white hot metal hooks of the bras against me. Ready to run, I hear shoes shuffle on the concrete floor. The red-headed woman stands glaring at me. She wears tight black pants, a red sweater. Her hair, curled up in ringlets, shimmers in the light. Beside her there are two large men in uniform. Policemen. Big grins on their faces. There is no way out. Not through them, not over them, not away from them.

The red-headed woman pulls a pistol and shield from the back of the black pants and says,

We've been waiting for you, you son of a bitch.

She smiles. She approaches me. I watch the gun hand, watch the hands of the men and I let out a long breath, one I have been holding for years and years and I say,

You're a cop.

I'm a cop, she says. And these are my cop friends.

I didn't expect it to be you.

Perverts never expect a woman.

The two men in uniform close in on me. I know that they have no experience in close combat. They are careless. Loose. Laughing, they joke about catching the Underwear Bandit, the Panty Pervert, the Braless Bandido.

I know that once the red-headed woman holsters her pistol I can take them—all three, take them down and leave them gagging, bleeding, perhaps dead—but instead I hold out my hands, palms up. I say,

Are you going to cuff me?

2.

In my apartment on Third Avenue, high up on the eighth floor, the light is dim in the hallway. The carpet is plush blue, not too plush, not too blue. Silent, not too silent. I watch the two men open drawers where my cache hides—a thousand pairs of white panties—lace panties, silk panties, crotchless panties, hip huggers, thongs, panties with little red hearts embroidered on them. Panties with the days of the week emblazoned across the pubic bone—all of them white.

Out come the bras, D cup, C cup, A cup, DD cup— strapless, with straps, with clear plastic shoulder straps all white. Then the assortment of slips and half slips, body stockings, leotards in all sizes from mammoth big women's down to tiny size three, all white.

As the men stack up the booty the red-headed woman says,

I'll be a son of bitch.

That's hard for you to do, isn't it? I say.

Metaphorically speaking, asshole.

Why do all you law enforcement people call men like me assholes?

Because who but an asshole is going to be stupid enough to hoard this kind of shit. You know something, smart ass?

What?

She holds up a white bra. She says,
I never wear white undies.
So what's your color? Red?
Emerald. Red-heads look good in emerald.
I should have known, I say. All that white and you a red-head.
White or no white, we've got you asshole, she says. You shouldn't work the same gig every night.
I had my reasons, I say.

3.

I remember nights when I lay in the dark smelling my own fetid breath, waiting for the footfall of men with packs on their backs and rifles in hand. Men trudging up mountain paths in moonlight, feet cracking loose an occasional pebble that, in the closeness of the night, clattered and ricocheted with the scream of an avalanche. And then, rising from the earth's shadow, I took their blood, took them down and Suki, like a viper striking once, twice, three times took them down to the soft burble of bloody air.

I remember the one time I was taken in ambush. In the mountains outside Arequipa. One night. Cold in the highlands. Feeling safe and secure with a string of dried ears around my neck, I let down my guard, fell into that easy grace of camaraderie born in the friendship of shared killing with men I relied on and trusted. And then gunfire lit up the night, shot hard and yellow venom into the bodies of men beside me and I ran—dodging, fast—clambering over rock and dirt trying to find the place to hide, running into the black, the sole shield against the bullets.

4.

The judge sentences me to five years. He says,
Mr. Mitchell, how do you plead?
Guilty, your honor.

He studies me, his long gray face lean as a hungry wolf's, his black robe the skin of a hungry shark, his teeth clacking like the gnashing of a wild dog tearing flesh. He says,

Are you certain you don't want to reconsider?

I did it, your honor and I'll take what you dish out.

This isn't a smorgasbord, all you can eat for five dollars, Mitchell. It's a first offense sentencing.

Yes and no, your honor.

Yes and no?

It's the first offense I've been nailed for, sir.

His gray face reminds me of the swollen bodies laid out on the banks of the Rio Verde like pieces of drying jerky. All those bodies, each with its left ear cut off, all those bodies with their tongues hanging onto their chests drawn through the cut at the throat, all those bodies slipping one by one into the brown and quiet and meandering waters of the Rio Verde. The judge says,

I have to tell you, this is a first, Mitchell, I've never sentenced a defendant who has stolen a dryer full of women's underwear. Do you care to explain?

Sir, your honor, it's a weakness of mine, a fetish. You've got just one way to control it and that's to lock me up because psychotherapy has failed and shock therapy has failed and drug therapy will make me lose my hair and grow breasts and so you have to lock me up.

I don't see anything about that in your psych evaluation, so how can I believe anything you say?

He glances from me to his fingertips pressed together doing finger calisthenics—up and down, down and up—and as I watch, I remember the early days in the Oriente of Ecuador and the night time slaughter of a village of the Colorados, those fierce jungle warriors of the Amazon who painted their bodies a red that washed off in their blood as one by one we took them down in sight of the Anglo Ecuadorian oil rigs already drilling on their sacred ground

9

and I remembered the feel of the knife in the flesh. There is nothing like that feel, the sudden point of resistance as the serrated tip hesitates at bone after hacking into the dense and meaty interior of the chest just as the drilling rigs had penetrated the jungle and I remembered the smell, remembered the feel, the taste of blood and the ear count as I took my trophies one by one.

The judge clears his throat and he flexes his fingers, thin as the sinew of a decapitated man and he says, Well then, Mitchell, how does five years sound?

Thank you your honor.

I'm taking five years of your freedom.

I'm not free as long as temptation is my companion, sir.

So you don't appeal?

If you let me go there's no telling how many women will have to buy new underwear, your honor, so no, I don't protest or appeal.

I see the bright white hair tufts growing in the judge's ears and I remember the first time I cashed in my sack of trophies, dried now, each one tagged with date and time and place, some of them still loaded with the jewelry their owners wore, some of them—like the Colorados—still dyed red, blood mingled with earth, and I remember the clatter of the dried skin—how little there is to a human ear—a small flap of skin—worth one thousand dollars—the skin worthless but the body it came from priceless. The judge says,

Because you're so eager, I have half a mind to send you out on probation.

That would be wrong your honor because I am a thief, a coward, a liar, and a cheat and to be honest I can't say how much underwear I'll steal.

He looks at me, his eyes burning, and I remember the nights in the Atacama, the stench of the copper mines clouding my throat, I remember cutting the eyes out of women with rifles in their dead hands, because the DINA wanted eyes and not ears and I took them, took their communist eyeballs and strung them on thread and dried them and the human eyeball shrinks to the size of a lima bean in the heat and the thin air of the altiplano. The judge says,

We're not just talking women's underwear, are we?

This is your chance to save society, your honor.

All right then. Women do have a right to the privacy of their knickers. Five years starting right now.

As I walk out of the courtroom, the officer guiding me says,

So you got a jones for women's undies.

Fuck you, I say.

He jabs me in the kidney with his riot stick and he grabs his crotch and he says,

Where you're headed, asshole, you'll be sucking on this.

I smile and hold my tongue because his pain is the kiss of a butterfly compared to the hurt I have endured, compared to the feel of a hot slug ripping my shoulder, compared to the searing tear of a knife slicing open my chest down to the bone until the pec flapped, the blood gushing over my belly—his pain—he knows nothing of pain, he has no idea why I accept his handcuffs, he has no idea that even in handcuffs, I can break his neck, break his leg, break his arm and walk away. He has no idea that I can shed the handcuffs, he has no idea that I choose to accept them because I don't want to burden the judge, another man who saved my life.

5.

The first day I see him in the steel and concrete cage. He lies on his bunk, arms clasped behind his head, a great head of black hair that curls like rings of chainmail. The guard shoves me into the cell, slams the gate with a hard grunt and he says,

Your new cellmate, Grosjean.

I watch the eyes in the head of black hair assess me, startling black eyes that eat me like a gourmet devouring garlic snails and roast lark and pig's brains stewed in morel mushrooms. After appraising me, he turns away, dismisses me with a slow closing of his eyes. I stand there feeling a visceral attraction to Grosjean, an attraction I don't understand but an attraction I don't dismiss.

I sit on the empty bunk of gray steel with its gray wool blanket and its blue tick pillow that smells of sweat and the pale perfume of men left too long in their minds.

Days go by and not a word from him. Grosjean is all the name I know. But I know him—tall, muscular him, his large arms and the hair so thick it mats like black moss on a fallen tree trunk. And then, on the eighth day, like a latter day god recreating a world, he speaks,

What'd they bust your ass for, punk?

Punk. No one has called me punk since my first days at Oak View School for Boys when Cain rescued me from Charlie Goodson in the shower. I say,

You takin' a survey?

He faces me, his flat belly covered with his blue chambray shirt tucked into the waist of his prison denims. His eyes still hold mine like a raptor tracking prey. He laughs. He says,

You got balls, junior. No one pisses on my boots.

You're not wearing boots.

He laughs again, a belly laugh and he looks at me with glistening eyes and he says,

Okay. Truce. No more wisecracks.

I watch his mouth. Lips thick and swollen like the lips of a woman. I watch his nose. Thin, aquiline, and that head of hair so black it glistens like rain falling. I say,

Grosjean. You a Frenchman?

René, from Montreal.

He has weight. He has height. He has the gravity of big men and he is unrelenting. He is the one man who ever made me feel small. He is heavy, thick in the shoulder, and his thighs bulge in his denims. After that encounter, I dream of him for a week. Awake, I try to imagine his secrets—what did he do? Why is he here? Where has he been?

6.

I measure my cell in every way I can. I pace it lengthwise—five paces. Fifteen feet. Pace it across—four paces. Twelve feet. The width cut down because of the width of the bunks.

I measure it using the span of little finger to thumb. Its length is twenty spans of nine inches. One hundred eighty inches. Across it is sixteen spans of nine inches or one hundred forty-four inches.

Some days it feels so small it closes in on me, clamps on me like a vise. And always the air is the same—it smells of concrete and steel.

It smells of sweat and piss. I kneel on the floor to look at the glazed concrete. On my knees, I see the small cracks in the glaze like wrinkles in a face. In a certain light and at a certain angle, I see my reflection on the thin veneer of concrete.

The bunks are anchored to the wall and to the floor. The wall anchors are three-quarter-inch thick bolts embedded three inches in concrete. The heads of the bolts have been rounded so no man can twist them loose. The bolts snug the bunks to the wall so tight that no amount of shear can snap them. The floor anchor bolts are driven into the concrete and rounded so there is no wiggle to the bunk.

The window cuts into the wall—a single window letting in dim light. It is so high you can't see out in a straight line to anywhere, but up at an oblique angle the sky always has a ledge of gray cutting across the sill. At the top, the lintel blots out the rest of the sky. All the world framed in gray concrete.

The toilet is bolted to the wall. A solid piece of stainless steel with no sharp edges, no loose connections. It doesn't stain, it doesn't rust, it doesn't creak when you sit on it. There is no lid, just the hard cold stainless steel toilet that stays cold even in summer because the cell is a constant sixty-eight degrees Fahrenheit.

The ceiling is embedded with a single light fixture high enough to keep a man from reaching it, strong enough to keep him from ripping it out.

The sink beside the toilet is also stainless steel. It is anchored to the wall with a knee brace. Its bolts are sunk into the concrete so well that you can stand on the sink, jump up and down without budging it. They have thought of everything. They have built it to contain us. They have locked us up in a cage where there are no moveable objects but the gate that opens and closes for chow, for work, for visitors. They have thought of everything.

I lie on my bunk counting the cracks in the ceiling. Some of them walk like spider webs. Some of them look like scabs from knife wounds. Some of them zigzag for five or six feet before bumping into a solid expanse of gray. The cracks don't change or grow. There are no new ones, but when the light is oblique, you can see spots. Little glazed spots where men in their erotic fantasies have masturbated and, taking their semen in hand, have flung it to the ceiling. If you look at the walls in that oblique light, when the sun at a certain time of day angles light just so, you read names in that same clear glaze where men using their semen as ink have etched the concrete, written letters home, drawn little hearts and small cunts and cocks fucking. There are places where the palimpsests are layered six or eight deep in a crazy jumble. Each attempt blots out the story line where men overwrote their passion on the smear of their predecessors without perhaps knowing it or perhaps doing it on purpose.

Thin layers of semen glisten, the history of pain and lust cakes its chapters like the history of Byzantine emperors overlain each upon the other in a trans-generational fucking, a deliberate and erotic touching of semen residue by fresh fingers smeared with fresh hot cum.

7.

It is night. I lie awake, still not accustomed to the sounds of men locked away—snores, shouts in their sleep, grunts and groans and the deep guttural noise of a man coming and flinging his cum on the wall.

It is night and I feel his weight on my bunk and his hand on my crotch and my shorts loosening. I say nothing. I don't resist. He rolls me over and he slides my shorts to my knees and mounts me, hands groping from my back to my shoulders. I smell his breath and his sweat and I feel his hardness in me, listen to his staccato breathing until he cums and then, rearing back on his knees, he whispers,

Tu es une salope, mami.

I smile, listen to the tender words of this man who has no idea that I can with one hand tear his throat out, rip out his tongue, gouge his eyes out. I smile and I say,

Et toi, mami? Tu aimes mon cul comme c'était une rose.

He laughs, buttons his denims and he crosses his index and middle fingers and he says,

This is how it will be, mami. Toi et moi, comme ça. I'm your first, pas vrai?

Tu crois?

You were easy for a premier. You were thinking about it, eh?

I sit up, feel his semen sticky on my ass. A hundred million homunculi shriveling, dying—legions dead. Standing, I pull up my shorts while he sits on his bunk watching me like a lover caressing his poule with his eyes. He says,

You're a big one for a bottom. With a cock like that you ought to be le roi au lieu de la reine.

My father had a twelve inch cock, I say. Nature cheated me.

You got enough, mami, he says. That verge de cheval is a masterpiece. Where'd you learn Français?

Without waiting for my answer, he clasps his hands behind his head, the black ringlets drifting down over his pillow and he falls asleep.

8.

I have decided to write a book. Outside, I was moving too fast, staying ahead of the game, searching, destroying. But now, in here, there is time. Twenty-two hours a day, I'm in this cell. Chow time, shower time, work time. All fixed into thirty minute slots. I have decided to write a book and I will call it *The Patron Saint of Blood*.

Day after day. It's punishment, they say, locking men away from the world to show them what they are missing. But me, I shut out the noise, tame the vile taste in my mouth, lie under René Grosjean, feel his cock in my ass, and it is a way to live that is safe and out of the stream of death and I am relieved.

I've set myself a goal to write half an hour a day. In my handwriting, I get twelve hundred words. If I am able to write twelve hundred words a day I can have eight thousand four hundred words a week, and thirty-three thousand words a month. I can finish my entire life writing in twelve months. Then I will edit it. Refine it. Polish it for four years. That's my hope. Where to start? Do I start with my family? My past? My father? My sisters?

Geraldine, my older sister, married a Captain in the United States Air Force and her blood is on his hands because he went mad, a furia francesa, and in a rage tore out her throat leaving her without voice.

9.

I walk into the library. No one wants to go there so permission isn't questioned. I leave Artie, the guard, at the door, a shit-eating grin on his face as he closes me in. He says,

What's with the books, Mitchell? You a brainiac?

No, I say. I'm looking for toilet paper.

You're in the right place, asshole.

He keys the door. In the quiet, I smell the odor of musty paper, taste the dust in the air, see the thin veneer of dust on the table, on the lone chair, see the fine coating of dust on the floor—no foot prints, no tracks, as if this place once built, was abandoned, left to decay.

I flip on a light. The dull angry neon tubes buzz, suggesting bees in a flowering field, but there are no bees, no flowers, just the angry buzzing of the neons. A yellow glaze reflects from the table dust and in the air, I see the rain of motes settling. I take a deep breath, walk into the stacks.

The books are out of order—hardbacks stacked on top of paperbacks. The chaos of an earthquake unreclaimed but left as they fell—and the books are dusty, flung at angles to one another. I want to straighten them out, put them in order, and so I stack a few, feel the grit of years of dust like a fine facial powder between my fingers.

I read the titles—English Roses in the Traditional Garden. The Lilacs of Two Continents. French Dahlias. The Quest for the Blue Rose. Fifty books on flowers.

I line them up by size the way books are stored in the old university libraries in England and France.

In a few minutes, I've arranged the books on flowers and then I chart a course deeper into the stacks where books have not been touched for decades, their embossed letterings still pristine and pure, their bindings still unbroken, and I see that I have landed in a history section. But once again there is no order—Medieval History and the Hidden Statues of Amiens Cathedral followed by Ancient

Greek Stage Machinery followed by The History of Cornwall in the 19th Century—again, chaos.

But I'm not interested in what's on the surface. I have seen libraries. I know the secrets of books and that the secrets aren't always in the books because men hide their secrets and fetishes not high up, but in plain sight behind the known, behind the obvious, that's where the sins and perversions lurk. I pull books off the shelves. Three and four at a time. Looking for the jewels, the crimes left by the men who came before me and there, right at eye level, half hidden behind a book on the Lives of the Muslim Saints of the 10th Century, I spy a small volume—a paperback—and I recover it.

L'Étranger, Albert Camus. Its yellow cover dark with thumbprints, its binding cracked, pages leaking from the covers like sap from a punctured maple tree.

It is like an old friend in my hands. I remember the first time I read it, this small tome of Camus. I was in Grenoble, sent there by my father to stretch my mind, but all I had done was bend my elbow guzzling French wine while I chased les putes who cost so little I soon tired of them because, as I learned, good pussy is only topnotch if you have to pay top dollar for it and les putains de Grenoble were not at that time in that category so I turned instead to reading all the best French pornographers—Restif de la Bretonne, Donatien Alphonse de Sade. On one foray into an underground bookshop where the walls were lined with magazines of women in chains, women in black leather, men with spikes driven through their penises, men with hot irons branding their buttocks, I found *Le Retour au Chateau* by P. Réage and beside that book a copy of *L'Étranger*, as out of place as the history of the Muslim saints in a prison library. I tried to buy both but the cashier, an asthmatic woman with a bone piercing her septum, said,

Qu'est-ce que c'est que cette merdeux bouquin?

Camus, I said.

Camus? Tu connais ce con?

C'est mon frère, I said.

Ton frère?

She shoved *L'Étranger* at me and said,

Alors, un cadeau pour toi.

I pocketed the book. Back in my room, I opened it to find an uncut edition in the French style—the pages still bound in their octavo signatures, unread, unmarked.

The prison copy of *L'Étranger* in my hand, all my past flashes through my memory and I open the first page—Maman est morte hier.

It's in French. In the prison library. I feel like a teenager masturbating, about to be caught by his sister flinging open the bedroom door to shout—You're jerking off, you're jerking off—and then I hear the guard at the door, the squeak of shoes on concrete. He calls,

Hey asshole, get your sick butt up front.

Is it time to go, Artie?

I tuck *L'Étranger* in my waistband, feel it flex like a piece of soft leather as I walk and as I exit, Artie says,

Find what you're looking for?

No. Still not there.

What the hell do you see in this shithole?

The library? I see books. I see the ruin of a once hopeful civilization.

I know what it is, he says.

So you don't read?

What for? We got TV in the bullpen.

So you can't read.

What the fuck, Mitchell? You giving me the third degree like some high and mighty.

He rams the nightstick into my gut. I double over, kneel, pretending to be hurt. I know I can turn him into blood sausage with a finger to the Adam's apple. But I play his game. I look up at him, letting his power run over me like warm water.

Who the fuck do you think you are, Mitchell. You know
what you are? A con, that's what you are. Up on your fucking
feet. Let's go.

I lead him down the corridor, the sound of his boots
clacking on the floor, the hard metal call of the taps on his
heels like hammer blows and up the steel stairway to C
Block, to # 6. The gate opens and Artie waits, his riot stick
dangling from his wrist until I'm in the cell and then he says,

You watch your step, asshole. I got my eye on you.

I lie on my bunk, pull *L'Étranger* from my waistband.
Contraband. A book in the cell. No one reads books. They
have cable. They read letters and magazines. But a book. A
book can be a weapon. Even *L'Étranger*.

10.

For six days running I have hit my target. Twelve
hundred words a day. There's nothing magic about the
number twelve hundred, but I'm finding that it marks a limit
for me—a limit of my brain, the limit of my hand speed, the
limit of what I can recall in thirty minutes of my hand flying.
I slow down when I deviate from the truth and then only
until I get back on track. I have to tell my story as it
happened. And so I write ...

When I began to hunt human beings, I decided to be the
scourge of the race, to be the best at it, not to let anything get
in the way because killing is the last and final truth and
when you take a man's life you eliminate his facts, his
stories, his hopes and his failures and in so doing you rid the
earth of his poison.

Above ten thousand feet in the Andes, we ran a death
squad, Suki and I and four compañeros. We were a unit, a
fighting unit, brought in to take care of insurgents, the
women of insurgents, the children of insurgents, and we
were paid by the ear, a thousand dollars, left ears only.

The six of us in the middle days, made money. A lot of
money.

To hunt a man, you have to be vicious but truthful. You have to be honest and pure because you never get a second chance. Of all the animals, there is just one that is the supreme killer and so to be a killer of killers, you must be impeccable and pure.

In the rainy season, in the mountains, in Peru, near a small town called Yuncan, we infiltrated to exterminate a cell of agitators not because of any animus for them—other than they were humans—but because we were paid to annihilate them for the benefit of the Cerro Corporation.

In that part of the mountains there is a stillness in which you can hear the distant rush of the streams and rivers as they hum their way back to the sea. In those mountains the greenery is like a slow spreading virus that lives ten thousand lives. You slip over the rocks silent as water spreading and in that silence you hold your breath as you track your prey. Then with a quick attack you slash and you are alive and he is dead. You take his left ear then you disappear back into the mist and the silent verdancy and you wait among the orchids and the monkeys and the parrots that don't smell human blood or see the swollen corpse as a victory. We are myths, we are like ghosts to them.

I see them those small dark-skinned men in their white panama hats, small dark men with machine guns cradled in their arms, small dark men worth more to the company dead than whole villages alive. There is no altruism in killing for money.

As I write, I look at the ceiling, and on the ceiling they move, those men, like figures in a slow-motion film. I look at them in the shadows of my mind and I see their bare feet in their leather sandals, their black and red, white and brown ponchos and their AK47s.

I try to calculate the amount of blood that seeped into the soil around Yuncan until the killing stopped, until they pulled us out in the night, sliding down the river to the sea, our clothing soaked, our bodies cold with icy wet, leaving the towns not as we found them but with a legacy of terror, assuring the remaining men we would return. It is this same terror that besoils my sister's mind—terror of the erupting male, his power, the seed of damnation. It is a game played with the man on top, the woman on bottom. It reeks of all that is terrible, smells of the weakness of killers unchained and impure. It is a dance of sperm and egg driven by six million years of pressure to plant the sperm, to grow the egg, to nurture the offspring. I know it is skewed because my brother-in-law, that CEO in Charge of Death with his Air Force wings and his baroque blue class ring and his walnut desk at corporate—that omnipotent cock-bearing son of a bitch master killer mother fucking chickenshit butcher—is one human being who doesn't merit a place on top.

I remember the decay out there. What will happen in the collapse—what will they do with all of us? Unlock the doors? Turn us back out into their destroyed and dangerous world? Back out into the slaughterhouse? Back out into the river of blood?

We are not the dangerous ones. I think about the small men lying in the mud and rain, throats slit, and that is why I am in here—not for stealing a tubful of women's underwear, no, I am in here in some twist of divine injustice not for killing those little men but for refusing any longer to kill them.

Each day I do penance for them, but I don't ask forgiveness—it is too late for that—and there is no one to grant it. If I speak of it then I am the debtor and I refuse to be in debt. Today I feel good as I remember that I am alive— I came out of the mountains with blood on my hands but I am alive and I have the memories of those men I killed, although as humans they had no special purpose or reason for living. In remembering them I keep them alive and I wonder if there are others like me who see their victims at night moving across the ceiling in slow motion— shadowlands of memory, small men with severed throats and unbeating hearts—too late for redemption because not even grace can bring redemption. There can be no confession.

Yesterday I stayed in the library studying my manuscript and I am afraid it will not survive.

The paper is thin, so thin the red ink bleeds out like the spider webs of veins in pale white skin, so thin the ink spreads like blood from a wound, so shallow you wonder how the blood can hover there, beading up on the paper. For a second it holds, then, like a small dam bursting, the ink shoots out, webbing itself into the page. When I hold up the paper, I see light break through the webs and the words disappearing, bleeding together so that even when I peer close, I can't make out the difference between *kill* and *man*. The two words fused, in red, on the white paper—lost and lost to my memory.

I sit back, spread the tissue out on the hardwood table, watch the ink patterns shine through, and in that moment I try to recall what I have just written—but the thought and the memory vanish, victims to the act of writing that once I believed to be a way to seize memory forever but now I watch each page bleed my memory away. One day, I know, there will be nothing left to remember and the pages will be the witnesses that I ever was.

I have to find a better way.

I have to find better paper.

I have to find better ink than the marker pen with its nib of red felt that protrudes from the tube like the swollen gut of some wounded beast, its intestine leaking infection and dirt. I take a deep breath.

Camus didn't have this problem, but the Marquis had this problem. Genet also had this problem—finding the right paper and the right writing instrument after the authorities destroyed his work. I am having this problem, but I am a thinking, feeling machine and I can solve the problem. I have to solve the problem before all my memory has disappeared and I become a shell lost and locked in the gray and dim concrete and steel cage.

Leaving the table, I roll up the pages, tuck them into the hollow core of the toilet paper tube and I go to the stacks where the gardening books rest like dead men lined up belly to back. I open a space and I lay the tube of toilet paper to rest there, its mouth full of my writing—indecipherable— perhaps illegible, perhaps destroyed, perhaps lost.

As Beckett said—all I have are those words.

I step back from the stack, look at my work in its place, and for a moment I feel tears break at the corners of my eyes and I am ashamed—It is so hard, the writing. It doesn't flow, it doesn't scream onto the page, it doesn't cry to be made immortal. It hides all the sin and crime now in its red webbing on the tissue, blood red, broken red lines, nothing.

I have to become an archeologist of my own history if it is to survive and I want it to be vital and vibrant and eternal, because my life is unique and it deserves a place on the shelf alongside the greatest men who ever lived.

I shall find new paper and a new pen, one that doesn't leak ink out like the blood of a throat-slit man lying in the mud and rain. No, I am better than that. Much better than that.

11.

I am behind five thousand words. I can never make them up. Memory is dammed up in my brain looking for a release. Empty pages wait. If I had the energy to get my quota of words I could rank right up there with the greats. But I can't will memory. I can't push a button to turn it on. Memory is blocked but when it comes, it isn't what I want to come. It floods out of me and I take it down, waiting to see what it will be. Writing by hand is slow. I need a quicker way to capture it when the flood comes. I have no control, there is no direction, it just comes. I seek the sudden spasm of masturbation, the small white pure innocence of semen. It is a senseless spoonful of death that I fling against the wall of my cell.

12.

Each day I write, the pack of pages grows. Writing, I fill a page, turn it face down like a dead man tossed into a grave, and write the next one ...

The Rio Verde, a slender jungle river brown as chocolate, lazy as a tree sloth, meanders through Southern Mexico seeking a path to the Coast where it spills its dirty cargo into the deep and cleansing blue Pacific. In ancient times it flowed through a paradise. But the history of killing cut its scars and everything is now lost.

Before the killing, camp was always tranquil. A calculated silence broken by the soft rake of knife blades on steel. Suki, an Otavalo from the highlands, no more than five feet two inches tall but with a barrel chest and narrow hips, had the quickest hands I had ever seen in a man. He learned the knife in Guayaquil in a vicious style called La Costeña that involves two adversaries clutching a bandana between their teeth, each clasping a blade, and they cut until one of them falls maimed, butchered, dead.

Suki, the little man who saved my life half a dozen times, shed his first blood at sixteen and at nineteen was a master of the corte corbata, a genius at the quick slash to the throat that shocked and froze his victims. I recruited him from the docks in Guayaquil after watching him fight.

Disguising ourselves as night, we infiltrated, killed, and before light left corpses splayed like mysterious crucifixions, throats cut using the corte corbata—a lovely cutting that severs the throat, lets you pull the tongue from the cavity to hang on the chest like a necktie—the necktie cut—a technique I learned from Suki who learned it from the Colombians during La Violencia when the rebels there stopped entire busloads of people to slaughter them all except one—the Chosen One—they left to tell the tale and to spread the terror.

We were hidden in the thickets outside a tiny village called Tepeñiptlahuaca.

From the foliage I watched bare-breasted Indian women wash their clothes in the slow flow of the Rio Verde, women who did not wear underpants or brassieres. Watching them, I felt a kind of Rousseauvian nostalgia for that kind of purity, but as I lay in wait, I also felt the hardness of the steel of the AK47. We didn't use the M16 or the Uzi because we wanted ambiguity left behind. We had been deployed to get rid of resistance, to kill communists, socialists, progressives getting in the way of corporate conquest of the jungle and its hidden economy.

In early afternoon, the women left the river carrying their laundry in reed baskets on their heads. Their breasts bobbed up and down as they walked but the baskets didn't budge. There was no shame in their nakedness, no lust, no desire. A dog licks its ass in the middle of a dinner party and there is no shame. A cat licks his balls on the front porch in front of the minister and there is no shame. A woman walks naked through the jungle and there is no shame. But steal a laundry cart full of women's underwear and you end up in prison.

As the sun set, the mosquitoes swarmed—drawn by the smell of lactic acid oozing from our bodies—to dine on blood. We didn't use repellent because in the jungle a whiff of that is like a siren calling attention to you. As we lay in wait, I remembered the hardness of my bladder and so I rolled onto my side and was taking a leak when Suki hissed at me. I rolled back, crushing the little vergonzosas, the delicate jungle fern that collapse like women shamed at the first touch of a hand. With my cock still hanging out I saw, at the river where the women had washed their clothing, the band of fifteen rebels—Guatemalans who had infiltrated Mexico seeking refuge. With a nose for the scent of prey,

Suki had led us to them. Suki understood the art of the knife. He understood the mind of his prey. Our goal was to kill them all.

They settled down, hunkered down and stripped off their gear, feeling safe in the waning light. I stuffed my cock back in my pants because no man should go into battle with his dick hanging out. Like an invisible wind, Suki, guided us down to the river. I stood. Opened fire and six of them went down. Before the others could react, Suki with his knife slashing took out three men lying on bedrolls. The others ran, leaving their gear and their weapons down to the hats they wore. I heard thrashing in the darkness and the sullen thud of a body falling.

Bodies lay leaking blood on the soft slope of the Rio Verde where just hours before the Indian women had washed their clothes. And then Suki emerged from the jungle, panting, gleeful, his hands bloody, his knife dark red. As I watched he took the left ears of the corpses.

Mosquitoes had settled on a corpse, covering it like a black web, and as Suki sliced away the ear the cloud of insects lifted as if the man's soul held down by the weight of their bodies had broken free.

I remember the smell of blood and dirt and the uneasy smell of shit and piss on the stained and jungle-wet clothing and it wasn't a sad smell at all. It was the smell of money.

Like a scavenger I went through the packs looking for tags, IDs, maps, journals, diaries because, as Fidel Castro once wrote, a diary can get lost in a knapsack. I wanted anything to identify these men. As I dug, I rolled one of the bodies over and found a woman. She was young with black hair and black staring eyes. There was a slanted rip in her chest where the bullet had entered at an oblique angle and torn her open. Through the rip, I saw her heart ready for the plucking as if some Maya priest had cut her to sacrifice her to the rain god.

Suki knelt for her left ear, blood dripping from his fingers. We dragged the corpses into the river, set them to float, letting the slow current bury them. And then Suki squatted. He wiped his blade on his pant leg. He looked at me. He said,

You want to track them cojudos down tonight?

No, let's get some rest. They're helpless without their gear.

We left the riverbank and retreated to the vines and the brush we had just crawled out of, retreated to our pure water and our camouflage.

In minutes Suki was asleep, eyes covered with his campaign hat. I saw a dotted line across his chest where the artery of one of his victims had showered blood and on this bloodline a cluster of mosquitoes had lighted. I tried to count them but in the dark, the bodies became a single black line pulsing, expanding, contracting, a thousand bodies working as one living thing.

I am efficient. I have a skill at destroying people, houses, dreams. I kill idealistic Guatemalans because my brother-in-law, the Chief Executive in Charge of Death, pays me to. Killing them makes him richer. The seed of death is planted deep in me. I am human. I have two choices— oblivion or murder. In this I'm no different than any other human.

13.

From the doorway to the laundry room I watch René. He's bent over so I see just his butt and his feet. Panting, hips driving up and down, down and up, a dog humping a leg and I hear his usual merdemondieu merdemondieu merdemondieu as he orgasms, cum gushing automatic as a mongrel salivating at the sight of fresh meat and then he straightens. His hair, black ringlets falling, coils of black wire to his shoulders, shakes, a dog shaking water from its body, and then he hitches up his denims. I hear a laugh. He says,

You ain't much, mami, but you'll do in a pinch.

Mami. He calls all his men mami. It is like he has hit me in the mouth with a rock and I am bleeding. I have to get the hell out of there but I can't because watching him is magnetic. Watching the heavy thighs, the broad back. And then, his bitch of the moment stands in the doorway tucking in his shirt. I am sick. He is a young kid. New. About twenty. Not a man at all but a little girl in a boy's body looking bewildered and wild and afraid. And then I hear René laugh, that hideous deep chest laugh, mocking and satyric, that sinks deep like a hook in the heart. He kisses the boy on the lips and he says,

Next time I fuck your mouth.

I pull back then, listening like a gossip at the doorway to a harem room. Betrayal, a knife in my chest, takes my breath away.

Behind me, in the corridor, I hear the sound of wheels on concrete and then the door opens and an inmate named Ernie rolls a laundry cart heaped with towels and sheets and the blue chambray shirts that even at twenty feet stink of sweat and semen—the hard odor of men in a cage.

Hey Mitch, he says. Whatcha doin?

René emerges from the laundry room, hair swinging like wild snakes, a grin on his face. He says,

Mitch, Ernie, you guys been here long?

And then he walks past me and I hear washing machines click on and the rumble of running water. Ernie says,

Gotta get this load in, Mitch.

He pushes past me.

I watch René leave.

At the door, he glances back. I know then that I'll have to kill him for his treachery.

14.

René lies, as always, on his bunk, hands clasped behind his head, black ringlets of hair spreading out over his pillow like snakes writhing out of his head. I sit on the edge of my bunk looking at betrayal, studying deceit as it sleeps in the peculiar innocence of a man who thinks he can do no wrong. He has no idea of the pain and anguish in my heart for having yielded to him, the first, the last, the one man I have ever let into my body and he throws it away like the peelings of a poisoned apple.

I shake his shoulder. He opens his eyes. He grins and rests his hand on my arm. I say,

You cheating bastard.

He sits up, back to the wall. Sneering, he says,

Mitch, mami, tu es jaloux, mais je t'ai dit—I fuck who I want.

15.

I am the last man in the laundry room. It is quiet, the heat of the dryers hangs like a hot fog in the air, and the stench of bleach boils poison gas in the air. The odor of detergent—that plain unadorned unperfumed detergent—clings to the towels, to the sheets, to the chambray shirts, masking for a moment the smell of sweat. I wait then, in the silence, pull one of the machines away from the wall, rip and, grasping the motor, I bend the fan blade back and forth until it cracks free.

It is a flat blade.

It is ugly and it is metal.

In its raw form, I see the shape of the shank in the steel.

I see it in its perfection, its killing form.

I see it burnished, shaped, polished, sharpened.

I see it planted in René's treacherous heart.

Hands quaking, heart pounding, I look around, check for eyes. Finding none, I shove the machine back against the wall. Stuff the blade in my waistband. Walk out of the laundry room stopping like a pilgrim at a shrine before the table where René took his boy. For a moment I am happy because from their union there will be no issue. In the universe of fucking men, there is no creation.

I feel the rush of death, feel the sin of betrayal, feel the sweat break out under my arms and I am glad René will die. I will kill him before he has another chance to create a replica of his lying, cheating, treacherous self.

Merde, mami, he says, I use bitches like toilet paper. Use'em and throw'em away and if they got a kid, who gives a fuck. There's just more of me out there.

No more of you, René. No more of you.

And then I rap on the door and the guard opens. I say, One of the machines is on the fritz.

Yeah, yeah, he says.

16.

I want the shank to bite like a shark. Want it to sink into his skin, rip at his bone, crush it to powder. The Greeks have a word for death—thanatos. The French have words for love—l'amour fou, l'amour lointain. No one has a word for his betrayal because in him there was no conscience, just the animal drive to plant his seed in as many bodies as he could find. The Greeks have a word for forgiveness. The French have a word for redemption. Dante has ten thousand words for the eternal hellfire I hope René burns in.

The shank rises from a flat slab of steel. Black with oil, gray with dust, flat and black and gray it lays on the table. A piece of clay I can mold into anything—a flower, a bird, a butterfly—but like a sculptor addressing a block of stone to see the one true real object hidden in the crystal, I see one thing—a death machine.

I work it—day after day—scraping at the edges until they shine. Then scraping more until the shine of the metal yields its blood to the stone floor, until the stone floor digs away the steel hiding the shank, digs it away, carves at it until it reveals itself—an exact image of platonic perfection—a shank that fits both the hand and the mind, a shank that feels balanced as an ashwood arrow nocked in the bow of a yeoman, a shank with a life of its own as if it alone, fed by my will, can find its way into his body, penetrate his skin, burrow into his muscle, chip away at his bone leaving death buried inside him the way he had buried his cock in me.

When I hold the shank to the light, I see the drippings of blood, the smear of semen, the juice of death and I shudder with joy, but still it isn't ready, is not yet perfect and so for days I file away at the haft to unveil the grip, a slender shaft of steel that I wind with thread pulled from the weave of a white T-shirt he had wiped his cock on so many times. The dried semen stiffens the threads until, on the shaft, the handle takes shape, phallic and stiff and wound tight. To secure it in place, I eschew glue or paste or tape—No, I want this angel of death to be part of me. I want to sink part of me into his treacherous hide, to sink into him like poison from the fang of a viper.

So, at night, as I lie on my bunk listening to the snoring men in their steel and concrete cages, I jerk off, saving the semen in a plastic cup until I can smear it on the string handle of the shank where it dries hard enough to hold. When it is hard and stiff, I study it in the sunlight streaming through the cell window, adore it, worship it like one of the Lords of Xibalba worshipping the dying and resurrecting corn god and it is death.

It lays in my palm, fits my hand with the perfect feel of an erect cock about ready to explode, like a pistol at the moment the bullet breaks from the muzzle screaming death all the way, but as with all blades, it is quiet and straight and stiff and it is ready.

17.

I set a date and a time for his execution and that day I
follow him from our cell to the laundry room, to the heat and
smell of soap and bleach and the dry ugly scent of men's
underwear permeated with the crust of their impossible
dreams, encrusted with the fantasies locked up in their loins
and bursting out leaving them helpless and wanton. As René
turns to roll up his sleeves, I draw the shank from my sock
and hold it to the light and he stops, left hand on a half-
rolled right sleeve. Those black ringlets of hair glistening
with the sweat already dripping from his skin in the heat of
the laundry room and then he commits a crime even more
heinous than his treachery, more despicable than his lustful
fucking of the blond-headed boy I had seen him humping
like a dog—he laughs. He says,
What's that, mami?
René, kneel and beg for your life.
Fuck you, asshole. I didn't marry your ass, I just fuck it
and you fucking bears are all alike with your marshmallow
verges and I know you don't have the guts to use the blade. I
know you're a chickenshit.
He laughs. He turns his back to me. The ringlets now
oily with sweat swirl like eels in water and I take a step, grab
his shoulder, spin him around. His face is a grinning face.
His eyes are haughty, daring. His body a sacred vessel,
immune to the profane world, that I am going to profane
with the shank. Locking onto his eyes, I smile, and then I
ram the blade into his chest between the third and fourth
ribs, just at the base of the heart and his face breaks open
with surprise. I step back. The shank handle glistens with
sweat and blood. I am proud that my sweat shines on the
threads of the handle, awakening the semen I laced there to
harden.
René looks down at the blade buried in his chest. The
first blush of blood blooms around the blade and he
crumples to his knees. He opens his mouth, his tongue slips

33

between his teeth, lays on his lips pink and flat and dying. He whispers,

Et toi? Pourquoi tu me tues, toi?

I know his blood is filling his chest cavity. There is no salvation when the blade slices at the heart, when the metal bites the muscle there, when the snake buries its fangs.

I watch him tumble face down, the handle of the shank driven deeper into him and once and for all and forever he is dead.

18.

I solved the paper problem with my manuscript by going to the library and cutting blank pages out of the signatures of books until I have half a ream of trade-size paper, enough for another forty-five thousand words. The ink now flows smooth as blood and the pages don't smear. I have to get another pen or new ink, because I will have to copy all of my first pages over—leaving just the small problem of legibility. The pages are a mystery—each one for sure a treasure—but to unveil it will require a lot of work because as I write the pages, I find that I can't remember anything I've written. I don't remember where it came from. I read it and it's like the work of a stranger. My choices are to stop here, go back to the beginning and copy over—but the memory problem will still be there. Or, I can push on to meet my quota of twelve hundred words a day until I get to the end—but that in and of itself is a problem because I don't know the end. Do I target my release day and call that the end? Or do I target some distant future and let it run until then?

One additional problem is what to do with the toilet tissue pages—destroy them or keep them after I copy them. Version control. I'll have to work on that. But the memory problem poses a bigger threat right now. I'll have to figure out what's going on.

19.

Yesterday I killed René. I think it was yesterday. It all melds into a shower of red and hands and that blade planted in his chest. I see the blue shirt, red spilling out like a flower blooming. And his face, the grimaced questioning. I listened to his last gasp, that peculiar rale of the breath as it leaves the body, buzzing, flies carting off the soul. The Greeks called flies psychopomps, but the Greeks didn't have a word for René's deceit.

I left the blade stuck in his heart, the handle protruding like the flesh-colored stem of a bright red poppy. I turned away, feeling nothing. Just as I felt nothing when my father died. The flies of death ported feeling away like maggots to a netherworld where there is no sensation.

In his heart, the shank—second-cousin to a stone—a shiv made from a fan blade, ground to a point on the hard flat surface of a concrete floor. The crimson poppy of death blooming on his chest. There was no other way—but with the crudest weapon.

The scent of blood still reeks in my nose. I still feel the shock of the shank slipping between his third and fourth ribs. I still see him pitched forward, blossoms of blood spilling on the floor. In the quiet of steel and concrete, the rush of blood in my ears muffles all other sound but the coughing of men in their sleep.

And then there is a flash, the ominous click of heels on steel, the argument of light and night and the torch glares in my eyes and the guard, the night guard whose eyes are soft and puffy with the alcoholic red of a man who doesn't sleep well, whispers,

On your feet, Mitchell. The Governor wants you.

My breath catches in my chest. The breath lays there unwilling to come out. I say,

I'm sleeping.

The gate swings open. The guard slaps my foot with his nightstick. He says,

I have to haul your sick ass outa here in a wheelbarrow, you're goin.

I stand, hands behind my back, but he taps my elbow with his hardwood nightstick and whispers,

No cuffs, Mitchell.

I smell his breath. That hard alcoholic breath of a man trapped in a skin from which there is but one escape. I lead him out of the cell, down the corridor, my feet tuned to his tread. We march as one footfall down the steel steps, silent to the first floor to the dim lighted hallway to the Governor's office where the guard pokes me in the back, shoves me through the door into the room where the Governor sits at his desk. A single light blooms a flower of yellow on the dark wood. He looks up at me, his face gray. In the light, I do not see his hands, just the gray face, the thin gray lips, the gray eyes, the gray skin, the gray hair clipped short and flat on the top like the hair of a drill instructor. On the desk, a white cloth lit by yellow light. Under the cloth, there is a lump. I stand at attention. He says,

Sit.

I sit.

He looks at me. He says,

You have any idea why you're here, Mitchell?

I'm a thief, I say. I steal women's underwear.

He laughs. It is not a good laugh, not the amused laugh of a man who has heard a good joke but the cosmic laugh of a god getting ready to shit on the world. He says,

You think I'm stupid?

No sir, I don't think you're stupid.

You think I haven't read your sheet?

You know why I'm here.

I need a man like you.

I look at him. I wanted to see the shank I had buried in René's chest. I wanted to see the bloody shirt with his life staining it. Instead, I see the gray eyes hard as steel

36

searching my face like an insect gnawing away bark so it can lay eggs in the wood. I say,

That's sort of upside down, isn't it, chief?

I've been watching you, Mitchell.

He opens a drawer in his desk. Lays a gray file folder on top, opens the folder, slides a piece of paper out, looks at it, then he says,

I need a man like you to keep things in line out there.

Out where?

In the yard.

How long?

Two extra hours a day, he says.

You've got personnel.

Do you know what I'm asking of you?

Spell it out.

I need a man who gets things done. A man who keeps all these honyonks in line. A man who can knock heads so it won't fall back on me.

He smiles. A gray smile. Gray teeth. Gray lips. I say,

You want an enforcer.

I want a man like you.

I'm just a con busted for stealing undies from a laundromat.

He looks at the paper on his desk again. He says,

You talk to no one about this. But if those shitheads get off the mark, you hammer them back into shape.

Why me?

He sniffles. Shrugs his shoulders. He says,

Do you want the job?

If I say yes, what do I get?

He lifts the paper from the desk, slides it at me. It is a color photograph 8½ by 11 on glossy paper. It shows a body pitched face down in a pool of blood in the laundry room. Heavy black ringlets of hair coil down and dip in the blood like black snakes frozen in a red sea. My throat tightens. My gut clamps. My breath burns in my chest. The Governor retrieves the photo, seals it in the envelope and opens the desk drawer. He looks at me.

Weekly verbal reports. The yard is yours. Break heads. Okay. Kick ass. Fine.

I stand. Wobble on my feet. Taste bile tearing up my throat. The Governor says,

One more thing, Mitchell.

I take a deep breath. I watch his hand lift the white cloth in the yellow light of the desk lamp. The cloth slides away and on the desk I see my shank with its semen-encrusted shaft, its blue steel blade still tainted with René's blood. The Governor prods the shank across the desk. It glistens. I let out my breath. I look at the Governor. He says,

Now get out of here.

I turn to the open door. The guard hovers in the gray light, his badge glistening like a gold spider, fangs sunk into his chest.

He follows me, silent, back up the steel stairs to my cell. He closes the gate behind me.

My bunk is hard. The mattress stiff. It stinks of sweat. I listen to the sounds of men asleep, the low rumble of the deep snorer, the thin, wispy pleading snore of thin men in the agony of dreams and then I look up. The guard is still at the gate, one hand on the bars. Leaning in, he says,

What's with you and the Governor, Mitchell?

He showed me a picture of René, I say.

René? The clown who got shanked in the shower?

The same.

What did he want?

He wanted me to finger the cunt who did it.

What did you say?

I told him it was me.

The guard laughs. He says,

You're a weird bitch, Mitchell. You know that? A sick weird bitch.

He turns and walks away.

20.

It is sunny. The fog has lifted. The smell of the ocean washes in, a clean sweet and salty smell. Just over the wall, just beyond the rush of the freeway, just past the beach, the ocean sweeps itself over the sand cleansing, washing away the detritus of the night and the tide.

I am tired from a night of bad dreams. I haven't written a word since the Governor showed me his picture of René dead. He has me where he wants me.

I squat on my haunches, my hands damp with dirt. In the ground in front of me, a small flowerbed lies, its plants in rows exuding the smell of marigolds, gleaming with the bright sky-blue shine of asters, arrayed in the brilliant rainbow of chrysanthemums. Blossoms the color of orange sunsets. Green and fresh as morning mist.

And beyond the bed, close to the fence with its razor wire tangled like angry black adders, I watch two cons face to face, nose to nose, hands still at their sides. Even at that distance I smell the scent of arousal that oozes out of men only when they face off toe to toe.

I smell blood, I smell death.

Standing, I brush away the fresh dirt from my hands and walk toward them, listening to the threats, watching the hands ball into fists, watching the fists come up like sledge hammers, watching the arms bulging and tattooed and warlike.

And then the one whose name is Freddie slams his fist into the gut of his enemy who pitches over vomiting a gush of air. Before Freddie lands the coup de grâce, I snatch his arm, spin him around and, grabbing the fallen by the neck, I ram their heads together. They drop.

I stand over them. I say,

Not here, not now boys. You fuck up, I break your arms.

They look at me, both of them on their butts on the ground, like lost sheep asking what happened to Little Bo Peep.

I turn then and go back to the Governor's flowerbed, to the dirt, to the rows of marigolds gleaming in the sunlight and I file the aborted battle away in a little report.

21.

The library smells of moldy paper and the mystery of a long deserted place. The air hangs heavy. The odor of dust like a sick perfume hiding a rotting corpse. I turn on the lights. The neon flickers, goes dark, then flutters to a dim yellow buzz.

The door behind me closes. The guard raps on the glass, holds up ten fingers twice—twenty minutes—then draws his thumb across his throat.

The library has a single table—oak—six feet long. Four hard backed chairs—oak. The floor is concrete. On the concrete a thin layer of dust—no footprints, no marks, no residual tracks of the men who were there before me.

I walk into the stacks. Six feet high, ten cases of books and I thumb my way through the volumes looking for anything on roses and gardening. As I touch them small clouds of dust kick up. Fine, choking dust.

In the yellow light, the backs of the books look sick. As I pull them off the shelves, I feel their weariness, but for every one that has been opened, there are a dozen that have never had their spines cracked. Row after row after row.

Then, in far back corner, high up on the top shelf in the shadows, I see the spine of a book on English roses.

Dragging a chair from the table to the stack, I climb up to pull out the book. And there, behind it, against the wall, its front cover facing me like the visage of a prisoner in a long forgotten cave, I see *Notre Dame des Fleurs*.

I check the time. My twenty minutes are up. I crack the book, expecting to find a translation. The cover is loose, open, the pages in French. They have been marked and dog-eared and even in the low yellow light, I see marginal notes in a crimped and obscure hand. "Qu'est-ce qu'il veut dire?"

The door open, the guard shouts,
Time's up, asshole, let's roll.
I stuff *Notre Dame des Fleurs* back in place, hiding it
with the book on roses. The guard says,
Get what you needed, Mitchell?
Next time, I say.
He clicks off the lights, and in the half-dark, I smell dust
and the faint odor of decay and then I lead him back to C
Block.

I lie down on the bunk, hands behind my head, and with
my eyes closed I see the marked and blackened and dog-
eared pages of Genet's masterpiece. It is there, hiding in a
place where it shouldn't be. I have to check it out again. It is
a forbidden book. It is a handbook of sin, a worm in the
heart of decency. Irresistible. I remember first reading it in
Tulle. I remember finding it in a small bookshop. A clean
edition with the pages still uncut. *Notre Dame des Fleurs*.
Written while Genet was in prison. It is like finding an old
friend in a foreign country. I want to shake his hand, to ask
him to join me for tea, to sit down at a table and talk about
our lives and the mistakes we have made.

My chance comes the next week. This time I pull the
book down and spend an hour going over it. It is a mess. The
words have been underlined and circled in red and blue and
black inks so heavy, entire lines are blotted out and illegible.
In some cases, a few words poke through, isolated like
prisoners in a cage, one to one to one but with their
neighbors smudged. It is impossible to say with exactness
what they mean. Who had loved this book enough to mark it,
but in decoding turned it into an obscure hieroglyphic tangle
no one could read again?

And the marginalia are as perplexing—some notes are in
a French hand, but others in a crimped Cyrillic hand,
possibly Balkan. In places the ink of the pen has smeared
leaving even the margin notes unintelligible. There are no
names here, no one claiming credit for insights. Only the

41

name of the author—Genet—is indisputable, only the title of the book is unequivocal— *Notre Dame des Fleurs*.

My time is up.

I return the book to its safe place and then, as I stow it, the book of English roses falls over. Behind it, in a corner, I see *Les 120 Journées de Sodom*—the Marquis' masterpiece.

It takes my breath away.

In that place, hidden as if the writer himself had put it there out of reach, out of time, the book shimmers in the quiet darkness like a black jewel.

The guard again tears me loose from my pleasure and I walk away, amazed that two volumes in a forbidden code hide in the stacks whispering their ciphers like voices oozing from the walls.

I lie awake for hours. My mind buzzing. My brain hungry.

It is two weeks before I get back to the library but I have permission from the Governor for two hours of work. As I tell him, I need to do more research if I am to make his little flowerbed flourish so I return, feeling like a thief sneaking into a treasure cave.

From the shelf, I pull the *120 Journées* and open it.

I smell blood. Dust. The scent of old paper and again I see that the text, on every page, has been marked. The words are underlined and circled but the writing is different, as if a dozen hands have marked and read and marked and read. There are overlapping notes as if the readers didn't agree with one another and were arguing on the page about the meanings of the text. The result is the same. I know the book. I know who wrote it. I have read it in another time and place, stirred to my depths by the Simple Vices, puzzled by the Complex Vices, stunned by the sheer bravura of the writing, but here, the text itself is a mystery as if written in code and illegible.

It makes me sad. It makes my heart beat fast. I imagine the hours men spent trying to decipher the meanings hidden

in the lines. I envy the first man who read the text before it
was marked and distorted, read it when it was still pure and
hard and true to the hand that wrote it. Here and there, a
sacred line is still legible, a few words left intact like shards
of a vase in an archeological dig, but the sense is obscured.
Each word is a small crumb on a hidden trail—just enough
to tantalize, never enough to satisfy hunger.

I remember *L'Étranger* with its markings and obscure
notes and I remember how my own writing on toilet paper
disappeared like blood seeping into sand leaving the illusion
of a story but no single word is readable.

My time is up and so I stow *Notre Dame des Fleurs* and
the *120 Journées* in their hiding places and return to my cell
and think of the obscured meanings under the black marks
like palimpsests. Their truth lies buried but unlike the
palimpsest, there is no way to remove a layer to find the
hidden meanings.

22.

It is another week before I return to the stacks. I take
my time. I have convinced the Governor that I need to clean
up the library before worms eat the books and mold
disfigures the pages.

I move the *120 Journées* and *Notre Dame des Fleurs* to
a new place deeper in the stacks. No one ever comes to the
library, but I take the precaution anyway. Squatting on the
floor, I study the *120 Journées*, searching for some insight
into why the readers needed to mark the pages.

And then, in a corner, hidden, I find a small French-
English dictionary and it becomes clear—the readers wanted
to understand the writing but didn't know French and so the
markings were their effort to decode the language. But in
decoding it, they had blanketed it with layer upon layer of
incomprehensibility.

Notre Dame des Fleurs like Camus' novel, is marked in
places until many of the words had been blotted out, had lost

their integrity, their drive to meaning—the Xs of the plurals blurred until you have to decide from context. It is all archeology now, retrieving the bits and pieces of lost and wonderful things from destroyed worlds—what the meaning is. That word again, meaning—qu'est-ce qu'il veut dire?

Notre Dame des Fleurs hiding its meanings behind the underlined and blacked-out words, points like a spear at René. Am I fingering the same pages René felt? Did he come to the library? Did he discover Notre Dame? We were both enforcers—me, a bear who loves men, René a priapic monster who took his pleasure when and where he found it. Maybe I am too hasty. Maybe there was more to him than I saw. I never asked why he was in prison. He never offered to tell me. There are secrets in every grave but like Perceval, I am at fault for not asking the right question at the right time.

I see now that I have to make up time—have to write like mad, have to find the river of words to atone for my failing, atone for giving in to my addictions.

One hundred days since René died in the prison laundry with a knife in his deceitful heart. I am death, I am killer, the killer who hides inside a bag of flesh and blood pretending to be shocked and amazed at the terrible callousness around me. I respect nothing, I respect no one, I want what I want when I want it and I want it now—but in the dark as I re-imagine *Notre Dame des Fleurs*, as I pore over the memory of *Les Cent-vingt Journées*, I see myself reflected in the evil De Sade documents in this terrible, truthful book—alone. You're never alone even in the depths of your despair because at any minute the bars open and faces jut out of the shadow, masks of fierce men with tattooed backs and mayhem in their hearts and they own you—there is no time alone and so at night, hidden in the warm folds of a prison blanket, you feel the secret arousal in your loins, feel the eruption of hidden desire, the surge of past gratifications and you hope the bars remain closed until you have let out the pent-up lust that cannot be satisfied in a normal way.

Normal. There is no normal anywhere—it is all skewed, slewed, slanted, bent.

As I stare at the bars I do not see anyone. When I raise my hands to brush against the cold hard steel, I remember that I am locked away, freedom stolen by theft. I am ashamed because even in here there is shame, my shame, if my fellow inmates ever find out that I am here because I stole a dryer full of women's underwear. No one knew but René and now he is dead—is that why I killed him? There is once again blood on the hands of a Mitchell—although my mother always called me Henry, my father called me his idiot son—while in here I am Mitch—one syllable, clean pure hard real Mitch. René knew of my transgression but now he is dead and I write about death.

23.

In the jungle where you move at the pace of the vegetation growing, you never know who or what will ambush you, and so you walk like a man on death row—one foot held up before planting it, a pace, another hesitation as you listen for the crack of a limb or the snap of a rifle clip.

No training can prepare you for the actual moment of attack that comes not with the shrill blast of a whistle and the exhortation to charge. Nothing measures death like the quick and quiet gravity of a man on your back, his knife ripping at your throat. Death comes with the abrupt heave of a springe snapping your leg and hurling you into the air like a trapped animal. You feel it, you know it is coming, and you do not want to die and so you act before death grabs you— you hear the knife a second before it lands, you hear the rustle of a sleeve, the catch of breath as it, the knife, is raised and you act as a simple animal—say a platyhelminth—a worm-like, amoeba-like reaction. You react and if you are lucky and if you are quick and if your enemy is slow, you gut him before he guts you and that day he lay in fatigue green, a campaign hat thrown back on his head held with a leather strap, the strap at his throat like a severed artery and he groaned, hands clutching his belly that lay open, his gut spilling out through the green fatigue like a giant green turd from an inhuman beast.

I knelt, pressed my left hand over his mouth and sank the still hot and bloody blade into his heart and he bucked at the last instant but I leaned into him, into his blood and I smelled the severed gut, smelled the half digested food in his ruptured belly and then he lay quiet and I, on my knee, searched the jungle for movement, saw the green and dusty jackets of my squad, and I knew that I had escaped, that the enemy alone lay dead and already decomposing and that moment is fixed in my mind like the steps of a ballet, fixed and immutable because death can never be reversed and every death is unique.

24.

I write my twelve hundred words, put them down on paper that I hide in a tube of toilet paper in the mattress. If the guards find these pages, and if they read them, they will know that I killed René for fucking a boy in the laundry. I should have killed the boy instead—there was a choice—it was as if I were back in Guatemala, on patrol, knife in hand again, no choice, René, there was no choice—he was unfaithful just as my father wounded my mother with his endless womanizing and so I killed him. Knife to the heart as if he were nothing but an animal.

25.

I ruminate over Camus, *L'Étranger*, searching for some hint of the truth beyond the words on the page, but the words are masked, hidden, each one a small cipher. What does this one mean? Can I ever know?

My new cellmate comes out of the ranks of the innocent and the unredeemed. He made a mistake his first day here—

he looked an inmate in the eye and that alone means either he wanted to die or that he was in love. The one thing saving him is that they think he is mine.

I might tattoo him with the shamrock and sixes centered in the leaves. But if I do he will cry as the ink bleeds into his skin. Yesterday, he sat whimpering on his bunk in his little femme way and had to tell me his story, his sordid little life story about his mother who was a whore who worked out of a trailer—stop, I told him, You're making me horny, but this hopeless wreck of a human being did not know his father. He was raised by his granny and his wicked mother who, as he described her, reminded me of Mrs. Wilson, one of my father's many women. His granny thought he was cute when he was drunk and by the time he was twelve he had already been joyriding. When he turned nineteen that joyride turned into grand theft auto which he thought was so cool until I explained it to him that in here his ass was worth more than his mother's ever was. I tell him I will have to use him in order to save him. He thanks me without knowing what he's thanking me for. He understands nothing. He is an ignorant little Valley boy who has never read a book.

26.

I'm still alive. I'm writing. I've met my quota for eight days in a row. Twelve hundred times eight equals ninety-six hundred words and the stack grows thick and rich and wide as a river. I no longer can hide it in the plastic sack in the toilet under the shit and piss because it has grown too large. There is a second complication, an unexpected one with the pen and paper, because the ink spreads when it hits the paper that is so thin the words run. I am not writing a mystery but my writing is a sordid mystery and I will never figure out what I have said.

Now and then I can decode a word, a phrase, sometimes even an entire sentence, but as soon as I put a word down, it

disappears from my mind and there is no memory left to
compare it to. The ink runs off the pen just as writing pulls
memory out of my mind. Sometimes whole paragraphs are
intact and so without effort I join the ranks of the great
writers—writing indecipherable shit that no one can read
and which, if they could, would bore them to tears but it's
just in the writing because my story is so unique, so pure, so
true and untold before that it will shake literature loose from
the Chekhovian Joycean DuJardinean meander that has
held it in thrall for two centuries. The lone caveat will be that
I have to peel away the layers of the obscure to reveal the
truth and I remember with a great sadness how the barons
like my brother-in-law in charge of filth and defecation have
peeled away everything until there's nothing left but the scab
of an earth, nothing left but cows and pigs and horses and
cats and dogs and sheep and shit and everything else is dead
or dying.

27.

I lose myself in the writing. At times I glow in the
sudden and free rush of words cascading from the pen as
though it, the pen, lives its own life, as if I am there only to
hold it upright against the paper while it does its work ...

I remember the monster I saw in Guayaquil. She sat on
a steel gas can in a pile of trash—banana peels, orange rinds,
pineapple bodies—and in her mess she was not recognizable
as a woman. Her legs had swollen up like pig bladders, her
face puffy as a corpse, her lips thick and cyanotic as if the fat
had choked off all the oxygen in her body leaving just the
hulk, the bones, the blood turning black. On her shoulder
there was a small monkey with a collar around his neck and
the collar had eaten away the hair and dug into the monkey's
flesh. There was a festering pusiness that oozed around the
leather and the monkey lay on the woman's shoulder like a
wounded soldier. I saw those monkeys in the jungle later
when I was on patrol with Suki and in the trees they are

robust and strong and alive but as the hardwood trees
transform into tables and chairs and armoires for matrons in
Boston, the monkeys migrate and die and rot until the last
survivor ends up on a chain around the neck of a human sick
with elephantiasis, her skin stretched so tight over the bones
you expect her to burst the way I saw corpses in Hamiltepec
explode, scattering rot and putrescence on the trees until for
a hundred meters around you approached at the risk of
gagging and vomiting at the smell. Now, as I write, I see how
they peel away everything, not just the trees, but everything,
leaving me without family, me with nothing but the knife
and the AK47 and the Beretta that I used to blow open the
heads of the rebels who had no idea my body was paid for by
the banana barons and the coffee chieftains to gut the
opposition. I was good at it, not as good as Suki who had no
qualms about taking the left ears of his child victims,
whereas I shied from it but had no compunctions about
taking the left ear of a man or woman until in a fit of
enlightenment I saw that my sack of ears— while it paid me
my bonuses and bought the bodies of whores in
Tegucigalpa—my sack of ears was money in the bank of men
such as my fascist brother-in-law, that chief executive in
charge of death, and I was sickened at my own life because I
was one of the peelers, the man with the knife paring the
scalp of an insurgent, the man with the bulldozer peeling off
the layers of soil down to the sterile rock where nothing
fruitful can thrive and then moving on to another place just
as I moved from Guayaquil to Guatemala and from
Guatemala to Mexico where I peeled away the skin and flesh
of men I was told to slaughter.

And now as I lie awake at night waiting for my eyes to
close, I see my brother-in-law with his broken leg and his
fractured arm—the price he had to pay for what he did to
Geraldine—as the winner. He wins as he sits at his desk,
hidden behind his walnut paneling, guarded by his secretary
who will not permit normal men into his presence unless

they beg so that he lives rich and high above. But my justice
is knowing that he has to breathe the corrupt air he creates
and in breathing it he further corrupts it until soon it will no
longer be fit to breathe and he will strangle, like the rest of
us, on the filth spewing out. What a grand day that will be.

28.

I think about my new cellmate—Donny Farmer, a
simple boy—who lies on his bunk crying at night because he
is alone and lost, a mere boy with no experience of blood,
who came into prison for stealing a car. When he cries, he
sounds like a small child. He doesn't understand why he is
here, he doesn't understand that the men who put him here
hate him. He doesn't understand that if I met him in the
jungle in Mexico or Ecuador or in the copper-rich mountains
of Chile, I would take his ear without question, I would gut
him, I would cut his throat, I would leave his tongue hanging
on his chest.

I don't tell him that he is one of the lucky ones, one of
the chosen lifted out of the slaughter and the butchery of the
abattoir by reason of his thievery and that out there the
killing goes on and on and on and no one knows why, while
in here as long as he sucks cock and agrees to be the soft and
lovely bottom men twice his size desire, he will survive.

I don't tell him that in here his ass is worth more than
his entire body out there. I don't tell him because he will cry
and whimper and I have heard enough of men whimpering
as they, on their knees, begged me not to kill them—but why
not? Their ears were more valuable than their politics and so
we took their ears and earned our bonuses and my poor little
innocent neophyte car thief doesn't understand how blessed
he is.

I wait for him to return one day bleeding, his ass torn
open, his mouth bruised—maybe then I will tell him the
truth. What will I tell him? I'll tell him that no matter what
happens, it will be blurred on the page, uneven, a cipher as is

every word that's written in here, out there, everywhere there is a man with a pen and paper aching to tell the truth about his miserable and unpolished existence.

In the yard he hangs around me like a lost puppy begging me for protection. As long as he has my mark on him, he is safe and when we work out, he changes the weights for me and hands me a cloth he lifted from the laundry as a sweat towel and because he is mine, he is safe.

I remember the first days I was here, how unafraid I was. When René died the space around me grew bigger. Only fools tangle with six feet four inches two hundred and seventy-five pounds of man-eater. Squeaky, my little puppy-dog companion, knows just enough to understand that.

29.

Twenty-one days into our relationship he kowtows and scrapes and he is more than willing to let me use him in any way I want. He screams like a little girl when I fuck him and so I give him a name—Squeaky. With my mark on him he can go alone to the laundry, to the yard without having to walk with his back to the wall.

When he made the mistake of looking a blood in the eye, I saved him. It was over fast—the nail of a finger to the chest of the blood with death in his eyes. I shook my head and he backed away, lowered his eyes, turned. If I don't save Squeaky he is a moving target, prey, the lamb. But I stand between him and the predators. I remember how I hated it when my sister Geraldine acquiesced to her husband, that CEO in charge of death and degradation and piss and I remember how I hated to see her train her daughter to bow and scrape and give in and defer. I see defeat in Squeaky— the defeat of the little man. You are measured by how men bow to you. I know that in here, at least, there is reason and logic but out there it is pure reactionary biology. In here, there is the logic of terror—when you rip a man's head off and shit in his neck everything becomes clear. The word gets out and there is peace until a new batch of convicts arrives, all proclaiming their innocence. They are feisty and cruel and you have to teach them logic one at a time until they see the system and they lower their eyes when the teacher walks past. I am that teacher. The supreme logician.

Squeaky admits that he is a thief, a rotten little thief who had never seen blood beyond a bleeding nose. When I fuck his mouth he gobbles up my cum like it is ice cream. I show him my scars, the white worm-like scars on my chest, my left shoulder. He knows he has found a knight.

Because he has a soft mouth I will write him into my manuscript. I don't have to knock his teeth out. I didn't have to write him in, I can't write it all in, not even Genet could write it all in, but he is a little flower with his own perfume and so I will immortalize him. He says,

Do they ever get off your case?

As long as you have my mark, you'll be okay.

What about when you leave here?

What makes you think I'll leave here?

You only got five years.

Shut the fuck up.

I lie awake. I hear him breathe, quiet, peaceful, his ass worn out, but his blood unspilled and then I write.

30.

I write until my hand cramps and my eyes itch with dryness. I get my twelve hundred words. None of it as mysterious as the first hundred pages and that makes me feel good—I have a book, I have Squeaky, I have this satisfaction of knowing that when I reach page one thousand I will stand with the greats—Genet, De Sade, Camus. I write and tomorrow I read. I am alone. Squeaky still has his teeth. Without me, he would not have his teeth.

31.

The guard stares at me through the dimpled glass of the library door, his nose pressed to the pane, his chin a greasy blob on the glass and I rap on his chin and he opens and he says,

What the fuck do you want, you pervert?

I want to see the Governor.

Yeah and I want a new truck.

Tell him.

Sure Mitchell, sure. Soon as I finish picking my teeth.

As the door closes behind me, I glance at the stacks where my manuscript sleeps between *Notre Dame des Fleurs* and the book of English roses. I'll have to find a way to get an unmarked copy of the *120 Journées*.

32.

Back in my cell, I lie on my bunk studying the cracks in the ceiling, watching the wispy strand of a cobweb flutter in the air batted back and forth by my breath. Squeaky lies on his bunk curled up face to the wall. I am afraid that today is the last time I will ever put pen to paper. Artie the guard raps on the bars, his nightstick long and black and deadly as a snake. He says,

Gov says I run your perverted ass to his office, Mitchell.

You're so nice to me, how come you are?

I stand, place my hands behind my back as the gate opens and he clamps the manacles tight. The steel bites hard and deep. I know there will be blood, but the pain is a reminder that I am still alive, still the blood is red, still the breath flows, still my eyes see the gray and dim inside of the steel and concrete cage simple as the inside of a coffin and as we march down the steel grated steps, the guard nudges me in the kidneys with every stride.

You like that, asshole?

Like what?

My stick in your ass.

You don't know what I like.

I got an idea, he says.

The door to the Governor's office is open. He sits at his oak desk in an office chair big enough to be a throne and behind his head the light from the oval window filters down on him like a ray of sunshine striking the corona of a saint. He looks at me, his gray eyes cut like swords. He has to be a hard man to deal with hard men and he says,

Close the door, Mr. Miller.

Artie pulls the door shut. When we are alone, the Governor says,

What's so urgent, Mitchell?

I need paper. And pens.

Why do you need paper and pens?

I'm writing.

You'll play hell too.

If I don't write, I'll die.

You think I care if you die?

No one cares if I die.

I already gave you the garden. I already gave you a new cellmate. I already gave you time. What do you want?

I need paper and pens because I'm losing everything.

What do you mean?

I mean I'm writing but I can't remember.

A lot of cons have that problem, Mitchell.

I put it down on toilet paper and it blurs and I can't get it back.

He stands. He comes around the desk. He sits on the edge of the oak top staring down at me. His gray eyes unblinking, he says,

Tell me what I need to know.

I had to bash a few heads in the yard.

You got it under control?

It's under control.

What happened?

My cellmate looked at a blood and didn't apologize.

You call him Squeaky?

He's like a little bathtub toy, I say.

A little rubber ducky for you to play with?

He's got himself into a mess.

See? A little thing like that means a lot to me, Mitchell. You don't make much out of it, but from where I sit it's good to know someone is watching the backs of the new queens.

Not watching his back, sir.

You know what I mean. Okay. How much paper do you need?

A dozen yellow-lined tablets and black ballpoints.

You can't have ballpoints.

You want me to stay on top of things, I need pens.

The Governor sniffles. Clears his throat. He turns, sits back down in his arm chair, sits in the halo of sunshine. He opens his desk drawer, hauls out the envelope where he keeps the picture of dead René. Tapping it with his fingernail, he looks at me. He says,

Okay. Paper and two pens, but if one of them shows up in the neck of a con, it's your ass that's going to fry.

Thank you, sir, I say.

Don't thank me yet, Mitchell.

33.

It was night. Suki and I lay behind a blown out adobe wall listening to six Senderos tell stories about the women they had butchered by cutting out their cunts and slashing their breasts. As cigarettes were crushed on stone and as yawns turned to snores, and as sentinels let their caps slide over their eyes, Suki and I rose up like a plague infecting a disease spreading to a sickness.

In Goyllarisquizca, at fifteen thousand feet, there is no vegetation. The air is so thin a scream carries from the knife digging into the skin to the ear. We took out the six. Bodies sprawled under moonlight—it is always moonlit at fifteen

thousand feet because there are no clouds. Then, as they lay
blood yellow, throats gaping, Suki and I took ears, one by
one. There was no rush, no push to a higher meaning. It was
business. It was pleasurable. Sticky blood on our hands, still
warm flesh of severed ears, the welcome stench of bodies
shitting as dead sphincters soiled already wet camouflage
dungarees.

Quiet moonlight settled its yellow dust on the stones. I
see my mistake—killing the Senderos before they had run
their course, killing the killing machines was a mistake
because with their awful and wonderful efficiency, swift and
sure as the Khmer Rouge, they would have made my work
easier, ridding the Altiplano of its two-legged lice. Too late
did I see that the Khmer Rouge were right—civilization is a
scourge on nature. We can't wash our clothes without
fouling the rivers. No human invention will ever mitigate
human destructiveness. But then, that night, that day, that
year, all that mattered were the bags of ears. Cut and dried.
In six months four bags of ears. A hundred thousand dollars.

In the end they trapped Guzman, the thinker who
spawned the blooding, and El Sendero Luminoso died. Yes,
it was a mistake killing them because it opened the door for
corporations to make the dollar de facto official currency of
Ecuador. I did that. I helped do that. I was the gatekeeper
who took out the resistance and the protesters and the
politicians all who stood in the way of my brother-in-law and
his corporate cronies hiding behind their walnut desks,
dining in their mahogany hotels, fucking their thousand
dollar whores.

My sister Catharin is a whore. She is a disease. Her
Disease is my Disease. It is the Sickness of each and every
one of us. No one controls the corporations riding in their
Silver Clouds, bleeding the country white, sucking out its
metal until, one day, the whole nation will collapse—spindly
legs butchered, eyes gouged out, guts ground into sausage,
anchovies to cat food. But then the corporations will find

new bodies to slaughter. At the time, unthinking, I took ears and collected my bonuses.

I am one of the Chosen—a killer of killers, the poison in the well, the edge of the capitalist blade, while Catharin, seeking sainthood, went to India to spread the poison of her aromatic Jesus of the Rose of Sharon and the Lily of the Valley butchering the ancient beliefs and opening the door for corporations to rape and murder a billion Hindus in the name of The Holy Mother Pelf. Jesus Pelf Christ. Jesus Dollar Christ. Jesus Fuck Them Until They Bleed Christ.

34.

Exhausted—Today I have my twelve hundred words down, black on white. I hear steel doors open on the landing and the harsh hammer of steel tapped boots on the grates echoing like the slow slothful crush of a beast gone mad. I tuck the new pages under the mattress of my bunk. Heavy, swollen, thick pages, thick and diseased. I am proud of my work. The guard stares at me and I at him. He rattles the bars of my cell and then walks on by.

And I feel a rush of forbidden pleasure. It is like the time I came home from Grenoble. I was seventeen, diplômé, and carrying a grammar of sex and love and death and I came in Mrs. Wilson's warm and wet cunt and my knees went weak and my breath came in short gasps.

35.

My mark is on Squeaky. He's alive because I'm here, just as I'm alive because of Cain. I remember the day. September. Hot. The live oaks dusty green in the sunlight. The smell of dry grass in the air. It was my third day at the Oak View School for Boys. I hid in the gym shower for half an hour waiting for Charlie Goodson and his crazy buddies to go away because I was afraid, and every minute I stood there listening to the water drip from the shower heads, I

hated my Father for sending me to Oak View where I was
supposed to learn how to be a man, but instead I learned I
was about to be turned into a punk because Charlie Goodson
and his gang pissed on all the little guys and made them suck
dick in the barn or behind the curtain in the auditorium.

It took me two days to figure it out and I hated
crouching in the dripping water. I heard footsteps sounding
like a herd of devil mustangs hammering down the hallway,
but horses didn't giggle. I hugged the wall, shivering,
knowing they'd find me and it would all be over, my mouth
turned into a cunt and I'd be a punk and they'd never let me
forget it the way they did to Lloyd Whitman yesterday.

I took a deep breath, smelled the disinfectant soap and
the anti-fungal powder the gym teachers made us dust with
to keep athlete's foot away. I held my breath because I knew
they could hear me breathe, hear my heart pound, hear my
knees creak, my teeth chatter and then I saw a face peering
around the corner of the shower room.

A grin. A crooked finger saying come here you little shit.
I pushed against the wall and grabbed a shower handle and
held on. The face of Charlie Goodson followed by his big fat
body slid up against me. He said,

I got him, guys. In the shower. Our little girl's hiding in
the shower.

He grabbed my arm. I said,

Let me go, Charlie.

You scared? You wanna call your daddy and your
mommy to come and save you?

Then there were the other two—big boys, tenth graders
with flat top cuts like soldiers, and big arms and hands and
they wore black engineer boots and Frisco jeans and they
wore white T-shirts and around their necks there dangled
silver crucifixes on silver chains. Emblems of the rape club
they ran. They stood around me. Charlie Goodson ripped my
hands free from the safety of the shower.

He pushed me to my knees. He unbuttoned his Frisco
jeans and he said,
Lunch time, Hank. Take a bite of tube steak little buddy.
Today you learn to play the skin flute, Hank.
He laughed. The other two—Bill Collins and Ted
DeLoach—laughed and Ted said,
I get him second, Charlie.
Charlie Goodson grabbed my ears. I heard him cough.
He lunged forward, falling across me. I rolled free.
I looked up as Cain smashed Ted DeLoach in the mouth
and blood flew out like rain and he slapped Bill Collins and
grabbed him by the nape of the neck and forced him to the
shower stall floor and then, turning back to Charlie
Goodson, he picked him up by the nose, two fingers in his
nostrils and blood flared out and around Cain's fingers and
Charlie's eyes, open wide, had the look of a small child being
eaten by a wolf.
Cain then kicked Ted DeLoach in the gut and Ted reeled
back and fell to his knees and out popped his lunch and the
smell was dead and dying and Bill Collins whimpered,
Jeez Cain, don't don't.
Cain lifted him by the left ear and stacked him on top of
Ted DeLoach and his vomit and then he grabbed Charlie
Goodson by the balls and dragged him on top of Bill and
then he turned on the shower.
Hot water sprayed scalding over the stack of jeans and
boots and blood and puke and silver crucifixes. The water
plastered Cain's white T-shirt to his chest. Standing with his
hands on his hips like a general looking over a wasted
battlefield, he smiled. He was massive. He was huge. He was
hard. He was tall. He looked at me and he said,
You okay, Hank?
His voice was already deep and thick like a full-grown
man. I said,
Kinda.

He laughed. He knelt in the water raining down on him and the three boys and he said,

Chuck, can you hear me? Ted? Billy? If I ever find out you've been hurting this kid, I'll cut your nuts off and ram them up your ass then I'll skin you and Ted. I'll put you in Chuck's hide. And Billy? I'll pull all your teeth and jam them into Chuck's eyeballs. Now. Do you hear me?

The three wet ones on the shower floor grunted and flopped like three carp wiggling on a hot sidewalk and Cain arose from his haunches and he towered over me and he said,

Come on, kid.

He dropped his thick arm across my shoulders. He led me out of the gym and into the afternoon sun. He said,

So, how do you like Oak View, Hank?

I've only been here three days.

I hear you've got sisters, Hank.

I've got two sisters. Geraldine and Catharin. They're coming to visit on Parent's Day,

Are they good-looking, Hank?

Why'd you save me, Cain?

That's what a big brother does.

You're my big brother?

For now.

You're a Senior, I said.

That's right.

You look out for all the guys?

Only the little ones who've got sisters, Hank.

Aw, Cain.

Look. You know how to fence?

Fence? Wow, yeah! My dad says a man's gotta know how to use a bow and arrow and he says if I don't learn l'escrime, he'll kick my ass.

He calls it l'escrime, huh?

Isn't that right?

That's right. I made Nationals last year, Hank. In sabre. You know what sabre is?

A sword, I said.

He laughed.

You don't call it a sword, Hank. That's what the bushwas call it. It's a weapon. You learn to use a weapon and no son of a bitch is gonna punk your ass like those shitheads tried.

You didn't use a weapon on those guys, Cain.

Oh yeah. I used the best weapon.

I didn't see one.

Fear, he said. You gett'em pissing in their pants and they're shitting in their heads and they don't give you a hard time.

But you're huge, I said. I'm skinny.

I wasn't always. You're what? Ten?

Just ten, I said.

Well, I'm gonna get you into the weight room, Hank, and I'm gonna pump you up.

Why're you helping me, Cain?

I told you—you got sisters.

My dad fucks Mrs. Wilson, I said.

He looked at me kind of funny then he laughed. He said, Every body fucks somebody, Hank.

You want to fuck my sisters, Cain?

Again he laughed.

No, Big Boy. I just want to take pictures for my collection.

Your collection?

Yeah, I got a collection of sisters from the guys who go here.

Even Charlie Goodson.

Yeah, even Charlie Goodson.

Did you save him?

We stopped at the door to the dining room. Cain turned to look at me. He grabbed my arms with both hands. He squeezed, not too hard, but I felt his steel hard fingers bite into my bones.

Flex, he said.

What?

Let me see a biceps.

I flexed. He laughed.

Yeah, we're gonna pump you up on carbs and lay some muscle on those bones, Hank. Before I finish with you you'll be as big as I am. You like that?

I like that, I said. Then I can save the little guys, right?

Only the ones with sisters, Hank. Only the ones with sisters.

36.

The guard, a chubby Delgado with a pencil-thin moustache and short black hair, has the eyes of a slaughtered pig. He raps on the bars with his nightstick. He says,

Hey asshole, you've got a visitor.

Where's Artie?

Artie's got the day off.

He never takes a day off.

He had a funeral.

A visitor. I have a visitor. I have had no visitors, no one to see, to call, to stare at across the table, no one. My chest seizes up with a hammerlock and my throat freezes. I sit up, swing my feet off the bunk and rub my eyes, feel the grit of a dead night, feel the grime and grunge of bad dreams about small brown men with their throats slit bleeding into the pristine waters of a mountain lake and I say,

You got the right asshole, asshole?

Getchur wormy butt out here, Mitchell.

The floor rolls as I stagger to the gate, routine, hands behind my head, and the guard clamps the manacles on my wrists, locks them tight. The cold metal, heating up as it cuts into my wrists, soothes away the pain.

The gate springs open and I walk out feeling the swing
and sway and rock like I am going to vomit, seasick vomit.
The guard closes the gate and I walk ahead of him, down the
three tiers of steel grates and iron locks of the solid cage
holding us in and then into the blue and white and
fluorescent lit corridor where humans walk in shoes that
squeak on waxed floors.

At the glass door that says Visitors, Delgado unlocks the
manacles and the numbness stings as blood rushes back into
my hands.

I see her at the table, her hands folded on the hard
wood, and my heart hammers in my chest harder than it did
the first time I killed a man and my throat, already tight,
locks up.

I can't breathe as I look at her. She lifts her head, those
eyes springing loose a torrent, and she rises and holds out
her hands and a looseness comes over me as if someone has
yanked out my spine and I have become jelly. I sink into the
chair opposite her and she wipes at her eyes. I grope for the
table, rocking like a boat in violent white water and I say,

Geraldine, what are you doing here?

She clutches at her throat, those fine white fingers lace
across the whiteness of her skin and she picks up the pen
lying on the pad of paper lying on the table and she writes ...
Henry, I thought I'd lost you forever.

My mind flashes to her husband, my brother-in-law
Carl Fairweather. I remember the day I broke his leg with
the bat, broke his arm with the bat, wanted to kill him with
the bat and I remember him writhing on the floor, his face a
white sheet of pain and I remember saying That's for
Geraldine, you cocksucker and if you ever touch my sister
again, I'll cut your guts out and stuff them in your asshole
and set you on fire. He whined like a whipped dog. I say,

How did you find me?

She writes, quick-hand flying ... Catharin tracked you
down.

My throat locks up again and when my breath returns
and when I can speak again I say,

I don't want you here.

She writes ... Your niece is eight and your nephew is six
Henry and they want to know about you.

Tell them I don't exist.

She writes ... I won't do that, but you have to tell me why
you are here.

I can't tell you that.

She writes ... Catharin has been hurt, Henry.

How?

She writes ... In India, she was beaten and raped and
now she's pregnant and she has lost her faith and she's left
her mission and is now staying with us.

I feel the weight on my shoulders like a chang, that
heavy wooden wheel of punishment the Chinese used to load
onto the necks of their criminals. Geraldine reaches across
the table, her hand moving a thousand miles from out there
to touch me, her hand, soft and small, and she squeezes my
hand and my lips quiver and then she writes ... Is what you
did so awful, Henry?

Don't ask me that.

She writes ... We can get you out of here, no matter what
you did.

Will Carl pull strings, Gerry? Will he be the one to
spring me? Will he and his bloodthirsty friends hire me or
cut my throat?

She writes ... He forgives you, Henry.

Do you forgive him for killing your voice?

Small tears leak from the corners of her eyes and I say,

Your daughter will never hear your voice again but you
forgive him?

She writes ... I need you, Henry, and Catharin needs
you.

Catharin needs no one, I say.

Geraldine writes a long passage, her hand skimming and I see that she has overcome the loss of her voice, she has found a way around the wound and the pain by writing almost as fast as she ever could talk and she turns the pad and I read ...

In her New Delhi mission, she adopted some street urchins and they turned on her and held her captive for a week and they raped her and now she's pregnant and broken and has lost all faith in Jesus, but you and I can save her, Henry, we're all she has left and if we let her go, I know she'll kill her child. She's sinking back into the same darkness she lived in before she was reborn into the blood and wounds of her Christ.

I remember Catharin in her zeal as she headed for India, convinced that she and she alone could save those untutored souls, she alone could bring salvation to two thousand million souls who had not heard the word of her worm-eaten androgynous bloody Jesus Christ of the Rocks of the Cross of the Sword, her Jesus Christ who now filled her belly with another mistake waiting to be born into the festering abattoir of human existence.

I tear the sheet of paper from the pad and ball it into a tiny sphere and Geraldine draws away, fear in her eyes. I see the scar at her throat, the small white scar where the surgeon's knife had cut into her skin trying to save her voice. I say,

Gerry, there's a virus in me that will infect you.

She writes ... It's in me too, Henry, you know that, you remember that? But without trying, what chance do we have to be pure?

Catharin rejected me, Gerry. Despised me, labeled me apostate, a whore lover, an infidel and she told me that I'd forever rot in the earthly sphere, that I'd never achieve Purity. What's purity, Geraldine? Do you think I'll rot in hell?

Geraldine again reaches for me and, her eyes pleading, she squeezes my hand.

She writes ... You're all we have left, Henry.

I say, He's still in your life, Gerry.

She writes ... I'm a woman with a daughter and a son and no voice what can I do?

And I say,

Does he know you've come to deliver me?

And she writes ... He walks with a limp, Henry. His right arm is so shattered that he's learned to write left-handed.

I say,

Is he still the same bastard he was before?

She writes ... He doesn't touch me, Henry.

Does he know you're here?

She shakes her head, No.

I whisper to her. I'm a killer, Gerry. A killer of men and women and you don't want me out there, you don't want me close to your children because I know that in their purity, they'll see the truth hiding under my skin.

She writes ... Why have you shaved your head, Henry?

I say, The mark of Cain, sister, and I am his scion.

Her eyes break again and then the guard comes to the door, raps on the glass, opens it and he says,

That's it Mitchell, time to crawl back into your hole.

Geraldine writes ... I'll come again, Henry. I need to know you're all right.

I lean forward and cover Geraldine's hand with mine. I say,

Don't ever come here again, Gerry. Never.

I release her hand. Her pen is tucked into my palm. I slide it up my sleeve. I walk away and do not look back.

37.

I am not an innocent, I have not been innocent. I feign innocence. I am one of the rotten ones. On my eighth birthday, Geraldine bought me a BB gun. My mother hated the BB gun.

She said, That BB gun is an instrument of the devil, Henry. Guns are meant to kill and this family has been killing through four wars.

Geraldine was in a hurry to see me grow up—never guessing that I would send a BB through Mrs. Wilson's upstairs bedroom window or that I'd end up in prison where, I might add, things are not as bad as they seem if you stay clean, keep to yourself, and try not to antagonize the powers—and there are powers here—men so evil they sweat pellets of evil, men so terrible they can't sleep, men who have horrible dreams, obsessive dreams about the crimes they have committed.

When I compare us to Meursault who was in prison for murdering an Arab on a beach, Meursault is a saint. I read about his descent into pain and his refusal to let a priest save his soul, because, like me, he has no interest in religion. Despite my mother's training, despite my baptism, despite the fact that I went to Methodist Fellowship Meetings to watch the girls and hope for a moment of neglect and a display of white panties.

I have no interest in God or Jesus or Mohammed or Buddha. My mother would have been ashamed to see me in prison with blood on my hands but there is no way to redeem the past. I read Camus' *Stranger* and I wonder who left the novel in the stacks where I found it hidden like a secret code to be deciphered in the dark. As I finger pages, I feel the sweat of the men before me who found midnight solace in Camus' prisoner, a relief from the tedium and bored existence of prison life. Meursault didn't know how lucky he was to get a reprieve from the river of blood.

I remember taking the BB gun, loading it that day and shooting a sparrow, watching it flutter and fall, wounded in the breast. I felt nothing. Later, I graduated to squirrels then to cats and dogs and of the two, I learned that the cat is the harder target because the dog, trained to heel and to sit, is easy to kill while the cat, distrustful and wary, moves at the last instant as the finger on the trigger squeezes as if it can feel death looming.

So while I scored a few feline trophies, my main source of joy was the dog.

38.

I remember how my sister, Catharin, first fell into the path of evil—she was predestined to fall because as middle child, she was the forgotten one while Geraldine, as first born was always my stiff-legged father's favorite while I, as the last born, the baby, and the only boy, was his genetic successor. Poor Catharin—all but forgotten in the middle, turned to cutting and to pain early and for some reason I didn't know she slid, ever so fast, into other wickedness. Once or twice I watched her with the blade dig at the soft places—under her fingernails, watched the tears flow from her eyes, watched the blood ooze around the blade slaughtering her pain, killing her pride, feeding her loss, while all I did was shoot dogs and birds.

But Catharin, heiress to the small fortune our great grandfather built on the backs of West Virginia coal miners, wanted to convert Hindus in India to the one true divine faith to which she attributed her salvation. She uses her own descent into drugs and sex as a model of redemption for her Hindus, most of whom can have no idea what she's talking about, but this deafness doesn't destroy her lust for Jesus.

Geraldine, always true and pure without having to call on the Lord for a reason to be pure and true, fell in love with her Fascist So Full of Hate who in his greed and depravity became Satan's foster child. Death ...

Death, in Camus' little book, hangs in the background, a dark omen of truth, and I discover every day a new smudge on a page where a man in pain before me dwelt over the words and I see the lines marked with pencil or pen and ink, sometimes so thick the text is hidden—like Catharin's God—hidden until as reader I have to guess and in guessing, reinvent like an archeologist, filling in the gaps in an undiscovered civilization. What was here? And this is there, so Camus must have written this, but this still undeciphered Rosetta Stone reminds me of how my mother looked, that quizzical look on her face the day Geraldine married Carl Fairweather, her fascist, angry Captain promoted to Major of the Air Force who taught courses on Just and Unjust Wars.

My mother, already so full of pain, masked her anguish, hid it under her hallowed camouflage the way Camus' words are hidden. I envy the first man who read this short pure little book in this cell, for I can imagine the book has been there since the beginning of time and will remain here until the end. Then it will all be black and red, ink and pencil, every word blurred until no one will know what it says.

But I have descended today into this place where I didn't plan to go. Today, my mother died, or was it yesterday?

39.

The corridor smells of bleach and mold, the acrid odor of soap and wax and the sick sweet scent of Artie's cologne.

Behind me, his smell spreads like a noxious cloud and, in a one-two rhythm he nudges me with the butt of his nightstick. Can he feel my smile?

At the door to the Governor's office, Artie stops.

I wait.

Like a teenage drama queen prepping for a prom date, Artie sweeps his hand over his hair, brushes at the tunic of his crisp uniform and polishes the face of each shoe on the calf of his trousers.

Then, with a smile, he raps on the door and stands back at attention.

He looks at me. Worried. I smile. His face clouds but then brightens as the Governor calls, Come. I say,

You think he loves you, Artie?

And I open the door.

The Governor sits behind his white oak desk. In the light from the window behind him his head looked like the halo of a saint. He glances up, the shadows in his face dark and demonic. Artie says,

Mitchell, sir.

Close the door, Mr. Miller.

I wait until Artie is gone, a guilty, sheepish look on his face before I face the Governor.

He keeps reading papers on his desk, turning them like a man turning pages in a prayer book. Then, finished, he closes them in a folder, sets the folder to one side before looking at me. He says,

You're a few days early.

It's not about the yard.

What is it about?

I need a typewriter.

He looks at me. Then at his clasped hands on his desk. In the light, the shadow of his head falls on the desk long and dark and gray. He laughs.

A typewriter. Why do you need a typewriter? What's a typewriter worth to you anyway?

Hard to explain, sir.

I gave you a new cellmate, little what's his name.

Farmer, I say. Donny Farmer.

And you've got the library.

Yes sir.

And you had a visitor.

My sister.

So why do you need a typewriter?

It's hard to explain sir.

I've got all day, he says.

I'm writing sir.

If they find it, they'll burn it and I can't protect you.

They won't find it.

If they catch you, I won't know anything.

I'm not asking for a favor sir.

Sounds like a favor to me, Mitchell.

It'll look like equipment for the library.

Nobody but you goes to the library.

I watch his eyes. He is a hard man used to dealing with hard men. He gives nothing without getting something back. He says,

What've you got for me, Mitchell?

Nothing.

He stands. He walks around the desk. Sits on the edge. Hand rests on his thigh. His eyes rake mine, back and forth. In the light his gray hair, clipped short, looks like a steel helmet. His eyes, gray in the light, hold me like prey. He clears his throat. A minute goes by. Two minutes. Three minutes. He says nothing.

Then, he returns to his chair, to his desk, to the halo of light. I feel his absence, the emptiness of no stare, the hollowness of release.

I stand. He says,

Are you really keeping me in the loop, Mitchell?

You think I won't?

How bad do you want that typewriter?

I need it.

And I need someone who keeps me in the loop. Guards and cons stealing me blind. And I don't hear anything from you. You need a typewriter. I need information. I want every scrap, every crumb, every shred of gossip.

What happens when word gets out I'm your snitch?

Snitch. I don't like that word. I think of myself as a businessman.

A businessman? Like my brother-in-law?

He laces his hands together, sets his elbows on his desk and he stares at them for a long time. The light behind him shifts, moving the shadows to the left, making them longer until they look like they have been stretched and made out of rubber. I watch. It is the first sign of time I have seen in a while, that shift as the shadows move from day closer to night. He says,

You do what you're supposed to do, you get your typewriter.

I need paper too, sir.

Next thing you'll be wanting chocolate candy and a flower on your pillow.

A couple reams will do.

You get one ream every time I get a good report.

He looks at me, hands still planted on the desk. He calls out,

Mr. Miller.

The door opens. Artie stands in the doorway, looking like a martinet. Shoes buffed, hair slicked back, tunic crisp and neat. A small spot of grease on his chin.

Yes sir.

Take this reprobate back to his cell.

Yes sir.

I step outside. Artie closes the door. He says,

Reprobate. What'd you do to piss the Gov off, asshole?

I laugh. I say,

Artie why do you call me asshole?

'Cause I can, he says. And you can't do a fucking thing about it. So what's the deal with you and the Gov, asshole?

He wants me to upgrade the library.

Who in the fuck goes to the library?

The smell of the corridor is no longer moldy, the scent of Artie's cologne no longer so noxious.

Hey Artie, I say.

Yeah.

If a guy wanted to get high, who would he talk to?

What?

High. Get high. Whacked out.

You wanna get high, cook yourself up some pruno.

No, man. I mean really high. You know. Stoned.

I'll nose around, he says. What's it worth to you?
My bitch likes to suck cock, I say.
Fuck that shit, man, I ain't no faggot.

40.

I hate change. When I killed René I knew I would be fed another sacrificial lamb. I hate change as much as I hate being alone but when Squeaky came, I saw that I could use him the way you use an old sweater or an old pair of shoes for comfort and ease when you need it.

Now they've brought the new guard who makes me nervous because the old guard had a one-word vocabulary—asshole—no name for you, just asshole you've got a visitor, asshole you've got mail, asshole get your shit out of that cell so we can steal your contraband, asshole.

When a new guard arrives you always expect the worst because they are criminals in charge of criminals. We are all criminals but some of us have been caught—I for stealing a tubful of women's underwear, Squeaky for grand theft auto. The guards haven't been caught yet, have not yet been punished. Maybe that's what happens to the old guard—caught fucking an inmate, caught selling coke—like Artie, caught poaching candy from the gift packs and so the new guard arrives. One guard is like the next.

He's young, wide-eyed and just out of training. He's white and nice and he's clean and not yet corrupted by the air and the breath of murderers behind steel. He still has a sparkle of humanity in him and so of course I will have to kill that. Squeaky's worried about the change because he's learned to keep his back to the wall, he's learned to keep his distance from the killers, he's learned that without me he's dead and so he hangs onto me like a limpet, his teeth close to my skin and he says,

What if this guy is a shit?

He is a shit, Squeaky, he just doesn't know how bad he smells.

What happened to Artie? I liked Artie.

He was dirty, Squeaky.

How do you know, Mitch?

I know, that's how I know and now he's gone and we've got a new boy to break in. Are you up for it?

Whatdya mean break him in?

Train him so he knows shit from graham crackers.

Why do you give the guards a hard time, Mitch?

They're zoo keepers, Squeaky. You gotta keep them on their toes or they doze off and the worms eat their brains.

What worms? Squeaky says.

41.

The new guard raps on the bars to my cell. He stands at the gate smiling at me. He says,

You Mitchell?

What's your name?

Martin, he says.

What do you want?

You got a letter.

A letter?

I jump up, heart beating fast. Not one letter in one year and six months. No letter, nothing from the outside. I want it. I don't want it. I'm afraid of it, I need it. I say,

Who's it from, Martin?

From your girlfriend, maybe?

Standing at the bars, I look at Martin. Misty blue eyes, peach fuzz on his upper lip, lips wet with saliva as he grins. He hands me the letter then steps back a step, turns on his heel and marches down the grating. His boots ring on the steel. He is fresh. He goes by the book. Neat and clean. The way it's supposed to be.

The letter is in a blue envelope the color of a robin's egg. There is no return address but I recognize the florid, girlish baroque hand of my sister Catharin. Catharin who sold her ass in Golden Gate Park. Catharin who ran off to India to save two billion Hindus from eternal damnation. Catharin who broke my mother's heart but who has now found me.

I fall back onto my bunk, turn the letter over. On the back flap there is a line of Xs and Os running like a fluorescent pink necklace around the seal. Pink. Neon pink. Bright pink. Woman.

With my thumbnail I slit the seal. Slow. Listen to the glue release with little paper sighs, careful not to tear the flap. I work it loose and then it pops open and I see the pages tucked and folded and it is a thick sheaf of blue paper the color of the sky. I pull the letter from its envelope. It falls half open and I see that there are eight pages of tight clean but florid writing. I check the date. No year just 5-22 and the first words ... Dearest Henry.

I stop there. Read them again ... Dearest Henry. I take a deep breath, refold the pages, tuck them back home, lay the envelope on my belly. I'll go slow. Take my time. I have time. Three and a half years. Lots of time.

42.

I lie on my bunk listening to Squeaky snore, his mouth open, eyes running in deep sleep like a child dreaming.

Catharin's letter weighs on my chest like a concrete block. I don't want to read it, I don't dare read it and when I get up to hit the head I think about my manuscript with its bleeding ink and thin transparent paper hidden in the library in the garden section on the shelf with books of flowers resting beside *Notre Dame des Fleurs* and the *120 Journées* and I realize how much I need the typewriter. With a machine to handle the pages I can rewrite the splotchy pages while I forge ahead with the writing, maybe get to an end, find a place to stop, but I don't know if I can stop and the Governor still hasn't gotten the typewriter.

With Catharin's letter holding me down I'm frozen in place, my feet locked as if chains with heavy steel links hold me to the bunk.

I hear Squeaky stir, his snoring stops.

I shift. The letter slides to my side like a knife cleaving me, and I take a deep breath, sit up holding the blue envelope with its pink neon ink spreading across the page like watered-down blood. I slip the letter from its envelope, feel the eight pages heavy and dank. In the pale and dim light of my cell I read the first line again ... My Dearest Henry, I'm back at Geraldine's now with her babies. I'm lost and my belly is swollen with child. I have lost any faith in Jesus. He betrayed me and ... The loops and lines of her letters are thin, precise, clear.

I fold the page, savor the words. Catharin crucified on her beliefs, pregnant with the sick sperm of holiness. I don't want to finish, I don't want to know how far she has fallen, how deep she has planted her hate. I feel a surge in my groin, the hardening of my cock as I remember Catharin and her boys, Catharin who started fucking boys at parties and ended up raped by her Hindu rogues who laughed at her bleeding for Jesus Christ of Deception and Lies, stinking and reeking of the spoiled promise of his Eternity. I crush the letter, twist it, mangle it but regret it as if I am strangling Catharin, drowning her in her own Jesus shit and Church vomit and I shudder, imagining her lying prostrate begging for redemption while her Indian boys fuck her until she bleeds. I want to know how she took it—did she fight, did she scream or did she sacrifice in silence the way she was silent when, in parks in the City, she sucked men off? Why be ashamed of her bleeding now? She needs just what she's always needed—someone to hold her. Why did she go dark so early while Geraldine held out the light of truth and love?

I smooth out the pages again. Open the heart of my sister. She is my sister even though she damned me, laid me out alongside the Lutheran apostate bastards of all time, but she is my sister and I smooth out the page, wipe at the hatred. In the wrinkling I lose the purity of the pink neon ink laid down with open heart and love. In the faint yellow light of the cell I re-open the letter, page one ... Henry, I am writing because I can't let you see what I have become. My feet and legs are swollen and my belly is blotched with stretch marks as if I have blood poisoning in my limbs. My belly is so full I waddle when I walk.

I remember the street monster in Guayaquil her skin stretched as tight as drum heads, her legs swollen with elephantiasis, rotting. A monkey wrapped around her neck. I am disgusted by my sister, now ruined by her Jesus of the bloody and worm-eaten cross. But I continue to read ...

I came back from New Delhi sick, Henry. Sick in body. Sick in mind. Sick in my soul because the church betrayed me. When they found out my condition, they cut me loose. They cast me out, a pregnant woman as if there were no lesson in the scripture. They cast me out knowing that this was not my doing. I have been redeemed and purified, Henry, but the Bishop sat across from me in his holy office and refused to weigh the facts. I had been taken prisoner. I had been raped. I had been beaten and all he saw was his precious Catharin with her missionary zeal bloated and bruised like a fat pig. He said, and these are his words—It won't do for you to be associated with the mission now, Catharin. He sent me home, raw and swollen. I am a disease and I'm afraid I'll infect Geraldine's babies. I can't go outside, Henry. I can't go out into the sunshine because my faith has turned me into a freak.

I refold the first page, tuck it back into the blue envelope. I can't finish it. I don't want to finish it because deep down I know that we share a hatred of salvation and I know that Catharin had hoped to find a spark of redemption and immortality and even sainthood in her good deeds while I, knowing the truth about humanity, understood that there can only be death and that I am the angel of death and the small brown men I left gutted, their ears severed, on the sand and rock of the Atacama were mistakes. I should have started by killing the Bishop in his sick black robes and

sanctimonious dogma-fed hypocrisy, the bishop who
sacrificed my sister, who took her two million dollars before
bleeding her of hope and purity and tossing her out dried
and betrayed and rattling like the ears of men I slaughtered
to make way for the Missionaries of Industry like my
brother-in-law, that son of a bitch CEO in charge of death
and corruption who needs to have his guts ripped out a foot
at a time and stuffed back into his murderous craw.

I want to vomit, to puke, to swallow my own
putrefaction, to wallow in the stink of corpses because that is
the purification possible for men—to float with their own
dead in the river of blood.

Squeaky stirs and sits up against the wall, the bunk
groaning in its steel frame and he says,

Hey Mitch, you asleep?

I cross the small space between our bunks and I hold
the ballpoint pen out to him and I say,

Kill me, Squeaks.

What?

Right in the heart, the eye, the throat, take this pen and
kill me.

He draws up tight against the wall, knees clutched with
shaking hands and he says,

What the fuck's goin' on, Mitch?

I sit on the bunk, feet on the floor and I look at him, his
little boy face with the wide eyes, the tender mouth and I
say,

Squeaky, what I tell you right here, right now dies with
you.

Jeez Mitch, why doncha lay something heavy on me?

Squeaky, I killed over two hundred men.

Holy cow, Mitch.

I killed the wrong ones, I made two hundred mistakes. I
took their ears and I cut out their tongues.

Squeaky gets off his bunk and squats in front of me and looks at me, his open blue eyes as pure as a mountain dawn and he says,

You're shittin' me, aintcha Mitch, you ditten kill two hundred guys, didya?

Women, too, I say. Took their ears to earn my bonuses and now my sister's lost because of me.

What'd you do to your sister?

I let her go to hell, Squeaky, I cleared out the rubble so she could march straight to hell and now Satan's getting even—he's killing my whole family. You can't see it, but he's coming for me so I want you to kill me before he arrives.

Squeaky grasps my hand with the ball point pen in it and he says,

I didn't know you believed much in Jesus, Mitch.

It's just a way of speaking, Squeaky.

Okay, but you ain't gonna cut me loose in the yard, right?

What?

Sometimes you just scare the shit outa me but I know you was just testin' me, huh? You just wanna know if I love you, doncha Mitch, doncha? I'm a dead man, without you, Mitch, 'cause you're my savior. You gotta see that, right? You're my savior?

43.

Today is the first day I've written since I got Catharin's letter. Four days running I've missed my twelve hundred words. Four days since I opened the manuscript, four days since I saw it rotting from the inside, infected with time, bloated with the blood of worms and now I'm sick with fear that I won't finish my story, won't find the guts to pull up the detritus of my life. The typewriter arrived, but I know it is too slow. I know that I need a computer.

With a computer I might find a way to get back inside, find a way to remember everything the way Genet had to find it after the scum-sucking beastly guards in La Fresne found his work and burned it. He started over from the beginning like a nest of ants destroyed by an oso hormiguero, having to find a way to wring the past out of time once again to find their destiny. He rewrote, recreated, refound his story and I can do it too.

44.

They call Squeaky out. We're in the library. The door opens. It is the new guard, Martin. He's right out of training. He still stinks of human nobility, bloated with salvageable altruism, pure. Thinks there's hope and destiny and redemption. He doesn't know that at the end of his night stick death lives its eternal blackness tainted with blood and the brains of the victims. I see him dead, so easy, a quick finger to the throat and he will gasp for breath, two fingers in the eyes and he will crumple to the ground and I will snap his neck, yank his head, tearing the spinal cord from his brain. He says,

The Gov wants your helper.

You want Squeaky?

I don't want Squeaky. The Gov wants Squeaky. I can't believe you call that kid Squeaky. Why do you call him Squeaky?

I call him Squeaky 'cause he squeaks.

I call Squeaky out of the stacks where he's reading The Descent of Man and, still holding the book, he stands with his little boy radiant face open as an angel with God's cock in his ass and I say,

Go with the good man, Squeaky.

Are they sending me to the yard, Mitch? I ain't goin back to the yard.

The guard says,

Gov wants to see you.

Leave the book, Squeaky, I say.

He lays the book on the table. At the door he looks back at me, farewell, his eyes wet as a maiden's at a train station. The door closes.

I take a deep breath, feel his absence like a hollow in the pit of my stomach, like a stone, an ache and I don't know why. I remember the times I hurt him and how he whined and cried and begged me to protect him and he said,

I'll do anything you want, Mitch, just don't cut me loose, okay.

Taking the blue envelope from under the typewriter, I open page five to read Catharin's words. She writes ... and he wanted me to have a baby, a pure baby, you see. But I could never have a baby with him. I couldn't bear the thought ...

I stop there. Try to figure it out but I can't see the threads, can't read between the lines. I think that maybe on page six or seven she'll tell me what he meant, but until then I can only think about her when she first ran away to the City, leaving at night so that my mother, waking and calling us down, found Catharin gone and she cried and I wanted to know why Catharin had left and I asked Geraldine if our father had done something to her and Geraldine as always the pious pure and good daughter defended him even though he fucked his women in the back seat of his BMW in full view of the house where my mother wrung her hands in silent anguish and yet there was nothing I could remember, no fleeting incident to show that he had abused Catharin, so why had she gone? The words—wanted me to have a baby with him—what did they mean? But like all words they floated first on the page in their pink neon ink then in my brain like butterflies never landing.

With Squeaky gone, the library is silent but in the distance I hear the rumble of equipment, the hum of steel and concrete, the thud of a hammer or the slamming of steel doors. I sit and listen to the music of confinement and I am alone.

I go to the shelf of books on roses and grasses and I pull
my manuscript from its slot. It is now thick, heavy, tied with
brown hemp twine. I lay it on the table beside the typewriter,
lay it out like a torn and flayed animal. I regret having
written it on onion skin so thin the ink blurs and masks the
true meaning of the story. I turn pages. Try to follow the line
but the splotches are like sudden stop signs jerking to an end
at the edge of a precipice. The smears are bloody wounds in
a body and the words remain opaque. I can't remember what
I wrote. It's as if in the writing my memory bled out of me
like the blood of a dying man mixing with water until it left
no clue but then on a page deep in the manuscript, I see a
few clear lines, the words ornate, pure, stylized, the
sentences delicate and balanced, a work of art just in the
script, but the content is black and bloody and drowning.

45.

I remember the slaughter on the banks of the Cauca, I
remember Suki shedding his gun belt, I remember his ammo
pouch, his boots, I remember him jumping into the Cauca
River to snatch out the dismembered bodies of the Rojos
and hauling them to shore, I remember that he whacked off
their ears—starting over—starting over because he had killed
them and he wanted his ears for the cash, for the bonus, for
all it could buy, for the refrigerator he'd get his mother, the
new dresses for his sister. Suki was family, a family man
needing his cache of ears. My family ...

46.

And then the door opens and Martin—with his smiling
Christian pure redemptive clean breeder Jesus loving full of
rotten fish mouth not yet twisted with the full realization
that we are behind bars because we are the killers, the
rapists, the butchers, the petty thieves—opens the door and

Squeaky re-enters the library and he looks pale and thin and his hair is wet with sweat. Martin says,

You all right in here, Mitchell?

Good as gold.

He locks the door and leaves. Squeaky stands, hands at his sides looking at the floor. I say,

What do you see down there, Squeaky?

What?

The floor, I say, what's so interesting about the floor?

He shuffles his feet. He looks at me. He smiles.

What did the Governor want, Squeaks?

He ambles to the table where my manuscript lies open, a gutted animal already decaying, and he sits and he raises his face and his eyes are wet and his lips tremble.

I ditten tell'em nothin', Mitch.

Tell who nothing?

He asked me a whole bunch of questions, Mitch.

Nothing wrong with questions, I say.

About you, Mitch.

He asked you questions about me?

You won't cut me loose now, will you, Mitch? Not after what I give ya, okay? You won't do that will you?

I get up, walk around the table to his chair and I lay a hand on his neck, feel the pulsing blood there, feel the heat of betrayal there, feel the vulnerable openness of his neck, his soft white woman's neck with its silky hair sweat soaked.

Tell me exactly what he asked you.

Squeaky looks up, his eyes plead

He asked me what kind of shit you tell me.

Did you tell them I'm fucking you?

No, Mitch, I ditten tell'em, how am I gonna tell'em that, okay? But he kinda knew, you know.

So what did you tell him?

Mitch, I ditten tell him shit.

Did he offer you a cell alone?

I don't want a cell alone, Mitch.

So what did you tell him?

I told him I ditten want nothin' 'cept bein' with you.

Did you tell him what I told you? I told you about killing and about the ears because you're my bitch, Squeaky, and you owe it to me not to tell anyone anything I tell you.

Squeaky looks at me and his eyes run with tears and his mouth trembles and he whimpers,

I know I'm a bottom, Mitch, and I gotta tell you I like being your bottom, but do you think I could ever be a top?

I rub his head. I say,

Tell you what—you start working out seriously and when you weigh two-fifty, Squeaks, maybe I'll let you top that new guard.

Not much chance o'me getting to two-fifty, huh, Mitch?

47.

I have to get a computer because the typewriter is too slow, too clunky. Martin raps on my cell bars and he says,

The Gov wants you, Mitchell.

In just a few weeks, new worry lines scar Martin's face, hiding in the shadows of his sunken cheeks. He has been inside the belly of the beast for a month and it turns him into what he never wanted to become. His transformation takes shape in the slope of his shoulders, the invisible burden that bends men's backs as they bear the truth about the butchers behind blue steel and I say,

Not feeling well, Martin?

He perks up, his sunshine face clear, but I see the acne scars deep in his cheeks, the acne scars like small soul worms eating their way out of his bones and he says,

I'm doing okay, where's your buddy?

He's in the laundry.

Is that right? I didn't know he worked the laundry.

Why does the Governor want me?

They don't tell me, you know that, Mitchell. They just say go get him and I get you so let's amble on down there, what'dya say?

I lead him out of the cell, down again over the three tiers of steel grating that rattles under our feet like some gruesome machine chewing us up and I expect to see the blood and squeezed intestines of dead men oozing through the mesh but the journey is uneventful. At the Governor's door, Martin stops, silent now, and I see the larvae of pain inch across his face, burrow into his hide. As he looks at me I see the hollow core of a man sucked dry by the knowledge that all his high ideals and his vision of a better world have yielded to the utter and bitter truth that his sole purpose is to keep the killers off one another. He has abandoned his dream of social perfection. He is ripe for the taking. I say,

Your soul's getting thin, Marty.

He starts. Glares at me. The door opens and I step into the presence of the one man who knows my truth.

The Governor looks up at me, his wrinkled face a field of deep pits as though his own rot is oozing out of him but his eyes are cool and blue as steel. He glances down at a piece of paper on his desk and he says,

You got connections, Mitchell.

What do you mean, sir?

He holds up the paper and in the light streaming through the window behind him like an x-ray beam, I see the letter head in gold and blue, a red seal and he says,

They want you out.

My feet squish like I'm standing in soft mud. I lose my balance, stumble, hold onto the corner of his desk.

Who wants me out?

The people who wrote this letter. They want you out.

I don't want out.

This is a letter to the board.

Can you release me without my consent?

Every man in here would give his left nut for this.

I step back from the desk and a huge gulf opens up and the Governor is the enemy and my finger curls around the trigger and I see his brain splattered across the window and the Cauca River flows across the polished top of his desk and the bloody earless heads that Suki hurled back into the water bob like hairy balloons.

I don't want to go back out there, sir.

Who is Carl Fairweather, Mitchell?

My brother-in-law, sir.

Well, your brother-in-law knows some powerful folks and these folks pay my wages and they want the board to let you go.

What do I have to do to stay here, sir?

You're a goddamned crazy son of a bitch, Mitchell.

He hurls the paper at me and it glides like a sharp blade and I snatch it from the air, crush it into a ball without looking at it.

Sir, I'm thinking maybe I need a computer.

I'll tell you what you need. You need to have your fucking head examined.

He shakes his head. He says,

Now what the hell am I going to tell these people? That you don't want out but I should give you a computer?

Carl Fairweather, my brother-in-law, is the CEO in charge of death for the Cerro Corporation, I say.

The Governor sits back in his chair.

The Cerro Corporation.

Yes sir. He plays golf with the Chairman of GM and he bowls with the chief architect of GenSoft.

Mitchell, why didn't you tell me your brother-in-law has his foot half a mile up my board's ass?

I gave you Artie, sir. I'm keeping a lid on things.

The Cerro Corporation?

Sir, I say, You talked to Squeaky three days ago. You're not planning something for him are you sir, because I need him.

Like you need a computer?

I need a computer for my work.

What do I tell your brother-in-law?

Do I have to kill another man to stay here sir?

Mitchell, he says, you crazy bastard get the fuck out of my office.

Will you get me that computer?

I get you out of the laundry, give you the garden. You leave the garden and go to the library and I get you a typewriter but now you want a computer. What do you want next, Mitchell? How about a plasma TV?

Is that what you talked to Squeaky about, sir? About me moving to the library?

You don't need to know what I talked to Squeaky about.

It's safer in here than it is out there.

You really want that computer, right Mitchell?

Yes sir, I say, It'll make my work a lot easier.

Okay I'll tell you what, I'll get you a computer if you take this offer and hand over all your contraband.

Contraband, sir? What do you mean?

I mean, he says, the pornographic pictures.

I don't have any pornographic pictures, sir.

That's not what I hear.

Is that what Squeaky told you? Did he tell you I sell contraband?

There are rats who'll sell your ass out in a minute for a pack of Camels so tell me who's spreading those poisonous porno pics.

I think he's doing the world a favor sir.

And just how is he doing the world a favor?

He's lowering the world-wide sperm count, sir.

I'll be goddamned, he says. This is the craziest shit I've heard in twenty-five years of keeping you scum behind bars. Get out of here.

What about the computer, sir?

Get me the son of a bitch selling the porno and you get your computer.

And Squeaky, sir, I need him.

Yeah, I'll bet you do.

On the return trip to my cell, Martin pokes me in the back with his nightstick. He says,

How'd it go with the Governor?

Marty, what do you know about the porno racket?

I don't know nothin'.

Somebody's setting me up, Marty. I want to know who.

I don't work for you, Mitchell.

We can fix that, Marty.

48.

Squeaky is still in the laundry. He has been there a long time. I lie on my bunk staring at the ceiling. Carl Fairweather pulling strings makes me nervous. What does he want? Catharin is there. What's he doing to her?

I pull her letter from its blue envelope, peel out page four. I see the splotches smearing the ink, great blobs of smeared ink where Catharin's tears fell as she wrote.

I try to decipher the words under the splotches but it is like a pentimento in a used canvas, I can almost make it out.

Squeaky returns from the laundry. He smells like soap and bleach. I sniff the air as he enters. Under the soap, I smell sweat. No semen, just his sweat and the bleach. If he reeks of semen, I kill him on the spot. He says,

Reading her letter again, Mitch? What's she say? Can I read her letter, Mitch? Please? I never saw a letter in neon pink ink.

Does it get you hot, Squeaky? Knowing my sister's got a rape kid in her belly? Does it get you hot knowing she got tied up and fucked by a bunch of Hindu cow lovers?

And Squeaky trembles as he looks at me and he says,

You don't have to dump on me, Mitch, I just kinda feel like I know her.

She was a nun, Squeaky.

I'm sorry, he says.

Squeaky hovers on his bunk looking at me with his liquid puppy eyes and he says,

Did I say something wrong, Mitch?

49.

I fold up the letter, stuff it back in the envelope and stand at the bars holding it like a dead bird. I recite the last words of page three, the words not destroyed by the ink bleeding through from the back ... Henry, I don't know where to turn or where to go. I'm like a homeless child, Henry. The church was home to me, Henry.

It was sanctuary, a place to hide from my sins, but the church cut me out, Henry, like an infection. Remember Joan of Arc, Henry. The English kept her prisoner, raping her over and over and over to make her repent of her heretical vision, but she held true, Henry, while I cannot, and did you know she was pregnant when they burned her? She carried her baby to the fire in her body and I, Henry, I am there, I want to burn it up, to cut it out, die.

Jeez Mitch, Squeaky says. Who's this Joan broad?

I turn back to Squeaky sitting on his bunk, his eyes wet, his round mouth a temptation, and I say,

She was a saint, Squeaks.

And your sister knows her?

No she doesn't.

But this cunt Joan, she's knocked up too?

So it's all about pussy, Squeaky?

He laughs. He says,

Don't I know it? Do you miss it, Mitch, the pussy?

No Squeaky, I don't.

Why not, Mitch?

Because where there's pussy, there's more little humans and my job is to cut down the breeders. That's why I like your ass, Squeaks. When I fuck you I know there won't be

any little Squeakies running around with Squeaky snotty
noses and Squeaky wet eyes. When I fuck you the killer gene
dies.

Squeaky laughs and he says,

Breeders, right Mitch? You call them breeders?

I sit beside him on his bunk and I take the letter and I
lay it on his thigh and I say,

Read it to me, Squeaky.

He hesitates, looks at me, his hand covering the blue
envelope and then he says,

Huh uh, Mitch, no way. You read way better than I do.

I pluck the letter from his thigh and I tuck it inside my
shirt.

50.

It is the most frightening dream I've ever had. All my
life I've had moments when—sudden attacks of truth
clouded my every-day web of lies and deceptions—I see
things in gray. Always in gray. The Building of the Hundred
Hound Heads comes back to me in pieces—the bridge with
the heads of the hounds that, when I get close, shows the
heads to be smashed, but at a distance they are like the
heads of greyhounds, and the windows have these awful
white and black crosses on them. It's an exodus across a
bridge of tears and there are thousands of people, all
faceless, clawing their way over the bridge going where? I
don't know, but the doom is coming, the end is near. And
then I see a float and on the float there is a man and a
woman, both baring their breasts and the man's breasts are
as ripe and full as the woman's and she is coy with her
nakedness. She has a vest that just covers her nipples and
she's embarrassed, but the vest opens to expose her breasts.
The man has long hair, makeup, he's not a complete man,
nor is he a complete woman. Below the float, on the gray
ground, I see men fucking other men, and the bottoms are
soft and loving as Berdaches in the throes, and the tops

penetrate them. There is no hostility, no resistance, just the soft slow fucking.

And then the dream ends and I wake up sweating, overwhelmed, wet, jittery, anxious, afraid.

I see it everywhere—the decay, the decline, the degradation. Rot. Putrescence. Putrefaction. I lie awake at night, hands clasped behind my head. I run my life tape, see the missed choices, see the wrong choices, see the places I should have gone, watch all the people I've betrayed fall down like cattle pole-axed in the head in a slaughterhouse— and I see decline, I see decay, I see great shit piles as though some great god had crapped on the world and left it filthy and stinking as the muck in a barnyard and it withers me from the inside as if something were sucking at my guts pulling me down inside myself. Soon I will collapse—decay, putrescence—at the core—core, from Latin cor, the heart, at the core the hole is big, the ribs of the structure diseased, the blood of the beast impure—and there is but one resolution— one answer to the question—what is wrong? Life.

Every day things are getting worse. When I was a boy I visited my uncle's farm three summers running.

The first year, I remember, the roosters in the barnyard were enormous—their eyes hit me at eye level and their terrible yellow beaks slashed like razors and I ran away, pecked on the cheeks and bleeding.

The second year, the roosters had shrunk and no longer looked me in the eye but their awful beaks struck at me chest level and I was afraid and I still ran away because I had not yet learned to throw rocks.

The third year, the roosters had shriveled into tiny creatures, beaks now no threat as they rose up to my knee. I didn't fear their eyes and I no longer ran.

The rot infects deeper every day. I smell it in the air, taste it in the water, see it in the red eyes of hopeless men— locked as I am locked inside steel cages behind thick concrete walls, tied to the floor by our misdeeds—I see it

everywhere now—in the city, when I last rode free—in the
BMW I inherited from my father—hunting for women,
hoping that not only his magical seed burned in me, but
magic connection to him through his miraculous BMW
would land a woman in the seat and I would take her the
way he took them in the back seat, their underwear strewn
on the floor, their hair mussed, their breasts bare, their
throats aching from the stiff thickness of his cock. In the
city, the streets cave in, the roads rot from the inside, sink,
the water stinks with the slime of decaying matter and the
scum of death. I didn't see it before, but now, in my bunk at
night I am cut loose from the rot and the stink and it is like
being four years old again—here someone cooks for me.
Here someone tells me when to eat. Here someone washes
my bed sheets, tells me when it's time to change. Here
someone tells me when to go to the playground, when to
come back. Here routine pulls me out of time and there is
just one clock—the running of your sentence. Some men
hate it, need to get back outside, but I know that as long as I
am here the state will take care of me. Do I need to be free? I
don't.

The putrescence seeps into and out of men on the
outside—because they think they can get ahead, do better,
make a difference, while I, locked in here trying to write my
story, I know that getting ahead is an illusion and as I think
of Squeaky and his soft mouth it's strange how a killer can be
so gentle, treat him like a small animal, small, soft strokes,
touches to the crotch as prelude, scratches on the arm to
heighten desire, the slow rolling over and the gentle
penetration—so slow and loving—so pure and clean. Why do
I want out? Why does Carl Fairweather want me out?

51.

In here everything is reversed, everything is upside
down. We are the dregs, the impure, the rotten shut away
from the good outside and the clean outside and the pure

outside for our rotten deeds, but in here I find things I never found before—love, gentle, pure—while out there the streets run pink, the buildings sink into their slime, the air is unfit to breathe, the water poisoned, and the barons of industry (of whom my great-great-grandfather was one) rip apart the fabric that they built and depended on for their livelihood. In here, there is no escape from our sins. If you mess on the floor, you clean it up. If you are dirty, you wash. If you are naked, you dress. And I didn't know, didn't see, I thought it was just the wolf mind of men gnawing their feet off, but then I fell into my own traps, ended up here, and it takes that jolt to let me see the light—I remember how Geraldine looked after Carl Fairweather beat her—her face, swollen, her lips bruised, her eyes blackened. I tried to imagine her agony, but unable to speak—he had crushed her larynx—she couldn't tell me what she felt, what she wanted and that was the trigger that made me seek him out—her fascist Air Force Major—seek him out to break his legs. There is a comforting feel to the crack of a baseball bat on a hated man's bones— the sudden thud yields to a sharp crack and the bone snaps under the thousands of pounds of force and you feel, for a moment, the resistance but the sharp yelp of pain masks it and he collapses and then in an ecstasy of revenge, you flick the bat again and an arm pops, the pain not so great this time because the agony of the shattered femur blunts the crushing of the radius.

He writhed on the floor. I squatted beside him. Watched the pain flicker across his face and, tapping his broken leg with the bat, I said, Does it hurt, Carl? Do you want me to call a doctor? And then I walked away, back to the bruised and swollen Geraldine and I sat beside her bed and I told her what I had done and how it felt and how the only sound he made was a shout of pain as his femur cracked and I think I saw her smile but in her own agony it might have been a twitch of a nerve relaxing.

In here there is sex and hate and fear. In here there is death. In here routine keeps men from going mad as they count days. In here there is love while out there rot spreads like a cancer from blood to meat to bone to brain.

52.

Good morning, assholes, work detail.

The, vile, decadent voice of Martin cracks open the day with his daily dose of poison. I rise sick. Vertiginous. Ready to vomit. The gate swings open and I step out, stand at attention. Squeaky follows. I lead our posse down the three tiers of steel grating, down to the ground floor, down to the library where the typewriter sits bolted to the table. Martin stops at the door. He says,

What're you working on?

I'm redoing the catalogue.

What catalogue?

Victoria's Secret, I say. You can proofread it when I'm done.

Right. See you in three hours.

Martin exits, locks the door. He was nice. So nice. But now he's not unlike the asshole guard with the one word vocabulary and I am now certain that I will have to kill him. The corruption has already burrowed into him. He is a breeder, a cocksman, a handsome, thin, female-loving gonadal Jesus Christ of Copulation who will sire a dozen offspring. He has to die.

I look at the books, at the rows of books in stacks from floor to ceiling. Books that no one reads. I go to the garden section where my manuscript stands tucked between two volumes on roses and I take it from its shelf and it is heavy and floppy as a corpse and I carry it to the typewriter. I lay the manuscript on the table, and, my hand trembling, I untie the brown hemp string and look at the stack of pages. I feel a rush of fear, of helplessness, of loathing because I know what it contains—a history of my mistakes, a catalog of my failures, a ledger of the wrongful dead.

I am sick. My skin feels cold. The man in the manuscript is a killer of killers, a cheater of cheats, a liar to liars. He is me.

53.

Like a man undressing a lover, I pull Catharin's letter from the envelope, lay the pages out on the table in the library. The blue fuzz from the folds drifts down, a light snow melting as if Catharin is wasting away each time I read her writing. I push the blue fuzz into a thin ridge then scoop it up using the lip of the envelope and drop it inside. I spread the delicate pages out, an archeologist separating sacred sheets of papyrus that yield their secrets the slow way a tortured prisoner yields his truth and I lay out the ink-spotted back of page five, pick it up where I left off and the words come like a hammer ... Carl Fairweather, writes Catharin, has decided to run for Congress, Henry, the Senate, and I'm afraid because he is a ruthless demon who doesn't care who he hurts so long as he gets elected.

I look away from Catharin's words, curled jewels crafted onto the page so intriguing that I can stare at them for hours as if they are a secret code or charms on a gold bracelet. I know that under the pain there is a secret. I don't read too fast—I want the letter to last. I have the typewriter, its heavy keys, its black platen, an antique, but I am slow. I hunt and peck at the keyboard, the machine is awkward, the letters don't strike clean and straight so the lines zigzag like drunken men dancing. The letters blur. They shield the just-typed words—is that *kill* or *fill*? Is that *rut* or *rot*? I don't know. I need a computer to preserve Catharin's pain because I no longer trust my memory to hammer the words onto platen to keep her words straight. The last words ... a ruthless demon who doesn't care who he hurts.

I see him, a killer in the Senate, a killer who paid for the deaths of thousands of the small brown men I slaughtered, paid for political power, killed entire villages so his corporate friends could pillage the metals buried in the mountains and turn the dollar into the national currency and now he'll sit in the Senate and pass his murderous laws and his lies will spill from his mouth like filth from a broken sewage pipe.

Frothy bile rises in my own mouth and then the door to the library opens. I shove Catharin's letter under the typewriter, careful not to damage it further because it is as precious as a Rosetta Stone. Martin stands in the doorway and he says,

Hey Genius, the Gov says I'm supposed to give you this.

He shoves a cart through the door and on the cart there is a computer, a keyboard, a printer, a monitor and a small packet of paper. I stand, touch the gray case, the cool metal like salve on my fingers. Martin says,

How long did you have to suck the Gov's dick to get that, asshole.

I laugh because Martin is now six months in the prison, six months watching killers and rapists and thieves weave their little webs of intrigue and in six months he has shed his pristine shell of innocence and out of it comes not a butterfly but a spider with cracked skin and the claws of a monster. He has been fucked by every one of us and not one of us laid a hand on him. I say,

Welcome to Hell, Martin, where a good blow job can get you just about anything you want. What do you want?

You asshole, did you really suck the Governor's dick?

Did I?

You give me the creeps, he says.

He leaves. I dwell on his word, asshole. Just four months ago he called me a gentleman but the poison inside the blue steel cage is so caustic it turns a peachy-faced boy into a foul acid-mouthed Satan.

I know that somewhere his night stick will taste skull and bone and blood and it will change him even deeper until all his sweetness sours in the blood of his first victim.

I pull the cart to the table, lift the machine, touch the keyboard, touch the printer, finger the monitor with its glass shine. I am lost because I don't know how to turn it on. I sit back at the table, stare at my salvation—I never needed a computer until now and now that I have one, I don't know how to use it.

And then the door opens again and Martin Mister New Death enters and he says,

Hey Shakespeare, I betcha need this, huh?

And he hurls a booklet at me that slides across the table, skids to a stop against the typewriter and then, laughing, he's gone.

I draw Catharin's letter from under the typewriter, look at the neon pink ink, look at the smears and smudges and the ink spots blotting out the words bleeding through like the severed artery of a dying man and I know that with the computer I'll save her, save her anguish, save her pain.

I pick up page five again, the verso, to read her words ... Henry, someone has to stop him ... and there her hand quakes and I see the staggered line of the T in stop, the scrawled cross of the T in stop and in that scrawl I read the truth deeper than in the words and I know, without reading more, that He, Carl Fairweather, has used her, hurt her again. I tuck page five under the envelope—save the rest for later when reading can turn to action but for now there is nothing I can do from inside the steel cage but fold the envelope and the eight blue pages in a file, place the file in the stacks between the two books on roses alongside the book of grasses where it will be safe until I learn to use the computer, learn to type using its magic.

I return to the table and look at the door, expecting it to open as it did six days ago, the day Squeaky entered. His face pale, his voice trembling and he said, Hi Mitch, I'm late and then he collapsed on the floor and I knelt beside him and I said, What happened, Squeaky? And he looked up at me, his eyes wet and pleading and he said, They was two of 'em, Mitch, two o' them bastards and they hurt me pretty bad, Mitch. And then he keeled over, face down on the hard cold concrete floor and I picked him up, like a wounded animal, and he was limp and shaking and I smelled his blood. I called Martin, beat on the door until the glass rattled and Martin running answered and I said, Where were you, Martin? I carried Squeaky out of the library and up the flights of steel stairs to the infirmary. And now I wait for the door to open again and once again there is nothing I can do and I have to make a decision because there are two of them and I will have to punish them together or one at a time because that is something I am very good at. I will harvest their ears, both of them, and I will dry them and I will put them in a pouch and give it to Squeaky.

54.

I sit on my bunk, close my eyes and run over Geraldine's visit. The truth is clear. I see that my sisters are in pain, my sisters are in danger and I see that Geraldine wants me to do what I am good at, wants it so much she'd use me to get it.

I am angry with her for masking what she wants but I am proud that she thinks she can come to me even in here and yet I am insulted by her presumption that I can save her. I lie back against the wall, feeling the chill of the concrete. I am trapped between my fear of being set free and my need to get out where I can set things right. Do I give Geraldine the truth that landed me behind bars?

The gate swings open again and Martin stands in the doorway and he says,

Gov wants to see you again, Mitchell.

What happened to asshole, Martin? You don't love me anymore?

Why don't you just build a highway to his office, asshole?

So you love me after all.

Only in your dreams.

Martin turns his side to me, ushers me out. I lead him again down the tiers of steel mesh down to the Gov's office where Martin opens the door and I walk into the office and wait, hands behind my back, until the Gov looks up at me. He says,

Mitchell, everything connected to you is crazier than hell.

What do you mean, sir?

Carl Fairweather is coming here and he wants to talk to you about your release.

When is he coming, sir?

And the Farmer kid, your cellmate. He was in the infirmary.

Yes sir.

The doc had to tell me he was raped.

Yes sir.

The doc says the two inmates who put him there are cut.

I'm sorry to hear that, sir.

Whoever did it took their left ears and cut out their tongues. What do you say to that?

You've got a trophy-taker, sir.

He opens the drawer to his desk and he pulls out the envelope and he slides the photograph of dead René from it and he shoves the photograph at me.

Sweat breaks out under my armpits, a prickling sweat that I get when I watch a man bleed out, not believing he is dead until I smell the shit in his pants. He says,

Remember this?

Hard to forget, sir.

This is your get out of jail card. I will play it. When Carl Fairweather comes, you're going to okay whatever in the fuck he says because I want you out of here.

It's going to take ten guys to do what I do for you, sir.

You didn't tell me who cut the ears off those two dingleberries, Mitchell. And their tongues? What kind of shit is that?

You know what will happen if I'm outside, sir?

What goes on outside is not my concern.

What if I talk?

Who are you gonna talk to?

If I'm outside, Squeaky will die for sure.

You're not his guardian angel.

I have a right to serve my entire sentence.

You're not the only blade in here.

If you wanted me dead, sir, I'd be dead.

Go back to your cell and get your head straight.

When's he coming, sir?

What?

Fairweather, when is he coming?

Tomorrow.

Shit, that doesn't give me much time.

For what? To commit suicide?

I'm not that kind of girl, chief.

Get the fuck out of my office, Mitchell.

55.

You're never first. They bring you in like an animal in a zoo, lead you in with a rope around your neck, your ankles shackled in case you break loose and go wild. Martin opens the gate, stands waiting for me.

He looks spiffy—khakis, with sharp creases, a new gimme cap with the logo on the crown, and polished black boots. I say,

Don't recognize you, Martin. I can see my face in that shine.

You're always just one step from the edge of the cliff, Mitchell. One of these days you'll wake up and they'll find you dead and no one will miss your sorry ass. Out.

I lead him back down over the steel mesh, the echo of his boots hollow against the concrete and in the corridor to the visitor's room, the lights are dim, two bulbs, one at the far end, one at the close end. I say,

Is this where you slit my throat, Martin?

And he shoves me in the back, closing the distance between us to killing range. I marvel at how easy it is to provoke a clueless man, how easy it is to lead him into a trap, how easy to turn his pessimism into a mistake and I measure that closeness, knowing that I can take him, crush his throat, gouge out his eyes and castrate him before he can draw his nightstick. I say,

Martin, you touched me, does that mean we're in love?

I ain't your bitch, asshole.

At the end of the darkened corridor I stop, look through the glass. In the room the lights are down, the figure behind the glass just a dark shade against the concrete. Martin opens the door and without waiting, without his usual punishing thrust in the small of my back, without his usual parting taunt of Keep it in your pants, asshole, he turns and steps back into the dark. I hear his footsteps fade far off and then there is the silence of dead men in the place between Martin's world and the world of the dim room. Then, I enter, step into the smell of Jean Vadé, a cologne that I know, into the scent of fifty dollar cigars filling the room with their precious smoke, into the reek of shoe polish and hairspray. I say,

We have to quit meeting like this, Carl.

56.

Carl Fairweather, my brother-in-law, Lord of Death and Perversion, CEO in charge of rape and fornication, High Corruptor of the Flesh stands with one hand on the edge of the table. His frame lists to the right like a ship taking on water, the tilt from the leg I shattered with the baseball bat. He steps forward. His right foot drags as he walks. I say,

Does it still hurt, Carl?

All the time, Henry.

I lean on the table, pitch forward to peer at him in the darkness. I say,

You've got a lot of pull, Carl, getting here at night, getting them to cut the glim, getting a one-on-one, giving the guards some jerk-off time. Is that so no one recognizes your shit-eating whore-mongering, money-grubbing murdering face?

He pulls out the chair. I sit, back to the glass door, the position reserved for the visitor because that way the guards can see my hands, check me for sudden and futile attacks and I laugh. Fairweather the criminal in the hot seat, faces me. He says,

You haven't changed, Henry.

I've changed, Carl, I've drunk too much blood, cut the guts out of too many men, fucked too many assholes not to have changed. The one thing I regret is that I didn't kill you, you turd. What do you want with me now?

Henry just why don't you want out?

I don't want anything you ever smelled, tasted, farted on, or held in your death-dealing, motherfucking hands.

Three years, Henry, you can live a lot in three years. I lift a pen and you're out of here. I can even make this little peccadillo on your record disappear, like you never served a day.

Make it like I never existed, is that what you mean, Carl? I hear you're going into politics, is that right? You wanna quit your scum-sucking death-dealing corporate sinecure to make laws for the rest of us to live by, Carl?

His eyes shimmer black in the dim light, but I see the flicker of yellow like a snake blinking and I wait for his tongue to part his lips, his heat-seeking serpentine tongue to lap up the air as he targets my throat. But he says,

What kind of a charade are you playing here?

Oui ou merde? Senate or the shit can, Carl?

You don't belong in here.

Everything I need is here.

I need you to clear out a few brambles before I make the leap.

Why are you talking to me?

You're more valuable alive than dead, Henry.

And that's why you want me out. How's Geraldine?

Geraldine is my business.

Still can't speak, can she, Carl?

Why ask a question you already know the answer to?

I should have cut your nuts off and I should have slit your throat and pulled your tongue out onto your chest.

Corte corbata, Henry? The Devil's Necktie. You are good at that, aren't you?

What did you do with all the ears, Carl?

I had my chef deep-fry them. With a little salt they taste like pork rinds.

And he clasps his hands on the table in front of him in a cathedral of fingers that have signed blood checks, signed death warrants. The heavy gold Rolex takes a glint of light. His gaudy Air Force class ring is polished bright. I see that his right arm is bent, the bone now held straight with a steel plate. He says,

I'll be honest with you, Henry. I do need some ears.

In the shadowy light, I watch the lips move like rubber flaps, watch the filth tumble out of his gutter mouth. He says,

I need a man I can trust and I know I can trust you to hate me and to want me dead but I can trust you to think about your sister and your nephew and niece. No one else has that attachment of blood.

So if I don't do what you want, you ... what? Butcher your own family?

How thick is blood, Henry?

I reach across the table, grab him by the throat and pull him, gagging, to me, like a greasy hunk of meat into a table saw. I say,

What about Catharin, you ass-licking dog-fucking piece of pig shit?

I let him go. He gasps and slides back into his chair like slime oozing into a hole. He says,

What about Catharin?

She wrote me a letter, Carl.

I don't know anything about any letter, but your sister is a whore, Henry, she's been a whore since she was born and no injection of Jesus juice will ever change her. Your precious little sister fucked everything in India with a cock and ten rupees Henry. She's a whore in a nun's habit.

What she wrote is true?

I don't know what she wrote. What I do know is that both your sisters like the cock and there's nothing you can do about that because it's in the blood.

I stand, turn my back to him, feel the blood hammer in my ears and then I sweep around the table and I pin his face to the wood and I say,

Carl, I can snap your neck like a Christmas turkey.

But you won't do that, will you, Henry? I know you won't do that. You have two sisters and a niece and a nephew and you don't know what will happen to them.

I let him go. He sits up, looks at me, straightens his tie and collar. I smell his cologne polluting the night air, smell his sweaty face, the odor of sweat tainted by fear, a scent I have smelled hundreds of times. He says,

Think about it, Henry, think about walking out of here but don't think too long because thinking isn't what you're good at.

I knock on the glass door. Hammer at it until it shakes like a rattler's tail, hammer it until Martin skids to a stop outside the glass and glares at me and I say,

Take me home, Martin.

I walk out the door and quick-time it back to my cell,
Martin following, breathing hard.

I remember killing nights in the jungle of Oxapampa,
running and running, feeling strong as a jaguar, knowing I
could run all night and all day carrying my weapons and my
ammunition and never getting tired and Martin says,

What's the rush, Mitchell?

57.

In the cell, Squeaky lies curled into a tight little ball, his
hands tucked between his knees. He sits up as I enter.
Martin calls lock-up and the gate screams closed.

Squeaky huddles like a small scared animal and Martin
trudges away, taking the hard steely sound of his boots with
him. I sit on the edge of Squeaky's bunk and he half-grins.

I remember the first day he entered the cell, wide-eyed
and innocent without a clue about how to get through the
daily gauntlet. I remember the first time I touched him, how
he quivered the way a burro quivers when you load him up
and stroke his flank and I remember how he opened up to
me and admitted that he liked what I did to him because it
made him feel wanted and needed and loved.

He touches my hand and I get off his bunk and cross to
mine. I lift the mattress and yank out the cloth sack I have
tucked there. The white cloth is dirty and blood stained and
ragged where I ripped it. I lay the sack on Squeaky's lap and
he looks from me to the sack like it is poison. I say,

You don't have to worry anymore, Squeaky. Go ahead.
Open it. It's worth two thousand bucks. A little present to
make you feel good.

He unties the top of the sack and spreads the mouth
open and there on his lap lie two ears, crinkled and crisp as
cold toast. Squeaky glances up at me, tears in his eyes. He
holds out his hand. I take it and lie down beside him and,
while he clutches the ears in his fists, I fuck him and it is like
the first time over again and he comes and the scent of his

semen is like a rich thick perfume wafting up from a bed of luxurious night blooming jungle flowers in full blossom.

58.

From my perch high up in the crotch of the giant sycamore tree, I watched Mrs. Wilson and my father writhe on her bed. Through the second floor window I saw his one good leg stuck out straight, no shoes, no socks, his wounded and shriveled one dangling like a piece of wet spaghetti. Mrs. Wilson screamed—I think she screamed because her mouth opened and she clutched at my father's head buried between her legs. This was not the first time I'd watched my father at work.

Often, he'd return in the BMW with a woman. Upon hearing the car arrive, I would hop out of bed, sneak to the window to watch.

In the beginning, I had no idea what they were doing but I knew that I couldn't ask my mother or either of my sisters. I knew better than to ask my father because he would either smack me around for spying or ignore me. I liked watching naked women—or half-naked women—because sometimes my father made them keep their clothes on, removing only their underpants—in the back seat of my father's BMW do things with their mouths that made them gag because of the size of my father's cock.

He never told me how big it was, but I knew from gym class and later in high school that he was, in a word, a phenomenon—and somehow that huge dick made him famous—and this was before pornography took off and huge dicks were common on film, on tape, on video—But then, well, my fetish didn't extend to an obsessive need or desire to measure other boys because I knew—by instinct—that this man was unique and in that sense no one could compare to my dad for the enormity of his prick.

Often I wondered though, about the effect of this on my mother and perhaps that was the root of the look of perpetual pain on her face—although it didn't seem to affect Mrs. Wilson in that way because, as I watched, she had nothing on her face but an open-mouth look of awe and joy. My fetishes, by this time, had a grip on me and if I wasn't trapped by my black leather fetish, it was the white panty fetish that owned me and if not the white panties, then the ruby lips of my sister Geraldine who, as I learned, later had no qualms about oral sex because I spied on her many times before she met her fascist Air Force Captain and—like the women my father used in the BMW, she had sex in the Captain's Corvette—and of course I learned from them what to say at the right moment—oh God, oh fuck, Jesus, come in me—so that later when I had a chance at Mrs. Wilson I knew just how to do it. She said,

Well, you are your father's son, aren't you?

I knew she wasn't impressed by the girth of my male member. By then I had learned—listening to the Captain and Geraldine—that sex, if it's done right, is at least as enjoyable as skiing or swimming or even racquetball—but it is not as strenuous as Karate—which I had mastered up to the black belt because my father, always a warrior, even with the one damaged leg that gave him his limp, made certain that I, his lone male scion, would never be the brunt of boyhood bullying and so he insisted,

One—that I learn to box

Two—that I learn Karate

Three—that I learn L'escrime because, he said, l'escrime is the last true vestige of real manhood—the sword, long, powerful, hard, steel is man at his most erect and proud. He said,

You will learn to fence.

And I did.

But Mrs. Wilson made no reference to my father's hard steel projection of manhood other than that first day when— I think—she might have been disappointed. But I had learned to service a woman in many ways, none of which

107

required anything but my tongue and in this, I am sure, I surpassed even my father and for certain Geraldine's fascist Air Force officer.

From the crotch of the huge sycamore tree that day, I watched Mrs. Wilson rise from her bed on the second floor, come to the window, naked, her breasts high and firm. It reminded me of the day I spied on Catharin in the shower— no fetish developed around showers—and in that regard, I am normal and ordinary, but it was the first time I had seen a girl naked other than the daughter of the banker in Colorado Springs the first summer I went to stay with Geraldine and her fascist Captain soon to be Major—but the banker's daughter was just a child while Catharin was already, at fifteen, a full-bodied woman with breasts, pink nipples, and pubic hair.

As I watched Mrs. Wilson I realized that the female form takes many shapes from the classic trim and thin frame of my mother to the buxomness of Mrs. Wilson. As she stood at the window she looked right at me cringing behind the trunk of the sycamore. She waved and blew me a kiss and then she turned away and I saw a thick waist, broad hips, far broader than my mother's and she was gone but I saw my father still lying on the bed, naked, his huge cock flopping to one side, his wounded leg twisted at an angle.

I slid down out of the sycamore—caught, afraid, terrified that my father would collar me, flail at me with his black leather belt or, worst of all, confine me to my room or even gouge my eyes out for what I'd seen.

Later he limped into the kitchen, his tweed jacket draped over his arm, his tie loose at the neck as if he was returning from work. I knew that Mrs. Wilson hadn't squealed on me. I knew that I had a secret bigger than any of the secrets I had before because while I had no idea of the names of the women my father abused in the back seat of his BMW with his huge penis, I did know Mrs. Wilson's name—

Grace—and I knew Mr. Wilson—Edgar—but I was too young to know how to exploit that power.

Years later I asked Mrs. Wilson why she hadn't told my father she had seen me in the tree spying on them. She explained her own fetish, which was that she loved to be watched and that, in fact, that day, Mr. Wilson, Edgar, had been hiding in his own spy box peeping through a hole as my father had unrolled his twelve inch weapon to use on her and that, she explained, was the only way she could orgasm. Her confession made me realize that I had no real power over her except when I used my tongue.

59.

I haven't written in four days. Four days without my twelve-hundred words. Four days lost because when I sit down to write I think of Catharin. Carl Fairweather's accusations about her burst into my brain, deep hurting words—Your sister is a whore. She's fucking everything in India with a cock and ten rupees.

It's like everything I've copied from Catharin's letter into the computer, the hours spent learning to type, the careful secreting away of her manuscript as though it were a sacred saint's relic, all of that is either a lie or Carl Fairweather is the liar telling me those things to jerk me around. I have no way to know or to find out the truth. Do I know for certain Catharin's pain is pure?

Squeaky, sitting on his bunk crosslegged, says,

It makes me nervous when you're too quiet, Mitch, you gotta get outa bed.

I imagine stepping out of the steel cage, I imagine taking Carl Fairweather's offer to swim again in the river of blood, to step back into the slaughter and the murder, back into the liar's world of deception and sliding slippery allegiances spurred by dollars and cunt and breast and ass and I am stunned by how much I want Squeaky, want to be with him, want to touch that poor tortured skin, touch his liquid mouth. If I take Carl's offer, if I accept it, I lose Squeaky, lose the safety of the steel cage, lose the special place I've earned and I say,

Squeaky, what do you do if I'm not here?

Uh, I crash on my bunk, sometimes I sleep.

No, I mean what would you do if I go away for good?

He looks up from the twin dried and clicking ears on the string and his hand clutches the ears to stop their dry rattle.

Oh shit, Mitch, without you, I'm dead, they eat me for breakfast.

He crosses no-man's land, the five feet of concrete separating us and he kneels and he touches my groin with his hand.

You ain't gonna leave me, are you?

Not yet.

I'd just as soon you kill me, Mitch, 'cause I'd have to do it myself and I don't know if I can do that.

I remember a time, when I was twelve, a time before the blood and the knife, a time before the rivers turned red, a time when I climbed the wooden ladder up to Julianne's treehouse where she kept her dolls and where she had a blanket, a bottle of water, and cookies, oatmeal raisin cookies her mother baked. I remember sitting cross-legged on the blanket and I remember Julianne's white panties as she spread her knees just that instant before her skirt fell like an iron door covering the flash of innocence. The taste of oatmeal raisin cookies always brought back that flash and the soft white thighs as she slid the skirt over them. We sat and talked and as she combed the hair of her dolls I told her about my brother-in-law and how he had sex with my sister in the back seat of his Corvette before they were married and Julianne blurted out that she would be a virgin when she got married. I remember wanting to touch her and I wondered how different my life would have been had it not involved the twin poles of sweet innocent Julianne and the sluttish Mrs. Wilson and her voyeur husband Edgar who watched

her fuck my father with his huge cock and his one bad leg. I
wondered whether, if it hadn't been for that fleeting vision of
Julianne's white panties, I'd have remained pure, a man with
no blood in his dreams, a man without a taste for the asses
of men captive behind steel bars. Sometimes I bring
Julianne into the steel cage, bring her to her knees beside
my bunk and the hand I feel on my cock isn't Squeaky's and
Julianne opens her mouth and her teeth are white and pure
and her breath is clean and fresh and I see her with me on
the bed and she sheds her plaid skirt and her white panties
and she straddles me and I am in her and she groans with
joy and there is no blood, there are no ears, there are no
arms and legs torn and ripped and bleeding and Squeaky's
hand slides into the fly of my jeans and he says,

You're so hard, Mitch.

I push his hand away, and I look at him, look at his
liquid eyes, his ruby mouth, his flat belly. All that will
disappear if Carl Fairweather is telling the truth, if I take his
offer, if I walk out of the steel house and back into the river
of blood and I say,

Squeaky, I've got a problem.

He's hurt by my rejection, by my distance. He looks like
a jealous little girl, he looks like Julianne at thirteen, his skin
pale, his mouth quivering, and he says,

You don't care about me now, Mitch?

The problem is that I can get out of here if I want.

Oh shit, Mitch.

He covers his face with his hands and the dry ears on
the string clack like the teeth of a skull and I see that I have
ruined him, turned his ass into my playground. I have used
him the way Carl Fairweather used my sisters.

I try to remember other times before the killing, times
before Julianne, times after, but it is almost all a blank. As I
write my manuscript the past disappears piece by piece into
the pages until I can't recall any time before I was a killer,
and it is what I am and that is why I began again, with

Squeaky, trying to regain my innocence, trying to begin a
new life free of old memory, building a new life one day at a
time, one fuck at a time, one kiss at a time, building a new
life inside the steel, a new life with its own pool of pain and
purity and its own river of memory and its own rainstorms
of forget as I come in his willing body waiting for him to cry
out, to tell me to stop and I know that I will have to write
this out as well, turn it into forget, start over again and again
and Squeaky says,

I can't cut it in here without you, Mitch.

In his words I hear the same plea for help that
Geraldine sent me in her notes, the same plea for salvation
that Catharin sent in her eight page letter and I know that I
don't care if she lied to me. I hate Carl Fairweather, hate him
more than I hate the blood. I clasp Squeaky to me, feel him
close, a second heartbeat and I stroke his shaven head and I
whisper to him,

If I go, Squeaky, I'll kill you so quick you won't feel it.

I love you, Mitch, He opens my jeans, opens his mouth,
and I close my eyes and it is not Julianne.

60.

I recall the day my Mother carried Geraldine's first baby
home for the first time. Tiny, no hair, skin wrinkled like the
face of an old man. Alone in her room, Geraldine held the
baby at arm's length as if it were a monster that had crept
out of her womb, a toothless monster with a piercing wail, a
Maenad tearing her apart piece by piece in an orphic frenzy.

Geraldine on her natal bed looked at me, looked at the
monster she had birthed and she whispered,

How do I kill it?

She wasn't the pure sister of my illusions, but a monster
showing me that our seed was tainted by my father with his
twelve-inch cock and his lustful pursuit of women, tainted as
was Catharin who, despite her name taken from the purest

of the pure, was perfect in no way except in the ways of fornication, prevarication and excess.

This was and is my heritage—five years in prison to atone for having been born of a man who lived as faithless an existence as any man ever lived. But there can be no atonement, no redemption. Nothing will smooth out the wrinkled past. Geraldine's baby died. She killed it. Her fascist Air Force Major of a husband who taught willing cadets the virtues of just wars, was, in his own sick and perverted way, responsible for baby's death.

Geraldine, once pure and real, had no idea that his seed could produce purity but would only produce the wrinkled tainted abstract human being much as my father's seed could produce a mere façade of wholesomeness that had the perverted and artless even monstrous reality called me, my sister Geraldine, my sister Catharin.

And in all this there was my mother who, despite her obvious and lustful fixation on my father's enormous prong, was a pure woman who never had an impure thought and who, in later years, did not understand why Catharin strayed, didn't understand how her daughter could earn a living sucking the pricks of men in parks in San Francisco and who would have been mortified to learn that she had birthed a killer not once but twice—one in short skirts and crisp starched blouses and white tennis shoes, the other with a lust for men's cocks in his ass and a passion for knives. Why didn't she just leave him?

I never told Geraldine I knew she had murdered her baby. She never questioned me and I wasn't about to divulge the truth to her fascist Air Force Major whom I hated and who led a double life of his own as dutiful husband and father and money man for contract killers and money man as trainer of killers.

I took to discipline the way some men take the heart and soul and blood and words of Jesus Christ the Insane Sufferer into theirs. I couldn't bear to look at him with his

hypocritical half-shaven head in the style of Curtis LeMay
whose goal was to bomb all enemies back to the Stone Age
and kill a million little brown men in one fell swoop—but
now as I look at the bunk where René once lay I know that
even though he was a killer, even though he loved to feel the
knife slide into flesh, he was better than my fascist brother-
in-law, better than my faithless father who fucked Mrs.
Wilson while Edgar watched.

Even a killer can be pure, no compunctions, he said—he
didn't use that word—but at night as we lay together, he
talked to me about the joy of death, about the freedom it
gave him to watch the god-like power of the knife as it took
the life from his victim—and of course the truth of that is he
died with a six inch blade in his heart, another killer better
than he had taken him down, laid him down in his own
blood, torn open, a small wound but large enough to leak his
life away just as his semen had leaked from me after he had
taken me at night. The purest I had ever been I was tainted
with the fluid of a killer.

61.

In the desert of fucking men, there are no offspring. I
remember René, the hours I spent with his cock in my ass. I
remember every time he came in me I killed a hundred
million of his sperm. I remember the hours I spent
masturbating as I read *Notre Dame des Fleurs* exhorting the
trapped and condemned Genet as he hurled his semen
against the steel bars of his cell, defiant, hating life and
understanding it all so well.

Sometimes when I lie with Squeaky and he mutters as I
come in him, I whisper,

Be assured, Squeaky, you're doing the planet a favor
because there will be no little Squeakies running around.

Feeling him tense as his own orgasm rockets out of his
stiff cock, I laugh, pull out of him and he lies on his belly, his

face in the mattress, immobile, his seed sticky between the mattress and his prick, and I say,

It's okay, Squeaky, you're not the first bottom to come screaming.

I'm ashamed, he says.

Why?

Because I like it, Mitch, I ditten see how I could ever like it, but I do.

Burroughs liked it. You know Burroughs?

Is he that guy down in D Block who works out of the kitchen?

No, he doesn't work in the kitchen. William Burroughs, a writer.

Sort of like you, huh Mitch? Squeaky says.

Nothing like me, but he liked to be topped, Squeaks, and he screamed like a slut when his top came in him so you're in good company.

Squeaky rolls over, his flaccid cock wet with his own sacrifice to Onan, and he says,

You don't hate me, do you Mitch?

Squeaky, I don't hate you, I like your ass when you open—remember how tight you were the first few times?

And Squeaky looks away, blushing and he covers his cock with his hand and faces the wall and I leave him, his bare ass mooning the neon lights.

62.

I have decided that a writer has to write about his family. Eugene O'Neil said that hell has no fury like a human family. So I write about my family ...

My father died on a Sunday. I didn't feel a thing. He was a hateful man with raging eyes the color of coal. I was glad when he died. I didn't want to bury him. I wanted to leave his carcass out in the sun for the vultures to tear apart but there are no vultures in our town and my mother said the stench might give people the wrong idea.

He was a small man, my father, with a hairy chest and a dick as long as a horse's schlong, He loved to shower naked while I watched. He'd say,

You'll never be hung like this, son.

He was a talker, my father, a mouth full of smut that he liked to smear on women. He talked at the dinner table about the women he'd hosed. My mother always left the table but we kids had to stay. And then she'd come back and as soon as she'd stir the peas on her plate he described in detail the breast and cunt of the clerk in an office he had laid on the floor. My mother died a little more each day and I don't know why she took it and so when my father died, after we buried him—no vultures in our town—I asked my mother what his hold had been on her.

She was sitting at the dinner table, our first meal without his raging eyes and smutty mouth. Geraldine, my older sister, married to her fascist, was at home with her two children while Catharin—at eighteen already hooking in San Francisco before her religious conversion—was gone to us, dead to us. My mother looked at me, her eyes that intense black a woman's get when her anger burns in her throat, and she said,

Children. How will I take care of you three alone?

She turned away, then, to the meat on the plate, to the mashed potatoes with gravy, to the apple sauce with its dusting of cinnamon, and she ate in silence.

My father had three cars.

A classic Studebaker Commander, restored to its pristine luster.

A brown non-descript Chevrolet that he forced my mother to drive to the store to shop, to haul children to lessons. The Chevy was a standard car—useful, ugly, uninspired, American.

And then there was the BMW—black, sleek, powerful, German, the car he used just for his women.

Sometimes when he came home late he left the BMW open and I snuck into it to smell the perfume of his ladies. I tried to imagine those lustful women crossing their legs in temptation and what they felt when my father used that horse-sized dick on them and whether it made them cry. I imagined them to be very unlike my mother who wore modest basic dresses, long to the knee, loose at the bodice.

My father left a will. In the will, he left all his shares of great grandpa's company to my mother as restitution for the pain he caused her. Ten thousand shares for every woman he'd whored with his twelve inch cock—every share a reminder of his filth but it left my mother a widow with money and a heart bleeding with all the pain a faithless husband engenders in a moral woman.

It was she who sent out the detective to find Catharin on her knees sucking men's cocks in San Francisco parks for a few dollars a pop. There is a flaw in the genetic makeup of this family and when Catharin came home I asked her why she had run away—at eighteen but looking thirty-five—she just smiled. I did not know what sent her away anymore than I knew why Geraldine married her fascist. It's the flaw in us, a deep flaw, a wound that appears as the stigmata on a crucified Christ and that leads me to ask—what is my flaw? Is there only one? When will it appear?

When Catharin came back after my father's funeral, she learned that she was a rich woman because my mother's pity and great love of her children paid out with shares of great grandpa's company. Catharin, sensing redemption, had found Jesus—the sickening, horrid, bloody, crucified Jesus of mystery and the eternal throbbing heart.

I'm sure my mother had no idea she was unleashing demons on the world. Catharin, cleansed of her sins and as intimate with the body of Jesus as she had been with the cocks of anonymous men in her runaway time—her conversion was swift—and her embrace of her dead god was complete—and mother hoped Catharin would never again open her legs or mouth to a man, never again kneel to worship at the turgid meat altar that spews its god-milk.

Catharin raised herself up, a resurrected temple-whore buying salvation, like a medieval nun whose womb had been excoriated with her monkish sins, but instead of buying an indulgence, Catharin cashed her shares in and bought a ticket to India where she sought to cleanse the rotted souls of a hundred million Hindus tainted with the impure and unholy preachings of Buddha. Sometimes I wonder if Catharin's fall wasn't related to the size of my father's dick. Did he, in that BMW, take her cherry one night? Did he use her the way he used the women in their black stockings and their skimpy panties shoved aside to take the thrust of his meat—and their ruby lips? I didn't know, but I do remember and will remember Catharin's enigmatic Monalisa-esque smile when I asked her why she had left us.

Did Geraldine know? How do you ask a sister if her father has been fucking her? I didn't. Maybe to spare my mother the shame—I'm sure she didn't know—but something did happen to Catharin—and before she can be a saint she has to fall into the clutches of evil for to the fallen alone can resurrection be anything more than a philosophy.

My father was capable of everything. I wanted to cut him into pieces, cut away that horsewhip of a dick and pickle it in brine flavored with dill and anise, cut it up like a sausage and feed it to the dogs like after-dinner scraps.

But my mother—rich and careless—was right. The stench and horror of a decaying, dickless corpse on the front lawn might have given away the stench and rot at the center of our family and it wouldn't have done a thing for her standing in the community.

63.

Squeaky stands waiting, fidgeting, hands fluttering to his throat like a little cunt waiting to be fucked and he says,
Jeez Mitch, what am I 'sposed to do?

I want you to keep reading, Squeaky.

Read what, Mitch? He says.

Go read Chekhov, I say, fill your little brain with his words, now get.

And he disappears into the stacks.

64.

The manuscript gets longer every day because I have set a goal to write half an hour every day and that gives me twelve hundred words times seven equals eight thousand four hundred words a week which gives me thirty three thousand words a month so in one year I'll have three-hundred ninety six thousand words and that is far and away more than Camus put into his little *L'Étranger*. Camus imagined a killer in prison. I am jailed because of my lust for white panties—a small and insignificant fetish that began with the banker's daughter—Julianne—in Colorado Springs the first summer I stayed with my sister Geraldine and her fascist.

Julianne took me into her treehouse where she showed me her white underpants and I was stuck—it was as if something connected in the way a certain chemical connects to a taste bud—and I am sure that not every man who sees a pair of white panties becomes obsessed with them and so I can only posit that I was born with the white panty receptor in my brain and it landed me in prison—of all my weaknesses, flaws, and fetishes, it is strange that the white one got me this dark place with its gray walls—gray is the color of the suicide, three AM is its hour.

I never considered it even though I had let myself get caught in such an ignominious way—with an entire clothes dryer full of white underwear—bras and slips and leotards—in my jacket. I was never caught before—I wasn't when I spied on my father having sex with Mrs. Wilson, I wasn't when I spied on Catharin in her shower and no one caught me as I watched my sister Geraldine in the back seat of her

Air Force Captain's official US Air Force Chevrolet, and no one caught me playing doctor with Julianne, but the white panties got me.

And I'm ashamed—not of the fetish—it gave me the focus to begin writing this. In prison every day is like the day before and the routine is designed to punish us and so everything is the same day to day. Punishment takes away the freedom to change but most of my fellow inmates can't change because they have genetic propensities too and they are trapped not just by the bars and guards but by their own bodies and minds and their flaws and weaknesses. I understand both the root and the consequence of my weaknesses while my fellows have given themselves over to their obsessions.

The inmate in D Block just across the way from my cell is tall, thin. A hard nose. Big white teeth. His arms and legs are wiry and bird-like while his feet are so flat they turn up at the toes. He wears prison garb but he is so rangy his arms stick through the sleeves twice as far as mine do and so he looks like Ichabod Crane. His obsession is hair, long black hair. He is in here for tying up Mexican women and cutting their pubic hair and weaving it into pendants. When the police arrested him, he was found with a hundred and eleven pendants, each one hanging from a fishhook in the ceiling of his trailer.

65.

Somewhere out there, I probably have a child. I'm not a father, but I have more than likely sired a child. We do things—no, I can't speak for humanity—I can speak for myself because it is a man's responsibility to speak for himself. I have done things, not all unspeakable, but things I'm not proud of. If there is a child of my blood out there, I will never have to sit down in a chair to explain how I have done horrible things. I am my father's child—that is a given even if I can never be certain who my father is—but I am not

Jesus, a god born from the womb of a pure Madonna. No, my mother knew my father was human—although I can't be sure my father is the man she slept with every night, nor can I be sure my father is the man who taught me to box. I don't mean to demean my mother nor to cast aspersions on her virtue because she had—I now see—a horrid life with the man she married. Whether he is my father or not doesn't matter in matters of her virtue—although there were times when I wished he wasn't—like when he taught me to drive. Most fathers would be kind, teaching in increments, but my father, with his wounded and shriveled leg, sat me behind the wheel of the brown Chevrolet he let my mother drive—he kept his Commander for work and his BMW for sex and neither of them could ever be mine. He sat me at the wheel of the Chevrolet and handed me the key and said, If you wreck it, I'll kick the shit out of you and make you eat it and then I'll whip your ass for making a mess. I started the Chevrolet. Having watched my mother at the wheel I already knew what to do and I drove around the block with one ear open to my father's grunts and groans as I made a turn—he said nothing—using the signal and another and then stopped at a light—before driving back to the house on LaVerne Terrace where I parked in the driveway just as I had seen my mother do and shut down the engine. My father didn't say a word. He held out his hand. I gave him the key. He got out of the car. I sat behind the wheel triumphant on two counts—I hadn't done anything wrong and my father hadn't whacked me upside the head. That day I was certain that if he had been my real father—what doubt is there of that?—he would have told me I'd done a good job. Somewhere there is a child with my blood and the blood of my father and that child has no idea who sired him. I hear men talk about their bastards with pride, talk about the cunts out there they left with full bellies. Being in prison they have no responsibility to their offspring and this, although I am not pure, this I find despicable because despite my own odious behavior (who

ever heard of being thrown in jail for stealing a dryer full of
white underwear) I take responsibility and in fact even tried
to track down the mother of my child who, I found out, was
fifteen when I—well, I can't say made love to her because it
wasn't love, it was sex in the back seat of a car on Skyline
Boulevard and it was fast and sloppy and when I finished
she looked at me and said, You're a real beast—and she
didn't smile and later, when I went to her house to ask her
out again, her father, a big man with a mashed nose and
narrow pig eyes stood in the doorway and said who the fuck
are you and I said I was a friend of Richie's and he said she
ain't here and I said when will she be back and he said she's
knocked up and in a home till her little bastard is born and I
said which home and he slammed the door and I walked
away but every day I wondered—was the bastard my
bastard? Was Richie having my baby? Where was she? And
so for a week—at least—I tried to track her down, but no
luck. So I suspect that my child is out there—lost—and
perhaps it's a good thing because I am not an example of
fatherhood gone right. I'm in prison, a victim of my own
flaws, my own fetishes, my own evil. At least my father was
open about his immorality and didn't hide it even from my
mother and sisters. He didn't hide it from Mrs. Wilson, who
told me that she loved my father because of the ham hanging
between his legs and with him it was the only time she ever
felt like a real woman because most of the men she fucked
were endowed with small dicks whereas my father filled her
up with his tree-sized cock and she loved him for giving her
that feeling and as I lay with her I didn't feel envy or pain. I
listened to her. I tried to fill in the gaps because my father
was a man who had killed men, who slept with every woman
willing to bed him, who owned fast and expensive cars and
had spawned at least three children—and that made him
exceptional although he talked just once about his killing
because as with most men who had killed in battle, the
memory and the facts to him were pure pain and not

something to brag about except that one time. At the dinner table for no reason he said in a clear and simple voice, I killed over twenty men and all of them with a knife. He looked at me, my mother, at Geraldine, at Catharin and then he went back to his bloody roast beef dinner and I, even now, can't imagine the tape that was running in his head. How often and why that day? Never again did he mention it. I cornered my mother in her bedroom later and I said did he really kill twenty men with a knife and she said they were the enemy Henry, the enemy, and he had to kill them and I said is that how he got his shriveled leg and she said not directly—he stepped in a trap and bamboo spikes poisoned him and that poison shriveled his leg but he was wounded twice and the shrapnel scarred his skin and he is a wounded and incomplete man now.

You have to unravel the mysteries to find the secrets and hidden truths and from that time, although I hated him for his ugly ways, I had a new vision of my father as a man who had enemy shrapnel in his body. The poison in his leg poisoned his soul as well and that is why he spent his hundreds of millions of sperm in as many women as he could find.

66.

Love. A strange word, nuanced like fine shadings in a rainbow. Did Meursault love his mother? Did James Joyce love his daughter? Did Samuel Beckett love James Joyce? Did Jean Genet love Jean Paul Sartre? Did Marcel Proust love Edouard Dujardin?

All the heartbreak, all the loss, love is gone and where does it go when it dies? Love comes just once. It rockets into your bones, you know love because you want to be with that person and it doesn't matter who sees you as a fool, it doesn't matter if you taste those lips while hiding in a broom closet in the laundry or you taste them lying in a bed, you know that until you see that person again you are dead, your

heart beats, your lungs respire, but you are dead and you
resurrect only when that person—that object of desire—
shines again in your eyes. And you feel whole only when that
person fills your eyes and you remember the moments in the
dark, the oil of those hands on your loins, the surge of blood
in your face, your turgidity, your breathlessness, the sudden
wet feeling all over your body—and today that is all a
memory and memory can never give back the sweat and the
love. I remember fucking Mrs. Wilson, who told me secrets
of sex and as I smelled her pussy she directed my tongue to
her secret place and I felt the surge in her sex and she
showered me, soaked me in her fountain of cum with its own
musky smell and sweet taste and oily feel. But it wasn't love.

Mrs. Wilson fucked my father and Edgar and she fucked
me because she was waiting for the one Love to appear—but
he never came for her. As I wait, I feel tears in my eyes
because I know that now and forever I will be alone. I try to
fathom it, the vastness inside that contains a universe that
can be filled by one touch—and I try to imagine his blood as
it spilled from his body and who and why but there are no
answers, no culprits, just suspects and he is dead. I
remember Shelley's poem to Keats—Weep for Adonais, he is
dead. Blood spilled in a great circle around his torso. The
blade of a knife, wrapped with string and fixed with semen,
rammed into his chest, in his heart that had beaten for
thirty-two years and I weep for him but I don't let the tears
out, no, I stifle them, guard them, as if he is in them and if I
cry I will send him out to another death. The cut in his chest
was an inch wide. How can life seep out of that small wound
so fast? It takes nine months to create a body but a minute
for it to die.

Catharin was right, Catharin with her whore's mind and
her slut's heart and her slattern's eyes—she was right—God
created the world then he went crazy and, showing us his
sense of humor, he left us to ferret out the meaning in his
joke and his joke is a shaggy dog story. And so my question

to my mother I understood only after René died—I was born to love and if I hadn't stolen that woman's underwear, if my panty fetish hadn't controlled me, I'd never have found love in its perfection—knowing that without the accident of one in a hundred million sperm I would have lived obsessed with black leather and white underpants but now I rejoice because in his death I find the answer to my question to Geraldine. I lie on my bunk feeling the thin bump of Camus' novel under my pillow. I understand that I am given one chance—one sperm, one body, one love, one mother, one father, one, and I am alive with death now that I have felt the stiffness of his cock in my ass and the sweet taste of his mouth on mine and you see, I see, that it was as Mrs. Wilson said—recreational sex opens the door to true love and I have known it.

And so I write. Writing is the thing that saves me. No offspring, just the pages stacking up, corpses—what is left of me is on the page. The only place I can find immortality.

In prison you have time to think about all the things you didn't do. Lying awake at night, hands behind your head you play a tape of your life and you see what you left out—great holes in time filled with missed chances.

Sometimes you kick yourself for getting caught up in your own stupid dreams that were not important—like new clothes. All the money I spent on clothes, all the time I spent in a barber's chair, all the money and time I spent on cars not because I gave a damn but because I needed people to see me cool.

Now, as I lie awake at night, I hear the guards march on their rounds and I know what I'd change. Clothes—one color, one style, never have to make a decision. Like now, I wake up mornings, pull on my denims, pull on my chambray shirt—no decisions—the shoes, one pair of black and white canvas sneakers—high top sneakers without a logo because in here no one gives a shit about fashion. Hair—let it grow, let it go long, down to my waist, no thought of cutting it off,

no thought of letting somebody haul away my body parts in
a garbage truck. No decisions about pomade or gels. Hair—
just tie it back with a piece of string—because in here,
nothing matters except the circle of fear you build around
yourself to keep the bastards away—and some of them are
rotten bastards, stinking bastards with gaping holes in their
moral fiber, bastards who have killed not to eat but for the
sheer joy of watching blood flow. Cars—how many cars did I
own—buying every two years, and all that because my father
and his goddamned BMWs ruined me for cars. I was raised
to think you had to have a big one, a big black one, a great
big black powerful car with a top of 175—but in here I see
that owning is a disease. I make plans for my exodus—no
car—walk, hell, take a bike, no hair cuts, no clothes bought
anywhere but Salvation Army—possessions don't matter. I'm
human and like everybody else, I got sucked into it and I
regret nothing, but in here as you lie awake at night, you
think about all the things you didn't do.

67.

I continue to write about fear and my father and how I
hated him and wished him dead ...

My father was a hateful man but he had one redeeming
quality—he insisted that I get an education because, he said,
he didn't want to support me for the rest of my life and
education was a way to get me out of his house. He said I
was his blood, his seed, miserable as I was, and a poor
excuse for a human being but nonetheless his seed and as
such I would learn and so he sent me to schools—private
schools, public schools, summer schools, and later to a
university where I learned such things as why my mother
named my sister Catharin with such an odd spelling—
Catharin with a C and no E at the end.

My father, never the sentimental pater familias, had
children and then hated us except for Geraldine, his first
born and his namesake, whom he showered with attention

and expensive gifts, while Catharin and I suffered in silence. I suppose this is why Catharin had no children and why I could see no reason to marry. If there are other children out there with my father's seed I know nothing about it. In those schools he didn't praise me no matter how well I did—but then he didn't beat me if I failed because I think he saw me as a lost cause and no amount of success or failure was going to change that even a little bit and so off to schools I went where I learned—among other things—that my father was a gifted man not just for the size of his cock, but for his ability to make money. His male member was by any standard extraordinary and this I learned by observation of the range of boys I met in school and the men I encountered in the university and killers I knew in the army. After experiencing that range I knew this for a fact—my father had been born with a cock the size of a stallion's and he knew how to use it and though this particular gift didn't come down to me in its entirety I didn't resent it because just as one can't choose one's parents, neither can one choose the size of one's genitals.

I know little about my great great grandfather except that he came out of the Great War with lungs tortured by phosgene gas. He forged a small empire in the coal industry. Using a bank loan he bought a dozen dump trucks that he hired out to haul coal from the West Virginia mines into the cities where every house had a coal-burning furnace and a basement with a coal chute.

My great grandfather—though I know nothing of the size of his male member—parlayed the dozen trucks into a fleet of hundreds and had the good sense to sell before the great coal strike John L. Lewis called in 1949. He turned the proceeds into a company that supplied parts to General Motors, which turned him into a very rich man who metered out his money like a miser. He adored my mother, his granddaughter, and didn't understand her fascination with my father. He nevertheless saw to it that she didn't lack

anything and when he died he left her the bulk of his
fortune, which was in shares of the auto parts company that
had wound down and by the time I was born the fortune was
a memory—or so everyone thought until my father died.
That wounded leg of his with its dose of Vietnamese
shrapnel gave up its load and wound its way into his brain
and so Ho Chi Minh killed my father forty years after the last
battle when the metal shard inched its way to my father's
brain felling him on a golf course, on the fourteenth hole
when he was six under par and playing for a thousand
dollars a hole.

When my father died, my mother discovered that while
he was a faithless and hateful man who fucked a hundred
women in the back seat of his various BMWs, he was,
nonetheless, an artful investor who had taken the trust of my
great grandfather and with inspired stewardship, saved it,
watched it flourish and grow so that my mother, who was
raised with a golden spoon in her mouth, returned once
again to that domain. I wondered why we had lived in the
three story house on Laverne Terrace all that time if my
father—who was not profligate—had all that salted away. I
don't think it was because of Mrs. Wilson. When I asked
Mrs. Wilson what she saw in my father, she said,

You mean besides that enormous hunk of meat
swinging between his legs?

I was afraid she would compare me to the
incomparable. I had learned many things at the university,
one of which was that a man's tongue can perform miracles.
While procreative sex has just one purpose, sex as
entertainment has a hundred thousand variations many of
which I tried on Mrs. Wilson who was reduced to six words—
Oh My God do it again. By then Mr. Wilson was dead but
Mrs. Wilson still lived in her house on Laverne Terrace
where I first watched my father do her while Edgar spied on
them from his hidey-hole.

She told me she didn't care that my father was a rich man, nor that I was an educated one, but when I told her why Catharin's name was spelled in such a peculiar way, she was impressed with my knowledge of Cathar history and said that she knew nothing about them. I explained that Catharin was born on the 730th anniversary of the massacre at Montségur, where all but a few of the Cathars were annihilated, and that my mother, a student of religious history was convinced that Catharin was a reincarnation of a Perfect and that's why she had no qualms about letting Catharin spend her inheritance trying to convert Hindus to the one true and pure religion based on the word of God and transmitted through his one and only son, the tortured and bloody and crucified and fruitless Jesus Christ.

68.

The words come easy today. Sitting back, letting my mind race, I write ...

Mrs. Wilson was in her kitchen wearing a clingy blue dress, her hair down to her waist held back with a black rattail comb as she stood at the range stirring a big pot of peaches she was canning. I sat on a rickety chair at the table with its cracked tile and I watched her. She looked ripe and full. Speaking with her back to me, she said,

When your father died, I didn't go to his funeral.

It's okay, he was a rotten son of a bitch with a mean streak a mile wide.

He looked out for you.

You weren't his only woman.

Some men are like that. Here, taste this.

And she dipped her spoon into the pot of peaches and dipped her finger into the curdled peach jam on the spoon and she turned to me. I saw the little beads of sweat on her face, her eyes crinkled as she headed toward me and I saw the dab of yellow jam on her finger. She held it out to me and I sucked it into my mouth, and she sighed and said,

You have a soft lips, like a mare taking a bit into her mouth.

I let go of her finger and she looked at me, lips wet, eyes open. The buttons on her blue dress strained to hold her breasts in place. At the neck, where the dress stretched over the tops of her breasts, I saw her rosy pink skin. She said,

Sweet enough?

Yeah.

She took a deep breath, wiped at her forehead with the back of her hand. As she raised her arm, the dress tightened over her breasts and I saw her nipples hard against the fabric. Hand to her forehead, she posed, raking me with her eyes. Then she turned away, the blue dress draped over her broad ass, and I blink and she is gone and I understand, lying on my back at night, how my father could love my mother and still sleep with Mrs. Wilson—that peach skin of hers and the long brown hair of hers and that broad hipped frame of hers and that mound of breast always about to burst past the buttons—I understand because in those moments, I know a real man would have taken her hand with the peach jam on it and pulled her down and set her on the table to open her up and eat her like a ripe peach.

Mrs. Wilson is dead. And I lie awake at night cataloging things I didn't do. Still writing, I go back to other times ...

The peach canning time with Mrs. Wilson came just a few years after Geraldine, my older sister, gave birth to her second baby. For the second time I was an uncle and the baby was the grandest thing I'd ever seen. Holding her in my arms was nothing like holding Mrs. Wilson because the baby was pure and clean and didn't reek of body fluids. Caressing the baby, my hands felt reborn to a time as pure and clean as the skin of the baby in my arms. The baby was soft but demanding, needing everything, having nothing, dependent on Geraldine who this time had no regrets about giving birth. You saw it in her eyes and the loving, almost desperate glow in her face as she stroked the baby's skin—as if she were trying to regain her own purity by osmosis, as if purity were a liquid she could drink like water.

I remember how the baby grew week to week that summer. I tried to fathom how Carl Fairweather, such a worthless murdering son of a bitch, could spawn such sweetness. She was light while Carl was dark. She was wide-eyed while his eyes were narrow slits in a donkey-shaped face. She was dainty while he was a rough mountain of skin and bone. Nothing of his wickedness had leached into the skin of the child.

I know I am as rotten as my father, as impure as Mrs. Wilson, as perverted as Mr. Wilson who loved to spy on his wife while she lay sweating and cumming with my father's twelve inch cock buried in her wet cunt. I know that no child of mine will be as pure and clean as Geraldine's baby even with her malignant sperm donor of an Air Force Major. No, my baby will have been born with a pitchfork in one hand and a leer in his eyes already just one inch away from jail. Is it for the best? I'll never know. I'll never know but still, it's something I didn't do. In the end all you have is the sum of what you did. I'm no saint—not by a long shot—you don't end up in prison with murderers and rapists if you're good and pure and you change your underwear once a day and wash your fundament at night and use deodorant.

As Geraldine's baby grew I watched, expecting the bad seed to germinate, to turn foul, but a little angel emerged like a white vision from the shell of childhood.

Each summer when I saw Geraldine and her fascist pig of a mate, I was amazed to see how the baby became more human, softer even than the day I first held her—softer at five years than at five months.

And so I did the one pure true thing in my life. I had nothing to give her except money. When my father died my mother liquidated all her shares in Great Grandfather's company. I took my share and put it in trust for the baby with the stipulation that she never know the money came from her diseased uncle.

69.

I write about the day my mother made lemonade for me ...

I was eleven. My mother was in the kitchen and I was at the kitchen table sweating from a game of kickball and thirsty for the lemonade she was squeezing using the hand squeezer she preferred.

Mother, why was I born?

She stopped with one hand on the squeezer and she stood straight. She said,

Henry, what a question.

She poured sugar into the pitcher and filled it with water and cracked a tray of ice cubes into the pitcher, dropped ice cubes into a glass and filled the glass with lemonade. She ruffled my hair and said,

Is it sweet enough?

It could use some more sugar, mama.

Go take a shower. You're all sweat and dirt. Take your lemonade. Go. Upstairs and shower.

What if I break it?

You won't break it.

What if I spill it?

You won't spill it.

She went back to the kitchen sink and made noise and I left her in the kitchen and went upstairs to Geraldine's room. She was lying on the bed wearing a pair of white shorts and a red bandeau top and her hair was done up like an old-fashioned woman in a French movie. I sat on the floor holding my glass of lemonade and I said,

Mom won't tell me why I was born.

Geraldine sniggered and she rolled over and I watched her mess with her hair and she said,

Do you like my hair?

Why was I born, Geraldine?

Tell me if you like my hair and I'll tell you why you were born.

Okay. I like your hair.

Well, it's pretty obvious why you were born, isn't it?

I drank some of the lemonade and watched my sister fiddle with her hair and then she said,

What're you looking at?

It's not obvious to me why I was born.

Well, you know about the birds and the bees so you know why you were born.

She plopped back down on the bed and crossed her legs at the knees and looked at the ceiling. I got up and went to Catharin's room, which was moody and dark because Catharin even at fifteen had taken to the dark side and her room had candles and incense burning. There were black curtains on the windows and it smelled of perfume and she always played Gregorian chant very low so it sounded like there were men under her bed.

She sat cross-legged on the floor in her favorite yoga position and her black-dyed hair hung down over her shoulders like a thick veil. I sat opposite her and I said,

Mom won't tell me why I was born and Geraldine says it's obvious because of the birds and the bees.

Geraldine is stupid, Catharin said. She's a baby machine in the making so everything to her is obvious—motherhood is sacred and the womb is its own mystery.

Why was I born, Catharin?

You were born by accident because there were a hundred million yous who died when our father ejaculated into our mother and so you are an accident and there is no meaning to your wretched eleven-year-old existence. You are a stupid biological machine who will go out and do something with your tiny little penis. It's called the biological imperative and you're it.

I drank some lemonade. It was tart and cold and tasted good on my tongue.

That's it? I said. I'm a biological imperative?

Do you believe in God, little brother?

I don't know.

I believe in God, Catharin said. I believe in a God who went crazy after he'd seen what a stupid mistake he'd made creating us and then he left and we're the spawn of a crazy thing.

You want some of my lemonade? I said.

Mom always scrimps on the sugar, she said.

She resumed her yoga position and closed her eyes and I finished my lemonade and set the glass on the floor and went to shower and I got an erection when I soaped up my cock. I thought about my father and his hundred million dead babies and how lucky I was to have made it and as I rinsed off I wondered if it hurt the women when he used his enormous cock on them and what happened to the hundreds of millions of could-have-been-mes that didn't make it. Did they die? Go to heaven?

As I dried, my erection went away and I stood looking at myself in the mirror measuring my luck—a hundred million didn't make it but I made it—and so I got dressed in some clean jeans and as usual I left everything on the floor of the bathroom because I knew my mother would pick up my clothes and put them in the laundry.

I went back downstairs to my mother who was in the living room sitting in her chair reading The Joy of Cooking and I said,

Catharin says I was born because God went crazy and I am one in a hundred million and there's nothing special about me at all.

My mother looked up from her book and she closed it and she patted her knee and said,

Come here and sit with me.

She looked at me, felt my still wet hair with her soft hands and she said,

Catharin has been reading the Existentialists.

Geraldine says it's obvious why I was born, I said.

You're one of the lucky ones then, aren't you? She said.

A hundred million and any one of them could have made it and it would have been a different me here.

Shhh, she said. You don't need to know any of these things.

But I've got to know.

Life's a mystery, Henry.

I left my lemonade glass upstairs. Does that bother you?

A mother's work is never done, she said.

And I left my dirty clothes on the floor.

Are they wet?

Don't you wonder why you were born, Mom?

I was born to make sure you were born, she said.

But I could have been anyone of a hundred million so would you still love me if I'd been one of the others?

A mother's love is unconditional, son.

Does Dad wish I'd been one of the others? I said.

Catharin has no business filling your head with that nonsense, she said.

Did God go crazy?

Well, she said, maybe he did and we'll get a chance to ask him won't we?

I don't believe in heaven.

That's your intellectual side, she said. Your spiritual side has another view.

Do you think God put us here for a reason?

God cares what we do.

I still don't believe in God, I said, but if he did put us here why did he put us here and not on Mars?

Why don't you go get your lemonade glass?

I ate all the ice.

You'll crack your teeth on the ice and have to see the dentist again.

Why here?

When you're older you'll understand.

Do you understand?

I know I love you.

You'd have loved any one of the hundred million?

Of course.

So Catharin's right—I'm nothing special? I'm an accident. And if I'm an accident then Catharin and Geraldine are too.

It doesn't matter.

You don't know, do you Mom?

I know I love you.

But you don't know why I was born.

I love you, that's what matters.

But if I'm nothing special how can you love me?

Maybe I'll have the minister talk to you about love.

That creep makes me nervous.

But Henry, he's a man of God, she said.

Does God ejaculate a hundred million sperm?

That Catharin. She'll learn to hold her tongue, she said.

70.

Writing empties me out. Each time I write I feel hollow. Words pour out of my brain eating memory until at the end of each writing session my head is anesthetized. I know that I have just so much left and once I write it out I collapse back into myself—a volcano sucking back a last spit of lava.

But the printed pages look good on the screen. Perfect. Aligned. Each letter clear and clean and exact—no smudges, no smears, no tear stains, no bleeding of ink through the paper—precise as if carved in stone and sterile. I type at Catharin's letter, fingers staccato on the keys, each word appearing on the screen. As I read the lines there is no

passion even in the words she wrote ... He made me suck his
cock, Henry. He said one sister is as good as the other and
the most painful of all is that Geraldine knows. But I'm
helpless. I have no where to go. I have nothing left but my
swollen belly and my swollen ankles and the pain in my
pride of knowing that I betrayed my sister ... I look at the
words on the screen, page six of her hand turns into a mere
half screen with its tiny letters and there is nothing left of
her pain in the script that she bled for each time, nothing left
of the quake and quiver of her hand that shook in her
anguish, in her pink ink ... his cock ... where the K wiggles as
if it were alive and I know that I will have to go back to the
handwritten pages for the truth, back to the handwritten
pages to find the anger and the anguish and the angst and
then, as I print the meager half page—Page Six Full of Pain—
page six reduced to a precise and beautiful but sterile half
page, the door to the library opens and Martin enters, his
face blackened by two months more of truth. There is terror
in his eyes, defeat in the slope of his shoulders where the
weight of a huge stone bends him, cracks him, and the
sunken chest—a void where his heart once beat, He slumps.
I say,

Martin, you're not getting enough sleep, you look like
canned dog shit.

He lifts his cap from his sandy, boyish head of hair, the
last innocence left in him now and he says,

Asshole, you got a visitor.

Martin, there's a lot of pleasure in an asshole so I don't
mind your epithet.

My what?

Your epithet. asshole. You say it as though it is a bad
thing but behind the steel curtain, Martin, an asshole is a
precious commodity and he says,

You cunts are all alike, Mitchell.

See, you grow each time I teach you something.

You can't teach me shit, asshole.

I shut down the computer, turn off the screen, tear the half page of Catharin's pain out of the printer and lay it in the folder and I say,

Can I have a second? I have to file this.

I ain't the one waiting.

I take the envelope, the eight pages and the printed facsimile of Catharin's words that I've already forgotten and I carry them to the stacks and plant them between the book on English roses and the book of French roses where the other pages of her life swell like seeds in dark soil. I return to Martin whose sloped shoulders look like the bent and twisted bones of a skeleton.

71.

He marches two paces behind me. I walk fast, stretch the distance to make him speed up and I lead him to the visitor's room where I see Geraldine seated at a table and she wears a red dress that looks like cascading fire eating her body and her hair is curled in long ringlets. As the door opens she stands and I see her face lined and weakened and her eyes are red.

I sit across from her and I look at Martin, see the pain again in his eyes, the sheer pain of a man in hell unable to admit who and what he is, unable to pull out because the pay is so good and he is in debt and his blood is starved for money and the cost of his SUV keeps him in the steel cage, the steep rent on his condo keeps his hand on the nightstick and I say,

Geraldine, this is my guard, Martin. He's been here for six months.

Geraldine nods and turns her eyes to the uniform and the nightstick and the sloped shoulders and Martin. For the first time ever I see color rise in his face as Geraldine holds out her hand and he touches her and she's electric and he lights up like a bulb.

Geraldine's shape is still that of a young girl and her breasts under the hot red blouse are heavy and her hips, in the tight red skirt, full. Martin's eyes widen. He takes her in, eating her from breasts to belly, from waist to thigh. He is seeing a goddess for the first time in his life, a goddess of blood and warm flesh, a fecund goddess whose breasts leak milk and honey, whose thighs open wide to receive him like the grave and he drops her hand and I say,

Geraldine's my sister, Martin.

Ma'am, he says.

She can't speak, I say. Her husband beat her up and crushed her larynx.

Martin backs away, backs through the glass door where he stands like a statue as Geraldine sits.

I face her and she takes her pad of paper from her purse and the ballpoint pen from a pouch and she writes ... Henry, why do you refuse parole?

I don't want to go back out there, sister.

She writes ... I need you, Henry, Catharin needs you. She had her baby.

I see in the curve of Geraldine's hand the curve of Catharin's hand and yet they are as different as rain and stone and I say,

A boy?

Geraldine nods and her lips quiver the way Catharin's hand quivered when she wrote about her captivity and her rape and about her violation by Carl Fairweather's cock and I take a deep breath because now there is, in the world, another Mitchell male, another killer, another carrier of the plague and I say,

Catharin wrote that Carl raped her mouth.

Geraldine's eyes flood with tears and she nods and I say,

Does it continue?

She nods again and I say,

Geraldine, is Carl going to run for the Senate?

Geraldine's lips break open and her eyes gush tears and she nods and she writes ... No one will ever stop him then, Henry.

I turn the pad, take the pen and scribble ... What are you telling me, Geraldine? What do you want?

She flips the pad, rips two sheets of paper from it and, taking the pen, she writes ... What you told me. Is it true? You really kill?

I seize the pen from her fingers and print each letter— the words run out of the pen, imperfect, true, absolute, pure, slanted, curled, blurred—feeling truth again in the black ink flowing from the hand as if flowing from the finger immediate and true and hard and real ... I can't say yes and I won't say no.

She again takes the pen and writes... Please? He still abuses Catharin.

She lays the pen on the table and I pick it up and write ... Does he know you're here? And she answers ... If he's Senator, the children are in danger. He'll use them.

And I hesitate before writing ... Has he abused Eleanor?

She shakes her head no, then, taking the pen she writes ... I'm sure she'd tell me.

Did Catharin tell Mom about Dad?

She looks at me, quizzical puzzlement clouding her face. She shrugs. I say,

Does he know you're here?

She sighs, lifts the pen and writes ... He thinks I'm in Colorado. Private school hunting.

She watches me, her eyes haunted, her skin flushed and I say,

You put yourself in danger coming here, Geraldine.

She turns the pad, writes in a quick script, her hand convulsing, head bobbing and she slides the pad and pen back at me and I read her words ... I'm afraid of what he'll do, Henry.

As I look at her writing, I see her mind at work in the thinness of the letters, the skipped parts of words where her hand moves too fast for the ink to spread—leaving small gaps—lacunae, as she speeds to the end of each thought ... of what he'll do ... the DO is faint, a hint of a word. I say,

Why does Carl Fairweather want to spring me out of here?

As I speak the skin of her cheeks first blanches then turns fiery, embarrassed, as if ashamed I've found her naked in the shower, and her lips tremble and she writes, her hand quaking so the letters tear at the page the way Catharin's pen gouged out holes in her pain ... Has he been here again?

Her eyes tear up and I cover her hand with mine, feel the hardness of the ballpoint pen and the cold clammy skin under the pen. I say,

Carl Fairweather asked the Board to release me.

The fear turns her face sweaty, and her chest heaves like the quick beating of a small bird caught and she scribbles at the page, the pen digging into the paper shoving wads of it up like bulldozed dirt and she stops, pulls the pen from the page and, taking a deep breath, begins again, printing in large capital letters ... DON'T TELL HIM I WAS HERE. I whisper to her,

Geraldine, he wants me out so I can take ears for him.

She jerks her head as if jolted by a bolt of electricity. She shakes her head and shrugs in question. I say,

What do you want? Tell me the truth.

She looks down, her eyelids fluttering, small wings beating, and she then locks her eyes on mine and still staring at me, mouths the words ... I want him dead.

She looks at me, her eyes pinning me, and then she picks up the pen again, bends her head over the pad and her hand stabs at the paper, tears at it in a rush and then she spins the pad around and I read her river of words ... He'll kill us all, he hates us, only alive because he needs us for his

big step we can't stand it anymore, Henry. If anyone ever
needed to die it is my husband.

I look at her. Her eyes are not cold, not precise as the
words on a computer screen. But there is a ramrod
straightness to her now. Her lips no longer quiver. Her hand
no longer shakes. She lifts the pad, tears off the sheets
covered in her tortured hand and folds the paper and tucks it
in the opening at the top of her red blouse. Then she stands,
turns her back to me and leaves the room, leaves her note
pad, leaves the ballpoint pen. The sudden cold absence is
like an icy wind. I pocket the pad and the pen. I shove away
from the table, stand.

Martin at the door, his nightstick dangling at his side,
says,

What'd you say to piss your sister off, asshole?

You like that, Martin? You like that sleeve?

Sleeve? What do you mean, sleeve?

Cunt, Martin, cunt. You like that red hot piece of
snatch?

His eyes flash—bewildered—I say,

How about I set you up with my sister, Martin?

And again his face blushes in disbelief and I say,

Her husband is a friend of the Gov.

Martin's face freezes in that fixed neutral place all the
guards go to when you lay out the truth of the power
structure for them, letting them know just where they stand
in the pecking order and I say,

Martin, I've watched you age twenty years in six
months, how's your gut holding up?

You fucking asshole, you'd pimp your own sister?

I lead him back up the tiers of steel, back to the cell,
back to my bunk where I say,

Wouldn't be the first.

You're really a pervert, Mitchell. How can you sleep at
night?

I don't.

Your sister really knows the Gov?

Marty, I need some ink cartridges for the printer in the library, can you get me some ink?

And he looks away, checks the tier like a man crossing the street in heavy traffic and he whispers,

What're you trying to do, asshole, get me fired?

I can help you.

How the fuck can you help me?

Next time I see the Gov I'll put in a good word for you.

Fuck you, asshole.

He calls the lock up and the gate closes with its song of sliding steel and he looks at me through the bars and he says,

You been pushing me, asshole. Cut it short or you'll end up with a nightstick up your ass.

Dream about the sleeve, Martin, and get me the ink.

72.

The ballpoint pen in my sleeve, against my wrist precious as a jewel nabbed from a crown, I huddle back in my bunk letting the visit boil inside me—mad. Mad for letting myself confess my crimes to her, mad at Martin with his shit-brown hair and his fascist riot stick and so when Squeaky wakes from his nap, he sits up and says,

Hey Mitch, who was your visitor?

And I rise up from my bunk, step across no-man's land between us and I hold the ballpoint pen to his throat and I say,

Today's the day, you little punk.

I press the tip into his neck and he stiffens and his eyes widen and his hands, at first raised as shields, fall back to his sides. He takes a deep breath. I catch a whiff of rancid boiling sweat-filled hormones telling him to run run run as fast and as far as he can but my hand on his chest locks him down like the wretched prey he is and he whimpers his puppy dog whimper and then I pull away, let the pen pull loose from his neck leaving just a single blue point like the opening to a small cave in his skin and he gasps, and he says,

Jeez Mitch.

I stroke his cheek, feel the peach fuzz skin, the blushing hot skin still ripe. I lie back on my bunk, hands behind my head and as I fall asleep I hear Squeaky breathing hard like a man who has just finished fucking for an hour straight.

Later, Martin rattles the bars, his stick rat-a-tatting on the steel cage like a hard rain hammering. He says,

Hey asshole, your bitch sent you this.

A blue envelope skitters into the cell, a dying butterfly, a wounded dove, and I watch it drop on broken wings and it lays face down on the concrete, its blue body at an angle like a corpse twisted and I flash on the blood and the bone and the butchery strung out behind me. I say,

Did you read it, Martin?

I don't want no part of your fuckin' soap opera.

Right down your alley, Martin.

He scoffs, turns on his heel, nightstick in his hand and walks away.

This envelope is the body of all bodies.

Squeaky rises from his death bed, kneels on one knee and then looks at me and he says,

You have a new bitch?

What?

Marty said it was from your bitch.

Leave the letter alone, Squeaks.

I look at him on his knee and I remember the Rio Verde, always the Rio Verde where I left bodies on the banks of that brown, slow flowing river, left the bodies of the small brown men with hate dead in their lidless eyes. I breathe hard, feel the ballpoint pen in my hand like a dagger and as I look at Squeaky I remember Geraldine in the visitors' room pleading begging cajoling me to help her, I need you, Mitch, my babies need you.

I thought about why she had come—the desperation of needing to break away from her motherfucking shit head of a husband. She wants him dead. Squeaky, frozen in place like an ice statue—one hand reaching for the letter, the other in limbo—looks at me. I say,

Okay, Squeaky, give it to me, partner.

Squeaky's face breaks into a grin and he springs up holding the broken blue body then he sits on the edge of my bunk. He says,

Who's it from, Mitch?

I brush his head with my left hand, his silky blond girlish hair soft and he smiles and he says,

You really was gonna kill me, huh Mitch.

Not today.

You know I don't like it here, Mitch, so why doncha just go ahead and do it?

I take the letter. Turn it over. See the pink slanted writing. My gut turns acid and I want to vomit. My heart beats wild and the blood has emptied from my body. I see her hand, Catharin's hand, with its fine letters interspersed with broad strokes—the H, twin beams of wide pink connected with that slanted crossbar that had been her trademark, her signature since we were children and the M of Mitchell, angling to the left with her backward slant, the mark of her left handedness, the only one of us to write left handed.

I hold the envelope up to the light, feel the thickness of the letter inside, heavy as a cadaver, and Squeaky says,

Aintcha gonna open it, Mitch?

I look at his face, his little boy cheeks still peachy pink. I look at his mouth still with its teeth, teeth that I saved.

I lay the body on my chest, feel it land there, a small bird, and Squeaky squirms on the edge of the bunk and he says,

Is it from your sister, Mitch?

Squeaks, you chirp like a little bitch.

I am your bitch, Mitch.

He giggles and I fluff his hair.

I go back to the return address on the envelope, to the handwriting in pink ink so like Catharin. I remember her in her room, hiding behind black curtains and incense, her hair long wavy sparkling in the candlelight and I remember the short skirts she wore baring her long fine legs and I remember her, once at a party in the house on Laverne Terrace when mother and father were away and how she danced half-naked under the lustful eyes of half a dozen boys all wanting her and how she had taken them, one at a time, into her black den, into the incense, into the smell of her body and I listened at the door, waiting. One of them, coming back out adjusting his belt, looked at me hanging around the corner and he said,

Man, your sister's one hot fuck.

Yeah, it's from my sister.

Squeaky's face is still flushed with anxiety like a child about to open a birthday gift when I hand the body to him and he takes it and looks at the blue corpse. He says,

You want me to open it, Mitch?

Yeah, you open it.

But he hands it back to me, his eyes say I can't. I look at the shamrock and sixes I'd tattooed into his skin and I take his hand and lay the blue dead thing in his palm and I say,

I'm afraid of it, Squeaky. I don't want to read it.

He giggles, his little soft bottom giggle and he says,

If I had a sis and she wrote me, I'd wanna read it.

I reach for the envelope. The censor's mark in the corner spoils the purity of Catharin's high-school-girl script. The black mark a stain. Using my ballpoint pen I release the flap that is stuck with just three dabs of cheap prison glue. The flap flies open. Inside I see thick sheets of blue paper. I pluck the letter from its coffin and I spread it out, six pages of blue paper written in bright neon pink ink and the date was two days ago and the letter begins ... My dearest Henry, my dearest Henry.

I let my fingers crawl over those words, feel them like scabs on the blue skin and then I stop and fold the letter and let it rest on my belly and Squeaky says,

Aintcha gonna finish it, Mitch.

I slide the letter back into its envelope and I tuck it under my pillow and then I pull Squeaky down beside me and he nestles against me and I smell his body, the fear gone and he whispers,

Whatcha want me to do, Mitch? You want to fuck me, Mitch? You want me to suck you off? Just tell me what.

73.

Nothing. For three days, nothing. Catharin's letter in its blue envelope and pink florid writing in neon ink makes my hands tremble. I try to open the flap, but I can't pull the pages out. Three days and I haven't written my twelve hundred words. Three lost days I'll never make up, three days locked up inside like there are cold stones turning my hands into icy blocks with no blood in them, no warmth.

I can't close my eyes because I see the blue envelope, the pink neon ink.

I need to kill someone.

I have memorized every word in her letter, I can recite it. I'm in Purgatory, she wrote. Purgatory with a capital P. I have lost everything I believe in, she wrote, I have no present, no past, no future but I am no longer swollen with the disease. Her words sting—the Disease, she called it, her disease. Swollen belly, thick stiff legs, swelling breasts all signs of the sickness consuming her that one day erupts in a shower of blood and it cries and suckles and it breathes and eats and in it will live the virus that spreads like an unending wave, unstoppable and obscene.

They think they punish me by keeping me behind steel doors, locked in a steel cage. We all have the sickness. They are saving me from the virus that lies dormant at the base of my skull, waiting.

I study the letter, open it again with my icy stiff hands, pick up the last word ... disease ... taste it on my tongue, acid as vinegar, such a sweet word, like death, like blood, like the smell of a disemboweled corpse, like the song of the sharp edge of the knife. I dream.

I know that the sickness will not end until the last man alive kills the last pregnant woman and then slits his own throat—then will it be safe to unlock the steel cages, open the thick steel doors with their heavy steel locks, but then there will be no one to turn the key, to throw the switch and we will all die in here and then there will be peace ... Disease ... Catharin wrote, dwelling on the word so hard the pen gouged a hole in the blue paper the way my pen gouged holes in the onion skin pages I have stored in the library on the shelf with *Notre Dame des Fleurs*, on the shelf with the books of roses and grasses, the way my knife tore open the skin of every man I slew. Disease, she wrote and she wrote sick of mind and she wrote trapped by the body trapped in her and she wrote ... I have to decide what to do with it ... I read the word. It. I read it again. It. Doesn't she know the sex of the monster growing in her? She didn't want to know because if she knew, if it became human with a tag—boy, girl—she'd be trapped in its life and never end it.

I close the letter, tuck the tongue back inside the swollen envelope, eight thick pages pushing against the thin paper skin like a root ripping its way out of the darkness of a seed. I think about my manuscript and the ballpoint pen and the paper and I have to decide too—what to do? Out there, I will have no choice—I will kill my brother-in-law. I will tie him down like a pig and cut the bones out of his body and stack them on his chest so he can see the vomit that makes him.

148

74.

It's quiet. Quiet the way it will be when we're all gone. Everything is gone except my anger. I read and re-read Catharin's letter and I memorize each line of the pink script, the agonized script that masks her pain, but I see it in her hand when she reaches certain words—the quake of the pen with some remembered anguish like the sudden thrusting of a sword into her flesh and she writes ... They kept me in the dark, Henry, blindfolded with a rag that smelled of blood and sweat. I tasted it in my mouth, my own sweat, my blood mingled with their oils. I felt each of them in me, day after day until I have no idea who had fathered the thing growing in me. He is hidden and can't be found. Once when I had fainted with pain, my mind blank, I saw a light and in the light I saw Jesus. He was walking toward me. His eyes, it's strange, his eyes were bright blue like the sky. His mouth was open as if he wanted to speak to me, but there were no words. Then, his robe parted. I saw Christ's naked flesh and there was a gash in his side, not the gash of Scripture, Henry, but a vertical gash, bleeding like the lips of a swollen vagina. I saw the goddess in his bleeding vagina and I knew I had made a terrible mistake worshipping just the Man-God.

When she writes the word Man-God, her hand trembles. I close the letter, hold it away from me as if it had rotted. I try to see Catharin in a dark place, her hands and feet tied, her mouth gagged, her eyes wrapped, like a corpse and the anger grows in me—a hurricane blasting, tearing flesh from skin like roots from the ground—and I gouge at my arms, driving the nails into the skin, drawing blood, digging at the bone to atone, to punish, to redeem, to sacrifice in blood, to share my sister's pain.

I remember then, the feel of the machete. The more primitive the weapon, the closer to the body you have to be to kill. The machete is two feet of death, a steel extension of the hand. Its edge, sharpened, crushes, fractures, severs, maims, bludgeons, hacks, cracks bone. The machete sings its own solitary aria as it works deep into the body. It is the hand hardened in fire and bathed in blood, tempered until it chants its own oratorio. This is death, this is the weapon of weapons just once removed from the stone, the sound of metal cracking bone is the song of the machete. I'd have killed them all. Anything can be made into a weapon. That's our sickness, the disease for which there is no inoculation except death—a button scraped to a sharp edge. Like its brother the bone, it becomes a knife. A zipper torn from its cloth changes into a saw for slicing skin from bone. A toothpick planted in the palm of the hand pierces an eye as quick as a sword. It's all one. We are tool makers. I am the master instrument honed to its finest sheen but I can't help her. I would have killed them all. One by one. Cut their tongues out. Cut out their bowels. Cut their throats. Lifted out their hearts and sliced them to pieces. Her tormentors.

I lay the letter on my chest, feel my heart beat, watch the letter rise and fall as if it were alive and breathing. I close my eyes and see the words as she wrote them—a terrible mistake. Mistake. Catharin and I are one in our mistakes and I remember the Governor's words in his office as he released me from the garden and gave me the books. It's done, he said. Done. And now I have to finish it, my manuscript. My decision is a hard one—to salvage what I can of the manuscript by typing up the pages or to forge ahead using the machine to get it all down before it further fades. The last time I checked my pages, I saw that they are deteriorating day by day as if I had written it on paper that would crack and break into fragments, crumble the way papyrus crumbles when it hits the air after a long burial. I am lost because as I wrote the words, they left my mind and now I can't remember ever having written them. The pages are mnemonic that is fading and all I can decipher are a few isolates, lost children of the horde, and my work suffers the fate of *L'Étranger*—pages marred, ink stained, circled and underlined until only a few words are decipherable and those of little consequence to the story and I think about the machine in the library bolted to its table but still usable. I can type thirty words a minute, eighteen hundred words an hour, but it will take me two thousand hours to salvage my pages and I have to ask—what is the past worth?

The archeology of my own past eludes me. I made a mistake asking the Governor for the computer because now I have to finish. I pick up Catharin's letter, pull it from its blue coffin, open to page two, every word memorized to there, and I read ... When the nuns freed me, Henry, I was destroyed. I remember their hands, hot and sweaty as they slid the blindfold away, as they wiped my blood from my thighs, as they lifted me like saints elevating the corpse of Our Lord and Redeemer Jesus Christ and I remember screaming as the bands were cut from my ankles holding me spread out like an animal about to be butchered, the pain of the abrupt freedom almost too much to bear, the fear that it would start again leaving me impaled and again unable to move. But then, mercifully, I fainted. In that faint there was no Christ. No cross. Nothing. And I knew then that I was the sacrament. I am not a martyr, Henry. Not a martyr. But what do I do with the thing that grew inside me? What do I do with it ... Her hand shakes when she writes the words *the thing that grew*. I drop page two. See that page three is written on both sides. The neon pink ink bleeding through the blue paper blurring the words she has written. And I close my eyes. No. No. No.

Unfolded and refolded Catharin's letter wears thin in the creases. The paper drops a fine powdery fuzz that falls like blue snow.

I'll have to find a way to preserve it. Maybe I'll press it like a rose between the pages of a thick book on roses, maybe I'll flatten it between the covers of a dusty unread book on prairie grasses I've found hidden in the stacks, preserve it without ever opening it again. I lay out pages 1 2 3 4, each one screaming like a confession to be read over and over. I have saved that much of it, every word buried in my brain where no one can find it except me, buried like *Notre Dame des Fleurs* so no one can burn it like the dry and reckless foliage of a diseased plant.

I pick up page five, read it, letting Catharin's words worm their way into my brain and she writes ... There are so many things I regret, Henry. I regret damning you to hell. I regret all the times when you were little that I made fun of you. I regret having hurt you. I regret lying to you. I live with the sins of my past and I am marked as if I had been tattooed with the word WHORE on my forehead. That's why they hurt me, Henry. They read me down to the bone and as I lay there with my legs spread and they raped me, I thought, This is atonement come to smother me, my last payment on sin. You know that when I ran away to the City, I was ashamed but I never explained to you why ...

And there, her hand quakes. The pink neon ink smears as her hand stays on the page a little too long letting the nib bleed out. I lay the page on my chest, feel its weight heavier than the weight of the first four pages and I let out a big sigh and Squeaky sits up on the edge of his bunk, tugs his pants back over his floppy cock—no underwear for you, I told him, I want you quick and open when I want you—and he says,

What's the matter, Mitch, are you okay?

No, I'm not okay.

Jeez Mitch, I'm sorry.

Come over here.

He lies beside me, his skin hot and wet and I smell his dead semen on his body, on his hands, sweet as a decaying corpse, a hundred million dead Squeakies, and I say,

Catharin, my sister, ran off to the City when she was seventeen.

The City? Squeaky says.

San Francisco. She worked the streets, Squeaky. She was a whore. A stand up whore in Golden Gate Park, a whore on her knees sucking men's cocks in the East Bay Terminal at three AM. A seventeen-year-old whore taking men's cocks up her ass, Squeaky. My father hated her for doing what she did.

So, Squeaky says, she wasn't always a saint?

No, I say, she wasn't always a saint.

As Squeaky huddles against me, I remember the women I took on their knees in Guayaquil, in Quito, in Tegucigalpa, in Juxtalahuaca, each time thinking about Catharin whoring herself into oblivion and I remember other women I fucked then abandoned when night came so I could slit the throats of their men, take their ears, dry them until they rattled in the leather sacks like walnuts and then, with the bonuses for each sack, find a new woman and spill my seed in her mouth knowing that not one of them would bear fruit, all of them would die and it didn't matter if I killed them one at a time with the edge of a machete or killed them in a sudden splurting holocaust of semen into a whore's mouth. They were dead, all the men I killed would not ever—and for this I am proud—ever foster a child.

I recall Catharin's explanation when I asked her once why I had been born. Was I chosen? Was I special? And she said,

You're just a worm Henry, a worm that crawled up inside our mother to be born, a worm meant to breed other worms.

I pick up the letter, page five, find the last words ... Explained to you why ... and her hand quakes, palsied, and she wrote ... Our father wanted me to have a child, his grandchild. He hated Geraldine's Air Force demon, he hated Geraldine for marrying him ... I stop reading, stop memorizing as the sudden truth reels off the page and slams into me and Squeaky jerks away. He sits up and he says,

What's wrong, Mitch, did I do something wrong?

I pull him down against me, his body thin, and I go back, way back. Hated Geraldine? His favorite? He hated her? How could he hate her? Hate her babies? And it's like everything that ever happened stands on its head. Catharin's words ... He loved me more than he loved Geraldine, Henry. He came to the City once, found me, begged me to come home because, he said, Geraldine's spawning monsters and he wanted me to have a baby, a pure baby, you see, I could never have a baby for him. I couldn't bear the thought—Another accident, like you? A chance being? So I turned him away and he never forgot. After that I threw myself away, tried to sterilize my own womb, sucked men dry to keep them weak, spilling as much as I could—it was my duty to the world, Henry, never to be fecund, you see?

My hand trembles as I read her words. We are alike, my sister and I, killers of men, born from the same saint of a woman and the same evil man, and like a thunderbolt slamming into my brain, I see that everything I have done, every man I gutted, every woman I shot, every whore I fucked was part of a plan. I am the instrument of death. I made a mistake when I forced the surgeon to cut my vas deferens. By cutting my vas I killed generations of killers—a terrible mistake killing the army of killers.

Squeaky lays his hand on my crotch, inches from the letter, and he says,

What's the trouble, Mitch? You look like something's the matter.

Leaving his hand on my crotch, I stack the five pages together, unfolded, lay them on the envelope. I don't need the first five pages. They are rewritten, safe in the darkness of the page. I press Squeaky's hand over my cock and I say,

I'm going to castrate you, Squeaky.

He sucks in his breath and in his eyes there is the look of a small creature who knows it is about to die.

75.

I set a goal of twelve hundred words a day, eighty-four hundred words a week, four hundred thousand words a year, but I have fallen and I blame it on my father—no, that's not

fair—I have to take responsibility for my own weaknesses—
being here has taught me that I can't rely on, count on, or
blame anyone for anything but myself. I'm a lazy bastard—
no, not lazy, troubled. Troubled man with a lot of problems,
more problems than a normal man in my position would
have. Much of it stems from René's death—seeing him
swamped in his own blood—blood leaking from his chest in
short gushes then tailing off to a slow throb until he lay
inert, quiet, peaceful. From that day, my own vow to keep up
the pace has slowed like blood leaking from a wound and
although I have surpassed by far the meager, puny,
dehydrated output of Camus and his *L'Étranger*, I am far
behind Genet and *Notre Dame des Fleurs*—far behind and
now I fear that I won't finish before my release. I have no
one to blame but myself because, like a fool, I give in to my
addictions.

The strong man, the real man, doesn't give in to his
addictions. The others in here, weak men, murderers,
rapists, thieves, they have all given in, caved into their
nightmares but they have no escape. I count the actual
words I have written to see if beneath the words there is
meaning. Counting reveals no meaning, and so I look at my
vocabulary and I realize that I have unlearned, stripped
away, decapitated all but a few polysyllabic Latinate words
because I am a thief, a liar, a cheat, a killer, a sodomite and I
do not want to pretend to be anything else. I want to write in
the gutter language of the communal toilet, the sparse
Germanic gutturals of men sweating with animal blood on
their hands, the sharp short Anglo-Saxon utterances of men
conquered by effete French frog fuckers. That's what I want.

Day four hundred and I am at the beginning again—
back at Word One. My work is full of holes, weak, gutted by
desire. Perhaps I have given in to my addictions. In here,
you learn the value of time—you want it to vanish, you wish
for a time machine to hurl you forward to your delivery date
so that you begin again and you swear to go straight on the

outside. I thought about my early days, trying to find joy. I had no pets, no dogs, no goldfish, no cats because my father—an impatient and hateful man, said If you want to fuck around with animals, go live on a farm, but in this city no beasts allowed.

76.

I write to remember and to forget. By writing, I forget what was but can't yet see what will be ...

We lived on Laverne Terrace in a big three story house with a pitched tile roof in the California Spanish style and at night, when it rained, I listened to the gutters washing with water and imagined its journey from cloud to roof to gutter to river to the sea. As I lie on my bed I imagine his life was like that—water running—and I recall a moment in a film I once saw where an android, dying, says,

I have seen things you people would not believe.

I have seen ships on fire off the shoulder of Orion and all these memories will be lost like tears in rain.

I never had a deep desire for animals—I didn't need a dog or a duck or a cat—I needed to steal and to lie and to cheat like when I stole the dimes from Catharin's piggybank using a knife to lift each one from the slot so it lay on the blade like a sacrificed heart. In Guatemala I played cards with thieves, cheating them as if I were the god of poker, thieves and bandits and murderers I fooled as if they were two-year-old toddlers. I was myself by that time a killer with great expertise in the garrote, in death by knife (my father's number, I exceeded within my first year in the selva) by gunshot, by poison. These men, ferocious as wild animals, didn't lose with grace.

I learned then that a man's mettle is measured by his grace when he loses. I found that I wasn't the man I wanted to be because all too often, I gave into my addictions of self pity, self hate, self loathing, self gratification. I gave into jealousy, greed, lust and I failed to write until I felt like

Meursault in Camus' tiny little pitiful novel—a loser because I indulged my weaknesses and used my power instead of letting the torture and pain of loss take me into a new realm. And so by not writing I lost fifty thousand words in the river of time, words I can never retrieve. What takes the place of the words I failed to write? Are the words that come now better? Or a substitute for what might have been? I won't know if those lost words are the words that would have freed me. They are words I can never recover. I will never know what they would have revealed.

77.

I am an insect under siege by a horde of hawk-beaked monsters and somehow they know I am guilty. In here we are all guilty but there are layers of guilt and they have no proof any more than my mother had proof it was I who stole all the dimes from Catharin's piggybank. I did steal them but I threw them away because I knew even then that if they caught me with the coins my guilt would be apparent but if there were no coins who was to know I had taken them?

So it was with the knife I made to deal with that asshole René. René the betrayer. René who deceived me. He deserved to die.

I learned here that what I was running from I carry on my back like any immigrant seeking a new haven but instead of vanities and desks and tables and chairs I carry my weaknesses and fetishes forward. I wish I were dead because then they would see that I did what I had to do. What is it to die unappreciated? With no respect? What is it to die with no memorial?

But there is no one to take my confession in here. There is no one pure enough to bear the burden of my guilt. There is no one strong enough to bear the weight of my sins. If I speak the truth, it will crush any man I tell it to. I am no saint. I don't pretend any more than Suki could pretend he was not a killer because you saw it in his eyes, you felt it in the way he moved, never turning his back to you, always looking, those hungry eyes searching not just for prey but for predators and now I understand.

It takes enormous sin to open eyes to truth and the truth is that I am, we all are cozy, warm-blooded, heat producing, luscious, ripe fields of flesh and blood and bone ready for our killer to sink his teeth, his knife, his fangs into. We are worms on a hook. Our bodies are worm-like tubes with arms and legs. Suki, with his desperate eyes and snake-like movements was an efficient machine who knew how to kill with no regret, no feeling, no hope, no desire. You can never escape. The weapons are built into you.

While my father insisted that I learn karate, he had no idea I would hone my hands into killing clubs. When he made me learn to fence, he had no idea that I would take the simple fact of the sword and return it to its original design—butchery. He insisted that I learn to box not knowing the sweet science would turn my body into a death-hammer serving my sister's corporate husband, Chief Executive in Charge of Murder.

And so when the judge said five years for stealing women's underwear, he had no idea that behind me lay two hundred and twenty men dead, a score of women, dead, and a few children who died at the edge of mayhem and for whom I take no credit and took no ears although I know men who would not shy from that accolade. And today I spill my twelve hundred words onto pages that I will hide because if the guards come, if they dig into my cell, into the bag hidden in the toilet under the shit and piss, they will find the chronicle of my destruction.

78.

Today I'm falling further behind. It's impossible to compete with Camus or Genet. I'm falling behind. Eighteen days and no words. I'm behind twelve hundred words a day and I'll never finish. I recall my father saying, What kind of a man can't finish what he starts? I want to write, but I get stuck in my own meditations and so I look for clues in Camus.

I dissect *L'Étranger*. I want to know if the Meursault's inaction and ambivalence are his or is Camus writing about himself in those words? But my memory fails me. I can't recall the details and the story is lost behind the markings and the marginalia and the blots on the pages of the existing book. I need to know—

Was Camus in prison?

Did he kill his lover?

Did he steal a dryer full of women's underwear?

Probably not.

I need to write about destruction. I recall a line from a poet—funny I can't recall his name—was it a he? Maybe it was a woman. He wrote that without poetry we're a tribe of expert killers. We haven't found anything we can't kill. I am of that tribe of killers, the tribe without poetry, although maybe the poetry of my life is in the lies. Maybe the poetry of my life is in the deceit, in the weapons, in the sweet arc of blood spraying from a slit throat. I wait. What am I waiting for?

Here on this bunk waiting for an answer to the question I asked my mother—Why was I born? Why do I ask the question? I am a biological accident—I can accept the fact of my meaninglessness. Camus gave Meursault a project—to keep himself comfortable and cool—and that project defined his life and was meant to fulfill his project but I won't go in those circles. The corpses.

I write about destructions ...

Suki was so good with a knife. He stalked, approached, attacked, killed and then cut off the left ear of every man, woman, and child because without the ear there was no body count, without the body count there was no bonus. He found the meaning of his life in his bag of ears but he never once asked how the Bosses would know these were the ears of their enemy.

79.

Another day and I haven't written my twelve hundred words. I sit on my bunk waiting. Just waiting for today, the first day in thirty seven that I find the energy and desire to write. Memory fills me as I look at the walls, look at the floor, look at the ceiling with its sunken light-cage. My cage is full of objects but they are empty, meaningless, nothing. I remember the line from Jack Moodey's poem, I am a tortured Zero. A zero. A man reduced to his past, a man with no future, a man with no present, a tortured zero.

Objects can never fill you up because what you seek isn't tangible—it's tactile, it's propinquity. It is not tangible. When you have it you have nothing but you have everything. Being in the presence of what you desire is love and when that presence is dead you are lost and can never be redeemed again.

Sometimes when I'm working I get waking dreams and in them I see the corpses I have left butchered in the mud or on the banks of a jungle river. The gas-bloated corpse of a gutted woman sprawled in the vergonzosas beside a trail, the rotting corpse of a decapitated Indian still wearing his colorful poncho but an AK47 strapped to his shoulder, two men in green fatigues lying in a death embrace in the jungle heat then exploding, scattering viscera into the bush, scattering hunks of putrescence onto the trees. Humans dead, their throats slashed, their bodies heavy with decay. They are always there, but I can keep them at bay most of the time.

Still, I see them—jagged holes where their ears should be, the ears banked in leather pouches.

To the men who pay for those ears there are no friends. Any ear will count in the final payoff—even now I can't fill a page, day to day, with words, but hang back, waiting until it comes in a rush, as it's doing today, like an ejaculation soiling my blanket—my words are sperm on the page, a hundred million accidents caught on an empty page, and no matter how much I try I can't find a reason, a purpose, a direction. But as I read and reread *Notre Dame des Fleurs* I realize that I am not alone, that all of life is a biological trick played on us by our sperm, which wants just one thing—to be born and so the question I asked my mother is answered by the ejaculation, by the sperm-like words spewing onto my pages. My words are my children, and I see the corpses again in the lush ripe verdancy of the jungle, each corpse missing its left ear but I find no meaning in a corpse. I see my fascist brother-in-law, that Executive Vice President in Charge of Death—and I know that each ear Suki severed enriched my brother-in-law and every banana I ate and every cup of coffee I drank enriched him and oiled his killing machine. I remember the day he crushed Geraldine's larynx so that for the rest of her life she will never speak like a normal human being and I remember confronting Carl Fairweather in his teak-wood library. I carried a bat. I remember the feel of the bat as I slammed it first into his thigh, breaking the femur, then into his arm fracturing the humerus. I remember standing over him staring into his murderous eyes and I remember saying,

She's my sister, you murdering cocksucker, the mother of your children and I saw the fear in his eyes, fear that I would kill him, but I didn't want to kill him—a mistake now, I see—I wanted to maim him so that he would carry his shame out in front for everyone to see that he had become a zero. Instead of shame and nothingness he reaped bonuses and accolades and a golden parachute leaving Geraldine, stripped of her humanity, unable to speak to her children. As I sit on my bunk I count my corpses, each one etched in my mind, each one positioned like a piece of meaty sculpture. I want to know what that means. But I know they are the absence of poetry, they are the artifacts of the human being without grace—without poetry and grace we are efficient killing machines.

I search through Camus for meaning. I look at Genet but see only the bars, the grill that separates the free from the not. Yet I know that those on the outside looking in have no advantage other than a larger cell—they can move, but there is a limit to their movement. They can dream, but they can never escape. I don't try to escape. Escape? To what? Back out there to the killing and the slaughter? Back out to the abattoir where all that remains is to sever the left ear of each victim, to put each ear in your little savings sack that you then plop on the desk of your master in order to get your puny little reward? And what is your left ear? Who do you kill? Who do you butcher to get your puny little bonus? What is the ear *you* lay on *your* master's desk out there?

No thank you. I'll serve my time because I won't go back out there to the butchery, to the land of all my brothers-in-law who don't pay for their crimes. No. I've been out there and it's safer in here living with the killers and rapists, the sadists and thieves. In here, you know. You know the zero beside you in the chow line, the zero hunkering behind you in the laundry room, the zero who stalks you in the corridors of the library. You know they all are criminals and there is some comfort, some satisfaction, some relief in knowing what they are and what they can do and you are prepared for them and ready because you know they are coming. But out there? The killer hides behind his secretary, ensconced behind walnut paneling, and all he has to do is push a button and you are dead, your ear severed. You never see his face, but on his desk there is a sack of left ears—yours included— and they are of all colors and shapes. Some are hairy and some are pierced, some still have their earrings in the lobes and he pays for those ears. In here, I know who is who, it is all clear to me, and it doesn't mean anything because I am nothing. If I vanish tonight no one will miss me. My lone value is in being a number accounted for behind the bars, my lone value was as a collector of ears to earn my bonuses and when you grow tired of the blood and the butchery, there is nothing if you are not a poet. Genet, the poet, descending into his sea of semen, his dizzy swirl of ejaculations, his frenzied masturbation, Genet was a poet redeemed by his words and I will be redeemed by mine. I too am a tortured zero.

80.

There is no answer but blood. It has to be blood. I look for answers but find only blood. I remember the day Catharin my hyperreligious sister told me she was going to India to save Hindu souls. I laughed and I said,

Why don't you buy them rice instead of saving their souls?

Henry, she said, you will rot in hell.

I'm already in hell.

You are damned, she said.

We don't speak the same language.

She threw up her hands and said,

You're a monster.

No, your God is the monster.

God is in you, she said.

If he's in me then he's in hell.

Catharin went off to India still with the taste of semen in her mouth because she had just changed from sucking men's dicks in San Francisco to performing fellatio on Jesus Christ her Redeemer and nothing had changed. She cannot save Hindu souls no matter how many times she fills her mouth with the semen of her Savior.

Nothing will ever change until the blood stops flowing. Nothing will ever change until all the ears are severed.

I wish the gamete that produced me had come from a dog because there is no shame in a dog. No wishes, no hope, no dreams. A dog just is. But I am a tortured zero who can't

163

stick to his goal of twelve hundred words a day. I'm reduced to looking for meaning.

81.

Today I feel trapped. The weather in here drives me crazy—it never changes. The one thing I miss about outside is the weather. The weather lets you know you're alive. You're hot. You're cold. You're wet. Your body stinks in the heat. Your breath freezes in the air. Your feet slip in the mud. Your mouth tastes the rain and the fog.

I remember my first year in the Cordillera Negra. We hired little boys to collect weather information. We set up small white kiosks and we had the boys measure the rainfall, record the daily temperature, make a note about the cloud cover. We had them write it all down in small notebooks that we collected. They had no idea why.

No one told them that the data in those books went to the Southern Command where it was collated with the data from a thousand other observation posts and then shipped to DC where all that information went to the planners who drew up contingencies—what to wear above ten thousand feet, what rain gear to carry in the Cordillera Blanca, what boots to issue to the killers roaming the Junin Plateau, what weapons to issue for the mountains.

And using that information, we came in, silent, in the dark, with our night-vision goggles and our automatic weapons and our knives and we slaughtered the insurgents wherever we found them.

I remember one night in a small town called Paucartambo that lies between La Orolla and Santa Isabel. We waited until three AM, the death time, the time of the assassins. We were on the attack when all hell broke loose. Mortar rounds dropping, rapid fire, tracers. I felt fragments of dirt and rock slice into my neck. Around me the squad went down and gunfire poured out of those marked houses.

We retreated, pulling our wounded, fighting our way back to the river and then it stopped.

Quiet and bleeding we sat waiting for extraction and I knew that somewhere, someone had leaked our position. It was then that the entire method changed. Two man teams working at night. No more big assaults. Ears. Take the ears, leave the corpses. After that night, the ears in my sack grew heavy. When bonus time rolled around, we counted the ears out like ears of corn, like farmers getting paid by the bushel.

82.

Today is like the day before—the same sixty-eight degrees. It will be the same in the winter and the summer. Every day is like the day before and the day after. It never changes.

In the beginning, I watched Squeaky on his bunk whimpering.

He asked me why I was in here and I told him everything but the truth, He asked me what I was writing and I told him everything but the truth but as soon as he noticed, I knew I'd have to find a new place to hide the manuscript, which was growing so fast it got out of hand.

That was when I lugged it to the library where I hid it in the garden section alongside Our Lady of the Flowers because I knew that no one would look there.

I think about the hidden masterpieces still lodged in men's minds—the million stories not told. If I told Squeaky everything, his whimpering would increase and I would have to kill him sooner than I want.

How innocent he is still. I know that when I am gone, he will not last long because he is too beautiful. His curled hair is soft and his white skin is smooth and his hands as a young girl's hands. What a waste. All that destroyed for an unthinking little joyride that lasted an hour.

Sometimes at night I hear him in the throes of his orgasm and I smell the scent of his semen wafting like the perfume of a blossoming flower. Secrets leaking like sap from the wounds of a pine tree advertising his hidden truths. I do wonder if he is as innocent as he lets on or if his display is the pheromone of an insect calling a mate through the darkness.

83.

I remember how, in Guayaquil, I smelled the perfume of a whore named Artesia. I remember how much like a rotten flower she looked in her red and white dress, her hair black as ink, her skin that Spanish olive velvet with its own sun burning inside. I remember how she captured my eyes when I approached her and then like a Venus flytrap catching me up in her teeth she bit me. Being close to her, in her, once her body yielded, her thighs and breasts and cunt—being close, she smothered me with her needs until her touch became a poison.

I called her La Cobija—The Blanket. She smothered me with her needs and endless mewlings and begging for love.

Enrique, she called to me, will you return? Will you love me? Will you hold me again?

The perfume of her armpits and the scent boiling from between her legs turned sour. In the end, I left her to her hunger.

Leaving her, I was glad to escape back into the jungle, deep into the Oriente where we had to wipe out a cell of indigenous insurgents with red skin who didn't want the Alliance to pump their oil. We isolated the cadres, cut them down one by one always at night because even Indians can't see at night. Sometimes we took them still on their mats with their women screaming and always taking the left ear as measure because without the ear there was no accounting and no payment. And so we worked like sharks under cover of the canopy sleeping on dirt, dug into the belly of hibiscus, its perfume cloying in the sweet rotten decay of the jungle where everything dies, rots, sinks back into the soil digested. The predigested concrete world out there gives you too many choices, too many options. In the jungle, just as inside there is one rule—kill or be killed, eat or be eaten.

I don't tell my poor little innocent whiner of a cellmate the truth but my blade is what keeps him alive. Without me he will die. When he dies is a decision I make. One day I will make it. Do I take away the aegis of my power? Do I sacrifice him to the monsters in the yard?

84.

In my dreams I often see blood. It wells up and flows like red lava splashing against rocks. The smell, the stench of rotting blood—sulfuric, cupric, ferric blood—and I always wake up in a sweat frozen in place, my legs and arms paralyzed, my fingers dead as the stumps of sawn-off trees, my chest strapped with steel bands, my breath just a whisper. Am I alive? Dead? Dreaming still about being dead? Sometimes in the pale light seeping through the bars I see the knife I have used to kill men in the dark and in those flashes I remember blood seeping into the jungle floor and the flies hungry as small black wolves not waiting for the heat of the dead to dissipate before sucking up the still running river of red and laying eggs in the gashed wounds of the wrenched and twisted bodies. As my arms and legs come alive again I thrust up off my bunk, shirt soaking wet, sit up and pick up the pen and the paper because in the blackness of the night I see the faces of the men I have killed and I write. It's my duty to the dead to resurrect them from the hell where I cast them.

I remember Mrs. Wilson, now dead, Mrs. Wilson with her nasty little secret lying on her belly pleading for me to fuck her in the ass the way my father fucked her and I remember watching her on her hands and knees, naked, her ass thrust up in the air, her white skin pale against the brown skin of my father as he fucked her, bucking against her until she screamed Oh God damn you and then it was over.

Mrs. Wilson is dead and my father is dead and my mother is dead and Geraldine killed her firstborn because killing is in our blood and Catharin alone escaped into holiness, into her sperm-filled Jesus Christ of the seeping wound, the gash in his side bleeding like the courses of a menstrual whore. If Geraldine had lived two thousand years ago, she'd have killed not her baby but Roman legionnaires just as my father in his way killed the minions of Mao in the South Asian jungles, just as I, in the dark of the midnight altiplano in Chile killed the scions of Allende, took their ears, drank their blood, and now write their names in the manuscript that flows as red as the slit throat of an Indian in the jungle. We are weapons of mass extinction killing everything that moves.

Squeaky stirs, sits up on the edge of his bunk, his skinny little arms not filling out the sleeves of his T-shirt and he says,

You awake, Mitch?

Go back to sleep.

I'm afraid of the dark.

The dark won't bite, I say.

Lay down with me, Mitch.

I'll stay awake till you go back to sleep

Okay, Mitch. Sure.

I stand, face the bars, look out over the tiers with their layers of steel. It takes steel to keep the killers outside. It's a matter of time before I will pass beyond the steel barrier, the safe steel barrier of this prison to land again in the hateful world of death and destruction, lured again into the river of blood, the killing world of my fascist brother-in-law, that CEO in Charge of Death, that murderous bastard with his filed teeth and his blood red eyes and his millions in banks.

When I dream I see the knife. My right hand twitches with nostalgia for blood. The right hand wants me to let it loose again, the severing slash to the throat, because it knows I belong out there reaping flesh stalks, filling tanks with blood, spreading death and terror, while the left hand quivers with fear that I will have to do it again, enjoy it again, relish the feel of the blade sinking past the paper thin veneer of civilized vulnerability like a virus planting its siphon in the cell of a victim.

I look at Squeaky on his bunk, imagine his blood flowing from his slit throat, his blood tattooing the floor the way I inked his hand with the shamrock and sixes. I won't—not yet. I hear his steady breathing. He's asleep again, fallen again into the river of forget like a child who awakens from a nightmare to find the comfort of his mother's arms. I lie back down, fold my hands behind my head and stare at the ceiling, watch the play of shadow and light and I close my eyes and listen to Squeaky rustling on his bunk.

I think he'd be better off dead. I have to control myself, hold it in, because the disease—once it infects you—settles at the base of your spine, leeches itself up into the medulla, buries itself in the hippocampus that hungers for the stimulation of the scream of a dying man, addicted to the rush of blood. I shake, my hands locked together, fingers like handcuffs. Rising, I stand over Squeaky, reach for his throat, and in the half light I see his eyes widen, his face blanch with fear, his mouth half-open, and the breath heaves in my chest as I smell death so close.

He tries to sit up but I close my hands on his neck and he says,

Mitch, you're scaring the hell out of me.

I thought you were asleep.

Do you do this all the time when you think I'm asleep?

Just practicing, Squeaky.

I touch his face, his innocent little soft bottom face, and I touch his half-open mouth, my fingers trailing over his lips

warm and wet as the cunt of every whore I ever fucked from
Guayaquil to Tegucigalpa. He whispers,

Is that all you need?

I take a deep breath, feel the thirst slake itself just with
the thought of him dead and I say,

One of these days I will kill you.

He whimpers. I feel his body shake. I pull away. He
says,

You're really scaring me, Henry.

Don't call me Henry. Always call me Mitch, do you
hear?

He hunches his shoulders, his narrow round shoulders
and he bows his head and he mumbles,

I'll do anything you want.

I have half a mind to cut you loose in the yard.

Please, don't do that, please.

He wraps his arms around my thighs and I flip open my
fly and he sucks my cock straight into his mouth and I fuck
his mouth, butcher his throat, pound him until his whimpers
turn to tears, until I spill and he, gagging on my hardness,
swallows it choking and then, looking up at me, his eyes
watering, he begs me, those wet pleading eyes batting, not to
cut him loose in the yard and I pull away, leave him with my
cum on his lips and I crawl back onto my bunk, and lie with
my hands laced behind my head until sleep wraps itself
around me and I dream of the knife. It hangs in the air
dripping blood, small endless drops of blood into a large and
bottomless red pool.

85.

A celebration. An anniversary. But there will be no cake,
no ice cream, no balloons to commemorate the day. The
anniversary of the Place du Capitole in Toulouse. The Place
du Capitole in Toulouse sits in the center of the city. In the
square called Place de la Liberté during the Terror, the
Guillotine stood bloody, glinting in the sunlight as the killing

spread from Paris, ate its way into the heart of the Midi, unlocking all the hate and fear and blood lust that had been pent up for the seven hundred years after Louis the Ninth ordered the massacre of the Cathars at Montségur. And here I write the story of the Place du Capitole ...

In the square, in the sunlight, in a café I watched him, my target, seated at his table reading La République and smoking as he read. He was a tall black man with hair thinning from forehead to crown, but with tufts at the nape as if a lab rat had crawled up and draped itself around his neck. I watched him as the waiter brought him a tray with a pain au chocolat on it and a cup of espresso along with a glass of water.

He was left-handed. He held his espresso between thumb and forefinger. He wore a white cotton shirt, open at the neck, the sleeves rolled up to reveal muscled, arms. Black pants and black espadrilles, no socks.

When he looked up from his newspaper, I watched his eyes. They darted. Afraid. He knew I was there but he couldn't resist. Once prey, always prey. He sighed and turned back to his coffee and his newspaper and his cigarette and his pain au chocolat that rested on a thin sheet of waxed paper on a white saucer. The sunlight lay across his hands like a sword. As the crowd of pedestrians clustered at the corner spread out, I slipped in behind him and, without hesitating, slit his throat with the razor. The sudden gush of blood spurted across the table, splashing against his espresso cup but missing the pain au chocolat, which I picked up from the white dish, wrapped in its wax paper and stuffed in my jacket pocket.

I turned away, dropped the razor to the flagstones in the shadow of the arcade and then crossed the street. I looked back at him, fallen head down on the table on his newspaper, cigarette smoke still hovering in the air overhead. To my surprise no one screamed or shouted or

even noticed the dead man in his blood in the Place de la
Liberté seated at a café on a warm November afternoon.

I entered a shop called La Librairie Tolosa, where the
window was filled with a host of books on the Albigensians.
Standing in the window, I fingered the books, felt their very
French pages—that bible thin paper the popular editions
were cast in. I watched the Place du Capitole, watched the
waiter who came to the bloody mess of a man in his chair,
the sudden eruption of fear, the sudden search for a culprit.
The waiter's hands flew up, his mouth formed words in
comic, silent-movie slow motion, words I knew he would
shout—Police, Police.

I turned to the cashier. Holding *Pouvoir et purité* like a
chalice, I said,

Have you read this one?

The woman—smoking a Gitane, one of the silky Virginia
tobacco Gitanes favored by writers and bookstore owners
and exchange students who hadn't yet learned to smoke the
black tobacco of the working class—said,

Oh yes.

My sister is named Catharin after the Perfects of the
Heresy.

You know about the Heresy?

You can't walk a street in Tolosa without feeling some
vestige of the Heresy.

Or the Revolution, she said.

I heard the claxon, that peculiar French siren the police
and emergency vehicles use, and I turned to look out the
window. The clerk said,

What happened?

I have no idea. How much?

She flipped the back cover of the Pléiade Editon of
Pouvoir et purité, a History of the Cathars in the Midi and
she said,

Thirty francs.

I paid her. Taking the history, I strolled out of the bookstore and across the square where the Guillotine had stood for two years and twenty-one days, where the aristocracy of the Midi was butchered as much to avenge the death of the Perfects at Montségur as to rid the country of its parasitic rich.

In the late afternoon sunlight, I watched the police and the medics and the dead man and in the chaos of their comings and goings I felt pity and satisfaction. Pity for the cops lost forever in a sea of inexplicability as they mopped up the dead, deep satisfaction at the perfection of my work. As I walked the two kilometers to the train station I glanced at the History, searched the table of contents, always in the back in the French style, and looked in the index for the word Cathar and its hundred references. I remembered how my mother often said that she spelled Catharin with an A and no E at the end to honor the seven hundred and fiftieth anniversary of the Massacre.

At the station, I washed my hands in the lavatory. I ran hot and cold water over them. Saw the skin turn pink, smelled the soap, paid the attendant for a towel that I used to dry my hands.

Then I sat in the café and ordered a cup of coffee. I felt a burden lift. In slitting the man's throat I had crossed a wide river. The first one, I was told, you will remember always, but do not fixate on him. You don't know his name. You don't need to know his name or what he did or who he was or whether he had a family. You know nothing except that he has to die and die he will and die he did.

I counted my francs. I had enough to upgrade to a wagon-lit. It was a wise decision because as I boarded the train, I felt heavy, sleepy, worn out.

In first class, a woman in a mourning veil stared out the window at the scenery flitting past. Her reflection in the glass was dark and empty. The face obscured by the veil.

Taking my cabin, I lay on the bed watching the evening shadows stretch out like dead men across the fields where eons ago the horses and steel of Louis the Ninth had clashed with the Perfects of the Cathars, their flesh no match for the Damascus steel, their robes no barrier against the crush of horse and saddle and the iron-toed boots of knights, their skin no guard against the flames as they burned at the stake.

I slept. I did not dream.

The conductor rapped on the door, Gare de Lyon, he shouted all the way down the corridor, knocking all sleepers awake. Paris.

Paris where the Terror began.

Paris where I had a room at the Hotel du Vieux Paris.

Paris the heart and soul of France

It was 4:00 AM and so I walked to a park near the hotel. I sat on a bench and in the early morning air, I smelled blood. At 4:00 AM it wasn't an unpleasant smell but I wished I had washed my hands in the wagon-lit again. I was hungry.

I remembered the pain au chocolat in my coat pocket. I pulled it out of its waxed paper wrap and bit into it. It was the best breakfast I ever had—even without coffee—and then I walked to the Hotel du Vieux Paris, a fourteenth century building on Rue Git le Coeur, a place of stone with small rooms and windows that opened onto cobblestone streets and to the sound of boats on the Seine. The street door was locked and so I rang the bell. The night concierge, still sleepy, looked through the glass. He said,

Ah, M. Mendoza. You're back.

He opened the door. As I entered I smelled fresh coffee.

In my room, I washed my hands again. The stench of death sticks to your skin, sticks in your nose, and you have to scour away the truth. And the truth is that death always stinks. Do you ever get used to it? There comes a time when you no longer wash your hands because you have grown to like the cloud of death hanging around your neck, filtering into your hair, your pores, your sinuses, your taste buds until it becomes sweet and soft like the sound of a familiar song fading in the night.

In the Hotel du Vieux Paris I remembered my father's obsession with the near god-like qualities of the French. I could now tell him that a Frenchman dies the same way a Peruvian Indian dies. I could now tell him that a Frenchman bleeds the same four quarts of blood that a Colorado Indian bleeds. I could now tell him that a Frenchman shits his pants the way a Spaniard shits his pants when the blade severs the jugular and the body dumps its last deposit of human filth into the world.

That day, in the Hotel du Vieux Paris, I lay down and slept better than I have ever slept before or since. I think it was the pain au chocolat that rested me. Chocolate, they say, induces in us the same feelings as love. A euphoric feeling of wellbeing.

In the late evening I woke up, heard the rattle of boots on stone and the door burst open and a man pointing a nine millimeter Beretta at me said,

Armando Mendoza you are under arrest. Get up slowly, sir, and place your hands on your head.

He motioned to two men in blue who entered my room. They cuffed me in the odd menottes used by the French services and they led me down the stairs and into a Peugeot and across Boul'Miche to the Palais de Justice, which set me on edge because it was irregular and very un-police-like.

They tossed me handcuffed into a room and left me.

In the room there was a desk and two chairs. Milk glass in the door let in a pale gray light. Sitting, I smelled the raw black tobacco French bureaucrats are fond of. Caporals they called them. Untreated tobacco—no molasses, no honey, no additives—just pure Balkan tobacco cut, dried, and shredded. Under the scent of tobacco, I smelled a cloying mixture of cologne and perfume and the thick odor of Calvados as if someone had spilled a bottle on the floor. I heard the shuffle of feet on the stones outside the door and the thrum of a motorcycle echoing in the courtyard, and then a door opened and a tall Frenchman peered in at me.

He had a heavy moustache, thick glasses, his hair slicked back with pomade in the bureaucratic style. He wore a neat black suit pressed and clean and a single white marguerite in the buttonhole. He carried a manila dossier with a red tab on the edge. He entered. He sat down at the desk. I said,

The menottes, sir. Please.

I held out my hands. He opened the dossier. He said,

Why are you in Paris, M. Mendoza?

I came to visit the battlegrounds of the Great War.

Are you a historian then?

Our blood is in the soil of France. My great great grandfather fought with the Colonials at Chateau-Thierry and at Bois de Belleau. My great grandfather left large chunks of his body in the Ardennes. My father lost a leg in Indo-China.

And your great great grandfather's name, M. Mendoza?

Henry Emmett Mitchell.

But your name is Armando Mendoza?

Yes sir. That's what it says on the passport.

M. Mendoza, were you on the night train from Toulouse?

Yes sir.

And you were in Toulouse at four-thirty yesterday afternoon.

Yes sir.

Who are you working for? He said.

I am a tourist. I'm staying at the Hotel du Vieux Paris.

And you are a liar.

Yes sir. I am a liar. I am also a cheat, a rogue and a murderer.

And you speak French like no American should speak French.

My father believed no man to be complete unless he be a Francophone.

You use the subjunctive very well, M. Mendoza.

Your professors taught me well.

So who are you?

I'm a tourist.

And you are working for?

I'm staying at the Hotel du Vieux Paris.

What were you doing in Toulouse yesterday afternoon?

I visited the Museums in Toulouse, I went to Saint Etienne, I bought a book on the Albigeois. I'm interested in the Cathars because my mother has a peculiar affinity ...

Please answer the question. What was your assignment in Toulouse?

I killed a man in Toulouse yesterday afternoon. I do not know who he was or why I was asked to kill him, but I slit his throat while he was sitting in a café on the Place de la Liberté.

Place de la Liberté?

Place du Capitole, I said. He is dead.

You slit his throat?

Yes sir.

Did you wash your hands, M. Mendoza?

Yes.

The tall Frenchman then closed the dossier. He looked at me. He stood up. He walked around the large dark wooden desk and he pulled a key from the pocket of his waistcoat and he unlocked the menottes, took them off my wrists and laid them on the wooden desk. He said,

Do you smoke, M. Mendoza?

He drew a pack of Gauloises from his inside cigarette pocket that all tailored French suits have and, opening the pack, shook a cigarette out for me. I took it. He lit it with a Ronson lighter, the old style lighter with a thumb striker wheel like American GIs carried into France after the Liberation. I took a drag on the lit Gauloise, tasted the harsh black Balkan tobacco and then I remembered that smell as it hung around the body of the man I had killed in the Place de la Liberté. I had watched him drink his espresso, but I hadn't noticed his brand of cigarette. I had failed to notice his brand of cigarette. Then my interrogator opened the door. Standing aside, he ushered me out. He said,

Enjoy your visits to the battlefields, M. Mendoza. Personally? I'd recommend the Ossuaire at Douaumont or the crypt at Verdun.

86.

Every morning I wake up to see him asleep in the quiet gray pre-dawn, asleep in the gray of concrete, the blue of steel, see him before the light glints through the window, before it splashes the ugliness of day into the cell, before it shatters the quiet as it passes over the wretched and thick slaughter in the world outside the walls. In the block, men rise from their nightmares of blood and poison. They escape into the light from the harsh black terror of dreams and then, as the sun hits the concrete with its yellow hammer splitting the concrete into real and fake, into black and white, into gray and shadow, I stand at the gate, as I do every morning, to watch the beasts emerge from hibernation, watch their tattoos come to life. The snake winds its way around the arm and over the shoulder and down to the waist of the shaven-headed killer in D1 and the skull inked in red and black grins its rictus across the back of the rapist in D2. I know that pure evil has awakened in the bodies of the brothers of my brother-in-law and it is prowling, held in place by the steel and concrete that not even their fiery felonious eyes can melt while he, out there, calibrates death to blood flow to the slow swelling of his bank account with impunity.

Squeaky yawns his first waking breath of the day, the measure I've counted eighteen to the minute, one thousand eighty to the hour, twenty-six thousand to the day, and in that breath I hear the opening of death and on the horizon I smell danger the way a cat sniffs the air for prey, for predators, for water reduced to breath and air and the rations of dead animals consumed the way the cat eats the rat, chews the head off its bird. I turn to see him on his bunk, his bare feet not touching the concrete as if his purity has levitated him, I say,

Did you sleep okay?

He grins, his little boy white-toothed open-mouthed grin and he laughs and he says,

I dreamed you was teaching me how to write, Mitch.

How did I teach you to write?

He stands, stretches his scrawny arms, hairless, pale, no tattoos except what I put there, no marks except the two pink scars in his side like dual stigmata. Around his neck I see the silver chain strung with its twin dried ears, a necklace of skin that clicks like the teeth of a skeleton dangling from a gibbet and he says,

What?

How did I teach you to write in your dream?

I don't know. It was a dream. You just taught me.

I've been reading the letter from Catharin.

The saint?

I don't want to read it anymore.

Squeaky comes to me, stands beside me as I look out through the bars, to the cells in D Block where the tattoos make their silent ablutions to the day before masking their ink with cotton. Squeaky says,

I don't getcha, Mitch. You lookin' at those guys every day.

They are angels of death, Squeaky, locked away from their prey like caged eagles. I think about letting them out.

Squeaky lets out a long slow breath and he says,

Jeez Mitch. That's pretty heavy shit.

I had a dream, too, Squeaky.

He bumps against me, his night sweat still an aphrodisiac on his skin. I say,

It was about my brother-in-law.

Squeaky backs away from the bars. I say,

I chained him to a butcher block and I nailed his tongue to his chest and I cracked the ribs out of his body and stacked them on his belly and then I yanked the nail out of his tongue just to listen to the blood gurgle in his throat.

I stop there. Wait for Squeaky to say something. He turns to his bunk, pulls the new white sneakers from under it. I watch his feet disappear, his perfect pure feet with his square toes, watch them slip into the bone white sneakers and I know his time is running out. He looks at me. He says, So what are you telling me, Mitch?

I squat in front of him. I say,

While you were in the infirmary, Squeaky, he came to visit, my brother-in-law, he came to visit and he said he wants me out. He can get me out. But I don't want out.

You can get out?

I don't want to go out.

Squeaky touches my hand. It's a cool hand, a fine little cool hand that has learned its place in the pyramid of power, learned how to pay homage to the walking living god of death who gives him life and shields him, who can, with a word, cut his throat and feed his liver to the eagles in D Block. Squeaky whispers,

If you go, Mitch, I wanna go too.

I feel his fear in the sudden wetness of his palm. I take comfort in his fear because that fear tells me he needs me and I feel powerful knowing that I keep him alive. I reach for the twin dried ears dangling from the silver chain around his neck and I say,

He wants me to take more ears. He doesn't want me to change. He wants me the way I was on the Rio Verde, he wants me the way I was in Santiago. He needs me to clear the path for him on his journey to the Senate.

Squeaky's sweat evaporates from my arm. Looking down I see the imprint of his palm like a rosette, faint, emerging from deep inside.

It's okay, Squeaky, I don't want to scare you, but I've got to make a decision.

What's the Rio Verde, Mitch?

It's a place where bad things happened.

The shaven headed killer in D1 rattles the bars of his cage and shouts his morning filth at the guard. It is a ritual. Squeaky turns away.

Whydya read me your sister's letter, Mitch?

And then, Martin raps at the gate. He calls out,

Good morning, assholes. Get your balls in a row, chow time for all deviant motherfuckers.

I look at him. See the same blackness of corruption in the corners of his eyes that I saw seeping from my brother-in-law's mouth, the same blood I saw clouding my brother-in-law's eyes and I say,

Marty you're looking pretty sharp this morning but you've got a spot on your sleeve.

I ain't got nothing on my sleeve.

That sleeve's tight, Marty, but a man like you can loosen her up.

Martin glares at me and he nods and runs the nightstick up and down his left arm. He says,

Get outa my head, Mitchell.

I see it in his eyes. He is close. He smells it, tastes it, feels the flesh waiting for him. Which hand does he use? Does he cum in a folded Kleenex or does he cup it in his palm—his little puddle of death teeming with its one hundred million human vermin? Does he wash it down the sink? Or does he flush his life down the toilet? He is close. I can smell it. As he walks away, I catch a whiff of semen and I laugh. I say,

Gotcha dreaming about it, right Marty?

87.

The clock runs. I can't stop it. I can't change it. It ticks and ticks. I'm not yet halfway through my sentence and already I worry about the end. Seven hundred days. A milestone. I'm still alive. My manuscript is still undiscovered. I still write my twelve hundred words a day and the pile grows. As I sit in the library, in the gardening section, surrounded by field manuals on annuals and perennials, garden books on rhizomes and the ornamental grasses, I feel like a man in a zoo looking at the last of species, the captive ones hidden behind glass, the dying ones squeezed out of their habitats by hungry men burning the forest for meat space, killing everything that walks, crawls, flies, burrows—creating islands of death surrounded by the human desert, the wasteland of excess, the spread of the human virus, its virulence devastating and incurable. My fingers hunt for the words.

Only the complete and total annihilation of the human race will secure the everlasting and pure gardens abandoned to the money lust of killers like my brother-in-law, that Chief Executive in Charge of Evisceration and Flatulence who will not stop until there is nothing left to kill. Then will he and his tribe turn on one another with their knives to carve out the heart of the weakest, butchering their kin for food?

I thumb the pages of rose books, dumbstruck by the stupendous variety of roses. There is more truth in a rose than in all the human race with its infinite ability to murder, to slaughter, to destroy, to burn and to flay with no thought of what happens after. Tucked in among the roses I found *Notre Dame des Fleurs* hidden like a crushed violet in the thick and weighty pages detailing death and the sweep of the virus as it spreads around the globe.

I remember Richie Rogers that sluttish teenage whore who may or may not have borne me a child and I know that when I get out of here I must hunt her down, must find that scion and cut it free of breath, kill the seed she bore. To purify the world, you start by eradicating your own blood.

Never lie with a pure woman, never burrow into the womb of a breeder. I chose the fallen and dark women who were lost to hope, who had no dreams, no illusions, no deluded ideas of permanence or family. I chose women who had accepted that their mouths were the perfect vessel of death because in their mouths the young died before they are born, they spat the death seed into a toilet, wiped it from their lips onto a piece of filthy cloth, swallowed it, shat it out like a lump of rot and flushed it down to the sea. I blessed them because they knew, in their darkness of darknesses that there was just one way to end the killing and that was to erase the killer. Their wombs were sterile, unfecund deserts in the human legion creeping across the once verdant jungle, searing the once buoyant forest, destroying the grasslands and their treasures.

The books in the library are reliquaries in a museum preserving bones of the dead—dodo, moa, carrier pigeon, condor. I feel the urge in my loins as I read, feel the hatred of my own urgency, abhor the desire welling in my cock anxious to spew its seed even though the seed cannot flower because of the scalpel.

The slit in my scrotum where the surgeon sliced the vas deferens burns. He said,

But you're too young for this.

I'm already old.

I don't know if I can cut a healthy young man.

I am death, sir, I am death and to stop the killing you have to stop the killer.

The surgeon laughed. He said,

You have a good imagination.

I showed him the scar on my neck, the dollar sized scar from the shrapnel that missed the carotid artery by half a centimeter and I showed him the half moon scar on my shoulder where the serrated edge of a combat knife nicked the biceps but I didn't tell him about the ears I had cut from the dead, the ears I sent to my control who wrote me checks. I said,

I don't want to pass this on, this death machine.

He said,

Do you hate that much?

You created me.

I don't even know you.

You reap the benefits of my terror when you live well and eat the dead. You have no idea how many ears I cut for you.

I took an oath to preserve and protect human life.

At that point, I grabbed my cock and I said,

This is the scepter of death you son of a bitch and you have to cut me to make it end.

He looked away then, in a low whisper, said,

My oath to do no harm?

Hand on his neck and I whispered in his ear,

This is how death feels and you are one second away from it. This is the touch of a killer, the kiss of the abyss waiting for you. With this I cast you down but if you kill the vas you kill the seed and you save me the trouble of seeking them out.

He looked up at me, his eyes wet with fear, his cheeks wet with tears and he said,

But you are human.

That is the problem.

I feel the scar, a small knot at the lobe of my testicles and I know that I have, in one act, killed a hundred billion. I don't have to hunt them down one by one. I close the book of roses, close the book of grasses, close the book of rhizomes and I look at the caged light in the ceiling. I am like a plant in a pot and a plant in a pot is like an animal in a zoo, the last of the living, an icon of what was. Once you capture the animal in the zoo or sow the plant in the pot, you are its prisoner. You feed your captives and your captives prey on your moral conscience. Do you let them die? They have you.

I squeeze my thighs together, crush the testicles, think of Squeaky and his mouth and the ever-lasting agony of desire. And then the library door opens and two men enter, men I know, men with tattoos and scars, men who have tasted blood and cut the guts out of living things.

They are my shadow, they are me with their beefy arms and cruel down-turned mouths and they are shaved slick, heads like river stones, eyes like lumps of shining coal, faces like plaster death masks.

They stand on either side of my chair. They are large men with thick necks and heavy thighs and barrel chests. One of them leans down and he whispers, his voice a raspy high pitched voice,

We want your bitch.

I scoot back from the table, feel a hand on my shoulder pressing, squeezing hard, the fingers like claws. I relax. I say,

How did you get in here?

How the fuck do you think, asshole?

There are two of them, two laughable common men come to bust my ass.

What did you say?

We want to buy Squeaky.

Squeaky isn't for sale.

It ain't up for debate, asshole. We get Squeaky or the Governor knows about René.

What about René?

I push back before the hand digs harder into my shoulder and the red veil of death descends over my eyes and I feel whole and pure and true again.

In my hand there is the hard cover of a book and the book is *Notre Dame des Fleurs* and I grasp it like a blade, slice left then right and there is a guttural grunt of a throat seizing, that oh so familiar and sweet sound of death and both men clutch at their throats, eyes on me, eyes on fire and

I snatch at the testicles of the audacious one, the one who brought me the message and I squeeze his nuts until I feel them squish like eggs breaking and he gasps and collapses to his knees and I spear fingers into his midriff and squeeze until I feel his heart beat in my hands. He tries to breathe and his eyes glaze. I say,

I am the chief executive in charge of death here, you fucking amateurs.

I wheel and with the heel of my left foot, I stomp on the crotch of the prostrate hyena who threatened me and I say,

You don't fuck with the corporation, cocksucker.

I cradle the broken spine of Our Lady of the Flowers— blood on her leaves—and I close her wounds, set her on the shelf, slide her into her slit of a grave buried between roses and rhizomes.

88.

In my dream, the judge on his throne thumbs the dossier on his desk. Leaning forward, he squints at me through thick lenses. I am a gray shadow on a gray wall. He can't discern my features. He glances at his documents tinged with red flags and then again he squints at me and I say,

Where do they bury the dead, your honor?

What?

Where do they lay them down to sleep? Do they lay them down on feather beds? Do they scatter the ashes like seeds sown into sterile ground?

The judge pushes his lenses up on a hawk-like nose, a beak still dripping with blood and chunks of spleen and pieces of liver torn from living bodies, and he says,

You are an impertinent son of a bitch, you are the scum of the earth, you are a pustule on a carbuncle infecting the scabrous asshole of a diseased whore, that's who you are and that gives you license to ask me questions, but not to impugn my integrity.

They haul the dead away in canvas bags, your honor. I have seen them carted away in the night. Where do they bury them?

He pushes his thick glasses up on his nose. He sings a lullaby, a sleep-time chant full of the wanton sexuality of a nymph searching for her satyr and he smiles at me, his teeth bleeding like the veins in a swollen testicle, filled like the poison sac of a viper and he says,

The dead? I see no dead. I see no corpses, no bodies, no broken limbs. I see you—a scum sucking pervert with hollow eyes and filed teeth. I see the sprouted sperm of a man unwilling to face his reality.

He laughs. He closes the dossier. He says,

Mr. Mitchell, may I call you Mr. Mitchell?

As you wish, your honor.

I have read your dossier and I like what I see. You are a sick man on a slow boat to perdition but there is nothing in your records that merits keeping you in here one day longer so you are free to go.

I look at him, watch him peel off his binocular thick lenses and I say,

But what about the dead, your honor? What about the dead?

Standing, he swirls in his black robes, black as the wings of a vulture, his nose sharp as the beak of a raptor, his nails long and red and swollen as the vulva of a woman in high ecstasy and he says,

Ah. The dead. Yes. The dead.

And then in an eddying of filthy wind, he vanishes and I am alone and awake listening to the thump of my heart and the dull distant pounding of the machinery deep in the bowels of the prison.

I don't tell Squeaky about this dream. I don't want to disturb him.

89.

I am reading my pages. Reading them as if they are the work of someone else because I don't remember writing them.

On the Cauca, in Colombia, just outside Cali, we caught them in their boats fording the river and we opened fire, cut them to pieces, cut the boats to pieces, cut them up like tree limbs falling until the river washed thick with arms and legs and the twisted torsos of men bleeding into the flow. I felt the warm heat of the AK47 on my thigh as I rested the barrel there, smelling cordite and the sweet sweet odor of blood. Corpses floating down to the sea.

I fold the page over, try to recall writing about the Cauca, Cali, Colombia. But I don't remember it. I don't remember the writing of it. This writing is there, buried in the middle of the manuscript and I must have written it, but I don't recall writing that passage. The writing has pulled the story out of my brain leaving a hole yet to be filled with something other than Squeaky's squeals as he orgasms— meaningless spurts of death on his thigh writhing to their demise on the hem of a blanket.

Catharin. I remember the blue paper of her letter clotted with smears of her pink neon ink and I think of her belly swollen with the blood and semen of her Hindu converts who took the word of Jesus Christ of Our Lady of the Flowers and I think, in a rush, what if that child was meant to be my father's child, the tree of a new generation of killers? And I search back for the words ... I turned him away, Henry ... I threw myself away ... because because because. Why did you throw yourself away, Catharin??

90.

She slumps at the table, neck bowed. Weakness shows in the line of her shoulder, the surrender in the slope of her back and I hesitate at the door, smell Martin's heat. He preens, smoothing his hair, primping like a street-slut on the prowl, his crisp uniform and polished boots picture perfect, the perfect poster boy for his generation of killers.

I open the door, glance at him, and in his eyes I see lust as pure and simple as death. As I enter the glass shielded room, Geraldine sits up, her hands, clasped together, separate in slow motion. She wears black leather gloves so tight they fit like a second skin. She smiles. She wears dark glasses and her face is made up so thick I can't see the pores in her skin. The makeup leaves a thin veneer like gesso on canvas, a field open to any color. Her hair, black as soot, is now straight and parted in the middle, a single straight line from forehead to crown, and the long falls splay over her shoulders like a shawl.

She holds out a black-gloved hand. I say,

Geraldine, you know Martin. Martin's in love with you.

Martin, standing behind the glass, grins with a puerile innocence and in that instant all the poison in his system turns to honey and in that instant I see the boy who came pure and serene into the steel and concrete hole that has eaten his heart. Geraldine's right hand flutters to her throat, her flesh where Carl Fairweather in his rage tore out her larynx and as if she wants to speak, she gurgles a throaty gasp and I say,

For a price Martin will do anything we want, Geraldine.

She sits. I see Martin, eyes on Geraldine, adolescent innocence, lightning struck and immobile, a lustful glow on his face. Geraldine plucks her writing pad from her purse and writes ... Meaning what? And I say,

He's never seen a woman walk on water, never seen a beauty so pure it hurts just to cast a glance at it. She writes ... Stop it.

I need a photo of you, Geraldine.

I lean across the table, lift the dark glasses from her face and I shudder when I see the dark circles under her eyes, darkness like the deepest wound a woman can suffer, darkness close to death and dying, the darkness of shame. I touch her cheek, drop the glasses on the hardwood table and she looks at them angled on the wood like a twisted snake and I say,

What's going on Geraldine? Four months, not a word. Then you're here.

She shakes free, jabs at the note pad, writes ... Why do you need a photo of me?

For Martin and Squeaky. She looks puzzled and in her puzzlement, the darkness lifts and she writes ... Who?

Squeaky, I say. He's my protégée, my bitch, my bottom. I fuck him.

She sits back in her chair. She writes ... Don't need to know that. I say,

Why are you here?

She writes ... Catharin's baby died. Cat is ruined.

I turn the note pad, tear out the page. I say,

I got her letter. She wrote that you might have smothered her baby, she wrote that Carl might have killed it, she wrote that Carl is a pig.

She looks down at the black leather gloves and then at me. She pushes at the sleeves of her jacket. Her face is thin, helpless, the mascara no longer hiding the pain or the fear or the longing. Her lips tremble. She nods, head falling to a slow beat. I look up to see Martin at the glass, leaning forward, a scowl on his face, worry lines sunk into his forehead as if he has some proprietary lien on the woman wearing the black gloves and I say,

You want me to save you, Geraldine?

She picks up the ballpoint pen and she writes ... Too late, Henry.

Your shit of a husband is still trying to get me out, Geraldine.

She turns away. Rises from the table. Turns to the glass where Martin stands, the wire-glass separating them. I watch his eyes rove over her, up and down. She holds still under his gaze as if chained in place until, offering herself to him, opening to him, she lifts her head. A half-smile leaks from Martin's mouth, saliva, love-spittle, the wet mouth of a man who has just eaten the cunt of his whore until she came in his mouth and then, at last she breaks free from the lock of his eyes, turns to face me but I still watch Martin as he follows her hips. His eyes tell me everything. He will do anything I want him to do. I say,

You can sit down, Geraldine. You've baited the hook. Geraldine sits. She writes ... Going to help Carl? I say, The photograph?

She opens her purse again, pulls out her wallet, shuffles through the plastic panes, then extracts a photo of herself in red—red dress, her cheeks bright, her hair flowing over her shoulders but parted on the left side so the mat of hair looks alive as it spreads over the red dress. I hold the photo, feel its heat. Look at Martin watching every move inside the glass cage. I say,

How do you get away from him, Geraldine? She writes, the pen gouging into the pad, tearing at it, angry, full of hate ... He has Catharin.

He has her so he lets you go? Does he know where you go?

She writes ... The children are in school in Los Angeles. I tell him I'm going to see the children.

Do you? Do you go see them?

Her eyes prey on mine, then she writes ... They are beautiful, Henry. If you could see them, you'd say they are the most beautiful children on earth. I say,

I can't solve your problem, Geraldine.

She writes ... He's made his decision. He's going to run for the Senate.

I feel a stab of anger. I say,

So he's not waiting?

She writes ... He's like a flood. Sweeps it all away. Eats you up, swallows you. I say,

Sister, can't you just leave him?

She writes ... He'll kill me if I try before he's bought the election.

I look at Martin at the glass, raising his hand to knock, to point at his wrist. I say,

It's time.

Geraldine writes ... Henry, please. You have to help me.

This isn't the kind of picture I need.

I stand, go to the door, leave her in her wounded darkness and I walk out into the corridor, taste Martin's cologne as it boils off his heated skin. Returning to the cage, I say,

Martin, I need a hole puncher.

A what? He says. A hole puncher, a three-hole puncher to make holes in paper.

I ain't go no hole puncher 'cept the rod between my legs.

I've got an address, Martin. I give you a phone number, you give me the hole puncher.

Whose number?

Who do you think?

He stops. I stop. He punches me in the kidney with his night stick. I say,

She asked me to give it to you, partner.

Silence. Then he says,

She wants me to have it?

Next time she comes, Martin, you might get ten minutes alone with her in that glass cage.

He looks at me. His mouth open. His eyes darting side to side like a man walking through a cave full of spider webs.

A hole puncher, Martin. Just get me a hole puncher.

91.

You feel the knife. A bullet keeps you distant, you don't feel the killing, but the knife goes deep, it hesitates as it nicks a rib before entering the liver, and blood seeps around the blade cutting though skin, though flesh. The knife is one step

BLOOD

removed from teeth. Through the cell bars I look across the deck to the tiered cell block and I feel queasy from the dream. The images rose up dark and cold and I felt the knife sink into the flesh of my ear and slide down hard into that momentary burst of pain when the hot blood spurts but the meat hasn't yet shut down.

In the cell block across from me, I see men waking, groggy, sweaty, stinking, ugly men with tattoos like blood red and black seas washing their hides, walking shadows of men with murder in their teeth, their semen clogged up inside their murderous bodies. I want to set them free, to watch them once again spread out, a plague, vermin carrying a plague, viruses infecting the living.

And coming out of the dream the pain in my ear curls me up into a ball and I sit up, expecting to feel blood, to smell blood, to awaken to the damp flow of my blood. to find a demon with a blade hovering over me, dead. I stand dripping wet, sweat tightening my skin like wet starch drying. I wipe it off, look at Squeaky still on his bunk, mouth open, eyes closed, his left arm dangling to the cold concrete floor. I dreamed of being in him before the blood dream took me back to the spoiled earth. I stand at the bars watching the tattoos rise, shaking themselves awake, and then, behind me, Squeaky groans as he shifts.

I turn my head, see his foot poking from under the blanket, his erection as he dreams of fucking, and I envision again the dreamscape as it unrolled—first a blackness then the landscape turning red tinged with coppery green like a statue corroding in acid air and the air turned thick, the color of vomit as if the sky had become infected, belching putrid sulfuric, cupric, ferric odors that tasted like metal so thick it wouldn't slide into my lungs but hung up at the back of my throat until, gasping, I woke, my lungs burning and as far as I could see the earth had turned violent blue and green and red burning at the edges of a huge pit as if the entire

193

earth had been ripped open, turned into a smelter bubbling with hot metal. I hear Squeaky churn on his bunk. He says,

Whatcha doin' up, Mitch?

I watch the men, bare-chested and tattooed in the cell block across from me and I feel the slice of the knife again and that first spurt of blood as the tissue yields to the sharpness of metal and I look down at my hand. There is a blade, sharp-edged and tainted with blood and it lies buried deep in the cauldron of molten copper spewing like fireworks from the tortured earth. Under the knife I see a hand that reaches up to me and I kneel, touch the molten flesh, expecting the skin to pull loose from the bone, but the flesh holds and I drag a man from the molten copper sea and a small brown hand erupts from the seething mass and he is intact except for his left ear where a gold coin with an eagle stamped on it dangles from a tab of skin above the bleeding gash where the ear should be. In the pukish orange and red tinged sun breaking through the sulfur yellow and cerulean blue clouds of poison the small brown man holds out a hand and I recognize him as the insurgent from the Cauca, the revolutionary from Bogota, the freedom fighter from Nicaragua. I took his ear and sold it to my brother-in-law the CEO in charge of death. Squeaky says,

Mitch? Y'okay?

I turn to him, turn my back on the men rising in their tattooed red and black and blue misty sweat and I say,

Squeaky, I had a bad night.

He curls up against the wall of the cell, draws a blanket over his scrawny flat chest and he says,

You ain't gonna kill me, are you Mitch?

His hand shakes as he touches his throat. Fine fingers—not the fingers of a man but the delicate and lacy fingers of a secret—and I take a deep breath as the dreamscape slithers back in front of my eyes obscuring Squeaky. The earth cauldron opens again and I reach into the molten red and chrome yellow metal and I pull them out one by one, a chain of the dead, hundreds of them, pull them one at a time from the metallic river of forget and their eyes are red and green and their skin drips with the silvery drops of molten metal and each of them has a gold coin sewn to the skin over the hole where the ear once held place. They walk past me, eyes furious with hate and loathing.

I sit beside Squeaky on his bunk, feel him draw away. I touch his skinny arm that will never deliver a death blow and I say,

Squeaky. I don't want to kill you.

I'm really glad, Mitch, 'cause I don't want you to kill me.

You haven't seen the blood stain the water and you haven't seen the bones stacked like stobs in a bonfire and you haven't held the beating heart of a man in your hand. You haven't stolen the meat and potatoes of hungry women, Squeaky, and you don't sit in a board room ordering Kobe steak tartar and you don't drive a four-wheeled pig that sucks and spews and shits its poison into the air, so no, Squeaky, I won't kill you yet. But in my dream Squeaky, the earth opened up and I brought them all back.

Jeez Mitch, that sounds like a really bad nightmare.

He is so simple he can't see me for what I am. Does he believe everything I say or nothing? I watch the tattoos in the cell block rise, cover their nakedness with cotton shirts and blue denim and under the cotton the red and black and sulfur yellow of the hell bleeding into their skin disappears and I feel Squeaky's hand grip my thigh like a small animal sinking in its teeth and he whispers,

Do you need it now, Mitch? I'm ready if you need it now.

I look down at my hand, see the yellow scaly skin, the cerulean blue of copper poisoning. I say,

You don't want to fuck a dead man, Squeaky.

92.

It comes in a brown envelope with four stamps on it. It is addressed to me. Martin throws it through the bars the

way you throw a bone to a chained-up dog. He looks at me
with his death-camp stare, his eyes narrow slits as if the light
had to squeeze its way into his brain. He says,

Hey asshole, somebody loves you.

The letter skids across the floor, skips against the toilet
and dies there a wounded bird. Squeaky sits on the edge of
his bunk, his bare feet dangling an inch from the floor and
he looks at me and he says,

You want me to get it, Mitch?

Leave it, little man.

Mitch, I don't like it when you call me little man.

I sit up, face him, then, standing, I cross the no-man's-
land between our bunks, five feet of foreign soil, a mile thick,
years deep in pain where thousands of men had knelt,
mouths open, and I kneel and look at him and I say,

You think I want to hurt you, Squeaks? You think that?

So you was just talking, right Mitch?

I scoop up the brown envelope with its four stamps and
sitting on my bunk slit the belly of the little beast with my
thumbnail. I pull a white sheet of folded paper from the
wound. Wrapped in it, there are four photographs. There is a
note in Geraldine's hand, in her flowing florid script with its
curlicues and slanted crossed Ts, not in the hurried, jagged
writing of her note pad, the pad she used instead of a voice.
In the flowery script there is no pain, no hurt. There are no
tears, just her own sweet voice, the voice I remember from
times when she was pure and I was innocent, times before I
had ever witnessed our father fucking Mrs. Wilson, times
before Catharin ran away, times when our mother was not
ashamed to look us in the eye.

I read ... Henry, here are pictures of Eleanor and Tracy,
we call him Trick. The pictures of me are for your friend
Martin, the guard.

I feel my hand shake as I read her words ... for Martin.
Through blurry eyes, I study one of her photos. In it she is in
blue, bright, brilliant blue and her hair is swept down over

her shoulders like twin onyx waterfalls and she smiles. Her teeth have caught a sliver of light so her mouth twinkles and the sheer blue top she wears is tight and outlines the shape of her breasts. From the picture it is clear that she wears nothing underneath as though the fact of the photo has aroused her. The wanton look in her face says she's waiting for someone to peel the blouse from her skin. In the other photo she wears a sheer blue robe against a bright light. Under the robe, she wears nothing and I see her breasts and the faint outline of her pubic hair. She wears black high heels that stretch her legs and I see the rose tips of her breasts under the blue veil and my hand shakes because that photo is like cash to me. It is gold, it is silver and with it I can drain what is left of Martin's soul before I fuck him screaming against the flat hard table in the library. His voice tight and high, tighter than I have heard him in months, Squeaky says,

What's going on, Mitch?

What makes you think anything is going on?

I seen you in lots of places, Mitch, and I know when somethin's eatin' at you and somethin's eatin' at you right now.

I hand him the photo of Geraldine clothed and he takes it between the nails of his thumb and right index finger, holds it out the way a man holds a dewinged insect waiting for its final flutter. He whispers,

Jeez Mitch, she's beautiful. Who is she?

He looks at me. His eyes are wide and open and his chest rises and falls.

My sister, Geraldine.

You're shittin' me, Mitch?

He looks again at the picture and he says,

She don't look nothin' like you.

I laugh, the weight of hatred lifts from my chest and shoulders. I turn to the other pictures. The photos of the children, and in their pure and angelic faces, I see the world lost. In their eyes, open and curious, the faintest glimmer of light, a flash, a sparkle of hope. The girl Eleanor is eight and boy Tracy is six and they are what I once was. They do not appear to carry the pure evil of the Mitchell genes, but I know that buried in them is the death-lust, just as it is buried in their mother and in their father who cannot pull the trigger himself but needs the unleashed amorality of men such as I to do his work. Geraldine writes ... I send you pictures of them, Henry, I don't want you to hate them for who they are. I can't let you hate them for who their father is. I need you to save them, Henry because without you, I know he will ruin them.

I search for more about her picture for Martin and I find it on the back of the sheet and she writes ... I saw the way he looked at me, Henry. I have seen that look. I knew what you wanted. I know what it means. You can use me in any way you need ... I stop reading. My gut churns, hard as rocks tumbling. I look up from the writing, watch Squeaky's face as he searches mine the way a woman searches for the sign that her man has wandered. I relax, let the hatred slip off my face and Squeaky smiles, still holding Geraldine's photo. He says,

You had me worried for a bit there, Mitch.

Does she give you a hard on, Squeaky?

What?

Would you bone her?

He grins. Hands the photo back to me. He says,

I'd never betray you with a woman, Mitch, unless you want me to.

Squeaky crawls off his bunk. On his knees crawls to me, hands folded like a supplicant. He hands the photo back to me. He says,

All I want is for you to love me, Mitch.

I look at Geraldine. I know that is what she means too but that's not all that she means.

93.

Geraldine's photo lies in my shirt pocket solid as a pound of fish bait. Its fleshy odors rise to my nostrils, reeking with the scent of new sex, spilling out like the leakage of a slut's cunt. I smell her ripening, pheromonal signals wafting through the cold dead air of the concrete and steel cage. As I sit at the computer in the library I hear Squeaky wheezing as if he were Sisyphus pushing his stone to the top of his mountain. Dust of the books leaches into the air, torturing his lungs like the detritus of dead civilizations, the ruin of men, the wreck of culture. The books are trapped in here with us, tied to the same unchanging, rotting core, lashed like shipwrecks to a hopeless Medusean raft adrift in a senseless sea. I watch Squeaky as he plucks a book from the top shelf, dusts it, then reaches up stretching to replace it, his body arched up like a woman orgasming. I suck in my breath, feel the urge push against the harsh denim of my prison issue dungarees, my prick trapped in cloth, my body trapped in concrete, my brain trapped in hatred and lust and the relentless disdain for everything built, touched, cherished by men because at the end of my prick, of every man's prick, there is a fountain of youth that needs to be dried up, turned to dust, amputated like the diseased and putrescent vestige it is.

Squeaky is the one thing keeping me alive right now, but I can't, I won't, I dare not arm him with ammunition like that or he would own me. As he replaces his book, he lowers his arms and the sweetness of his form catches my eye. He turns, looks at me and smiles, and in that smile I see the last innocence in a reeking, stinking world, an innocence as yet untainted by desire, an innocence that is pure and perfect in its surrender to me, an innocence that shows what we could have been.

I turn back to the computer, to the pages of my manuscript, to the gouges and rips and the ink splotched pages still indecipherable as any Rosetta Stone before

Champollion, any Linear B before Michael Ventris, any
Maya glyph before Knorosov, and I know that all my truth
and pain will forever lie hidden from enlightenment. It will
be denied to the world that needs to know, to understand, to
see that the plague we are is unstoppable and that we, I, you,
all of us, we all kill the wrong ones. But this enlightenment
comes when it is too late, too late for anyone to say it's your
duty to slit your neighbor's throat and then to slash your
own wrists because that is the only way to redemption—the
complete eradication of the vermin.

Squeaky, silent as a butterfly, lands in front of me, his
cherubic face dusty at the cheeks with the gray prison pallor
of decay and neglect and he says,

Hey Mitch. I just finished dusting all the Rs. Every one
of them.

I jerk out of my reverie, feel the stiffness of my cock
surge, about to burst free. And then he coughs and his face
flushes and I see a sudden vision of him dead, stretched out,
bubonic, hemorrhagic, eviscerated and I say,

You got a cold, little man?

Mitch, I don't ask much but do you gotta call me little
man? You used to dint call me little man, so why do you
gotta do it now?

I'm sorry, Squeaky.

He sits on the edge of the table, legs dangling like a five-
year-old at a circus and he swings his feet back and forth, his
small feet in his white tennis shoes now soiled, and I watch
the slow rhythm of the feet, a metronome of flesh and bone.
He snaps his fingers, says,

Mitch, you with me?

And then the door opens and I see Martin the Septic,
Martin the Diseased, Martin the Poisoned, Martin whose
lust seeps out of his pores like the sweat of a blacksmith, lust
that smells like the crotch of a putain and he says,

Mitchell ... we ... gotta talk.

I look at Squeaky whose eyes are blue and open and wide as if there were no sun in the world, as if my cock had never buried itself in him, as if each day he arose virgin clean, unashamed, immaculate and I say,

Squeaky, why don't you have a go at the Ts, okay?

And he slips down off the table and, turning to me, grins and disappears into the gray canyon of the stacks, into the gray hollow death where civilization wastes away unread on the shelves of a prison library collecting dust.

What's up, Martin?

He shuffles his feet and clears his throat and I pluck the photo of Geraldine from my shirt pocket, feel it slippery as the wet lips of an aroused woman, swollen as the breasts of a woman in heat. I hold it in the palm of my hand and flash it at Martin and he lurches back as though I have smacked him in the mouth. A hand rises to his lips and I say,

She told me to give this to you.

He holds out a hand, but I lay the photo on the table. Martin looks at me, his face a blank, his eyes a question. He says,

Then let me have it.

It'll cost you, Marty.

He lunges at my hands, drawn to the woman in blue in the photo like a lion to raw meat and I clasp his hand under mine, Geraldine trapped between the table and my hand, sprawled between Martin's fingers and mine, and we both possess her, feel her blue heat, smell her musk, taste her perfume and I say,

I don't pimp my sister for nothing, Marty.

I got you that fucking hole puncher and I got you those fucking file folders and I got you ink for that fucking printer, what do you want?

I squeeze his hand, crush it until I feel a creak of joint over Geraldine squirming on the table, her breath hot against my palm, and I say,

I want what I can't get, Martin.

He relaxes his hand, limp, and he looks at me, a sideways glance, his faced twisted like a man in mid-orgasm.

What do you want?

I look him in the eye and I lift the photo of Geraldine from the table, feel the sweat on her skin, and I say,

Have you ever killed a man, Martin?

94.

A corrupt man leaks when he walks. You see the slime trail of a rapist, smell the rotten stench of the abuser, breathe the confused air of the thief. In here, a man breathes that air, smells that stench and it infects him, eats him from the inside out until nothing is left but the hollow skin sack.

Martin has begun to decay from the heart out. I see it in his walk, in the shuffle of his boots on the steel mesh, the halfhearted attention to his job. I expect him to fall back in on himself like a lava dome collapsing. I expect to see the vestiges of his moral fiber float away like motes of dry dust and then my job will be easier. Instead of a knife to the throat, all it will take is a short push, a finger breaking through the eggshell thin veneer of his humanity and he will be one of the walking dead.

I sit on my bunk in the gray predawn light. I am alone and waiting because Martin took Squeaky away four days ago, four empty days, four days I haven't written a word as though his absence has drained me the way writing drains my brain of memory. I've stayed out of the library, where Catharin's letter festers in its blue envelope, rots on the printed page like a shot-gunned rabbit in the sun. I'm afraid to touch it for fear of learning the truth about her because if Carl Fairweather is right then Catharin is corrupt and rotten and her putrefaction will seep through the words. I'm afraid of that because she was my touchstone, a saint on the prowl for souls, a virgin-saint-whore with a bayonet in her hands succoring the lice-like men I slew. If she is corrupt then I am foutu because if she is my pillar it has turned to salt if she is my touchstone it has shattered and even in my disgust for her puke-sucking Jesus, her choice gave me a rotten hope that maybe, just maybe the race had at least one pure being who didn't deserve to die. Without Squeaky next to me, I am alone and afraid and I can hear his words,

You ain't never been afraid of nothin', Mitch.

I see that in a backhanded way I was Squeaky's hope, but now that he is gone, there is a vacuum.

95.

I ask Martin every day where my cellmate is and he looks at me in that death-camp hollow-eyed stare all the corrupt guardians use to hammer us into submission but says nothing. I know his weaknesses, I sense his perversions that to another man seem mere aberration but to me are as big and perfidious as boils, as sickening as pus-filled suppurating carbuncles in the hide of a cow—visible and true and pure in their filth—and through them I know how to take what remains of his pride. I am resigned to the fact that Squeaky is gone for good, ferreted away in the jaws of the night-lions, strung up, raped, butchered like a shot deer, cut to pieces and wrapped and buried and I have to ask the Gov why—why did they take him away? It could be something as simple as an early release—why not? Carl Fairweather can procure mine, but Squeaky has no Carl Fairweather, no history of eating deep-fried ears—or does he? It could be something as clean as a voided sentence. But what if it is something as vile as the need of a Carl Fairweather, my brother-in-law with designs on the Senate, to pull Squeaky out of jail in order to pressure me because the Gov has told him of my affection and need for Squeaky. On my bunk. In the reddening dawn, I imagine Carl Fairweather strapped to a butcher block, his hands anchored to the floor, his palms nailed to the wood, his tongue nailed to his chest, and I strip him naked—his twisted leg, his shattered arm where I laid him out with the baseball bat when I found that he had beaten Geraldine, smashed her larynx so that never again will she speak. Yes, he needs a man with my special talents.

I have to decide whether to kill again without sanction and confess it in order to stay here forever or to take Carl's offer and walk back outside into the corruption and the stench of the slaughterhouse, into the river of blood he will ask me to spill for him. I imagine him again on the butcher block and I have moved up to his thighs, cut the skin away in slow rosettes through the muscle until the bone in his thigh shines through, the metal plates and pins of the shattered bone like the inside of a mechanical man, a robot with its metal skin peeled away. I imagine his shattered femur cut out of his body and laid on the stack of bloody bones on his chest. I close my eyes, take a deep breath. I have to get in touch with Geraldine, get in touch with Catharin if I am to know the truth, but how do you ask that question of a saint? How do you ask her if the church excommunicated her for whoring? How do you ask her if she did reform? Did she change from a street slut into a savior of souls? How do you ask that of your own sister?

96.

I have heard nothing new from Geraldine, no pleas to save her, no begging letter from Catharin begging me to rescue her. If something doesn't come soon, I'll have to ask the Gov for a visit to clarify things, to get an address, to make a phone call and so as the sun breaks the horizon, unleashing a river of red through the window and its steel bars. I sit up, walk to the gate, listen to the rattle of night sticks, watch the bodies of tattooed men swing off their bunks, watch the snakes buried in their skin writhe to morning light, watch the skulls stretched across their backs gape, and I wait for Martin to appear with his death walk, wait for his hollow corrupt eyes to lock onto mine, wait to see how much he has shrunk during the night, how much more of him has disappeared in the black cesspool of his

soul. I expect one day to see him dissolve, leaving a pile of
sawdust as his moral termites chew up the last remains of a
man. As he approaches, I say,

Martin, did you call her?

He looks at me, his eyes red and weepy, his cocaine nose
tortured red. His mouth quivers as he searches his toxic
brain for the words he used to spout like venom and he
sputters,

F Fu Fuck you, aaa asshole.

What's that on your chin, Marty?

He wipes at his chin with the back of his hand. There is
a smear of saliva. I say,

Say the word and you won't have to do it by hand,
Marty.

I grin because he is infected with the plague of avarice
and lust. If I touch him he will pop like a balloon speared
with a straight pin.

97.

I lift Catharin's letter from the manila folder unable to
hold it without trembling because I no longer trust her
words. Carl Fairweather with his ugly tongue has tainted
her, painted her with the whore brush, splashed her
excommunication across my mind and, as that plagues my
brain, I know Squeaky's not coming back but still I wait for
his return. He has been gone six days and I can't get Martin
to tell me where or why or when but I see the Machiavellian
hand of Carl Fairweather in his disappearance, a callous
using of Squeaky as a lever to blackmail me into doing what
he wants. So I pull out Catharin's letter, go back to the ink-
stained pages, back to the neon-pink ink and the gouges in
the pages to try, once again, to find the truth.

I lay all eight pages out on the table in the library, look
at each one and as I spread them side by side, I see the
erosion in the script, see the loss of detail in the letters as if
the more she wrote the more frantic she became. I go over

page three, that pivotal page three where she relates her capture, tells of being bound, beaten and raped, and there on the same page she writes of her confession to the mission director who, she said, told her she had to leave India because, pregnant, she was an embarrassment to the Church. As I read, I see the hand quake, the short stabs at the nib of the pen into the blue paper and I know there is truth, if not in the words, then in the gouges in the blue skin, the angled rips like sword slashes.

I jump to page seven, to the release from captivity where she writes about Carl Fairweather, writes about how he limps into her room, kneels beside her bed and buries his face in her breasts, rubs her swollen belly and then forces himself into her mouth where he cums and then, having used her, reviles her, calls her a whore, a street slut. Her hand quavers there as she writes that one day he will kill her—there is no doubt that this is truth.

Once again I tuck the letter back into the folder, satisfied, look at the typewritten pages I've copied using the computer and once again see how the machine has stripped away the anguish. The paper is flat, but each page has a depth of pain. It is all paper, but the magic of the hand is gone. The hand is different from the font. In the smooth, perfect, exact, machine-produced words there is nothing of the torn page where the pen dug into paper as Catharin wrote ... kill her... and I understand the hell she was in. I am there, trapped, helpless, waiting for the one person I care about to fill my eyes again, immobile as a monk in a monastery with a steel strap around my ankle. I can walk as far as the strap wills it—to the wall, back, then to the wall again and I know that Catharin—trapped by her own disease, bound up in the walls of Carl Fairweather's house, terrorized by the man with the limp and the utter disregard for the pain he brings—has written the truth of prisoners. I have seen him in full flower, Carl Fairweather, my brother-in-law, the CEO in charge of murder, extortion, corruption, pollution and diarrhea. I have seen him with sacks of ears on his desk counting the dead, transferring death into dollars and I know that Catharin in prison will write the truth and so I replace her letter and the copies on white computer paper, replace the file in the stacks with the book of English roses and *Notre Dame des Fleurs* and I return to the table, sit down, imagine again Carl Fairweather strapped to the butcher block, the bones of his twisted and shattered thigh cut from their meat and stacked on his naked chest, the bloody river seeping from his heart onto the floor. With a flaying knife, I cut his pectorals free, cut down to the rib cage and, because his tongue is nailed to his chest, I have to excise one pectoral at a time and to do that I yank the nail from his tongue and in that second, he screams but then I reseat the nail and his tongue spasms, jerks against the nail and I hear the deep gurgle of blood in his throat. I say,

Carl, a man with my special talents deserves to live in the steel cage as long as he wants.

And then the door to the library opens and I look up expecting to see Martin the Corrupt, sawdust trickling from the thin walls of his worm-eaten chest, but instead, I see Squeaky in the doorway and I am paralyzed with the limerence of seeing him pure and whole and intact and I can't stand.

He enters. He wears clean jeans, a clean chambray shirt, new white sneakers and he stands, a nimbus about him the color of an angel in ecstasy, and the aura bleeding from his body is radiant blue. I'm afraid to reach out, afraid that this apparition is as fleeting as Carl Fairweather's blood on the butcher block, as ephemeral as his imagined tongue nailed to his imagined chest, misty as the imagined bones cut out of his body and stacked on his belly. And then Squeaky says,

Holy cow, Mitch, aintcha gonna even say hello?

And I burst out of the chair, pick him up. He is soft and real and pink and I hug him, feel his heartbeat, taste his breath, let my fingers play in his sweat. I say,

You little fucker, where've you been?

I hadda go be a witness.

Someone could have told me.

I set him on the edge of the table, look at him, inspect his eyes see dark circles there, test his cheeks, see the rosettes of happiness blooming there, touch his lips, fingers tracing the cherry wetness there and I say,

I thought they'd killed you.

After you laid down the law, Mitch, ain't nobody touches me.

He flicks out the twin dried ears I'd made into a necklace for him and I see that he has restrung the dried ears on a new silver chain but the ears still rattle and clack like the teeth of a skeleton, and he says,

These got me thinking about you every day, Mitch. They gave me meat loaf.

Was it good?

Really good. Onions and tomatoes and they gave me waffles, too. I love waffles.

98.

The targets wobble on stiff legs, blood spouting from gun-burnt holes in their brown skin, wobbling, they dance across my pages and I taste their dying, wrinkled as prunes in hot sun, their blood sweet as raisins, and they couple— man-woman—arms tangled like cats twisted in balls of yarn. Always I see the blood-red moon spill over them, blot out their broken arms, blot out the slot where ears grew but blood drips like a dead drum beating. The targets dance across the pages, my words blotted out by blood, by the rip of the pen into the tissue soft paper and as I read each page, I try to refill my memory with my own forgotten past until I become what is written, taking it as my own. I punch holes in the margins, listen to the pop and click of the steel punch as it pierces the memory-page, pierces the paper as my knife in the blood moon night pierced skin, and the writing is all that remains of the act. I read and punch and stack the holes in memory left by the smeared blood-red pages, refill bit by bit and I know I have to decide—to stay, to leave. The pages, out of order, tell some story out of order, but is it the one I lived? Is this what came out of my memory? I realize that once it is written I can no longer tell if I lived it or if I am reading the life of someone else. Am I remembering things I forgot? Or am I remembering things I never knew? I can't tell. I have no way to check for truthfulness. No one to ask—did this happen? Am I dreaming? Did I imagine this? And every day the punched stack grows. It grows and keeps on growing—writing is infinite.

Squeaky emerges bleary-eyed from the stacks, holding the Descent of Man, its tattered hard cover a palimpsest hiding all the fingers that have preyed on its pages looking for an explanation. He sits on the table, holds the book between his knees, looks at me and he says,

Is it true, Mitch?

Is what true?

He waves the book at me and says,

I been reading this Darwin freak like you said and shit, this ain't American.

What do you mean?

I can't get it, Mitch. It's like he's fightin' me and I want to get it but I can't.

Maybe you get it but you don't know you get it.

The best I can tell, he's saying we all got monkey blood in us.

He looks at me, his pale skin ash gray in the grayness of no light, in the pale thin shine seeping through the clerestory of the library, and his face has the wan look of skin bleached in acid and worry.

You think he's got it right, Mitch?

Keep reading.

I pick up a page of my manuscript, one of the typed pages from late in my story and holding it the way a soprano holds the score of a sacred cantata, I read aloud—

In the jungle, where the night bleeds a reluctant moon through the canopy, I heard the laughter, then the quietness, then the light snoring of men in sleep and then with the slivered moon as torch, we slid into the shadows, the only light the glint of blood moon on steel and we took them out, one at a time, let the blood leak from their throats as we pulled their tongues from the mouth through the slit in the throat to lay it, signed, the way an artist signs his painting and then Suki, hands red in the yellow moon, took the ears— quick, the knife severing the ear from skull and in the quiet of the moon I saw his face, teeth bared, lips tight, then breaking into a grin as he held the ears in two fingers before dropping them into his leather pouch—

I look at Squeaky. He sits on a chair beside me, his pure and innocent face tight and startled as if he's seen a soul slither out of a corpse and he says,

Jeez Mitch, can you teach me to write like that?

Like what?

Like that, like there with the slivered moon as torch, we slid into the shadows. If I could write like that, I'd be happy.

You're missing what it's about, Squeaky.

I don't care what it's about, Mitch, I just wanna write like that.

Before you can write like that, you've gotta feel what I saw, Squeaky. If there ever was any doubt that we've got monkey blood in us, this will dispel it.

What do you mean?

If you ever doubted that we're just killers wearing khaki, this is proof.

Dintcha feel bad, doing that?

Squeaky, I haven't felt anything since I was twelve.

What happened when you were twelve?

I turn back to the manuscript, scan a page, try to place it in time, in the flow of the story—before Oxapampa, before Juxtlahuaca, before Hamiltepec, before Santiago? After Tolosa? But there are no time clues in the writing and my memory, now empty of all trace, can't find the place or the time and so I punch the holes, using the three hole punch Martin gave me in return for Geraldine's address.

Squeaky, I have something for you.

I look at him. He sits on his chair frozen in place, fragile as men I've seen just as the knife enters the hide, just before the blade twists past bone. He blinks. Shakes his head.

Mitch, that wasn't you in the jungle, was it?

I think that was me.

Wow, Mitch, that must really be something, I mean, wow.

I open the flap of my shirt pocket, pluck out the photo of Geraldine and slide it across the table. In the photo, she wears a red dress, and her hair snakes down over her left shoulder thick and rich and black. He touches the photo the way a celebrant touches an icon and his eyes trail over her features, slide down from face to breast like water sliding over rock and he says,

I gotta tell you, Mitch, she's beautiful.

She killed her first baby, Squeaky, choked it to death the way they used to when they couldn't carry more than one kid.

Squeaky jerks his hand away from the photo. Hot and fiery, his eyes are wet and his lips tremble and he gasps.

If you needed more proof, Squeaky, there it is.

His chest heaves and his eyes water and he tries to speak, but there are no words and then, he mutters,

I guess I'm the only one.

The only what?

The only one who never killed nothing.

You've killed, Squeaky. No one's clean, we're all killers. All of us eat the dead.

His face collapses, the muscles weaken, the skin sags. He comes to me. Crawls across the table, shoves the punched stack of manuscript aside and he slides into me and he's sobbing and he says,

I dint mean to, Mitch. Honest.

You're almost pure, Squeaky, you're almost perfect, but there's too much monkey in your blood for you to be saved. You're just one of us, lover, one of us.

99.

Martin worries me more every day. Mornings he comes to the bars, his eyes crusted with matter, his teeth tainted with the scum of bad sleep, his breath tangy as the flesh of a putrid corpse. He moves in slow jerks as though his soul has disengaged from his heart, the jerkiness of a mechanical man breaking down, and now, when he raises his riot stick to pound the bars, it falls with a hollow clunk, his arm no longer hammering at us as if he wants to send a message in code. He is at the right point, in the right place, and I know the one thing keeping him from collapsing into his demented shell is his masturbation fantasy over the photo of Geraldine. I see it in his eyes when he looks at me and I imagine him fucking her, his prick sliding into her imaginary flesh—the urge driving him to cum is the urge that kills the jungle, pollutes the rivers, fouls the air and I am happy that he spills his seed into the night, each ejaculation a reprieve. I sit up in my bunk, waiting for him to shout, Rise and Shine, assholes, grub in five and his voice is raspy from lack of sleep, swamped as he is in Geraldine's body and I say,

Hey Marty, you ready to take the big plunge?

He sidles close to the bars and he says,

What the fuck are you doing to me, Mitchell?

Quiet Martin, you'll wake Squeaky.

He glares at me. I say,

Just think about it, Martin. One man. You tap one man and she's yours.

He closes his eyes. Were I his eyes, I'd see her,
Geraldine from the photo, her mouth painted red, her lips
open, her breasts aching against tight blue sheer silk. Martin
opens his eyes, his sunken chest heaves, the khaki like a
brown shell of a molting insect split at the throat, ready to
peel down to reveal the monstrous killer hiding there. I
laugh.

Paradise, Martin. You'll never get close to a woman like
that the rest of your shit-eating life.

He growls,

Get off my back, Mitchell.

I turn to Squeaky. Eyes wide, hands still tucked between
his knees like a baby nested in some liquid utopian womb,
he licks his lips.

Martin turns his back. I watch his scrawny shoulders
push into the khaki of his uniform like a skinny bird trying
to fly and I remember his first day, the peachy pink skin, the
perfect little boy face full of righteousness and morality and
resurrection and I am so happy for his fall into his own
private abyss where he will, in sinister hope of one hour with
Geraldine, corrode what is left of his humanity. Squeaky
swings off the bunk, his bare feet dangling inches from the
cold concrete floor, inches from the gray that shimmers in
the morning light, a deep lake he will slide into like a stick
sinking and he will be lost and I watch his face, see the
question there, and he says,

What's he talking about, Mitch?

I reach across the chasm between us, connect again to
his skin, feel the softness of morning innocence because
each time he rises, Squeaky is reborn into the light and I say,

Martin and I are working on a deal, Squeaky.

I had another dream, Mitch. You were teaching me how
to write but I couldn't figure out what hand to hold the
pencil in and then it kind of explodes and this gooey black
stuff sticks to my face.

It's okay, Squeaky, there's nothing to it.

I'm hungry, Mitch.

He steps onto the gray mirror of the pit and his pure white feet glide over it like an angel walking on water. He pulls on his white sneakers, now stained black, the dirt and crusted trash of life sticking to the once pure canvas and his feet disappear into the holes. He is still alive, still clean, still wearing the necklace of dried ears, trophies of his ordeal I delivered to him and I stand, realize that for the first time in days I haven't watched the skins in D Block rise out of their black dreams, haven't watched the snakes and skulls and tormented trees twist in their morning light and for a moment I'm afraid I might have crossed some river of hope or been born into the same matutinal purity that Squeaky awakens to but then I hear the voices of the guards, hear wood on steel clanging the killers out of their coffins and I know that nothing has changed. The bleak and black truth still holds me in thrall.

100.

In the spring the light slices in at an angle, a blade carving away the edge of darkness leaking like blood from a wound. The dawn light turns from pale pink to Chinese crimson as the sun shifts itself, tipping into the cell where I lie on my side tracking the shaft of light through the thick dust-gray glass, through the webbing where invisible spiders, trapped by their hunger, feed on the scum of night, wings caught in the webs decaying into slender threads, shattered by wind and time. Light cuts through the dust, through the putrid air of the cell filled with the sweaty stench of trapped bodies, animals in a cage unfit for life beyond in full sun, unfit for anything but the driving ritual of rise and eat, eat and shit, shit and sweat, sweat and sleep. Light bridges the abyss between Squeaky's bunk and mine and the light spreads on his face, clearing away the crust of night clinging to his skin and he sits up, swings his feet to

the floor and in the beam of light I see him pure and clean
and true and he grins. He says,

Hey Mitch, you sleep okay?

No, I had bad dreams again.

He yawns, stretches. The white T-shirt tightens over his
pathetic pecs. I look away as the rumble of morning ratchets
up to full speed. The guards rattle their nightsticks on the
bars, spout their cruel grunts of Assholes, grub in five, hit
the deck you perverts.

Martin is working his way down C Block, his club
clanging on cages. At our bars he stops, presses his face to
the blue steel and he grins, his yellowed teeth gaping in the
center as if some absent-minded dentist has pried open the
space, turning him into a clown. But Martin is no clown and
he doesn't shout his morning greeting of Hey assholes, grub
in five, instead he leers at me and he whispers,

Mitchell, you got a visitor already.

Martin, I haven't had my oatmeal and toast yet.

He rattles the bars and he says,

If I have to come in there and roust you out, I'll shove
this nightstick so far up your ass your tongue will shake
hands with your nuts.

Now, Marty, that doesn't make a lot of sense,
anatomically, you know.

What're you talking about?

Aw, Marty, loving you is so much fun.

He stiffens, raps the nightstick in the palm of his left
hand and he says,

Let's go, Mitchell.

I swing off my bunk, look at Squeaky, his face lined with
worry and I say,

Don't go to chow without me, Squeaks.

The grate slides open and Martin steps back, the
nightstick tapping the palm of his left hand, and I march
ahead of him, listen to the thud of boots on the steel mesh,
listen to the growl and grumble of the tattoos in D Block

rousing themselves like ancient bears clawing their way out
of a winter's sleep.

Down the stairs, down the corridor, past the wire glass
of the visitor's room, down to a solitary unit with a steel
door. I stop. Martin behind me grinds to a halt and I say,

What is this? You said I had a visitor.

He says,

I do what I'm told, now in with you.

He opens the steel door and I step into a sharp harsh
light, an interrogation lamp, and I blink. When my eyes
clear, I see a hulk in the glare of the lamp and the door closes
with its heavy steel thud and I wait for the slap of wood on
my skull, wait for the fist, the crushing hammer hard fist,
but then the hulk in the lamp shifts and I track him, ready
for anything, understanding nothing, expecting anything.

101.

He is over six feet tall and he is broad in the shoulders,
thick in the chest, but narrow of waist and hips. He stands
legs apart, legs thick as trees. I look again at his face and I
shudder because I am looking at a copy of myself when I was
still human—before my shaven head, before tattoos, before
6s and shamrocks were inked into my arms.

Two chairs in the solitary cell, a table, and he, my mirror
younger self, sits. He looks up at me and I see the eyes, like
photos of eyes I remember, the eyes of my father, the chin of
my father, the hairline with its strong V shape like my
father's, and standing still. I say,

Who are you?

You're Henry Emmett Mitchell?

You know who I am or I wouldn't be here.

He clasps his hands on the table, hands I've seen every
morning on waking, hands that have held the knife and the
razor, hands like ghosts. He says,

I'm your brother.

My heart hammers and the blood coursing through my veins tries to eat its way out into the room. I stumble into the chair on my side of the table, shift it in the light, sit down hard and, seated, I look at him. He smiles. I see my father in the smile, the teeth, the chin, my father. I say,

Well, fuck me blind.

You even sound like me, he says.

What do you want?

I don't want anything beyond seeing you.

I study him like he's an insect on a pith board. He says,

Our old man was one busy son of a bitch, Henry.

Our old man?

I was born In Bramwell when the Company was still running.

Who's your mother?

My mother worked for the Company. He fucked her in the back seat of his BMW.

One of those. Do you have a name?

He pulls an envelope from the inside pocket of his blue suit jacket. He opens it. He unfolds a birth certificate and a set of photos. I read the name on the certificate. I see my father's name and the name of the mother and I see that his first name is Edward but his last name is Coddington.

Coddington? Your mother's name?

Couldn't take the old man's name.

What do you want, Edward?

He looks at me for a long time. This time I'm the insect and he's the man with the pin about to gore me and then he takes a deep breath. He says,

I found Geraldine. She told me you were here. I know a lot about you.

You didn't come for a family visit.

I need to know something.

What do you need to know?

He narrows his eyes the way I've seen my father narrow his before he pulled words from his dark place.

I need to know if I'm alone.

What does that mean?

Why are you in here, Henry?

You don't need to know that.

Sometimes I feel the urge to kill. It's like this white spot centers itself between my eyes. It won't go away.

What have you done, Edward?

It's not what I've done, it's what I want to do.

I sit back in my chair, look at him. He looks fit, strong, solid, powerful.

Did he train you? Did he give you boxing lessons and teach you to fence? Did he teach you to use the bow and the knife, Edward?

Edward looks down at his hands on the table. For a long time he looks at his hands and then he says,

I feel like I'm missing a piece, but I don't know how to fill it in.

I lean forward, smell the cologne on his skin, smell the Mitchell in him attach itself to my nostrils with its small death-hooks. I say,

Blood makes the white spot disappear, Edward. Blood releases you from the bad dreams of immortality. With blood you're in the present forever and eternity.

He sits rocking back and forth on his chair and the shadow of his head bobs across the table and, looking at his hands, he says,

I thought that was it. I have dreams that scare the shit out of me. I wake up sweaty with the taste of gunpowder in my mouth and the scent of blood in my nose and when I wash I expect to see stains in the water.

I watch his hands splay on the table in the solitary cell, like dead animals, the nails manicured, perfect, clipped short, compulsive, obsessive, careful. My hands are the same hands. He raises his eyes to mine, his eyes drooping sad and afraid, questioning and afraid, and he says,

Does it bother you that I came to see you?

No, it doesn't bother me. I need to know more about you.

Are you going to say something about my dreams?

What do you want from me, Edward?

I need to know, he says, if you have this feeling in your gut that you're meant to taste blood.

To taste it? I say. Are you a vampire?

You know what I mean.

He closes his eyes and purses his lips tight and white, and the hands on the table crack as he presses the palms into the hard wood. I say,

You think you've got it too.

Our father talked about killing, Henry, he talked about it all the time. He was hard on me, rode me hard, made me sweat, told me I had to learn to defend myself. He taught me to shoot a rifle. He bought me a 9MM Taurus when I was twelve.

He never bought me a pistol. He said the knife was better.

Oh yes, Edward says, he had killed men with a knife.

He told me he had killed twenty-two men.

Edward blinks. I scan his face. He doesn't look away. I see the placid demeanor of a man at peace. He says,

We're just like Dad.

He lifts those hands from the table and he clasps them together the way I remember our father clasping his and I see the tilt of his shoulders the way our father tilted his and the slope of his back is the same as our father.

So, now tell me why you're here, Henry.

For stealing women's underwear.

Come on. You look like me. You look like our father. Why are you here?

He laughs. It is, no doubt, the first time laughter has ever fallen in this room with its cold concrete walls.

I have to go now, Edward, my cellmate can't go to chow without me.

Before you go, just tell me—how do you handle it? Do you see death as your calling? Murder as your god, blood as your salvation?

I feel like he's inside my brain, tasting the blood I've tasted, feeling the blade slide into flesh, watching the spout of death gush into the sky. I say,

Go talk to Catharin. She's Our Holy Sister and Saint of the Resurrection.

It wasn't a dream, Edward says. I had to wash the blood from my hands. What's it like in here?

Edward, I fuck men in here. I fuck men because I like to. That's all you need to know about me.

I feel the cold steel of the chair against my back. He says,

I've spilled blood and I've felt flesh yield to a knife and I liked it but I knew I wasn't supposed to like it. I was supposed to feel anguish and remorse and guilt, but I didn't. In fact, just the opposite. He trained me to do this without ever saying it was what he was doing. It felt good. This is what I was meant to do.

I look at him. I see the square jaw of our father, the teeth in the same mouth and the force in the jaw and I feel kin in Edward. I say,

They worship the wrong god, Edward. Your conversion puts you in a holy place right now.

I stand back from the table, the steel chair slides under my hands. I say,

Have you been cut?

Cut? How do you mean cut?

A vasectomy?

No. No one touches me.

Good. You have a duty to death, my brother. I thought the gift was dead, but no. I see you have it so it's up to you to pass it on.

Pass what on?

The bent for blood, the taste of sliced flesh. Don't let them cut you, Edward. The demons you have gestating inside you are the angels of death. You and I are born to this.

Are you mad, Henry?

Never more lucid.

And that's why you're here?

Not for what I am, not even for what I did.

Why are you here then?

I'm here because what I want is here.

I knock on the door of the cell, call Martin who lets me out into the corridor, into the half light and as we walk, he says,

Guy looks a lot like you, Mitchell.

He's my brother, Martin.

Up the stairs ringing with the clank of shoe on steel, up to the top tier of C Block there is no talk until Martin locks me in. He says,

I didn't know you had a brother, Mitchell.

Neither did I. Are you ready, Martin? You look ready.

Ready for what?

To taste real blood.

He looks at his feet, wrinkles his nose. It's like a window opening into bright sunlight. I see the changes in him. The bent, decrepit soul straightens out like an angel unfolding its wings as it emerges from its gestational womb, the moral decay of his sawdust soul turning to solid wood again. I say,

I see that you're ready for the big leagues, Martin.

The big leagues.

She's waiting.

He looks at me, his eyes gleaming and in the glint of light. I see a silver streak like the cutting edge of a new blade and then he blinks and he nods and I think I hear him mutter a word and the word is Okay.

I look at Squeaky sitting on the edge of his bunk and I can see that something is wrong.

What's the deal, Squeaky?

He looks at me, his big wide eyes innocent and open and wet with tears.

I think I'm going to kill myself, Mitch. I been reading all those stories you told me to read by that Russian guy Chekhov and if I have to read another one I'm going to have to kill myself.

You don't have to read that guy if it makes you feel suicidal.

Then why did you make me read them?

You have to know what not to do.

Nothing happens in that guy's stories, Mitch, nothing, just like nothing happens in here and to tell the truth, Mitch, I'd rather read Darwin than any more of that Russian.

I sit beside Squeaky.

Tomorrow we'll go to the library and we'll gut Chekhov, how's that?

You're just trying to make me feel good, Mitch.

You always make me feel good, Squeaky, so I want you to feel good.

How come you come back feeling good?

Because my brother is going to have a thousand kids and every one of them is going to be like me and my brother and we're the solution to the problem, Squeaky.

I don't get it, Mitch. Can your brother get rid of Chekhov?

He can't, but he's ... well, Squeaky, you know how you don't like it when I read about blood to you?

Yeah, it makes me nervous.

The future is blood, Squeaky. The future is a river of blood and I am the God of Blood and my brother is my Disciple.

Just as long as I don't gotta read any more of that guy Chekhov.

I put my arm around him, feel his scrawny shoulders, smell his sweat and the faint odor of semen wafting up from his crotch. I say,

Were you jerking off, Squeaky?

He nods. Slumps against me.

It's okay. It's good. Get these little homunculi out of your system.

What's homunculi, Mitch?

Little Squeakies, I say. Miniature Squeakies swimming upstream in the river of death.

102.

In the library, in the gray light of no light, in the death gray light of pseudo-night I pry the seal from the envelope, glance at the bold clean letters etched into the sky blue paper of the envelope. It is heavy, the letter, with its single stamp the color of a blood-red sunset, obtuse color crippling the robin's egg blue of the envelope, butchering the bright pink neon ink. I breathe, sit back, watch the envelope where, in the upper left-hand corner rests the return address in its bold pink flowing like a blood river. I can't pull the pages from their blue coffin because I know that the corpse inside will reek of decay and the putrefaction of fornication and I fold the flap of the blue envelope back, spread it like the legs of a whorish slut spreading her stagnant swamp of a cunt to the rays of the death-gray light. I shake out the letter, watch it fall, flutter to the table where it splays open and in the gray light of the folded page, I see the words ... Dear Henry ... words pink as the inside of a woman's mouth against the pale blue paper and without reading, without letting the words leach into my brain, I type her words onto the screen. The computer screen with its pale yellow letters lets me transfer her words onto a solid page and I need that because I don't want to be seduced by her pain.

I know that if I read the words on the screen, if I then print them out, turn the neon pink to yellow and then to black and white, I will escape the anguish that shoves itself into the space between the words. The letter is longer than the first one, longer than the second, it is the length of a hangman's rope. In a fit, I finish typing, take a deep breath just as Squeaky emerges from the stacks, stumbles in the gray light of no light and says,

Hey Mitch, you paying the electricity now?

I take his hand, pull him down to me, feel his tightness, his softness, the stiffness of his erection and I smell the soap on his skin and the perfume of his sweat. He says,

Whatcha readin'?

Catharin sent another letter.

Saint Catharin. Mitch, if she's a saint and she's your sister, then you gotta be a saint too, right?

I'm not reading it, Squeaky.

But you can type it? Shit, Mitch, that's a miracle.

I hit the print button on the computer and the pages spill out like black-stained splashes of semen pouring onto the table beside the blue and pink and splayed pages of Catharin's letter. I catch words, black words etched onto pure white untainted by feeling or pain, clear of anguish, empty of emotion and I read ... suicide, blood, hideous way to die.

I pick Squeaky up like a china doll, set him on the edge of the table, a curious child watching the horrid truth of life spin past him and I gather up the spilled and sticky pages, wet with ink, smelling of sex and the open wounds of perversion and I read them, fast, faster, without having to witness the gouges and rips as the pen wormed its way under the skin of blue and the words are horrific ... my baby died or maybe Carl killed him or maybe Geraldine smothered it or maybe I poisoned it with the toxic milk of my sin swollen breasts, Henry ... Even from the printed page her pain pulls me into the roil of death. I scan the words zipping past almost blurring in their speed ... I've tried the razor but blood frightens me, Henry. He has his weapons although I doubt I could do that and so now I'm on a quest for poison because I have to die. I have to die because even in my post-partum blood, he takes me, ties me to the bed, spreads me like a sacrifice and I expect him to cut my heart out, to eat it, but he uses me like his slut while Geraldine, poor Geraldine, has to watch, Henry …

Squeaky says, Mitch, Mitch? Hey Mitch? What's she saying?

I look at him. My hand holding the printed pages quivers, shakes, trembles and my breath, ragged and putrid rots the air and Squeaky lays his hand on my shaking arm.

I shake his hand away, bunch up the printed pages and the envelope and the blue sheets with their pale bloody pink ink and I stuff them all into a folder and I raid the stacks, my legs quaking and I pull out the book of English roses and as I free it from its grave, the folder with my manuscript breaks free and falls, scattering the splotched pages like scabs into the half light of no light and Squeaky, behind me, tries to keep the still falling pages from complete chaos. But it is too late, the manuscript hits the floor, slithers out, ants running, rats skittering, snakes squirming away and I feel a sudden harsh sharpness in my chest like a knife has slid between my ribs and I stumble, lurch forward the way I have seen men lurch when a bullet slams into the backs of their heads and I am dead, my work splattered like blood in a whirlwind and I kneel, knowing I'll never get it back into a single form. Never.

103.

It is gray, the light seeping through the dusty window gritty on the outside, slick with the exhalations of a thousand men on the inside and I'm afraid to wipe at the glass, afraid that if I smear the grease and the dust, the glass will crack, leak in the poisonous air from outside with its stench of blood and the raw sewage of six billion bodies shitting their guts out in prayer to a dogwood-mounted Jesus whose rotten semen has yet been proven to save a single soul. I know the slippery knot of living is a Moebius strip with its blood soaked outside twisting into its semen slick inside, an endless race to extinction. I see the day when the blood rises up to the windows, the day when the plague-sick ocean of bodies stacks up to the rooftop, and I ask who will call chowtime for Squeaky? Who will dare to open the gates of the only sanctuary possible and spill us back out there into the hell of sperm and ovum and placental afterbirth? We will die in here. When they are all dead, we can lie down in peace.

I look at the neon-pink adolescent girlish writing of Catharin's fourth letter. The script has changed. The zeroes over the Is are smaller and tighter and the angle of the crossed Ts is more acute. I read these little changes, small glimpses into her mind as if she were standing in front of me talking to me about her anxiety. On the pages the pain still spreads like a broken bottle of poison and I see Catharin in her Holy Jesus Save The World Mode dipping her finger into the pus and blood-filled font in the Cathedral of Notre Dame de Paris. I ask myself why she has fallen back into the blood of that sickness, back into the fever of the Rhapsody and I read, in the gray light ...

Henry, I have found him again. I have rediscovered the purity of my faith on my back under Carl's sweaty body, tormentous, yes, but revealing, Henry, because in the torture he inflicts on me, I see the saintliness of pain and I understand that my captivity was a test of my faith ...

This is a letter I will not type into history because it disgusts me to see my sister again on her knees in the expectation of another miracle. She is the mystical one who, kneeling on the grass at Stonehenge, felt the warmth of the finger of Jesus Christ, the savage Redeemer transformed into a Druidic Jesus of Contradictions, the Jesus of the Slaughtered Priestesses, the Jesus of Blood and War masquerading as Hope and Water. Catharin alone, perverted in her faith, could betray her name—the martyrs of Montségur—Catharin alone could find redemption and salvation on her back with Carl Fairweather in her.

I fold her letter in quarters, look for a match to burn it
in fire, in blood, but then, the door opens and Martin enters
the library and he looks calm, peaceful, a sailor returning
from a journey in the turbulent sea of semen and blood.

I notice that he wears new boots and his khaki uniform
is crisp and clean and pressed, its creases like the blades of
swords and he smiles and his face is open, his eyes bright.
He closes the door, leans into it, his hands behind his back
and he says,

Where's Squeaky?

He's in the stacks with Faulkner.

There's three of you in here now?

Faulkner's a writer.

How'd he get in here?

It's okay. He's dead.

Martin glides from the door to the table where I sit
holding Catharin's quartered letter in my hand. He leans
down to face me, his mouth inches from my ear and I smell
his breath and it is fresh and clean and minty and I smell his
body under the smart odor of antiperspirant and he takes a
deep breath. He whispers,

I did it, Mitchell. Ask me how.

I don't need to know.

I found him in his study. It's a nice house, Mitchell, the
kind of house a man could live in for a long time and be
comfortable in, a real nice house. I used twenty-gauge wire
with wooden handles on the ends.

A garrote.

Cut his fucking head almost off.

Martin glances at his hands and I see the nails are clean,
trimmed, glassy with clear enamel. I say,

Did you wash your hands?

Oh yeah.

And you had a manicure, Martin.

Got some blood under the nails.

I'm glad you had a manicure. I'm glad you washed your hands.

I liked it, Mitchell. I didn't think I could do it, but I didn't just do it, I liked it. I can't believe how easy it was.

Geraldine?

What about Geraldine?

He smiles. It is an innocent smile, the clear open smile of a man who has reamed out the clogs in his soul to undam his spirit and he says,

You want to know if I fucked your sister, Mitchell?

Did you?

He glances at his hands again and then he says,

No.

Why not?

He takes another deep breath and he says,

Because I came when I felt him die, Mitchell.

The burden on my shoulders is lighter now, it has become feathery and I take a deep breath, measure it out in little exhalations and it feels as if I have given birth to God, as if I have felt the warm finger of the Watery Jesus on my forehead, as if I have felt the breath of Moses the Murderer on the back of my neck, as if I have smelled the odor of Mohammed the Malignant because I am more powerful than those liars. I have redeemed Martin, brought him back from the dead, given him a reason to hold the blade, raised him out of his nothingness to live in the clear light of the knife and the garrote and the bullet. I look at him and see a new man proud of his rebirth, proud that he has fucked the True Mistress called Death and found her orgasm to be earth-shaking everlasting. I say,

Catharin?

The Saint?

Yes, the Saint.

Was she there? Did she see you?

No, Mitchell, you don't have to worry. And you don't owe me nothing. I owe you because before you showed me the way I gotta admit I was lost.

He smiles. He turns. I watch him leave and now I see the winged back of a disciple of death—striding sure and straight and for a moment I am a god reshaping the blunted edge of humanity into a machete. It is a good change.

I unfold Catharin's letter, open it, looking for a sign, but there is nothing in the ink or in the pain, nothing, and then I read between the lines and I see that Carl Fairweather was her Jesus of Blood and Meat, her Savior. Martin, Saint Martin of the Wire is her double, the one who kills so that others can be saved. I smile, sit back, feel the cold steel of the chair. Then Squeaky emerges from the stacks and he stands in a shaft of bright light that rains down over him and in the light he shimmers and I expect to see him levitate, rise up into the beam of light but instead he says,

This Faulkner guy is weird, Mitch. He's got a guy doing this babe with a corn cob. Can you believe it? Are you hungry?

Did you finish dusting the Fs?

You know there's a whole lot of titles that start with F, I mean a whole lot, but you know, Mitch, not one of them Fs got read? You know? Can you believe it? All the Fs is Virgins, Mitch.

Just like you, Squeaky.

Yeah Mitch, just like me.

104.

In the dark, in the deep dark, in the cold deep dark I hear the hard breathing of men in mid-dream waking to the blood of their sins, waking out of the dark stream of their misdeeds, awake begging for light and love but they have sold their souls and in here the quiet of the dark is a reminder of their future and what they have done and I am one of them. In the dark quiet of the night I listen to

Squeaky's labored breathing, the asthmatic, phlegm-charged death rattle of a tubercular in last agony and I expect the shower of blood to spew out, like red foil shattering the darkness, sticking to me to the bunk to the bars to the floor. As if in a divine reprieve Squeaky rolls onto his side and I hear him groan his nocturnal pain, the wincing wail of a wounded animal and then he falls quiet and in the muffling dark, I hear the howl of a man caged in steel and concrete and then he too falls back into his own shadow swallowed by the immensity of his crimes and in the quiet I remember a day in the Quito as I waited in the shadows, waited, my heart beating slow like a clock as I measured out the last minutes of a life.

I remember how he came out of the doorway in a crisp clean shaft of yellow light and I saw his face for the first time. He was a sallow-skinned man with black hair and black moustache, dressed in a gray suit cut crisp and clean and as the driver of the Ford opened the door, I stepped out of the dark and quiet doorway. No sound. In that moment before blood flowed there was always an absolute eternity of silence and then the hammer fell twice and the man in the well-cut suit spun in the dark and still and quiet night, his back dotted with twin holes. And then the driver crouched like a wounded stag and then his head opened up in a dawn blossoming. I closed on my prey, fired the coup de grâce and then turning I walked away, back into the dark and quiet and at the corner I saw the first blood red wrinkle of dawn in the clear Quiteño air. At the equator, dawn explodes at breakneck speed, spills its rosy red streamer into the eyes, blinding and cutting and severing all ties to the now dead night. I lifted the dark glasses from my shirt pocket, placed them on my nose and I was once again invisible.

I hear Squeaky's bark, his bird chirp, his song of three AM as he squirms awake and in the darkness, in the dark and quiet grave-like quiet of our cell, he whispers,

Hey Mitch, Mitch, you awake Mitch?

Yeah, I'm awake.

Can I come over, Mitch? Can I?

I roll onto my side and I feel him slide beside me and he whispers,

Mitch, I just had the craziest dream and it scared the hell outa me.

Tell me about it, Squeaky.

He takes a deep breath. I hear the phlegm in his throat, hear the rattle in his lungs, and he says,

It was about blood, Mitch. I don't like to dream about blood, but it was everywhere and I was swimming in a river of blood and my mouth was full of it and I was drowning and there was no one to save me.

I wrap Squeaky in my arms, feel his soft flesh under the white T-shirt, the scrawny flesh, the soft and white and untainted flesh and I say,

You been with me too long, Squeaky, you've got my disease.

I feel him tense against me, his back hardened and I squeeze him. I want to crack that hardness open, peel off the carapace of his insect shell and release the predator in it. He says,

What am I gonna do, Mitch?

What you've been doing.

I don't wanna go back out there. I like it in here with you.

Even if you now have blood dreams?

I don't care. I just don't wanna go back out there.

And then, as he does when he has confessed, he falls asleep and his body goes limp and his breath evens out and I feel his heat against me, and then somehow, without wanting it, I fall asleep and when I hear the rattle of nightsticks on steel and I jerk awake and I see the streaks of sunlight raking across the concrete floor. I feel the threat of having been asleep, vulnerable, alone in the dark, a body of prey, and I hear the voice calling,

Okay assholes, come alive, drop your cocks, grab your socks, grub in five.

Squeaky rolls off the bunk, stands rubbing his eyes. I stand, walk to the bars, look at D Block where the tattoos rise out of their somnolent hell, out of the nocturnal resurrection of their sins and crimes, rising once again to face the days of regret and lament. The rattle of the nightstick stops at the grate of my cell and a face peers at me, a new face, a shining new face with thin peach fuzz on the lip and dark skin and black and innocent eyes and I say,

Where's Martin?

Motherfucker's dead, can you believe it?

What?

He turns aside, but I reach out and he pulls away, he says through clenched teeth,

Keep your perverted hands off me.

What happened to Martin?

Bastard capped some dude and I hear he got his ass shot for doing it.

I fall back into the blood-red rays of the sun and I feel my breath aching in my chest. Already a lost disciple. But he had no discipline. I didn't have time to train him right. I turn to Squeaky, who stands at attention, tense, tight and I look at him and he says,

Jeez Mitch. Ol' Martin killed some guy? I dint think he had the balls to kill some guy, did you?

105.

Touching his skin in the dark there is no difference between the soft perfumed skin of a woman and the hungry deliberate skin of a man. In the dark, skin is skin, the integument between blood and sensation.

Reducing him sometimes to a sack of bones makes me feel powerful and real, makes me remember how glass-like the skin is when it cracks—at first a line of red as the skin parts under the blade then splitting open the skin reveals its

measure of life and out it spills and you see the line between
life and hate, between love and jealousy.

Sometimes in the dark he moans and his voice, high and
tight, is all of the voices I've heard crying out for any number
of reasons—the whore in her lie, the young girl in her
orgasm, the butchered woman in her pain—guts tumbling
into the chalk white sand of a paradisiacal beach.

He stiffens. His thighs harden. His back arches against
me and I run my fingers up the spine, feel the tight muscles,
hands of a death-dealing masseur on the knotted hatred of a
body and I can't contain my loathing for the desire that owns
me, even as I thrust into him. I hate him for arousing me,
hate myself for my weakness, hate myself for having been
born into the turgidity of manhood, tasting mother's milk,
eating her body.

I do not remember the swell of her breast in my
mouth—was I born to wolves and raised by humans? I know
that she fed me her body every day, a hundred times a day if
needed, and she didn't know that my teeth had already
formed, my fangs had already emerged.

I feel the knots of his tension, my hands inches away
from releasing Squeaky into the night, into death, freeing
him from his own slavery, but for some reason I do not and
that reason is no reason—at this point, it is all automatic,
either/or, beyond reason just as the urge to spill seed in a
womb is beyond reason, but driven. It is the utter fear of
emptiness that too was born into my flesh by my being born
into the world through no asking of my own—no little
homunculus in my father's vas deferens begging to be
released from non-being. I again sense how easy death
comes to us—if I press there, just at the base of the neck,
ram a finger into the skin, I'll feel it tear deep, rupture the
artery. So easy. As easy as life giving. Anyone can do it,
anyone can fuck a woman, any woman can bear a child. It
takes will to refrain. Refraining is a contradiction in the logic
of semen and ovum that screams do it do it do it—and the

result is me—a monster buried ten inches in the flesh of the bone sack under me. He disgusts me. I disgust myself.

I yield to the urge that has driven us from the night into the light and he rears up, he mutters, his voice the squeaky orgasmic voice of a slut on his belly and I feel the sudden slickness of his skin, the sweaty slickness of his desire and I press my thumbs into the back of his neck, feel the throb of blood and heartbeat, feel the pulse of life under my fingertips and then he cries out, a little whimper, the whispery whimper of a child waking from night terrors and he goes limp, he dies that curious unconscious moment when life yields to death—la petite mort—the moment of blackness when the body bursts its stranglehold on life.

The man orgasms. Shoots his semen loaded with death into the nighttime sheets of a prison bed and he says,

Mitch, oh God, Mitch, I never knew it could feel like that.

I place my hands on his hips, feel the inevitable bursting of my own infertile milk into him, that one truth of mine. There will be no more of me after this cloud is eaten by the winds of death. I hold back. Wait for my own ungodly second of blackness. My own second of the divine knot between being and not being, that one second of death in life—that I want to extend, to expand the way the universe expands to infinity—and I know that I am an angel of death with bloody wings and red-painted nails and fangs like six inch spikes put here to slaughter and slaughter until there are no more of us. I hold back, still feel him under me yielding, waiting in his tenderness as though he expects me to stroke him, but he knows he owns me because of desire and lust and still I hold back, not wanting to give him the satisfaction of his certainty that I will not kill him because he is safe, his body a well where I dive like a seabird into the swelling, a lake where I wash away desire, leaving me simple, animal flesh and bone once more. He whispers,

Come on, Mitch, come on, come in me.

I flood into him, hate him for understanding me, for knowing me, for making me love his small ass, his tight mouth, love his human body because we fit, we mesh, we are one and the same all of us and I hate that and I lie against him, feel his sweaty skin. That thin land of desire where twin continents of bodies collide, slide, slip, convulse like the plates of earth crashing together to build mountains.

He whispers,

It's okay, Mitch. It's okay.

I break as I have broken every time and my breath, ragged as the claws of a crab, gushes from me just as my own sterile semen gushes into him and he whispers,

That's good, Mitch, oh God, that's good.

I hate him, hate myself, hate the force that turns me into a gushing fool, needy fool, human fucking machine.

In the gray light, in the gray prison light, in the stone and steel prison holding my heart in place, I separate from him, kneel looking down at his gray shadow sprawled on the gray woolen blanket and I see the sparkles of sweat on his skin. He says,

I like it when you hurt me, Mitch, I like it a lot.

Disgust driving me now, I get up, feel my cock's sudden limpness—bled clean of desire—and I return to me, return to the flesh of my own body and the skin of my own belly and the hardness of muscle. But I am empty.

106.

My manuscript is now hidden high up on the shelf between a handbook on Dutch Iris and Genet's *Notre Dame des Fleurs*. Thicker than a telephone book, its dirty gray binding looks sick. I stand on the library stool, pull it out, sense its heft, its weight, its gravity. Holding it like a Templar holding the Grail, I carry it to the table where the computer sits with its green face blinking at me. I set the manuscript down, it lands with a satisfying thump. Heavy. Thick. Solid.

I open the cover, look at my title page. It's been two months since I wrote a word. Two months without any effort to type up the translucent pages spoiled by red ink, blue ink, onion skin scabbed with clots of ink like blemishes on an ivory pale skin. In here, everything is scarred and wounded, even the paper you write on.

And now I'll never finish it.

I separate the typed pages from the autograph pages. Separate the onion skin from the back pages of the books I butchered for paper. Separate the red ink pages from the blue ink pages. Isolate the typewritten sections from the computer printed one. The clumps are fingers of time marking the passage from the early scribbling through the stolen ink pens from Geraldine down to the typewritten pages ending in the mechanical uniformity of the computer script. I set each of them in its own stack.

Four thousand pages. Enough to make me famous, enough to put me in the company of Genet and the Marquis, more than enough to make me a companion to Camus, enough to launch me into a universe different from the Belly of the Beast. Four thousand pages. A shelf of pages. Eighteen inches thick. As thick as an encyclopedia. I'll never have time to rework it.

Squeaky sits at his library table reading. I study him over the top of the computer screen. I see his boyish face, his forehead unwrinkled as if the pages he reads cause him no consternation. He reads *War and Peace* as though it were a comic book. *Moby Dick* as though it were a Sunday supplement to a newspaper. He reads the *Structural Study of Myth* with no more effort than he would use reading a want ad in a singles newspaper—SWF seeking fun-loving, sun-loving non-geek for afternoon walks on the beach. And none of it sticks to his brain, none of it rubs off on him, none of it changes him. He is untainted by his reading. He will be as pure and simple coming out of *Death in Venice* as he was going in. He is purity itself—cut, tattooed, raped, beaten but still pure and holy. In his purity he is a paragon of patience and emptiness, his mouth a paean to perfection, his buttocks as delicious as the mouth of the Nubian in the Song of Solomon. The purity of the rose. He is the model prisoner.

I watch him. I clear my throat. He looks up. I say,

Squeaky, listen to me.

His blue eyes are clear as they change focus from War and Peace to me. He says,

Yeah Mitch?

His eyelashes blink, his mouth half-open. In that second, time stops. I hold my breath the way Saint Teresa of Avila must have held her breath when first she saw her bleeding Jesus in an erotic vision, the ecstasy not yet rushing to her loins, the beauty of union not yet possible in that wet moment of exquisite eternity between lust and devotion as she held her ground before sliding into immortality, crossing the boundary between human and divine, mating with her lord God Jesus, coming to the taste of his tongue in her mouth the way Leda, raped by the Swan, tasted her god as a stiff prick melding forever the human and animal into a single being.

Squeaky rises from his wooden chair, his blond hair electric in the halo of light and he glides to my side and he stands beside me and I smell his body the way Saint John of the Cross must have smelled the incense of tapers in his dark night before emerging into the light of God. I say,

Squeaky, I need a favor.

Whatever you need, Mitch. I'm your slave.

Can you type?

I seen you do it, but I don't know maybe I can. I never tried. Why?

I look at him. Smell the odor of prison soap, the faint scent of semen still on his body. I take a deep breath. I say,

I need some help with this.

Sure Mitch. What do I do?

I open a sheet of the manuscript, one of the book back pages I cut from volumes on the shelves. It is smeared with blue ink in my scrawl. I say,

Can you read this?

Squeaky pulls away, stiffening. He says,

You're gonna let me read your book, Mitch?

I smile at him. Can't tell him I'm leaving the book in the library, abandoning it unfinished.

Well, you can write your own story if you want. Tack it onto what's here.

But you wrote it, Mitch. It's yours.

You can pick it up where I leave off.

I close the blue-ink pages, turn to the red-ink pages on onion skin. I say,

Here, read.

He bends over the table, studious, forehead furrowed. I watch the curve of his neck, the flow of his back down to his buttocks in their tight prison dungarees and then he stands back and he says,

This is about me, Mitch.

His eyes are wet, his mouth half open. He sucks in his breath.

This is about me in the hospital after those two guys fucked me and you killed'em and gave me their ears.

I did kill them, I say.

No one else knows it was you killed them, Mitch.

So you write your own version of the story, Squeaky.

You're going away ain'tcha, Mitch?

I touch his hand, the skin flushing pink. Standing, I gather up the pages of the manuscript, stack them up. It's now a huge stack of pages. Four thousand pages. Squeaky says,

I can't live in here without you.

I take the manuscript, replace it between the Dutch Iris and *Notre Dame des Fleurs* where it belongs with the other prison flowers, each with its own aroma, its own perfume, its own allure. And Squeaky retreats back to *War and Peace*. He looks at me over the thick finished pages of that masterpiece. He lowers his eyes and skims Tolstoi again.

107.

In the gray light, the smell of bodies rises up like a poisoned perfume, the sweat of men locked in horrid dreams full of blood and entrails and bloated corpses. I listen to the snorts and cries of men reliving their sins, raising again the knife to a young throat, plunging again the axe into the skull of a kneeling victim, twisting again the neck of a bug-eyed body already beyond sensation and as I listen to their involuntary atonements drifting between the steel bars of the cages like confessions, I do not envy them their sentimental attachment to a decayed morality because in death there can be no remorse. Death is the great relief, death, the common bond we can't escape.

Squeaky turns on his bunk, the scrape of steel on steel like a rusty rasp and I roll to my side, see him curled up, knees together in the birthing knot that he unravels in the morning when the tattoos awaken to once again don their masks of invulnerability—monsters aching to be human. I watch Squeaky and I am afraid because soon when the gates open and the sun rises and chow has been served, I will no longer be there to protect my little man.

I feel guilty—not a heavy guilt but a light guilt bordering more on indifference than guilt but still a feeling of shame because I will abandon Squeaky to the tattoos, the iron men who will prey on his slender body like hyenas gnawing at the meat and bones of a dik-dik kill. He knows nothing of my exodus and I can't tell him but he senses it the way a man who falls feels the last foot of his safety rope slip between his palms before he plunges into his abyss.

I turn away. He is a white flower about to be cast into brutal sun, no water, no stem, no root to anchor him. I know they will corner him, claim him like a prize bouquet at some ceremony.

I close my eyes. Carl Fairweather is dead. René is dead. Suki is dead. Martin is dead. I drift back half a day, see myself again in the Governor's office, the Governor behind his desk shaking his head and clucking his tongue. He said,

Mitchell, I've been behind this desk for twenty five years and you're the most enigmatic son of a bitch I've ever seen. Just who the hell are you?

A thief, sir.

Don't give me that crap.

He rattled a sheaf of papers, blue pages with red and white seals on them, official seals, the kinds of seals you see on Government documents or on classified tapes, the kinds of seals that lock up secrets for a lifetime, the kinds of seals whose keys have been thrown away. He said,

These bastards want you out, so out you go.

I shuffled my feet, coughed, tried to look humble. I said,

I told you already sir, I don't want to leave.

Look, damn it, your buddy Fairweather had pull but the son of a bitch behind this has a thousand ton come-along and the balls to make it work. So I'm telling you—this is the third time these papers have landed here and every time I've covered for you, but these bastards are power so you leave or I lose my job and I'm not losing my job.

I can still be useful to you, sir.

You've been useful to me, but from the looks of it you're more useful to the tycoons out there. So? You ever going to tell me just who in hell you are, Mitchell?

I have a suggestion, sir.

What's your suggestion?

Fake my death. Tell them a tattoo butchered me in the machine shop and you had to turn me into cat food.

I'll give you this, Mitchell, you have a sense of humor, but you're going to a judge in the morning. I'm sending a file that has nothing in it. When you stand in front of him, you'll be as pure as a snowflake in the Sierra. And you know what? That kind of juice says you ain't some two bit thief who's got a jones for women's underwear. Now get the fuck out of my office.

Sir, I said. There's nothing in my file?

Nothing.

Don't make me go back out there.

They've pulled the plug. You're out.

In the gray light of the corridor, I see shadows static and hard—gray permanent, eternal shadows that hang there year after year. Thin shadows of light cages, long thin shadows of bars and steel doors. I listen one last time to the snorts of men who will be in the same place next year and the year after.

And then, there is the clang of a night stick on steel and the call starts at the far end of the block.

Up and att'em, you lousy sons of bitches.

The guard, Perry, who replaced Martin, stands at my cell gate and he grins and he says,

Hey sleeping beauty, you want to get your animal butt up?

Perry, I say, fuck you.

Don't you wish. I heard about you, Mitchell. I heard all about your cutie in there—what's his name? Squeaky. Jesus, I like that. Squeaky.

He laughs and marches on down the corridor, his night stick banging. Squeaky stirs, relaxes his pre-natal coil and with a whistle of dark breath he sits up on the edge of his bunk, his eyes wide open, hands pressed palms down against the steel frame of his bunk and he says,

Mitch? Did I miss chow? Huh?

No, Perry just rolled by. You hungry?

I'm always hungry, Mitch. You think it'll be pancakes?

No, I think it'll be steak and eggs, Squeaky.

We deserve steak and eggs, huh Mitch?

Yeah, we do.

You okay?

What do you mean, am I okay?

You been real quiet, Mitch, and you know when you get quiet it scares me.

I got a lot on my mind, Squeaky.

You're leavin' aintcha, Mitch?

What?

I had a dream and you were gone.

I still got two years.

When you go, I'm gonna die, ain't I?

I'm not goin' anywhere.

I know you are, Mitch.

He stands. Faces me. He says,

Please don't leave me in here alone.

108.

The corridor looks dimmer than usual. My shoes creak less than usual. The air is thinner than usual. The smell of Lysol is less acrid than usual. Even the new guard, as cruel as the end of his nightstick, walks behind me without jabbing the butt into my kidneys.

The door to the visitor's room is open. It has never before been open. Always before the room had held a dozen men pressing their lovers for one last groping touch before returning to the cold sanctuary of steel.

Inside, the lights are low. I remember meeting Carl Fairweather in that same dim room—his Jean Vadé cologne, his Rolex encrusted with diamonds, the pale light casting shadows over his face, deepening the valleys of worry in his cheeks, the cliffs of anguish in the crags of his brow. But today, in the low light, I see Geraldine standing, back to me, her hair down to her shoulders glowing carbon black. Her waist, in a yellow dress, cinched with a black belt, accentuates her hips that flare inviting the eyes down to the buttocks curved and sheathed in yellow silk, down to her legs that shine like the scales of a wet fish, down to her small feet in red stiletto heels that tighten her calves and arch her back, thrusting out her pelvis as though she has just orgasmed.

She turns. Her face shines with pride and satisfaction. In her eyes, a bright confidence that has been missing for years. She closes in on me. I smell her perfume, a flowery scent fresh as a garden on a midsummer morning, and under the perfume, the half-sweaty odor of a woman clothed in a hurry. She rushes at me, arms around my neck, before the guard can say No touching. She pulls away. She looks at him with the fiery glare of an angry cat and she snarls,

Crawl back to your box little man.

Her voice crackles in an electronic monotone without cadence, without melody. It is a hard, static, unmodulated voice that sends chills up and down my spine. She clings to me, her hair smells of fresh shampoo and her body of a flower perfume that boils off her yellow dress like the scent of lilacs in bloom.

The guard, whose name I haven't bothered to read on his badge, wheels about as if he's been slapped and staggers out of the room and closes the door and stands back to the glass, arms behind him.

Geraldine relaxes, smiled at me and the glow in her face isn't just confidence but power like a dynamo under her skin drives the light inside her. I say,

You can speak now?

I've been able to speak for years, she says. They rebuilt me from the inside out. There's a computer buried in my chest. I'm more machine than woman. I came to thank you. Now there's nothing separating us, Henry.

She smiles. Her face, that, on her previous visits had been wrinkled with trouble and creased in worry now glows with that unnerving confidence. Her cheeks burn with the healthy rose impatience of a woman on the verge of losing her virginity.

She leans against the table in the center of the room where other men had confessed their crimes hoping for forgiveness from an inattentive god but willing to accept absolution from a woman with cherry red lips and smoldering black eyes. Geraldine's hips rest on the same table where those women, checking their Timexes, had spread their legs to take the hungry cocks of their men gasping for air as they came in the hurried rush of clothed clandestine copulation, panties thrust to one side before the guards pulled them away, separating them like copulating dogs, to drag them back to the steel and concrete cages where their lust bloomed in quiet solitary grunts. I say,

Move.

What?

That table's filthy, Gerry.

What's a little filth between us after all that's happened?

The filth will rub off on your dress.

You're worried about my dress?

But she slides away from the table, her yellow dress swishing around her thighs. She dusts her palms together, glances at the shiny steel surface. I watch the silk outline her legs. I glance at her face, at the eyes, the lips, the hair. She says,

I'm so glad to see you. So glad. Thank you.

Why would you lie to me? All those notebooks, the writing.

Tools, Henry. Tools, not lies.

Tools for what?

I needed you to do what you do so well.

I didn't do anything.

Well, Carl's dead and you're not and I'm free to run things the way I want to run them.

It's like she's slapped me in the face, rammed a fist into my throat. I float, dizzy, lightheaded and trembling. I turn my back to her, watch the guard fidget, rocking side to side, back and forth the way men with badges and pistols and roots in authority rock when they wait, men who've spent hours on their feet at perpetual attention. Geraldine touches my arm. Her fingers, hot as coals, send a shiver up my back. I say,

What will you be running the way you want to?

Everything I did was to get rid of Carl, that useless drone, that used up nothing of a man. The truth is that I knew you'd find a way that wouldn't blow back on me. Thank you for sending your man.

I didn't send anyone.

He came, she says. And he delivered us all from that worthless, toothless, gutless excuse for a man.

Geraldine. What's going on? Tell me the truth.

The truth, Henry?

In the dim light her yellow dress turns black and her black hair spreads like the black wings of a vulture and she isn't my sister, she isn't the wounded angel who begged me to save her, she isn't the pleading mother anxious for the safety of her children. She isn't the innocent and pure and clean tormented sister I knew. I'm empty. My head is fuzzy and I can't think straight and everything she says twists me up inside until my gut is knotted and I want to vomit. I say,

Martin is dead.

I know.

She turns to face me. Her eyes flicker yellow with fire and her mouth, wet, glistens with red like the blood of an eviscerated animal leaking from her lips.

How do you know?

Henry, Henry. You always were so simple. Always the little brother tagging along behind big sister, doing what you're told.

She laughs and the laughter is the screech of a vulture descending, tearing flesh, and I expect to see meat in her beak, meat in her talons. The death mask drips foulness from her blackened teeth. I say,

Catharin. What about Catharin? Her letters?

She covers her mouth with her claw. The nails, black, drip with pus. She says,

You poor thing. You believe everything you read?

I read her letters. She sent me letters.

Henry, Henry. You still don't see?

See? See? See what? I talked to Carl. He said she'd been living with you.

And then it comes clear just as she leans onto the table, claws spread out, talons yellow and sharp. She whispers,

Carl was a lunatic with his senate dreams. A deluded lunatic whose drug habit turned him into a zombie with maniacal paranoia. He would have destroyed everything, Henry. Don't you see?

Catharin isn't living with you?

Catharin is in India, Henry. She's saving Hindu souls from eternal transmigration.

But her letters.

I wrote them, sweetheart. I wrote them. They're pure fiction.

And then she leans close to me, her breath reeking of putrid fat and she whispers in that raspy, raucous croaking vulture voice,

She was never pregnant. She was never excommunicated. She was never abused. I know you, Henry. I know that if a maiden in distress calls, you'll come running like a dutiful puppy dog and you did and now it's over. I wanted to tell you, but I couldn't. Still, I want you to know all the good you've done because you are a saint.

Martin?

What about Martin?

Did you watch him do it?

Lord no. I was visiting ... a friend in Palm Springs.

He said you were there. I think. I think he said you were there.

I don't care what your man said, Henry.

Did you fuck him? Did you fuck him before or after he killed Carl?

If that was the price then I still owe him, but he'll never collect will he?

She smiles, shakes her head. The black water fall washes over her face, strands of black whip across her smiling mouth. She whispers,

Does it matter, Henry? Does it matter?

I look at her. At the face with its blooming confidence, the black eyes burning with control and power. Her claws change back into fingers heavy with diamond rings and nails painted red and I grasp her hand, her coal hot fingers. I want to strangle her. Want to squeeze her throat until her eyes pop, tear her tongue out, rip her to shreds, but she's my sister. I need an explanation. She rips free. I say,

You betrayed me.

I saved you.

How much did Carl leave you?

What?

Your future was paid for with the ears of dead men, Geraldine.

What has gotten into you, Henry?

Death, I say. Death has gotten into me.

You poor poor baby, she says. You still understand nothing. Don't you see? You're an angel of death and I have plans for us. I'll get you out of here—my man is arranging it already. You'll get a call in a while and he'll pick you up. Oh, there is so much we can accomplish, Henry. So much yet to do.

The guard turns to face me through the glass. He raps on the window with his nightstick and points at his watch. I shudder.

It won't be long, my darling, she says. In a few days you'll walk out of here into a bright new world where you'll make such a splash.

She shakes her head, her hair shatters in the light, a shower of diamonds that, if I caught them, would make a necklace.

109.

In the quiet gray of the cell, holding the pages, I could be a tenor sight-reading an oratorio, a soloist in a piano recital, the excitement of the pages, of the words on the pages, of the letters of the words on the pages, the excitement of not knowing what comes next, that takes the breath away. Squeaky lies silent, hands behind his head, listening as I read and in reading discovers who and what I was, as if by reading, I refill the holes in my memory, refind the darkness that I allowed to escape when I wrote it out so fast that in the writing my memory bled into the pages. As I read, there are gaps, holes where the ink blurred into the onion skin paper, each letter distorted, entire sentences reduced to mystery, whole paragraphs lost forever and so when I read to him, I make it up, fill in the slots and in the gray light, my voice echoes off the concrete and steel of our cage like I am an oracle speaking from a trance.

I didn't know the names of the dead. We need copper, they said. They said we need tin and I saw their faces at the moment they were about to die, as they pled for life. We need silver, they said. They said we need oil and lumber and we need fish and gas, we need what's buried in the sea buried in the mountains hidden in the jungles, and so when they told me to kill, I killed.

As I find that memory, Squeaky stirs, rolls onto his side. He looks worried. I am sorry because before, each night I read to him, it was with the energy and fire of a fairytale about the green of the jungle, the gold of the valley, the granite and ice of the mountain, but when the story turns red, Squeaky squirms. He says,

Mitch, I don't like the parts where you kill those guys. I'm not sure I did.

But you say you did.

I read what I wrote, Squeaky, I don't know what really happened.

You gotta remember something like that.

Maybe I want to forget.

So they died?

They had to die, Squeaky.

Why?

Because it's written that they were in the way.

What were they in the way of? Who are they? You keep saying they they they and I can't keep it straight, Mitch.

They are the men who told me to kill and they are the men I killed, I think, but I didn't know their names, I never knew the names because the names didn't matter and they didn't matter because they were in the way and they had to be removed and I removed them. I wrote it down and that's all I remember.

But the ears were real, weren't they, Mitch?

He swings his feet off the bunk. The necklace of dried ears—the ears I gave him, the ears of the two men who hurt him, took him, laid him up in the infirmary—the ears rattle on their silver chain. I say,

Lie down, Squeaky, I'll read some more.

No more blood, okay Mitch, I don't like blood.

He lies down, hands behind his head again. Shuffling through the manuscript, I find a page, a white page where my handwriting is in blue ink and the letters are formed and do not bleed into the weave, and I read,

Buenaventura rests in the curved arms of its bay, the blue and sparkling belly of the Pacific, and from the hills as you wind down dusty roads through acres of banana plants, you catch glimpses of the blue bay and the sparkling white walls of the city, jewels strung on a necklace and then, turning farther down into the dust into close tight streets, you smell the ocean, the salt like sandpaper in your nose and then, down deeper, diving between the white plaster walls

you roll into a square. In the center of the plaza, gleaming
like a hundred-foot angel you see the statue of Libertad, her
hair running down in golden tresses, her robe swirling round
her body so perfect the cloth swayed in the breeze and then
you come to a halt and all the green of the banana trees and
the blue of the bay and the dust of roads yields to the stench
of rotten oranges, yields to the call of men and women
hawking their lives for a few pesos and as you walk the
alameda, the arcade of Spanish-Moorish intricacy, you see
her, the woman seated on the stone. Her legs are swollen to
the size of small trees and her fingers swollen to the size of
bananas and her face swollen like an engorged mask, and on
her shoulders a monkey sits, its white face gleaming clean
against the deep blood-starved skin of the woman and in the
air there is the odor of urine and feces and the putrescence
of fruit gone sour and the wriggle of maggots. The monkey,
at my approach, hops from the woman's swollen shoulders
and, carrying a can with Nescafé still printed on it, hops to
me, rattles the can and chirps its helpless trapped chirp and
I see that there is a chain around the monkey's neck and the
chain is hooked to the swollen ankle of the woman and the
chain has dug into the fur and into the skin and into the
muscle of the monkey and there are maggots eating their
way between the links of the chain.

Squeaky sits up, clears his throat and he whispers,

God, Mitch, tell me you didn't really see that.

I don't know, Squeaky.

And the monkey?

I turn back to the pages of my story and I fall into
another memory hole, a spot where the words are written as
if in a code that even I can't decipher. I say,

I don't know.

So maybe you made it up?

Maybe I did.

In the dark any ray of light has the power of a sun and I
cling to the slightest glint in the vale of gray. I don't read

Squeaky the scenes about blood and sex. I ask him to read the descriptions of places. His innocence forces me to rethink every word until he acts like an editor even if he can't write a single declarative sentence.

What's a declarative, Mitch? He asked.

It's when you say something direct, I told him. Like you suck cock. That's a declarative sentence.

Squeaky laughs and the darkness lifts for a second but then settles back.

As I read I see why I have run from the story. Every story has a beginning, a middle, an end. I have no idea where my story starts, how to keep it going, or how to end it. I am every writer who ever put pen to paper. All brothers in a lost fraternity.

And there is silence and I look across the gulf between our bunks and I see Squeaky on his back, his hand dangling from the edge. He has fallen asleep. I fold the pages back into the envelope, count them—thirty six pages—but where do they go? Where in time and space? After Cartagena, I suppose, but the rest is blank, my memory gone. Without the pages, I can't find the story, without the memory I don't know where the pages go. I am lost. I am lost. I am lost.

110.

They're hot. They lie on the table in the library glowing like rivers of lava. Blood. Rape. Swollen belly. Smothered child.

All lies.

Pink ink thin as watered down blood—why didn't I see that before? Is that even Catharin's handwriting? It's been years since I saw it. It could be. But which lie do I believe?

I can't touch them. Heat waves roil up with the steady heat of a compost heap—the foul odor a stench, the rot of lies, every line a lie, every feeling a deception, every plea for help a fabrication—and I didn't see it. Catharin. Helpless Catharin on a bed tied down—a lie. Catharin beaten and raped until she bled—a lie. Catharin on her knees sucking Carl Fairweather's cock—a lie. Catharin's baby, her swollen belly, her dead infant—lies all. Fiction.

Geraldine wrote it. Plotted it out, swept me up in it— why didn't I see that before? Her voice? Three letters worthy of Lovelace, worthy of *Les lettres Portugaises*—masterpieces of fiction that fooled me and I can't touch them now.

I expect them to explode like small blue bombs.

Burn. Too hot to touch. Geraldine—my sister—a greater writer than I. A greater writer than Genet, than the Marquis. She caught me up, carried me along in her fiction that I believed like I believe in my own blood.

I look up from the letters laid out on the table like homeless children slaughtered—but there is nothing in them. They are light as feathers, hot as boiling oil. Geraldine.

Squeaky emerges from the stacks. I don't hear his footsteps. Don't hear his breath, don't hear the squeal of the chair as he pulls it away from the table, sits—it has all changed. I am in a spiral, spinning, spinning. I want to hold on but then the bottom falls away and the floor disappears and below me there is nothing but an infinity of emptiness— blue, deep, ugly, monstrous infinity—and I grab at the chair back but my hand passes through the wood like a bird through a cloud. I fall, falling, faster and faster and my head spins and spins and the room whirls and then with a crack, a smash, I hit the floor and my face flattens against the concrete hard and unyielding. Squeaky shouts,

Jesus Christ, Mitch, holy shit.

And he's kneeling beside me—where did he come from?

I try to sit but there are no bones in my body.

My arms are floppy as wet string.

My legs jelly.

My body spreads running like water over the concrete and I taste blood.

I look up, into Squeaky's worried eyes and I say,

Kill me, Squeaky.

Oh crap, Mitch. Crap.

He grasps my hand and my hand turns to mush in his tight fist and I whisper,

Kill me, Squeaky. I'm already dead but kill me again, please, don't kill me, I want to live, but kill me quick I want to die and there is a flutter of blue snow, huge flakes of blue snow and they are bleeding—each flake laced with curlicued rays of blood seeping weeping flakes of blood and a huge flake falls across my eyes and it is so heavy I smell shit and I feel the piss flood out of me and I know I am dead and unforgiven, unshriven but who gives a damn when everything has turned to shit and the only person who meant anything to you betrays you, you might as well die and Squeaky, squealing like a trapped rat says,

Mitch, Mitch, Mitch, what the hell, Mitch.

I read the bloody lines on the big snowflake fallen across my eyes and it says, Dear Henry you are an idiot, a fool, a little boy with a man's cock, a tool used by Mrs. Wilson, Carl Fairweather and Geraldine and I say,

Squeaky, how could she do this to me?

The floor gives way and I hang on by one slender silver chain and Squeaky says,

Mitch, you're choking me.

I smile. Squeaky. The one pure true real innocent thing ever in my life—no lies, no deceptions, no fakes, no fictions, just Squeaky and he has to die, they all have to die— Geraldine has to die and Martin and Carl Fairweather and Catharin and Geraldine's babies and in my fingers, tangled, I see a silver chain, the chain around Squeaky's neck tied to the dried ears I gave him, his trophies from the two bloods who fucked him raw and who are dead and earless and lying in their gray sacks in the ground dead and I sit up and let go of the chain and I say,

Sorry Squeaky.

Jesus Christ, Mitch, what's got into you?

It's all a lie, Squeaky.

What's a lie?

Catharin.

The Saint?

Geraldine.

Your sister? What's going on, Mitch?

Martin, I say. A weapon. She used me.

Who used you?

Geraldine.

I try to stand but the floor is a web of thin strings, elastic, sticky, and my feet tangle in the web and I can't move and in the corner of the library, far away, in the dark, I see the bright red eyes of a huge spider and I say,

She wrote the letters.

The Saint?

No. Geraldine.

The spider scurries out of the dark hole. The webbing under my feet trembles—I am lunch. I say,

She wrote the letters.

I don't get it, Mitch. Come on. Get up.

I can't. I don't have any bones in my body. She cut my spine out.

Come on, Mitch. You gotta get up. You having a heart attack?

Yeah. A heart attack. My heart. She tore out my heart, Squeaky. I was pure and she ripped out my heart and ate it and cut out my liver.

The spider dances out, her claws raised, tasting the air, kaleidoscope eyes hunting me—fangs. Long, silvery slick fangs poison oozing in small clear drops. I say,

Kill me, Squeaky. Please.

I'll call the doc.

Screw the doc. Pick up a chair and bash my fucking empty head in, Squeaky.

You know I can't do that, Mitch.

She lied to me all the way. She's a vulture. I have to kill her. Kill her kids. I have to get out. I can't stay in here. Gotta go. What am I going to do? Nobody left. Nobody to give a shit about me now.

You got me, Mitch.

But you have to die, Squeaky.

I know, Mitch. I know, but not right now, right? Right now we gotta fix you up, right, Mitch?

And he strokes my forehead and his hands are soft and warm and comforting and I hear him singing,

Lullaby, lullaby, go to sleep, go to sleep. That's all I know, Mitch. Lullaby, sleep. Lullaby.

The spider rears high up over me and her mouth opens and Squeaky keeps stroking my forehead and he doesn't see her, such an innocent boy, can't see the spider of death and her six foot fangs and in her maw I see myself and I laugh and Squeaky says,

That's better, jeez Mitch. You had me going there, I gotta tell ya, you had me going.

I pull him to me, feel his heat, his smooth skin, smell his sweat and the trace of semen on his skin. I fall and keep falling and the last thread holding me in place snaps and the spider sinks her fangs in my chest and I hold out my hands and they are covered with blood, no, not Squeaky—looking around, I see him struggle like a woman in labor to lift me from the floor and the clots of blood chunk together like curdled milk, red paint, and through the red I see Squeaky and his mouth moves but there is no sound.

I curl up on the table, still falling. I say,

I have to leave, Squeaky.

Sure you do, Mitch.

I'll kill her and then I'll kill her babies.

That's okay.

But I have to kill you first.

Okay, Mitch. You do what you gotta do. It's okay.

And I sleep. I don't care if I ever wake up. I am tired. Very, very tired.

111.

There is just one way to recover from Geraldine's betrayal—to write. No matter what, to write. Empty out the vessel down to the dregs of existence. And so I write about the only pure thing I know—death

Suki lay on a patch of vergonzosas, little ferns that when you touch them fold up like shameful virgins about to sacrifice their virtue to love. The moonlight yellowed his skin, turned the blood patch on his tunic gray. I knelt, felt his pulse. It had stopped. His eyes faded into that far away look of the dead. I unbuttoned his tunic, looked at the gash in his belly where his liver bulged as if some demon inside him had pushed its way out. The cut in his belly ran side to side like a wide leering grin. The stench of the ruptured stomach, the smell of blood, for the first time, made me ill.

In front of him, on the ground lay the man who had cut him. A hole in his neck where my bullet, too late to save Suki, nailed him. Blood pulsed from the wound.

I remembered the rush in the night, the gunfire as we attacked, and I remembered the hard counter punch as our targets, instead of yielding, instead of retreating, instead of rolling over, came at us. A dozen of them taking casualties as they hacked at us, and from twenty meters I saw the man with the machete low running, head jutted forward like a bull mad. I shouted, fired a round at him but he reached Suki and he slammed into Suki's side hard, then raised the blade slicing in and across and, just as my second round caught him in the neck, he swiped the blade into Suki's belly and Suki went down, kneeling, and the man keeled over and then it was quiet except for Suki's groan, Ay Carajo, he said, son of a bitch. He looked at his hands oozing blood in the yellow moonlight, the dark stained tunic, at the muck. I ran to him and he looked at me, regret in his eyes, and he wanted to say something but he fell back, knees up, feet tucked under his butt, and he died.

I knelt. Took the pulse. His eyes blank. I had lost men before. I had watched men bleed out, falling, dead, but this was Suki. As I looked down at him, I wanted it to end—wanted it to stop—because nothing had prepped me for his death.

I took his hand, already cooling in the heat of the jungle night, cooling with that undeniable coldness of the dead. The dead are like lost limbs and there is no way to replace your right hand. No way to replace the man who saved your life a half dozen times. No way to replace the man who showed you the truth of the knife. No prize for second place. Suki was dead and now there was no one left to save me.

Without him I was half a warrior. As I looked at Suki dead on the ground, I thought—that could be me and it was then that I wanted out.

I stripped Suki down to his olive drab shorts and T-shirt. Cut his sack of dried ears from the thong at his neck. I took his knife that had tasted so much blood. I took the small Saint Christopher medal on a chain around his neck. I took the.40 Caliber Desert Eagle he packed on his thigh.

The small dark man who had killed him groaned. Standing, I went to him, felt his pulse. He was still alive. He'd stay alive for a while.

I dragged branches from the underbrush, laced the branches with vines until a small raft lay on the ground. I laid Suki on the raft and gathered piles of dry wood, stacked it on the body and then I dragged the litter to the bank of the river where the moon struck a long golden streamer across its brown face. I set the boughs on fire.

As the wood burst up in flame, I watched the fire flicker, lighting Suki's face, eating at his flesh, eating the gash in his belly, eating the guts still distended from that cut.

And then I shoved the pyre into the river. Didn't care if any one saw it, I wanted to give him a warrior's funeral.

The Rio Verde is a slow, meandering river. Its brown water smooth as snake skin. The current picked up the flaming litter, turned, pivoting, rotating like a leaf in an eddy—slow and slower, spinning, and the fire rose high and bright and it sizzled as it ate the fat left on his small body.

I watched until, in the marriage of moonlight and flame, the raft tilted, dipped, still twirling, and then Suki's body slid off and into the water and the flames staggered like drunk men in the fusion of brown and yellow and fire.

Then it was gone and the river lay flat again, again brown, quiet again and still golden with its streak of moonlight and in the distance, like a ship slipping over a wide horizon the raft vanished and I was alone.

Behind me on the floor of the jungle lay twelve bodies. Ears still intact, still oozing blood, still stinking of sweat and piss and shit.

I unsheathed the flaying knife from Suki's scabbard, listened to the hiss of steel on steel. I set to work on the corpses, gathering the left ear of each fallen man, feeling the slickness of the blood of the dead. I added eleven ears to Suki's bag. And then, turning to the twelfth man, I knelt, checked his pulse again. Still there, still a beating heart. Blood seeped from the hole in his neck.

I rolled him over. I wanted him to look me in the eye as I cut his ears. He cried out, blood oozing from his mouth. One at a time, first the left, then the right, the blood stained black in the yellow moonlight. I tucked his ears in my bag along with the twenty-three already moldering there and, wiping the knife on the man's thigh, I slit his throat. He groaned one last time as the knife severed tendons, baring the larynx. Reaching up into the cut, I yanked his tongue down and through the slit in the corte corbata—the cut Suki had taught me—so the tongue lay long and pink like a fat necktie.

A weight lifted from my shoulders. Carrying the sack of ears that I was honor bound to cash in, and with one last glance at the river, I slipped back into the jungle. Numb, I didn't feel the searing nip of the mosquitoes.

112.

The electricity is off in the entire complex and they have confined us to our cells. Squeaky sleeps through it all. No worry, no fear, just sleep. The emergency lights cast a thin gray patina over C Block. In the dark, in the hot oppressive sweat of the cell, I think of all the men around me who cry innocence while I, knowing I am guilty, accept my punishment even though it is not and cannot ever be enough.

They hang themselves with ripped T-shirts.

They slash their veins with broken ballpoint pens.

They fry their guts with caustic lye.

They offer their throats up as sacrifice to men with tattoos and shaven heads.

There are too many to count. The dead.

As I stand at the bars of the gate to my cell, I watch Danny across the way in D Block Cell 33. He stands at the gate, hands at his sides, staring. He has been staring since 3:30 AM. Rigid. Eyes fixed on a point this side of infinity because inside you can see only as far as the next wall, the next block, the next set of bars. I've seen this look before.

Danny stares. I call to him.

Do it, Danny. Let the evil rotting inside you come out.

At 4:00 AM, there is nothing but the sound of men sleeping—the raucous snores of thick men with thick bellies, the nasal snores of thin men whose asthmatic nostrils clog during the night. There is the occasional shout as if the demons that brought a man to his cell surface in a dream to claw at his eyes from the inside out, to eat his liver. Even reprobates have a conscience in their dreams, the worst of them has a mother who, in their dreams, teaches them not to kill, not to eat their young.

Danny, still staring at his point of light, looks up and even at a distance I see that his eyes are deep hollow holes in a face once pink and flushed but now bearded and scarred. I say,

Go ahead, Danny, it'll all be over.

He starts, jerks like a body electrified and he reaches up to his throat and tears at the skin, rips at it with his nails until blood oozes from his neck and then he kneels and in a slow harsh dirge-like rhythm pounds his head against the steel bars, each thud a hammer blow and then standing, he backs up and in a full rush, a bull raging, he slams his head into the steel and I hear a crunch, a crack, a hollow thump and Danny falls, his face pressed between the bars—blood rushes from his nose, his eyes, his mouth then stops as his heart throbs one last time.

I lie back down, fold my hands behind my head and watch the sun ease its way out of the darkness and then there is a click and the lights come back on and I hear shouting. Sitting up, I watch two guards run down the corridor, nightsticks drawn. They stop at Danny's cell. One of them calls for the gate to open. The other peels off his two-way mike and calls a medic and I hear them, frantic little men, muttering,

Little cocksucker's killed himself, shit shit shit.

I turn away. Good boy, Danny. One less sperm factory. A hundred million sperm per ejaculation. Twenty times a month. Two billion sperm a month. Twenty-four billion sperm a year. Four hundred and eighty-billion sperm in twenty years, and not one of them will make a man. No more little Dannys. No more swollen bellies. No more writing on the walls.

I get off my bunk, walk to the cell window. Squeaky asleep, drawn up in his fetal wrap, knees tight to his chest, hears nothing. I scratch a line in the concrete under the window sill. Seventeen. Seventeen lines, seventeen men cut down, hammered into jelly by time and steel bars. Seventeen times four hundred and eighty-billion sperm, too many to calculate. I wonder if there's a way to speed it up, the slaughter.

In his sleep, Squeaky's sweat has plastered his white T-shirt to his body. I calculate the yardage in the cloth—torn into strips, each two inches wide. Tied together, braided, a single white T-shirt yields eighteen yards of cotton with which a man can braid his own death knot. A T-shirt is a lethal weapon.

Grunts and mutterings across the way in D Block draw me away from my calculations. Through the bars, I study the guards and now the doctor—the Haitian doctor who speaks his melodic, shaded French. The doctor who patched up Squeaky when he fell to his tormentors. The doctor, his accent eating at the guards, like acid says, Vous êtes bêtes, bêtes, idiots. Il est mort.

He kneels beside Danny, in the blood, and his hands turn grayish in the dim yellow light. He rises, shoulders slumped, and he says,

Carry him to the infirmary.

As the guards hoist the corpse, the doctor looks across the way, his eyes locked on mine. I smile at him. He lowers his eyes and walks off. His footsteps on concrete echo and then stop to the clang of steel and then the usual sounds begin—the stirring, the farting, the coughing, the sneezing, the grunting of the tattoos as they crawl out of sleep, snakes facing the light, hearts beating another day and in the air there is the faint scent of semen, the residue of wet dreams, the spillage of billions and billions of little angels of death writhing, drying, desiccating in the morning air—the sounds of toilets flushing. I smell shit, hear the sound of men pissing, so many men pissing it's like a sudden rainstorm, and then the laughter and the guards beating the bars with their nightsticks like town criers raising the sleeping—

Rise and shine, chow in nine.

Assholes and elbows.

You scum sucking swine.

The guard raps on the bars of my cell. He calls out,

Good morning, Mitchell, did you have sweet dreams you prevert?

I didn't get much sleep.

Too busy jerking off?

Too busy watching Danny.

Who?

Danny. In D Block?

What you're talking about?

The doctor just took him away, I say.

I ain't seen nothing, I ain't heard nothing, nobody tells me nothing.

Seventeen, I say.

What?

Seventeen suicides.

Well, fuck me, he says. Whatdya want me to do about that? Get your ladyboy on his feet, Mitchell.

He smiles, grinds his way down the block rapping his nightstick.

Squeaky stirs. He sits up. He says,

Jeez Mitch. I had a weird fucking dream.

I turn to him. Sit beside him on his bunk. I run my fingers over his head. I say,

When are you gonna wash your hair, Squeaky? It's getting greasy.

Oh shit, Mitch, I don't care.

You look like hell. Nobody cares about you except you.

You care don't you, Mitch?

Not when you let yourself go.

I look at him, at the little boy face, the mouth, the wondrous eyes, the cheeks that still glow with his peculiar innocence. I say,

Danny bashed his skull in.

Oh jeez, Mitch, that's awful.

Squeaky grabs my hand.

When did he die? He says.

Four AM.

Oh man, oh man, oh man. What's happening, Mitch? This is the end, isn't it? Everything's going to hell, isn't it? Oh man ...

113.

Where do they bury the dead?

What earth do they pour over the eyes of the dead who have given up their breath?

Where do they bury the dead when the sky hangs gray and pendulous like an axe?

What earth do they spread?

What seeds do they sow into the earth covering the dead who gave up breath in the darkness of a concrete cell?

Where do they bury the dead borne out of darkness and steel? Men who give up breath in the dark gray of concrete and steel cells hatching them like eggs in a sterile womb?

Where do they bury the dead they haul out in canvas bags in the night of surrendered breath, from the cold concrete and steel cells like the cells of a beehive where the queen lies tended, fat, fed, white and pulsing with eggs?

Where do they bury the dead who vanished leaving holes in the darkness, emptiness in the void?

Nothing remains but the echo of their howl.

Nothing remains but their stains on the steel and concrete floors where the dead lay last breath pushed from the colding body.

Where have they hidden the dead carted away in canvas bags like booty ripped from treasure chests?

In the calm afterglow of death when the blood has stilled like sparkling wine gone bad, I wait in the calm sea of skin cooling and I ask—Where do they bury the dead who have yielded breath to the dark, whose breath mingles with the air of living men held in cells like eggs unfertilized, sterile, incomplete?

In the calm coolness that remains like the cold chill after an explosion, I wait for an explanation.

JACK REMICK

But it doesn't come.
There are no words of piety.
No wailing and wrenching of hands.
No ululations hammering the dark.
No Salve Regina dripping from the end of a priest's finger dipped in water.

The dead who vanish here leave no footprints, leave no vapor trail streaking across an azure sky. These men lie in gray concrete wrapped in steel where no one asks directions to the grave, where there are no flowers planted from seeds sown in the gray earth and no crosses, no monuments, no stones to mark the grotto of no resurrections.

I hesitate to ask where they bury the dead. The doctor, his Haitian French fractured on the tip of his tongue, the Haitian doctor knows where they lie, the dead whose last gray breath broke free in the dim gray cell where men lie like eggs waiting to be fed sperm, their bowels swollen with semen, their mouths still holy sepulchers of semen spent, their teeth still glazed with love. The doctor knows. He carries them away wrapped in canvas, their blood still oozing from their wounds, their bodies still scarred with the cuts and slashes of memory buried in their brains like seeds in soil seeking light. Their memory leaks out of the body like the oil from a cracked cask. Their memory fades and when you ask, where do they bury the dead, there is no reply, there is no apology. There is only the question: What?

114.

I place my hands on his throat. He looks at me. His eyes wet as the eyes of a newborn calf. His mouth opens over his white teeth and he says,
Mitch, you're really doing it this time?
For little guys like you, Squeaky, it always ends in a corner with your head cracked open and grit in your mouth. You don't stand a chance out there. There are wolves who'll eat your feet and vultures who'll eat your liver. Little guys

264

don't stand a chance and when I'm out there, in here turns
into out there for you. You see? I can't leave you and I can't
take you with me so there's just one thing left—are you ready
to die? If I kill you, I promise I won't take your ear. If I kill
you, you won't suffer. You see? Little guys need a Cain, a
savior, like Cain saved me when I was a little man—a savior
keeps the wolves away from your feet, a savior scares off the
vultures, a savior watches over you and keeps them away
when they come for you in the night. I'm your guard in here,
but when I'm gone, I can't save you or guard you or watch
over you. You'll end up slumped in a corner in a tight ball of
boy beaten and bruised and bloody. You can't stop them,
Squeaky. You see what I'm telling you? If you lie down and I
kill you, you'll die with dignity. But if I go, they'll take you
and grind you into powder and leave you piled in a corner,
hunkered down, beaten and dead. I've seen it so many times.
I don't want to leave you here but I can't stay and I can't take
you with me. They're coming for me because they need guys
like me out there—they like to keep their wolves on the loose
and not cornered in some steel sanctuary out of the river of
blood—they didn't sharpen our claws and file our teeth just
to let us stay in here. You see what I'm saying to you? I'm
one of them. I'm one of their wolves and I smell blood and
death the way a woman smells perfumed flowers in her
garden and I can smell death on you, Squeaky, I can smell
death on you, I can smell the shit on your legs after they
pound you raw. I don't know if you can see. I don't want you
to suffer little man. I know you don't like me to call you little
man, but you are a little man and you don't know how to
fight the wolves and the vultures, Squeaky. You steal a car
and you wind up in here with the tattoos and the filed teeth
and the naked dicks, you see? You don't stand a chance if
I'm gone, but if you die in darkness, you'll feel no pain, no
hurt, it's over in a second. No pain. No more pain. Squeaky?
I love your little ass, I do, you know I do and you know I
wouldn't abandon you but they'll come for me and I won't

have a choice and I'll go back out into the river of blood, back into the abattoir, back into the slaughter. You see? You see what I am? You have to see, Squeaky, because unless you see what I'm doing for you none of it means a thing. Can you do that? Can you lie down in darkness and know that you'll never wake again, that you'll always be with me, that you won't be hungry or thirsty and you won't hurt anymore? You remember what they did to you in the laundry room? You remember the pain and the blood? And the scars? I won't let you suffer, Squeaky. I can save you all of that and I promise I won't take your ear. I wouldn't do that to you because I know how much you hate the blood. I want to remember you whole, intact, complete—so that when I dream of you, I'll see you as you are right now, always with those dried ears on a chain around your neck, wearing that lousy white T-shirt, wearing those dirty scruffy sneakers. You're beautiful you little cunt, and that's how I want to remember you. Go ahead, take a deep breath. That's it, lay your head back and bare your throat. It's easier that way—no blade, no stone, no gun, just the flesh, the most primitive killer of all, the hands—before we ever picked up a rock, these were our weapons—flesh on flesh. But when the wolves come for you, they'll slash and tear and rip and you'll end up slouching in a corner and they'll leave you dead and they won't remember you. You'll be a number on a card somewhere so unimportant they won't even enter your name in the computer. That's how little men like you end up—forgotten, bloody, your brains leaking on the rock, blood on the blade.

Oh shit, Squeaky. I'm going back out there and I'll get revenge for you, little man. They want to toss me back into the blood bath, okay, I go, but you're the last little man I skin and I promise I won't take your ear. So just lie back and bare your throat, open up like dog giving in and it'll all go away—and when you're dead, I won't let them stuff you into a canvas sack. No. I won't. I'll take you to the doc and he'll make them bury you under the flowers in the garden. You see? I planted the garden with poppies, Squeaky. The poppies are for the dead. They'll have to take care of you there after I'm gone. They can't hurt you when you're in the earth, you see? Just remember the blood and the scars and remember that I won't let you end up crumpled in a corner like a forgotten sack of meat. No, buddy. I love you too much for that. Are you okay with this, Squeaky? You see? You see how it's going to come down? On that bunk where I fucked you so many times. Not in a corner of the yard, not in a corner of the laundry room—it'll end here. Are you all right with that? I have to go, Squeaky. I have to walk out of here because I can't stay here unless I'm dead. I've got work to do out there for all the little guys. The way Cain helped me. You see? You see how it works?

I press my thumbs into the small soft spot just under his Adam's apple. He stiffens. His eyes, wider now, stare into mine and I see the first sign of understanding and he stops resisting. He relaxes. The tension flees from his body. He says,

Okay, Mitch, if that's what you want.

And he tilts his head back, bares his throat, surrenders to my hands. I press harder, feel the larynx pop, the hyoid bone snap and still Squeaky watches my eyes, still giving himself to me and then his arms flail in the involuntary spasm of dead men as the pain first charges their muscles before letting go as if soul and breath and muscle and electricity are one, leaving just the momentary and fleeting warmth of a corpse.

Rising, I let go of him, unlock the silver chain with the ears from his neck and holding the chain I lie on my bunk, listen to the silence, complete and utter and pure and my heart beats fast and my eyes are wet. For the second time in my life I feel the residue of childhood in me. For the first time, I understand the emptiness and horror a young boy feels when he kills something he loves. Wafting through the dark air of the cell, there is the smell of shit, the last farewell.

Ave atque vale. Morituri te salutamus. Rolling onto my side,
I sleep.

115.

When I awake, it is to the rattle of the nightstick on
steel, that reckoning of the living called to account for
another gruesome day. I stand.

Perry, the new guard, speaks,

Mitchell, rise and shine, chow in five and roust your
little ladyboy to hit the deck.

He's not feeling well, Perry, I say. He's going to miss
chow this morning.

That's his problem.

I need to take him to the infirmary.

If the little cunt is sick, he can walk himself there.

He won't be walking, Perry.

I grab the steel bars, lean close, smell the odor of Perry's
pussy cologne slapped on his skin like a coat of slut paint
and I glare at him and I laugh at his narrowed eyes and I say,

Will you let me take him to the doc, Perry? Pretty please
with sugar on it, Perry.

You cons, he says. Okay, go ahead.

He unlocks the gate. I wrap Squeaky in his gray wool
blanket. I carry him in my arms. Perry says,

Christ, Mitchell, has your twink got the runs?

You better back off three paces, Perry 'cause you don't
want what he's got.

What's with this little turd, man?

Don't worry, you won't get it today. Maybe tomorrow.

What?

The walk to the infirmary is long and slow and Perry,
keeping his distance, goads me with his nightstick, the tip
digging into my kidneys. He says,

Smells like that kid's pissed his pants, too.

He'll be okay as soon as the doc gets a look at him.

At the door to the infirmary, Perry stops, knocks. The door opens. The doctor, the young Haitian with watery eyes and a bald head beyond his years, lets us in. He says,

What's he got?

A case of death, Doctor.

He laughs. He says,

Don't we all? Over there. On the exam table. Jesu Marie, est-ce qu'il est mort?

Oui, je l'ai tué.

He looks at me. Then at Perry. He says,

I'll take it from here, mami.

He closes the door in Perry's face. He looks at me. He says,

Que'est-ce que tu as fait, toi?

Je l'ai étranglé, I say.

I look at my hands. He shakes his head. He goes to his desk. Picks up the phone. Looking at me, he speaks into the mouthpiece. He says,

Governor, I need some guidance here, sir. It's Mitchell.

Then, he listens before hanging up. He says,

Go back to your cell, Mitchell. A guard is coming for you.

Perry's here, I say.

The warden's sending someone special to handle you.

He rubs his face, the bald head gleams with sweat and light. I say,

In the garden, Doc. No canvas sack for the little man.

116.

It's as if I'm in a dream. It's hot and I'm tired. The air is stale. My lungs burn. The light is dim. My eyes water from the rotten air stinking of sweat and old floor wax rising like the mist of death. It is the cumbersome residue of cigars smoked so long the stench has eaten into the wood like acid leaching at the bones of decaying rats.

He sits up on his wooden throne. His spectacles slide down to the tip of his nose and I know him—

He is the last leftover of my nightmare, the final beat of a heathen feast, the pig roasted over the open fire. He holds his hands in that peculiar folded manner of judges as they sit high up, glaring down at the cesspool of rapists and addicts, killers and thieves, and his eyes, reddened by the foul air and the anguish of handing down death like a drunken chef larding on the mashed potatoes at a cheap buffet—all you can eat, death for your pride and your guts—his eyes seep goo. He coughs.

I expect to see raw sewage burst from his mouth, expect to see a river of frogs erupt from his mouth, expect a plague of rats to flow from his mouth. My hands, clamped together with steel bands, quiver, and he lowers his eyes behind the greasy spectacles and, bending his neck, he reads, his eyes moving, jerking like rats dying from an overdose of Warferin and he clucks as he reads. Clucks. Chills race across my back, over my chest, up my arms. He closes the folder on the hard wooden desk in front of him, the temple of damnation where the gavel of resurrection or the knife of death lays like a black wooden viper and he clears his throat. The room grows silent, even unto the breathing of the bailiff beside me, the vein in his neck throbbing quick and alive and silent and the judge, looking at me, says,

Well, Mr. Mitchell, you've had a long wallow in the pit of Purgatory since last your name crossed this desk.

Yes sir, I say. Nothing has changed. I am a degenerate. A killer. A thief. A liar. A beast of the cloth.

Spare the court your poetry, Mitchell. You plead guilty without counsel to crimes that may not have been committed and you say you want to die.

I do want to die, your honor.

He wipes at his mouth with the back of his hand and his hand slides free. In that second, I see the fangs and the red tongue and the drops of yellow venom dripping from the fangs and he says,

What has happened to you, Mitchell? And why do you want the state to kill you?

Because I am a beast, your honor. I have killed the men I loved.

He smiles. His eyes crinkled like crepe paper at the corner and he looks again at the papers on his dark wooden desk where the gavel of death lays silent as the blade of a guillotine. He says,

It's not the court's job to cure your delusions. The law is the law even if you're a bleeding faggot who looks like a bear.

I am an ursine butthole bandit, your honor, a cock-lover who's not afraid to fuck anything anytime anywhere. I'm a menace to society and I belong behind bars.

Your friends are powerful people, Mitchell, people who don't care who you fuck and who don't want you dead.

They are vermin, your honor. They want to save me because I am beyond death.

He laughs. In his voice I hear the gurgle of swollen bubones, the swollen nodes of death that I had heard in the voice of Carl Fairweather when he came to set me free. I say,

I have killed hundreds, your honor. I have killed women and children. I have taken their ears and dried them and strung them on wire and worn them around my neck as amulets for the men who want me outside again.

He holds out his right hand, the hand poking from the draped sleeve of the black robe. His fingernails are curved. I have seen them in dreams of the angel of death, long curved nails like scimitars slashing my throat until I woke gurgling in my own blood to discover that my dreams were my life and I was the angel of death slicing my own throat.

He says,

There's no evidence in the record of these things, Mr. Mitchell. I have the history of your thievery, of your minor perversions. But let me say this—what man hasn't dreamed of stealing a woman's underwear or getting fucked in the ass?

He smoothes his cheek with his left hand. The bailiff beside me chuckles like a teenaged girl with a boy's hand sliding inside the elastic of her panties. The bailiff grins at me. His teeth are black, his gums swollen. Iron bands hold his incisors in a silvery grip. The judge blows air from his lips and in blowing, his lips flap like a flag in the wind and I smell, even fifteen feet from him, the odor of decay wafting from the gullet of a vulture. He says,

Have you seen a psychiatrist, Mitchell? Have you? Have you had your brain probed for diseases? Is your homosexuality curable?

I am guilty, your honor. I murdered René, my lover. I murdered Squeaky, my little man. I connived with a prison guard to murder my brother-in-law and I pimped my sister to the killer.

The judge then whispers, his voice a dry rattle like snakes in sycamore leaves,

As I said, Mitchell, there is no record of a Squeaky in your file. The record shows that you've never had a cellmate. What am I to make of that?

Someone is lying, your honor.

And who are these people who don't want you locked up even one day longer?

They're barons of industry, your honor.

Do they have names?

You never know the names of those people.

They must have names.

They're invisible, your honor.

So you can't see them and they have no names?

How can I make you undestand, your honor, I need to die.

That's not going to happen by the hand of the law.

At least let me stay in prison for the rest of my life.

He holds up both hands, in mock prayer. I halt. He says,

When I first saw you, Mitchell, I had no idea who you were. I asked you why you didn't appeal the sentence. Stealing a woman's underwear is an admirable exploit.

White underwear, your honor. Thong panties, nippleless bras, half slips made of silk. Drawers full of it. Entire wardrobes packed in trunks in self-storage units, your honor.

And you served your time.

Your honor, please. Don't send me back into the river of blood.

Mitchell, the rest of us drown in the sewer of human existence. Are you so privileged you don't have to crawl there with us? I'm cutting you free.

I look at him, at the red gooey eyes, the thin wet lips, the dripping nose and I know he is right. I've had my time in paradise. With a deft movement and a jangle of keys, the bailiff unlocks the manacles and my hands fall to my sides and I am numb. Now I go back to hell.

117.

I close the door. The latch clicks once like a cricket then falls silent. The library is quiet. Under the concrete and steel I feel vibrations, the rumble of heavy machinery like devils drilling tunnels. I scan the stacks, the table where the computer rests, its screen dark. The keyboard askew on the table. A sheet of blank paper under the mouse.

The machines rumble in the soles of my feet. I stand in the center of the room for the last time listening, waiting. But I am alone now—Squeaky is dead, Martin is dead, René is dead, Carl Fairweather is dead, Catharin's fictional baby smothered under a fictional pillow. That leaves Catharin and her fictional letters. Who knows where Catharin is—lost, maybe, roaming India on a futile mission to save souls with no idea that there is nothing to save. She always was the innocent one. The dreamer. Pure and good and holy, Catharin, the Saint born on Montségur, martyred in San

Francisco in a park. In India, she's safe. No one can find her there.

I walk to the stacks, stand on the ladder, reach up to the top shelf where my manuscript lies between *Notre Dame des Fleurs* and *Les 120 Journées de Sodom*, covered by the English roses. It is heavy now, four thousand pages—a mixture of red ink on tissue paper, black ink on the cut back sheets of books, typewriter ink on 8½ by 11 sheets of twenty pound bond, and computer ink on the last two thousand pure, clean, precise, passionless pages. I carry it to the table and I lay it down like a corpse resting on a mortician's slab. I smell the dead things in it. I see the river of blood in it. I taste the cordite in it. I smell the shit and piss of dead men in it. I leaf through the pages, turning the red splotched and indecipherable first thousand pages with a slow twist trying to remember what I wrote, but my memory is blank as I stare at the black veins bleeding across the pages and it is as if another hand had written that story. In the three hundred pages of ink, I see my mind spewed over the pages. I read the names of places I say I have been, recognize arcs of blood captured in black images like hieroglyphics of a lost world—a vast and indecipherable world. Just at the edge of consciousness there is the thread of a tale and I shudder as I read the names and count the ears and then, turning deeper into the unknown, I uncover the fifty typewritten pages where my fingers stumbled like blind men walking over slick rocks, the typos as numerous as the words and in code as the ribbon of the typewriter faded leaving a light imprint of letters on paper—the trail of being disappears into indentations. And then to the last two thousand pages of computer printout, so clear, precise, detailed, a mask of hell. I feel joy as I tally the bodies that lie there reeking like ripened corpses in a hot sun and at the end where I have laid Squeaky, his larynx crushed. I feel an apotheosis. I will leave this little man here on the pages for someone to find, to resurrect in the reading, but I am afraid Squeaky will lie

forever a man no one will remember. I take a deep breath.
Close the manuscript and tie the covers over it like a shroud
sealed with bee's wax and semen.

For a moment, I feel a great loss.

The emptiness of completion.

The second I wrote the last word the river dried up and I
will never add to these pages. I will leave the manuscript in
its cosmic mystery the way readers left *Notre Dame des
Fleurs* and the *120 Journées*—their words blocked out,
circled, underlined by the invisible hands that preceded
mine.

I get up from the table, hold the manuscript like the
Eucharist as I return to the crypt where I place it back in its
niche, back beside its brother and sister— *Notre Dame des
Fleurs* and the *120 Journées.*

I have re-arranged the universe by placing *The Patron
Saint of Blood* where it belongs—on the shelf with Genet and
the work of De Sade. It lies in good company—a cascade of
blood between an ocean of semen and a river of pain.

My manuscript is home.

I turn. Walk away, refuse to look back but at the door I
hesitate. Wait. Listen to the rumble of the machinery driving
air and water and blood inside the walls.

I close the door.

For one moment, I'm lost. Afraid. Careless. But it
doesn't matter now. The story has been written. Where I go
now I'll leave no record. No pages detailing the opening of
veins and the bleeding of wounds. Bodies will appear on the
coast, in the mountains, in the wood, in swimming pools.

They want me out. I'm happy to oblige.

She wants to use me. I'm happy to be of service.

They want me back in the river of blood, back in the
abattoir of human existence.

She wants me back in the sewer and the filth and slime
of the breeders and the rich and I am happy to go there.
Now.

The guard waits at the gate. He wears the somber half smile. He is a diseased man whose vermin have not yet eaten their way out of his brain. He waits, his hand quivering with fever and lust.

I laugh.

I watch him breathe, watch his chest rise and fall, watch his nostrils flare. He is alive but walking on thin ice, the abyss waits for him and the monsters in the abyss are hungry for him. I say,

Have you read *The 120 Days of Sodom*?

What?

He looks at me, eyes widening as if I'm speaking a foreign tongue.

Notre Dame des Fleurs?

Mitchell, what the fuck are you talking about?

Books, I say. *The Patron Saint of Blood*'s in the library.

The library? That's for pussies, he says. We got cable in the bull pen.

Oh yes, I say. Cable. You must be proud.

What? Mitchell, you're a fucking mystery, you know that?

118.

I strip off the blue chambray prison issue shirt that stinks of sweat and soap and the peculiar musty odor of cloth that never sees sunshine. I step out of the prison issue dungarees until I stand naked. The guard sucks at his teeth like a man sucking loose the last bit of breakfast bacon. His eyes wander to my cock.

So that's Wonderboy?

This is nothing, I say. My father had twenty-four inches, soft. He had to rope it around his neck to keep from stepping on it.

You're a funny guy, Mitchell.

Get out of my way, before Wonderboy gets pissed and breaks your jaw.

He turns on his heel, walks out of the change room. I
hear his footsteps halt just outside the door.

In the dim gray light, the shadows look alive, like
crawlers working their way out of the concrete. The water in
the shower is hot. The smell fills my nostrils with the odor of
castile soap. Under the soap, the scent of Lysol tunnels like a
thick worm.

I let the water tear at my skin, feel the heat rip away the
grunge and grime and gray until my skin turns red, my eyes
burn.

I remember the day at Oak View School for Boys—I was
trapped in the shower where Charlie Goodson and his
friends tried to teach me to play the bone-aphone until Cain
stepped in and cracked a few heads—the enforcer. Cain. The
Saint.

Turning off the shower I listen to the water drip on the
concrete floor, little chirps like small hungry birds begging. I
reach for the rough terrycloth towel that smells of bleach
and detergent and the scorched odor of cloth left too long in
a dryer. I remember the feel of hot women's underwear
against my skin, the warmth against my belly, and it is a long
time ago and the woman with red hair and her handcuffs
and her Glock disappears, and there is another hole in my
memory and I float along on a deep brown river of forget.

Still wet, I look at myself in the metal mirror—no glass
here, no shards you shape into a shiv, no blades for digging
out the eyes of a man. I study my body. I see the belly, white
as pork fat but flat and hard. I see the chest of a man who
has stayed fit. I see the thighs with their bulging quadriceps
and I am okay. Only the head, shaven, its tattoos red scars
on the scalp, mar it. The tattoos on the fingers are the marks
of Cain, my protector, my patron saint who has kept me alive
for years. Cain who didn't give a shit. Cain who cut and
slashed until all other men stood clear when I walked by. I
hand-strip the beads of water from the thick black pelt
covering my body. With the towel, I scrub at my skin, feel

the hard threads of the terrycloth sandpaper away years of fucking, years of semen, years of sweaty bodies, years of blood and puke and shit and piss.

On the bench there is a package. In the package there is a pair of black slacks, a white shirt, a light gray sports jacket and a red tie. A pair of black penny loafers. A pair of black socks with gold toes and heels. A black leather belt finishes off the ensemble.

I step into the slacks—no underwear—slide the belt through the loops, pull on the white shirt, button it. Sitting down, I tug on the black socks and pull on the penny loafers and, last, slip on the gray jacket. It is a little snug in the shoulders. I look at the man in the mirror. I knot the tie in the half Windsor the way Cain taught me—without looking. You never know, he said, when you have to tie it on the run, you know what I mean?

I walk out of the change room where the guard waits leaning against the wall. He stands, hands on his hips, stirring a pile of gray dust with his boot toe. He looks up. He grins. He says,

Hey, there was a human being under that load of shit, huh Mitchell? Let's go.

He leads me out of the basement up three floors to a door locked with a magnetic code. He punches in the code and the door opens into another corridor, still prison dim and gray, still stinking of hot lard and the sweat of men and the stench of roasting meat. I see the guard in the light and for the first time, I see his skin as it is—the pock marks are not as deep as they seemed inside, his hair isn't as gray as it seemed inside. He stands at the last door and he holds it open and he says,

I won't lock this, okay Mitchell? 'Cause you'll pro'ly be back here in, what? A week? No, two weeks. It'll take'em that long to try you before they fry your animal ass again.

Overhead the lights are caged in thick wire housings bolted to the concrete, the bulbs buzzing with a low hum. My

shadow is a dull gray blob and under my feet I feel the throb
of the big machines, the breathing beating pumping
machines in the heart of our prison. At the end of the
corridor, there is a door the color of rusted steel and a small
glass pane cross-hatched with chicken wire. A gate swings
open into a hallway painted robin's egg blue. It smells of
Lysol and fresh floor wax. My shoes squeak as I walk and
then I realize that I am alone. No guard. The first time in
years, I walk alone. Another door. It springs open.

A hallway with waxed oak floors. The walls are painted
Saint Petersburg ochre. The lights—neon white—do not
flicker. My shadow sprawls out on the floor ahead of me. The
cool breath of air conditioning flows over me. The air is
sweet. I hear the distant thump of the machines recedes.
Still not free, but better. I take a deep breath.

Ahead of me, I see glass. Windows. A door with a push
bar. The upper half of the door is plate glass. The glass is
sparkling clean. Beyond the glass, I see walls that are
painted creamy yellow and on the walls the lights are buried
behind chrome sconces. I push the bar on the door. I feel the
cold aluminum under my palm, the first metal I've touched
in years that wasn't bloody or tainted with the shit and sweat
of sin.

The door pops open. I hesitate at the threshold. Wait
two heart beats, a lifetime.

Then I cross over.

119.

Outside, the air smells of heavy coal smoke. I take
shallow breaths, soot turns to acid in my mouth, the acid
leaches at taste buds martyring my tongue to the Industrial
Filth in the clammy air. It is always cold in the fog, in the
mist of an ocean hurling itself to death on the sand. Doors
behind me close. I stand still, listening.

The clatter of steel sends chills up my spine and I smell
the prison air drafting behind me mingle with the acid night

mist. I exhale one last breath loaded with the scent of concrete and steel. Wet with mist, my head, shaved, for the last time, turns cold and my shadow looms ahead of me strung out and wide and dangerous.

120.

From the last gate, a walkway leads to a parking lot and in the lot there stands a black limo. A dark red pool of ooze has formed under the radiator of the limo. It is thick, pasty like grease.

Beyond the limo, there is the street and beyond the street, the sand dunes and behind the sand dunes the sea stretches out to the night horizon. I hear the hiss of waves curling ashore, bearing the residue of a voyage ten thousand miles long.

As I walk, I listen to the pounding of waves and beneath the roar, the crunch of sand under the soles of my shoes. Inside, shoes hissed or squeaked on worn concrete.

At the back door of the limo, a chauffeur in full livery points a black-gloved finger at me. He wears a black hat, black jacket, white shirt, black slacks, black boots, the toes polished mirror bright. He wears dark glasses. He says,

Mitchell?

Yeah.

Shadows under the limo congeal into clots that float like icebergs on the red mass under the limo's radiator. The chauffeur opens the door. I smell the exhaust of the tail pipes seeping their gray white clouds into the pale night and I smell the brine. I don't want to leave that smell. It is a clean smell, moist, wet, pure, pre-human. I don't want to leave it because I know what will happen when I do.

A hand reaches from the open door of the limousine and crooks an index finger at me. I get in. The air inside is thick with a man's cologne. A deep animal musk. The scent of a fat boar in rut. There is the odor of shoe polish and the scent of leather rubbed with saddle soap. Outside the rear window, I see a skull. It is a weird skull—half white, half black like a painted Day of the Dead mask—half grin, half grimace. The skull floats on a surging wave of blood, its teeth pink.

The limo is big enough for eight. Twin banks of velveteen seats, side stools, a bar. In the overhead light, I see telephones and legs and a man in a black overcoat smiling at me. Over his shoulder I see a sack, a canvas sack with a draw string at the mouth cinching it up like stitches in a deep wound. I have seen that pouch around Suki's neck. I have seen that pouch on the mahogany desk of my dead brother-in-law. I have seen that pouch bloody and seeping and full of ears in campsites.

A woman with big tits and empty eyes and long legs sits curled up beside the fat man. Her right hand rests on his fat boar's thigh. The fat man says,

So, Henry, you like your new wardrobe?

The jacket's a little tight in the shoulders.

We can fix that. We can fix everything. Make you look good.

You mean look like you?

He laughs. He says,

Handmade in Italy. Chinese silk cashmere blend. The best money can buy.

He holds out the hand, the finger still crooked. I look at the puffy pink fingers, the big fat diamond ring on the fat ring finger. Shiny pink nails like the hooves of a soon-to-be-slaughtered sow.

I don't return the offer. He draws his fat little hand back. I say,

I like that ring.

He looks at me with gray eyes buried deep in white skin, orbs like the eyes of a guinea pig. He says,

She said you were a hard man, Henry.

Call me Mitch, I say. What do you want?

We have a job for you.

And the job is, Mister ... what's your name?

He smiles. It is a dead smile that spreads across his inert and lifeless face. He says,

You don't need to know my name.

I reach for the door handle, unlatch the door, shove it open. He sits forward, leans into the space between us. He says,

Just hear me out.

What do you want?

Ears. Your trademark is ears, right, Henry?

I close the door. He sits back in the dark corner. I see light reflected in his eyes, pinpoints of yellow—like fat.

The limousine lurches forward. The woman pushes back into the seat, her knees relax, gape open and her eyes rake me up and down, side to side. The limousine turns a corner, heads toward the sand dunes, splits the dunes, turns onto the Coast Highway, turns into a stream of headlights. I watch the river of blood sweep past the door of the limo, window high now, covering half the glass. In the flow of blood, bodies sweep by, careening into one another, bodies of small dark skinned men, bodies of tall black men with axes buried in their skulls, bodies of eviscerated woman all without their left ears and in the rising tide I feel the limo levitate. The river boils at eye level, the flood streaming past, and a flutter of white underwear zips by and then a corpse, a white corpse, a white grinning corpse, the mouth wide, the teeth bared like the fangs of a white and bloody beast and the Fat Man says,

Look, Henry. Mrs. Fairweather tells me you're good.

I watch his fat face come and go as the headlights cut into the half-darkness of the limousine. I turn away from him. It feels odd, moving so fast, so far. Inside I walked ten thousand miles but never went farther than fifty feet at a stretch. I look at him again. Feel nothing. Want nothing. Have nothing. His face is a face I've seen in photos of CEOs and CFOs and embassy attachés with connections to men with their names in the books of corporate boards.

I smell shit and piss and the odor of rotting offal rising with the bloody river cresting over the top of the limo and in the stream bones flit past like the bones of butchered cattle—floating—and in the mix, I see eyes, free-floating eyes glued to the glass of the limo door, eyes staring, unblinking disembodied eyes.

The woman crosses then uncrosses her long legs. For a second she holds her legs apart, inviting my look. The Fat Man leans forward again. He says,

There's a certain man in a certain country who's blocking our development plans. We want him to go away.

I look at the face, at the narrow rat-like eye sockets, at the sallow lips and then look at the woman, at her knees half-open. I say,

Do you know why I was in prison, mister? I was in prison for stealing women's underwear from laundromats. I like to sleep with it under my pillow. I had drawers full of it. Panties, bras, slips. All white. White's my specialty.

The woman giggles, separates her knees more. The Fat Man laughs. It is a nervous laugh. The laugh of a man who doesn't know what to do with me.

He sits back in the seat, sinks into the shadow. I see his black overcoat split by his legs showing the black hard creases in his trousers. Legs open like the woman teasing with her cunt no no no, but knowing she'll give in when the time is ripe. I glance to the side, see the river, the floating slaughterhouse, the charnal house, the butchery, the heads with no left ear, the corpse in her white underwear, her mouth gaping open in death's smile. The Fat Man says,

Maybe Mrs. Fairweather was wrong.

I slide across the space between us, a few feet, just far enough away that our knees don't touch. He curls back deeper into the shadows. His hands raised like pale shields as I close up to him. Reach for his throat. He gasps. In his eyes, pinpricks of fear. He sniffles. I release his throat. He says,

Henry, my man is armed.

Your man is a pissant.

You don't know what he can do.

I know exactly what he can do.

You don't seem very reliable to me.

When do you want this certain man eliminated?

I don't think you're the man for the job.

He presses a button on the arm rest.

I look away. I remember days in the tank, watching tattoos come awake, dreading this moment when the walls would disappear and they'd drive me into the river of blood. I think about Cain again. I think about Oak View School for Boys and the day in the shower when Cain saved me. He didn't want ears. He wanted photographs. I take a deep breath. Spreading my legs, I push against my bowels. Feel the pressure build up there, feel the hard knot of gas bulge against my sphincter, and then it explodes—a fart so thick and noxious it turns the air in the limousine blue.

In the toxic gas ball surrounding us, I kneel and with my right hand grasp the Fat Man's throat again and with my left hand, I jab two fingers into his rat-like eyes and I yank and blood surges out in a geyser and he gurgles, blind, his eyes nothing but goo on the tips of my fingers. He collapses into the seat, head lolling on a snapped neck. The woman leans forward, hands on her knees, hair swirling as her eyes switch from the Fat Man to me. I search the pockets of the dead man's silk and cashmere suit, I pull out his cell phone, slip it into my jacket. Then I snap his finger, rip the big diamond ring free, tuck it away.

The limousine stops. The door opens and the driver, his face dark gray shadows in the glare of onrushing lights, reaches into his coat for that automatic—Taurus, Beretta, Glock, it doesn't matter—because I seize him, drive my right palm into his nose. I hear bones crack and I yank him into the limousine, crush his throat with my left hand. Because he is a small man with small bones and a small mouth he dies very fast. His automatic drops to the ground beside the car. Leaning down, I sink my teeth into the fat ear of the fat man and rip it from his fat head. Spitting the ear into my hand, I then chew off the ear of the dead black-clad chauffeur and drop it into my hand and then I pocket the ears.

These are the last ears I will ever take.

I wipe blood from my lips. The river pours into the limo. The eyes watch me and the leering skull, half-black, half-white grins at me and the white corpse in her white underwear lips peeled away from her teeth hair streaming like a dark black cloud in the thick oozing blood drapes her arm around my shoulders and I smell the stench of earless dead men slumped on the seat. The woman says,

What about me?

Did you fuck him? The Fat Man?

Uh-huh, she says.

Did he pay you?

She holds out her right hand with a huge diamond on the ring finger and a diamond studded watch on her wrist.

Blood diamonds?

Uh-huh.

Come here, I say.

Uh-uh, she says.

Inhaling the scent of death in a deep breath, I feel the current of the river of blood swirl around me. I step out of the limousine, pick up the automatic, cock it, ejecting the cartridge already in the chamber and then I shoot the woman between the eyes before she has time to scream. I know she is a screamer. Unlike the women in the Altiplano who didn't beg because they believed in virtue and their cause, this one is a Fucker of Fat Men who, wearing her filthy dirty diamonds, will scream in the face of death. She plows back in the seat, brains scattered over the rear window, over the upholstery, her legs open, her pantiless shaven cunt now and forever useless.

Then, I close the door. Get into the front, slide behind
the wheel. Opening the dead man's cellphone, I scroll
through his list of dialed numbers. Check the numbers
against the address book. Alphabetical order. The order of
extinction. Name, number, species—CEO. CFO. Chief. Head.
President. Vice President In Charge Of ... That's all I need. A
name and a number. The Fat Man's phone is the first in a
new collection. After the Fat Man, Geraldine is next.

The key is in the ignition. The engine idles quiet. Setting
the limousine in gear, I nose her into the swelling river of
blood. The bow breaks the waves, sending sprays of red into
the copper scented air. And it is good. Very good to be free.

The cellphone rings. I flip it open. Peter Carbo.
Canadian Resources.

Yes? I say.

Did that salaud Mitchell agree to our terms?

Agreed, when can we meet?

5820511R0

Made in the USA
Charleston, SC
07 August 2010